OUTBACK

PATRICIA WOLF

echo
PUBLISHING

Praise for Patricia Wolf

'Tense, atmospheric and gripping. I adore Australian crime fiction and *Outback* doesn't disappoint. I eagerly await the next DS Walker thriller.'
Chris Whitaker

'*Outback* is a hot read, I highly recommend it.'
Lynda La Plante CBE

'Compelling, immersive and gripping, with a setting so vivid it's almost a character in itself.'
Becca Day

'Nail-bitingly tense, *Outback* grabs you from the word go and doesn't release the pressure until the very end. A startlingly well-accomplished debut.'
John Marrs

About the Author

Patricia Wolf spent her childhood in Australia and now lives in Berlin. She likes whisky and strong coffee, busy cities, surf beaches and wild places. A journalist for almost twenty years, Patricia is a regular contributor to newspapers including the *Guardian*, the *Financial Times* and the *Daily Telegraph*. She was formerly a design columnist at the *Independent*, and the Lisbon correspondent for *Monocle* magazine.

IG: Patricia Wolf, @patricia_wolf_crime
Twitter: Patricia Wolf, @pattywolfcrime

Echo Publishing
An imprint of Bonnier Books UK
6/69 Carlton Crescent
Summer Hill NSW 2130
www.echopublishing.com.au

Bonnier Books UK
4th Floor, Victoria House,
Bloomsbury Square
London WC1B 4DA
www.bonnierbooks.co.uk

Echo Publishing acknowledges the traditional custodians of Country throughout Australia. We recognise their continuing connection to land, sea and waters. We pay our respects to Elders past and present.

This is a work of fiction. Names, characters, businesses, places, events, locales and incidents are either the products of the author's imagination or used in a fictitious manner. Any resemblance to actual persons, living or dead, or actual events is purely coincidental.

First published in Great Britain in 2022 by Embla Books

First published in Australia in 2023 by Echo Publishing,
an imprint of Bonnier Books UK
Reprinted 2023 (three times), 2024

Printed and bound in Australia by Griffin Press

The paper this book is printed on is certified against the Forest Stewardship Council® Standards. Griffin Press holds FSC® chain of custody certification SGS-COC-001185. FSC® promotes environmentally responsible, socially beneficial and economically viable management of the world's forests.

Page design and typesetting: transformer.com.au

Cover design: Blacksheep

Cover images: Outback shed, © David Trood/Getty Images; Summer countryside landscape, © Olenka-2008/Depositphotos; Eagle in flight, © Krumpelman Photography/Shutterstock; Raptor flying against blue sky, © Sean Mahoney Photography/Shutterstock

A catalogue entry for this book is available from the National Library of Australia

ISBN: 9781760688509 (paperback)
ISBN: 9781471411700 (ebook)

 echo_publishing

 echopublishingaustralia

 echopublishing

For Bunty, who also loved the outback

Prologue

Saturday afternoon

Rita is watching the temperature gauge creep towards the red. The car, the one she didn't want to buy but which Berndt said was the best they could afford, is rattling along at its top speed, just shy of 100 kilometres an hour. The air conditioning hasn't worked since they left Sydney and the vents are blowing so much hot air onto her arms and face that she feels like she's sitting in a fan-forced oven. It's 12.30 and the car's dashboard says the outside temperature is 41°C.

The road stretches in a straight line for miles, shimmering like oily water in the heat. On either side are flat plains of pale grass, leached by the sun of any hint of green, endless and empty. The occasional tree, marooned in a sea of grass, flickers in the bright light, the haze of heat making it look as if it is floating above the earth. Rita's sunglasses, which looked so great in the shop, are no match for the intensity of the sun, and she feels the beginnings of a headache. Beside her, Berndt is asleep, head against the window, mouth open.

A red light is flashing on the dashboard and the temperature gauge won't stop inching upwards. She takes her foot slightly off the accelerator; their speed drops to eighty. Buying the car was a mistake, but thanks to Berndt's insistence she's behind the wheel of a fifteen-year-old Ford Fiesta that's been driven into the ground and is too old and uncomfortable for this long journey. It's taken them longer than they'd expected to make it this far, three full days, and the drive has been unremitting. The roads are bad. Single lanes in each direction, bumpy and with gravel verges that spit lethal pebbles onto windshields when huge trucks hauling three or four carriages roar past. The windshield is already sporting a spiderweb of cracks on the passenger side after they'd gotten too close behind one and its tyres had flicked a stone onto the glass.

She misses Sydney already. In their six months living at the hostel they'd made a good group of friends, all young and free and up for a good time. No boring discussions about the future, no stress about careers or life plans. That could all come later – for now, this was her dream life. She'd had a decent job at the Sportsgirl fashion chain, and got great discounts on the clothes. They'd partied hard, lots of late nights in the bars and nightclubs of the city, and hanging out in the hostel, drinking, talking and laughing. Even in winter Sydney was balmy compared to Berlin, and they'd spent long sunny days by the beach, weekends in the Blue Mountains, even a couple of trips to New Zealand and Fiji.

Then, a few weeks ago, Berndt had met a crusty older German who'd been at the hostel for a few days. She remembers him sneering at their version of backpacking: 'You are all sitting here, drinking your flat whites and cocktails, taking your Instagram pictures. You have seen nothing real. This is not travelling – this is just posing.'

Maybe I like posing, she'd thought, and brushed it off for the self-righteous posturing it was, but Berndt had been stung. He wants to be a traveller, to have a real adventure. In order to extend their visas and spend another year enjoying the easy-going beach life in Sydney, they'd always known they'd need to spend three months working in rural Australia. It's part of the deal and she'd almost been looking forward to it. But there was no hurry and everyone had told them to wait for the Australian winter, because summer in the outback is an inferno of heat and dust.

But after the contemptuous remarks Berndt thought of nothing but heading inland. They loved the heat, he said. Hadn't they both spent every summer they could on the beaches of Portugal and Spain? He even turned down the chance to work on a vineyard outside of Sydney. That was too familiar, he said. He wanted to work in the *real* Australia, the outback, and he spent days convincing her it was a good idea. It would be something to sustain them when they were back in boring jobs at home – memories of their three months as Australian cowboys. So here they are, in this shitty little car, miles and miles from anywhere. No Sportsgirl, no margaritas, no beach.

She was right about the car but wrong to insist they push on today. Berndt had wanted to stay in Caloodie, the small town where they spent last night. It was 'proper Australia', he said, the real deal, exactly what he'd been looking for since they left Sydney. Rita had also liked the Wild West feel of it when they arrived yesterday afternoon – the wide empty streets, the men wearing cowboy hats, the hotel with its veranda overlooking the main drag. But last night at the pub she hadn't felt welcome. They'd gone in for drinks and dinner, the room air-conditioned to a delicious cool that spread goosebumps up her bare arms and legs and cooled the ever-present sweat on the nape of her neck, back and thighs. The steak and chips they'd ordered were salty and satisfying and the beer was so cold the condensation ran down the glass.

The bar, a large wide U-shape, wasn't what she'd call busy, especially for a Friday night, but perhaps out here that's as busy as it gets. There were a few old men sitting alone, a few groups of men in twos and threes. Apart from the small children

3

belonging to a family in the dining room, they were the only customers under thirty and she was the only woman sitting at the bar. She'd felt eyes on her, a couple of men in particular undressing her with blatant stares. Berndt was convinced he was making friends with a guy sitting near them but to her ears his slow Australian drawl felt sarcastic. She'd seen one of the groups watching them and turning away laughing. It was the kind of bar you find in any small town – not cool, a bit sad and judgemental, and she hadn't felt any desire to prolong their stay.

But this morning Berndt had said he was tired from the long days of driving, that he wanted a rest day before they started the job. Wanted to spend a day just lying on their bed in the air-conditioned cool, maybe exploring the town, finding somewhere for a swim. The ranch could wait another day, they could make the time up at the end. 'It's Saturday,' he'd said. 'If we arrive tomorrow, we can still start on Monday. Come on, it makes sense.' But she couldn't shake the fact that they were already a day late for their work placement. They'd texted the owner that they'd be arriving on Friday evening but had underestimated the distances and the speed at which they'd cover them. They can't be another day late. Babs would agree with her, she thinks. Her older sister always looks out for her, but she knows that Babs thinks she's a bit of a flake, just because she didn't take school that seriously or have a career plan by the time she was thirteen. Still, she shares enough of the same genes as Babs to want to make a good first impression – but now it looks like the car isn't going to make it much further.

'Berndt.' She reaches over and shakes him.

He wakes, sits up, squints at her.

'I think we need to pull over. The engine temperature is really high, and this red light has been on for a few minutes.'

He reaches for the water bottle at his feet, takes a gulp. 'Urgh. Hot water with a flavour of plastic.' He grimaces, then leans over to look at the dashboard. 'That's not good. Yeah, we'll need to stop, let it cool down.'

He doesn't say 'I told you we shouldn't have driven on', which she might have done were the situation reversed, and she reaches out and touches his leg.

'Sorry,' she says.

He takes her hand and brings it to his lips for a quick kiss. 'No, you're right, babe, we do need to get there. Let's keep an eye out for somewhere with a bit of shade where we can stop.'

'There's been no shade for miles. I've barely seen any trees.' Rita feels a knot of anxiety in her stomach. 'We can't break down out here. I haven't seen another car since we left and it's so hot and we don't have a signal.'

'It'll be fine, don't worry.' Berndt pulls out his phone. She's right, there are no bars. They haven't had much in the way of signal since they started their journey. 'How much further do we have to go?' he asks.

Rita does a quick calculation: they're at least fifty kilometres from Caloodie and it's probably a hundred and fifty to the next town. They're in the middle of nowhere. Before she can answer him the engine emits a loud bang and she feels it lose power. She hits the brakes and veers onto the gravel verge, where the car skates a little, the back wheels shifting left and then right before skidding to a stop. Steam starts to rise from both sides of the bonnet.

'Jesus! Babe, what do we do now?' Rita's shock is palpable, pupils huge as she turns to Berndt.

Outside the car, the heat is staggering. The tarmac burns through her sandals, the sun scalds her skin, her eyes squinting into the light. Berndt has lifted the bonnet but neither of them knows a thing about cars. The steam seems to be lessening a little.

'Let's just wait, let it cool down, and then we'll try to drive on,' says Berndt.

The gravel verge is teeming with black ants as long as her fingernails. They climb over her sandals and across her toes and she shakes them off with a shudder, opens the car doors and sits on the passenger seat, lifting her feet off the ground. A dead kangaroo on the other side of the road, bloated like a balloon, gives off a putrid, fetid smell. She digs out a shirt from her backpack and fashions it into a kind of face mask to deaden the stink, and reflexively reaches for the hand sanitiser that's melting in the door's side pocket.

'I don't think I'm going to like this job,' she says. 'It's too hot here and everything is so dry and dead.'

Berndt, lying across the back seat, reaches his arm through the centre console to stroke her fingers. 'It'll be fine when we get there, babe. Don't worry. We'll try to restart the engine in a minute.'

The heat inside the car is unbearable, but standing in the sun is worse. They wait fifteen minutes, passing the water back and forth between them. As hot and plastic-tasting as it is, it helps. Berndt climbs into the driver's seat and turns the key. There's not even a cough from the engine. He turns it again. The click of the key in the ignition is the only sound.

Rita feels tears welling up. 'What are we going to do?'

'A car will come by soon.'

'I haven't seen one since we left Caloodie,' she says, wishing again that she hadn't pushed them into coming on. She can see he's anxious too, although he's trying to hide it.

'We can't walk fifty kilometres,' he says. 'It's better to stay here. Someone will come along, we'll be fine. And if not, we'll wait until the sun goes down, then we can walk back along the road.'

Rita's mouth is dry and she is starting to panic. We could die out here, she thinks. If we run out of water, we could die. A bird of prey is floating in lazy circles high above. Apart from the ants, there's no other sound or sign of life, not even the call of a bird or the hum of cicadas – just the endless red earth, pale burnt grass and the sky, a vast bowl that curves over them, a pale blue washed almost to white in the heat of the afternoon sun.

They're still debating what to do when they hear the sound of a vehicle. Both of them scramble out and stand in the middle of the road, jumping up and down and waving their arms, even though the car is still a speck of white in the distance.

'We're saved, we're saved!' Rita is yelling like an idiot, the relief flooding through her, arms in the air, legs weak with the release of tension. Berndt is doing a little dance. They're laughing, semi-hysterical.

. . .

He's driving back to his place, feeling pretty good. It's Saturday arvo. He's got a couple of cartons of beer, some meth. He's going to get wasted and relax. He'd like some company, but he wouldn't mess about with a woman this close to home. He'll have to settle for watching some porn.

The miles are flying by and he's almost at the turn-off when he sees the two of them jumping up and down on the road beside their car, which has the bonnet up. He's not really in the mood to play the Good Samaritan but as he gets closer he sees it's the young couple who were in the pub last night. The girl, pretty, slim with long dark hair. He usually prefers blondes, but beggars can't be choosers. The bloke is a wanker, long hair, brightly coloured hippy trousers, wearing some kind of sandals. Exactly the kind of waste of space he despises. He slows down and pulls over, just in front of their vehicle.

'Thank you very much! Thank you very much!' The girl won't stop jabbering, explaining pointlessly where they've come from and where they're going. Young foreigners, visiting for a few months, about to work on a property the other side of Smithton.

Their car is an old heap, should never have left the safety of the big city. The engine has overheated, a problem with oil or maybe the radiator has some kind of leak. He gets it going – probably it's just cooled down enough – but it won't get far without overheating again.

'I don't reckon she'll get youse back to town,' he says. 'Look, my place is only a few clicks up the road. If you want to follow me, I've got a radio and you can call someone from there.'

They are pathetically grateful – the bloke even pats him on the back when the car gets started. 'Great job, mate,' he says.

I'm not your fucken mate, he thinks to himself.

'We really appreciate your help,' says the girl in her Kraut accent. 'I don't know what we would have done if you hadn't driven by.'

He waits while the bloke gets in and starts the engine. It kicks over, the temperature gauge rising immediately to the red. They'll be lucky to make the ten clicks or so to his place. As he drives off and the two of them follow, he's cursing himself for stopping. He doesn't want them around, wants to drink his beers, have a hit, unwind. He flicks his eyes to the rear-view mirror to see if they're still on his tail. They are – he can see the girl on the passenger side, her long hair blowing in the breeze. Then again it could be the bloke, he's got equally long hair. He blows out a derisive puff of air, thinking, what a loser, that hair, those dacks, fucksake.

As he comes to the turn he slows and indicates, wondering if they'll come too, cursing himself again as he sees them follow, eating his dust on the dirt road that leads to the house.

• • •

Rita is savouring the sweet relief of being rescued. The guy seems grumpy or perhaps just not the chatty type, but she doesn't care.

At least they're not on the side of the road, burning up in the sun. Grumpy or not, he's the first person they've seen in hours.

They've been driving for less than ten minutes when they come to a line of trees running the length of a dry riverbed, and the car in front slows and indicates he's about to turn left. They slow and follow, turning onto a track that's barely visible, just more dirt stretching into the endless grasslands.

'Maybe we should just keep going,' she says, looking at the track. 'I don't think the car is up to this. If we drive slowly on the highway, maybe we'll make it to Smithton.'

'No way,' says Berndt. 'What if the car breaks down again? And anyway, it would be totally rude not to follow him. This is the best option, babe. We'll call a mechanic and hopefully we can still get there tomorrow.'

They bump and jolt over the red earth, the dust from the car ahead seeping in even through the closed windows and another red cloud billowing up behind them. Then the track curves to the right and they pull up in front of a dilapidated house with a large tin shed and a couple of smaller run-down wooden sheds beside it. The house was probably yellow once, but the colour has long since faded to a dirty cream and the paint is peeling.

The guy is standing beside his car, waving them forward. Berndt rolls up beside him and he leans down and puts his head into the passenger-side window. Rita smells his sweat, an unpleasant musk, and pushes herself back into the seat, away from him.

'Drive her in there,' he says, pointing at one of the old wooden sheds. 'It'll save her overheating in the sun.'

Berndt nods. 'Right. Great. Thanks.' They jolt over dry hummocks of grass, the guy holding the shed door open and then closing it and slipping the latch across when they re-emerge.

The silence is loud in her ears. The heat is a physical thing and every living being is immobile in it. The rustle of the grass as they step over it is the only noise she can hear. If this is his house, no wonder he's moody. The wilderness runs straight to his front door, tufts of white grass as high as her knees, red earth, more ants swarming over her feet. There is no shade, no relief.

She lifts her arms in a stretch, the heat of the sun burning across her bare shoulders. The house looks hot and dirty. There's a small veranda in front, with a solitary plastic chair under a drooping tin awning. Except for the big shed with corrugated-iron panels glimmering in the light, the whole place is run-down and unloved. She hopes they're not going to have to stay here too long. No doubt he'll offer them a beer or something. She touches Berndt on the shoulder.

'Berndt, we're not staying here a minute longer than we have to,' she says, keeping her voice low. 'I don't want a beer or a coffee or anything. I want to call the mechanic and get out of here.'

'OK, OK,' says Berndt. 'But I don't see how we can refuse a drink if he offers it. He's helping us out.'

'Leave it to me,' she says. 'I'll handle it.'

Berndt rolls his eyes. She can see he thinks this is all part of the adventure. Meeting locals, hanging out in a dilapidated house. He has his phone out, taking a discreet picture. He's probably already imagining the Instagram likes: #outbackadventure. But she's had enough adventure. In fact she makes her decision then and there, she's not going to stay out here and work in this heat. If the place they're headed for looks anything like this she'd rather cut the trip short and go back to Germany early. She'll talk to Berndt, as soon as they've sorted the car out. They'll drive back to Sydney and she'll probably still get her old job back.

She feels a surge of relief at the decision and it gives her the strength to be firm with this guy. She'll say they need to get the car fixed today, they don't want to hang out, sorry, no beers, thanks anyway.

The man who's saved them still hasn't introduced himself, she realises. He has his back to them and is rummaging around in the tray back of his vehicle, looking for something. She's preparing her speech as he finishes and turns back towards them. He's holding a carton of beer in his arms.

'Come on in, then,' he says. 'I'll see if I can raise Smithy. He owns the servo. He might be able to come and tow you back to town.'

'A tow all that way? How much will that cost?' asks Berndt. They don't have much money – that's another reason she wanted to get to this job quickly. She can see he's anxious, thinking of the $50 or so they have on them and the not-much-more they have left in their accounts.

'I dunno, couple of hundred, three maybe.' The man is already walking towards the house.

'Shit,' says Berndt, turning towards her. 'And it'll cost extra to repair. We don't have that kind of money.'

'Would your dad send us some?' she asks.

'Probably, but I really don't want to ask him again,' says Berndt. He takes a step towards the house. 'Is there any chance you could fix it for us, just good enough to get us to Smithton? We're a bit short of cash.'

The look of irritation, anger, on the man's face makes Rita quail. They're really imposing here.

He pauses for a second. 'I need a beer first, maybe gear up, then I'll have a look,' he says, pushing open the door with his shoulder and disappearing into the gloom of the house, the screen door shutting behind him with a clang.

Monday

Thirty-six hours missing

1

The sound of his mobile phone pulls Lucas Walker from sleep. Just as he realises what's woken him, it stops. He reaches an arm out, picks the phone up from the bedside table, still groggy, half asleep. The screen says *7.59, Missed Call Dan Rutherford* – that's Chief Inspector Rutherford, his boss at the organised crime unit of the Australian Federal Police.

The bed creaks beneath him as he rolls onto his back, phone in hand. His mind is still fuzzy with some half-remembered dream that slips into mist when he tries to grab hold of it. He usually wakes much earlier than this, but he and Blair had sat up late last night, drinking stubbies and reminiscing. It was gone 3 a.m. before they'd called it a night.

He lies for a minute, clearing his head. He's on compassionate leave far from Canberra at his grandmother's place in outback Queensland, so there's no good reason for Rutherford to be ringing him, though no doubt there are plenty of bad ones.

Above him the ceiling fan turns slow loops, moving the morning air over his broad, bare shoulders. It's early November, not officially summer yet, but out here in the far north-west of the state the heat is already unremitting. Even at this hour the air is overly warm, and the room, with its curtains closed against the light, feels stuffy. He's been trying to get his grandmother to install air conditioning for the last ten years but she's stubbornly refusing. 'I've managed without it for seventy years, love, I sure as heck don't need it now.'

The threat of his not visiting doesn't carry any weight. She knows he doesn't mean it – this has always been his true home, hot as it may be. He sits, pulls a pillow behind his shoulders and rests against the dark wooden headboard. The bed is an old relic with a lumpy mattress and pink floral sheets that match the curtains. If anyone he knows saw him like this, his street cred would be totally shot. He smiles at the thought as he looks at the phone again. Decides he needs a drink of water to clear his head before he calls Rutherford and finds out what drama is about to ruin his leave.

He pulls on a pair of shorts and walks out, barefoot and bare-chested, through the cramped living room, being careful in his hung-over state not to knock anything as he walks past the ornaments that adorn every shelf, nook and corner of the space. At almost six-three he always feels oversize in the small house. He winces as he reaches the kitchen and sees the empty bottles littering the tabletop. They'd set the world to rights last night, no doubt about it.

There's a plastic jug filled with cold water in the fridge. He fills a glass and drinks it; the cold liquid helps clear his head. Usually he doesn't like the taste of the water out here. It comes directly from the artesian basin far beneath the earth, emerging from the faucets warm, sulphurous and metallic. Icy-cold from the fridge it's just about bearable. He'd half thought of buying some bottled water; only knowledge of what his grandmother, not to mention his cousins, would say about his soft city ways prevented him.

Pushing the screen door aside, he steps out onto the veranda, the wood warm beneath his feet. Shaded from the sun by a deep awning and sitting on stumpy stilts a couple of metres above the ground, allowing the air to flow underneath, it's one of the coolest places in the house. He pulls out one of the chairs beside the rickety wooden table and stretches his legs into the sun. At the sound of his footsteps, Ginger, his grandmother's red heeler cattle dog, dingo descendant through and through, emerges from under the house, her tan ears pricked, her pale fur dusty from sleeping in a hole she's dug, her white-tipped tail swishing happily to see him. She's a true-blue Queenslander just like Grandma, thinks Walker with a smile. She'd been the runt of a litter, and when no one wanted to take her as a working dog, Blair had bought her as company for Grandma. For her own reasons, Ginger has always had a soft spot for Walker, and now she comes up to where he's sitting, leaning against his legs as he strokes her ears and her soft, knobbly head.

As he runs his fingers through her fur he revels in the stillness and quiet of the house behind him. He's due at the hospital to pick up Grandma this afternoon. They're sending her home, though for how long, no one knows. There's not much they can do for the cancer that's eating her up inside.

She's made her peace with it – more than he has. 'I don't want to live forever and I want to die at home,' she says.

There are plenty of people here to help her navigate these last days, but he wants to be here too. She raised him. He's closer to her than he is to his mum. Once she's back, the veranda will fill. His aunt Michelle, cousins Blair and Anna and their partners and kids, other friends of Grandma's, dropping in to say hello, ask advice or offer it, or chew the fat of another day passed. He'd better call Rutherford now if he wants any privacy at all.

When he first joined the Feds, he'd worked as an analyst. He'd inherited some of his mum's maths smarts and had graduated top of his class, but the desk job hadn't suited him. It was Rutherford who'd encouraged him to move into an undercover role.

'You're not political enough for head office,' he'd said. 'You'll do well undercover, and you'll like it better, doing your own thing.'

And Rutherford was right, working undercover suits Walker and his streak of independence. The last operation was particularly demanding but he'd gotten close enough to a key player in a big Lebanese organised crime group in Sydney to bring him down, and had been celebrated around the office. Feted enough that the top brass had signed off on his taking a couple of months' compassionate leave to spend up here with Grandma. He's planning to be here until after Christmas. They haven't had a family Christmas together for a long time and who knows how many more they'll have before Grandma passes. His bosses had wanted him out of sight for a while anyway, until things cooled down a bit after the last op.

'Alright, Walker?' says Rutherford when he picks up the phone, a question that doesn't demand an answer because he's barely said 'Yeah, good' before Rutherford is talking again. 'Look, I know you're on leave, but there's a misper case out your way. You're up in Caloodie, aren't you?'

'Yeah . . .'

'Right. Well, we've got a couple of young Germans, Berndt Meyer and Rita Guerra, gone missing. They were on their way to a station near Smithton, due on Friday evening, never arrived. You got email out there?'

Walker manages to inject another 'Yeah' before Rutherford continues.

'OK, good. Go and have a chat with the local fellas, find out what they know, where they're at. Best not to tell them you're from the Feds, just keep it vague.' Rutherford pauses for a moment. 'Say you've been appointed to be family liaison as their families aren't in the country. I'll let the Queensland Police know it's authorised.'

'OK. Sure. But why are we getting involved in this? Doesn't seem like our kind of thing . . .'

'Sorry, DS Walker, I forgot that you always need a full explanation of why something needs to be done before you follow a simple instruction.'

'If I know why we're looking into it, I might keep an eye out for different things.' Walker keeps his voice level.

'Just routine. They're foreign citizens, the local fellas are under-resourced. Foreign Affairs wants to make sure they're located, fast. Bad for tourism when people go missing and we don't find them.'

'Righto, I'll look into it this morning,' says Walker, noting down the details before ringing off. Afterwards, he sits for a moment longer on the veranda. He's happy to take on the job. Sitting around worrying about Grandma is eating him up. Hence the drinking session last night. At least this will give him something productive to do. But there is a less-than-zero chance in hell that Rutherford wants him to follow up an everyday missing persons case. He wonders what he's getting himself into, what's really going on here, then shrugs it off. He's had plenty of years working undercover in Sydney's organised crime world. Whatever it is, this should be a piece of cake in comparison.

He goes back inside, changes into a shirt, jeans and his boots, mentally shaking his head at the tourists who come to the outback so unprepared. No matter how many signs are put up, visitors are always underestimating the heat and the distances. The advice, and they publish it everywhere, is to bring plenty of water and spare fuel and to always stay with your car, but most of them think they can walk to the next town, especially Europeans who can't really wrap their heads round the idea that the next town might be 200 kilometres away. And that the heat, which will probably hit 40°C or more today, can knock people out in minutes, not hours.

His ute has been sitting in the sun and is already unpleasantly stuffy, the vinyl seat burning through his jeans, the steering wheel hot to the touch. He opens the windows, sets the air con to max. He's had the ute for close on ten years and she's looking a bit worse for wear, but the engine is good as gold and she'll go pretty much anywhere thanks to the four-wheel drive and high suspension.

Grandma lives on the edge of Caloodie, the last street before the bush starts again, but the town is so small that it's only a couple of minutes' drive along the wide empty roads to the police station in the town centre. The station is in a converted old worker's cottage, just three rooms and a small veranda. You'd hardly notice it was police, except for the small *Queensland Police* sign above the front door and a white Toyota four-wheel drive parked on the dusty driveway, with the distinctive red-and-blue roof lights and the blue-and-white chequered insignia of the state's police service.

A middle-aged woman is sitting at the front desk, wearing a flowery blouse and dark-blue skirt – a civilian receptionist, Walker supposes. She looks up as he enters and says a chirpy 'Good morning.'

'G'day,' he says. 'I'm DS Lucas Walker from Sydney. I've been asked to help with your missing persons case. I need to talk to the chief here about it.'

She looks at him, studying his face and attire, and seems to find him wanting. 'What's your connection to the case?' she asks.

'I've been appointed to represent the families of Berndt Meyer and Rita Guerra. They're in Germany and Foreign Affairs want me to keep an eye on things for them.'

'Let me check with the officer in charge,' she says, pushing her chair back and disappearing from sight into a back room. When she returns, she opens another door into the hallway and ushers him into a small interview room. 'Senior Constable Grogan will be with you in a mo'.'

It's less than five minutes before the door opens and a uniformed officer comes in, carrying a slim pale-pink folder. 'Senior Constable Dave Grogan, I'm the officer in charge out here,' he says, holding out his hand. Walker shakes it. Grogan is tall and big, with blond hair so pale it's almost white. His skin is pink, the type that goes bright red when it's hot, and there's a fair amount of stomach pushing at the buttons from under his shirt.

'I got an email from HQ that you're representing the families and that we're to give you every assistance,' says Grogan. 'Bit weird, isn't it?'

'Nah, yeah, I don't know. I'm a DS in Sydney but I'm from round here, back on a family visit. Reckon the Foreign Affairs department or the embassy or something put them in contact with me. I'm on leave, but you know how it is when the blokes at the top get a hold of something.' Walker is making it up as he goes along, the half-lies coming easily. Nothing he's said is strictly untrue, just short on a couple of details.

'Are they someone important, then?'

'No idea, mate. Just following orders, you know how it is.'

Grogan looks sceptical but opens the file he's brought with him and runs through the details. 'Pair reported missing on Saturday evening when they didn't turn up at Glen Ines station. They'd texted Andy Miles, the bloke who owns the place, on Friday morning saying they were due to arrive that evening. Never showed up. He thought they were probably just running late but then he called me late on Saturday, bit worried because they're young and foreign, don't know the bush.'

Walker nods. The harsh country out here can kill the unwary.

'As it happens, a young couple were at the Federal, here in town, on Friday night. I spoke to the publican and he said they'd had a couple of backpackers staying the night, heading out west for a job on a station, so I was pretty sure it was the same pair. I checked at the servo and they had CCTV of them fuelling up just before lunchtime on Saturday. You could pick the bloke a mile off, proper hippy traveller type, ya know? CCTV showed nothing unusual – they filled the tank and left. I called the Smithton servo but it seems they didn't stop for fuel or anything there. No one out there remembers them passing through. I took a quick drive along the Smithton road yesterday arvo just to check they hadn't broken down. There's been a few trucks on the road this weekend so I would have heard already if they were out there, but better safe than sorry. There was no sign of them so I've sent the details to the misper team in Brisbane this morning. They'll handle it from here.'

Walker is impressed. He knows that when tourists go missing out here it needs to be taken seriously and Grogan has done everything you'd expect him to.

Grogan hands Walker the slim file. 'My guess is they never went to Smithton and were too embarrassed or too hopeless to call in and cancel the job. Probably they turned round and went back to the coast, back where they came from. Wouldn't be the first time someone's changed their mind about working out here when it gets as hot as this.'

It sounds plausible to Walker. Caloodie is small enough and Smithton is definitely nothing to write home about – a servo and not much else in one of the hottest and driest parts of the state. After an almost decade-long drought, the earth around here is parched, those trees and shrubs that survive grey and wilted. He can imagine a pair of kids discovering they've bitten off more than they can chew and turning back round for the bright lights of the coast.

Walker knows that any digging around he does will tread on Grogan's toes, so he keeps it low-key. 'Great, thanks. Sounds like you've ticked all the boxes, to be honest. I'll do a bit of a follow-up, liaise with the family, keep them informed. If anything else comes up, let me know. Like you say, probably they've just taken a detour, changed their minds about going bush, and hopefully this is nothing serious.'

Back in his car, air con pumping, he eats a Cherry Ripe, savouring the dark chocolate and sweet cherry filling and running over the notes in the file. There's not much to read. Along with registration details of the car, there's a screenshot of Berndt Meyer's passport – the picture of a youthful face, blue eyes, light-brown hair almost to his shoulders. He checks the date of birth, calculates the age, twenty-four. The girl, Rita Guerra, is even younger, just twenty-three.

He's really not sure why Rutherford, or Foreign Affairs or whoever, has asked him to get involved. Although they're young, they are adults, and apart from the harsh country that they were driving into there's no real reason to suppose they've come to any harm. Perhaps it's just because, like most small outback towns, Caloodie is a one-man station and the officer in charge is only a senior constable, still relatively inexperienced. There's not much goes on out here; Grogan probably usually has nothing more than the occasional drunk to deal with, or a tourist asking for directions and travel advice. He's got a big patch, though, if Smithton is under his remit – that's a couple hundred kilometres away. But Walker reckons most likely Grogan's right and there's no reason for Queensland Police to do anything more than they have already.

He's still not sure what he's supposed to add to the mix, and the fact that Rutherford is involved is playing on his mind, but he puts his doubts to one side. He can at least reassure the bureaucrats that there's someone on the case who's more senior, though the bush cop seems to be doing just fine.

He puts the files in the glovebox and drives to the other side of town to pick up Grandma. With a population of close to a thousand, Caloodie isn't such a small town by outback standards, and because it's so far from the capital, Brisbane – a good seven hours' drive at least – there's a small hospital here. It's not set up to handle serious cases, really it's nothing more than a doctor's surgery with a couple of beds out the back, but Grandma refuses to go to Brisbane for treatment. 'Never had a reason to go there and I'm not going now,' she'd said.

He'd been pushing her to do it until the doctor pulled him aside and explained that, while it might prolong her life by a few months, the treatment would also make her feel much worse. 'If she's happier to die at home, I think you should respect that,' he'd said. 'We'll help keep her comfortable.'

So now, when the pain gets too bad, she spends a few nights here, with access to morphine and nursing care. But she's always busting to get back home as soon as she can.

He pulls the car up on the double yellow in front of the main entrance. Grandma is sitting in a wheelchair by the door. Her face lights up in a smile when she sees him. 'Take me home, Lucas, away from this miserable place.'

She needs his help to walk the short distance from the wheelchair to the car. She's always been thin but now she's tiny, with birdlike arms and bony shoulders, though she's not lost the inner strength that makes her such an important part of the community and the bedrock of his life.

Back home, he settles her in bed, turns on the fan and gives her the painkillers that they've sent back with her from the hospital, then gets caught up welcoming the stream of visitors who begin dropping in as soon as the news gets out that she's back. He's dispatched to buy lamingtons and sausage rolls from the bakery, and finds himself trapped by a succession of relatives, friends and passers-by who, after enquiring after her health and updating her on the day-to-day happenings she's missed, inevitably turn their attention to him and start asking questions about his life and his plans and his work. As he can't talk about his work, and doesn't have any specific future plans, these are questions to which, it turns out, he doesn't have satisfactory answers.

The misper case gives him a good excuse to avoid further interrogation. He takes the file and a couple of lamingtons on a plate into his bedroom. Ginger pads in after him and settles with a soft thud on the floor beside the bed. It's against the rules for her to be inside but if she won't tell, neither will he.

He starts by dialling the two kids' numbers, more in hope than expectation. It would be nice if they answered from a pub somewhere, having decided to forget about the job and get drunk instead. That way he could give them a piece of his mind about wasting police time and spend the afternoon shaking his head at the idiots he has to deal with. Instead he gets automated 'This phone cannot be reached' messages for both numbers.

He checks the time difference – it's 7 a.m. in Berlin. A good time: likely they'll still be at home and likely they'll be awake.

He dials the number for Berndt Meyer's father. The phone rings a few times and is answered by a brusque 'Ja, hallo?'

'Ah, yeah, hello. Do you speak English?' asks Walker.

'Yes, I speak English. Who is this, please?'

Walker introduces himself and explains the situation. 'This is just routine, nothing to worry about – we're just keen to talk with them both,' he says. 'Can you confirm when you last heard from your son?'

'Ahmm, OK, yes. I spoke to Berndt last week on Sunday, so eight days ago. He doesn't call us so often. When we spoke, he and his girlfriend were in Sydney and they were planning to drive north to take this job. You know Berndt is travelling with his girlfriend, Rita? She might be better than he is at keeping in touch. Have you talked with her family? I can send you the contact details of her sister, Barbara Guerra.'

'That'd be good, thanks,' says Walker, spelling out his email address.

'I will email it to you this morning,' says Meyer. 'Tell me, please, how worried should I be? Is he going to be OK? Should I come to Australia?'

Walker pauses. Except for the last – an emphatic no – he doesn't have answers to these questions. 'Ah no,' he says, finding his most reassuring voice. 'We're handling it here and I'm sure they're fine. Changed their minds about the job, most likely. Let's see what the next couple of days bring.'

Walker takes his plate to the kitchen and then walks out to the car and brings the map of the state he keeps in the glovebox back inside with him. He finds Smithton: it really is the arse-end of nowhere. Some 200 kilometres west of Caloodie, with nothing much beyond it but the huge expanse of the Simpson Desert. If they headed to Smithton, didn't like the look of it and changed their minds, there's no immediate turn-off they could have made, though perhaps they could have driven east towards Windorah, another tiny, isolated, one-horse kind of town, and then on to Longreach and from there to the coast.

He calls a contact he has at Lohan's, a nationwide trucking company.

'Did you have anyone on the Caloodie-to-Smithton road, Saturday lunchtime or early arvo?' he asks. 'And if you did, could I see the dashcam?'

When the promised email from Lohan's arrives it's with a note saying they had a driver going the other direction, leaving Smithton at around 9.30 a.m. and arriving in Caloodie just over a couple of hours later. Walker thanks his luck: if these kids went towards Smithton, the truck should have passed them. He fast-forwards through the dashcam footage, watching the highway spooling out, mesmerised by the sameness of it. For most of the journey the road is empty. When he sees a car approaching in the distance, he slows the frames. It's an old black Ford Fiesta that matches the description of Berndt Meyer's car.

There are two people in the car. He can't quite make out their faces but if he had to guess he'd say the girl is driving. It's 11.25 a.m., Saturday. The pair are ten minutes or so outside of Caloodie on the road to Smithton. It's good to confirm that they definitely headed in that direction, but strange that they never arrived. Somewhere in between they simply disappeared. Two youngsters, foreigners in an old car who don't understand the heat, the emptiness and the dangers of this part of the world, have vanished on a quiet road on the way to an even quieter town.

2

DS Barbara Guerra catches herself running her hand through her hair again. It's an unconscious gesture, one she makes when she's distracted from the task at hand and trying to force herself to concentrate, and it makes her short dark crop stand up in unruly tufts. She's sitting at her desk in the LKA Berlin office, where she's managed to snag herself a prime spot by the window. Situated on the third floor of the building, her window overlooks the busy traffic on Tempelhofer Damm and then the greenery of Tempelhofer Feld, the park converted from a former airfield. In the summer the park is a gift. She goes for a lunchtime run around its perimeter or meets friends and colleagues for a post-work 'Feierabend' beer in one of its beer gardens. She loves the old airport – despite its Nazi heritage it's a striking building, evocative of a more glamorous age of travel – and enjoys the wide-open skies that the large space affords.

But now, a Monday morning in early November, the view isn't calling her. The sky is dark grey, clouds heavy with rain or more likely sleet if the temperature dips low enough, and the park is windswept and empty. Despite it being almost 10 a.m. she has her desk lamp on. The office is busy but she is almost unaware of the sounds and movement of the others in the team coming and going, chatting about their weekends and cases. She's anxious, her thoughts endlessly returning to her younger sister, Rita. She had a call from Rita's boyfriend's father earlier this morning and learnt that the pair haven't turned up to the job they signed up for.

Rita left Berlin almost a year ago, to travel in South-East Asia and Australia. Barbara had encouraged her to go, helped her buy the backpack she was so proud of and waved her off without envy. At thirty-two she's probably missed the boat on the whole gap-year thing, but she loves her Berlin life and her job at the LKA, the detective division of the Berlin Police. Life is good. Her recent promotion to detective sergeant and the small apartment she's lucked into means she can now afford to live by herself after years of flat-sharing.

This morning is the first time she's spoken with Berndt's dad, Carl, though she's seen his name on a WhatsApp group that Berndt and Rita use to send photos and updates. Rita met Berndt early in her journey, at a hostel in Bangkok, and they've been travelling together ever since. The few times she's spoken to Berndt he's impressed her as a kind person who is obviously in love with her little sister. And Rita seems equally smitten. Berndt's father had seemed relaxed about the situation – the pair have probably changed their minds, decided to go somewhere and have fun instead of taking up this job. Barbara is less sure. It's not like Rita. She's easy-going, loves to party, but she's also a Guerra and that means it's been drummed into her that keeping your commitments is sacrosanct. She tries to tell herself that maybe Carl is right. They're only young, and kids can make frivolous decisions, Rita more than most. Barbara's police background means her first instinct is that something untoward has happened, when in reality, most of the time, there's a perfectly innocent explanation.

The time difference means it's the middle of the night in Australia, but she can't help checking and rechecking her WhatsApp. The message she sent to Rita is still unread, just the one tick beside it.

Perhaps she's turned her phone off overnight. Not that she's ever seen Rita without her phone to hand, but maybe she's more relaxed over there in Australia.

She ruffles her hair again, forces herself to focus on the tedious though vital work she's doing: a search of CCTV footage to see if they've caught any images of a man who's been responsible for a string of violent robberies in the Charlottenburg area. He's targeted wealthy older women who live alone and is getting more vicious with each attempt. The last woman was beaten so badly she's in an induced coma in hospital, and it's uncertain if she'll survive. Which makes it a potential murder case. They have a description from earlier attacks – tall, well built, local, given his accent – but he's been clever enough to have covered his face and avoided the obvious CCTV areas. She's called in footage from a wide geographic circle around the last attack, hoping that an image will jump out at her.

It's dark outside by the time she leaves work. She calls Monika. They've been friends since primary school. These days they couldn't be more different – Monika with her pink hair and her job at the art gallery is freer in spirit than she is – but they've been close for so long that it's somehow irrelevant. They'd been planning to meet for drinks and something to eat tonight but Barbara's not in the mood.

'Sorry, Mon,' she lies, 'it's work, I can't get away.'

'I knew you'd cancel,' says Monika. 'I woke up this morning, I put my "going out for a drink with Babs" lipstick on, but inside I knew you'd cancel.'

'Sorry,' she says again.

'Ah, no worries. The weather's shit. I can sit on the sofa in my pyjamas with a soup and Netflix.'

They're due to see each other on Saturday anyway. It's Anika's birthday and a group of them are meeting for drinks and a pizza. They bitch a little half-heartedly about the Saturday event: Anika, recently married and with a baby on the way, is the first of their friends to eschew single life. Conversations with her now inevitably turn to baby preparations, the new flat the couple have moved into and other household topics. She and Monika usually need to go for a drink on their own afterwards to wash away the domestic vibes.

'It's not that I don't like Olaf,' says Monika for the ten thousandth time, 'it's just that he's so goddamn reliable. It's boring.'

Barbara rides her bicycle home in the drizzle, the streets wet and slippery, especially along the canal where the leaves are damp on the ground. She likes autumn. It's a time for burning candles, eating heartily, meeting friends in warm bars. She embraces the chance to hibernate a little bit. But tonight she's cold all the way through by the time she arrives home and wishing she'd left the bike and caught the S-Bahn instead. She takes a long hot shower and puts on her pyjamas, a pair of thick socks and slippers. She doesn't really need them – the flat is warm and she's made it cosy with rugs and throws and candles – but she's still anxious about Rita and she wants to feel cocooned.

Her mind is racing over possibilities, each worse than the last, and she doesn't enjoy the bowl of pasta she prepares, or the big glass of red wine she's poured. Every time she calls Rita or Berndt she gets the same message.

By 11 p.m., which is 8 a.m. in Australia, she's getting properly worried. Rita never switches her phone off. She's from that generation that use it as unconsciously as they use their right hand. She calls Carl and he answers immediately.

'Have you heard from them?' he asks. She realises he's more worried than he's let on.

'No. Nothing. Rita's phone is off.'

'I've been trying Berndt's number too. This is very unusual. He has his phone with him all day, every day.'

'Yeah, Rita is the same. Can you give me the Australian

policeman's number? The one who said he's working for you? I'm police too – I work for the LKA. Maybe if I give him a call, he might have more to tell me, professional to professional.'

'Would you? That would be good.' Carl seems as desperate as she is. 'I'm going to kill Berndt when I talk to him for all the anxiety he's giving me. I'm sure he's having a great time somewhere, drinking beers and not thinking about us at all.'

She murmurs a kind of agreement but her police experience, her tendency to expect the worst, is gnawing away at her. The two phones turned off doesn't feel good.

She calls the Australian number that Carl has given her.

'Lucas Walker, g'day.'

She's so startled not to get an automated message that she's momentarily silent.

'Hello?' he says.

'Sorry, hello.' She takes a deep breath to give herself time to prepare what she wants to say. Her English is rusty, and out of practice. 'This is Barbara Guerra. I'm the sister of Rita Guerra, who is with Berndt Meyer. The young Germans that are missing. You called Berndt's father, Carl Meyer, this morning. He's given me your number.'

'Ah, right.'

His accent, a slow drawl, is soothing somehow and transports her to a vision of Australia, beaches and surfers, the Sydney Opera House.

'I'm also police,' she says. 'I'm a detective sergeant with the LKA in Berlin, the CID. Can you tell me if you have any news? Have you found them? Are they at the farm . . .' – she looks down at the paper she's holding – 'Glen Ines?'

'Glen Inn-es,' he says, correcting her pronunciation. 'Yeah, nah, sorry. I can't tell you much more than I told Mr Meyer. They haven't turned up to the job. They were seen on the road headed north and there's no sign of their car having broken down or any indication that they're in trouble, so it's possible they're not missing as such, just travelling further afield and haven't checked in.'

Barbara thinks of Rita and her live-life-in-the-moment, have-fun mentality, but discounts it almost instantly. Rita isn't that selfish, she wouldn't worry them like this.

'No,' says Barbara. 'Rita wouldn't do that. She's pretty good about keeping in touch.'

'I'm sure she is, but out here you often don't get mobile phone coverage or internet connections so it might be that they can't contact you.'

Barbara feels a flare of hope. 'Do you think that's possible? They just don't have phone access?'

'It's definitely possible. We're pretty isolated out here. Only the biggest network has a signal, and even then not everywhere. And you know how it is with kids on holiday – perhaps they don't realise that not turning up for the job has us a bit worried.'

The fact that they might not have a phone signal is good news but it's been nearly three days since they were seen. It's too long. She says as much to the detective.

'We are taking this seriously,' he says. 'We're doing everything we can to trace them. If you give me your number and your email, I'll let you know when I have more information.'

She's not listening. These are words she's said to families of victims herself. A vain attempt at reassurance when there's nothing to say. She has to call her parents, tell them the news. They'll go to pieces. Their beloved Rita, her beautiful, impetuous, free-spirited little sister, the baby of the family and everyone's favourite, is missing.

3

A shaft of sharp light filtering through the venetian blinds and slashing across his face is what wakes him. His mouth is dry, his lips are parched, he's sweating like a pig and his body aches all over, his neck twisted and sore from the way he's been lying. He groans and drags himself to sitting, feeling like shit, the usual post-high emptiness, a bleak stain washing through him. He's on the sofa in the living room. Empty beer cans all over the floor. A bottle of rum, dry but for the dregs. The pipe and his bag of meth on the coffee table, nearly done. Thank god he's left a little for this morning, hasn't used it all. He needs a hit, can't be feeling as shit as this.

As he leans over to pick up the pipe, he sees the sandals on the floor, hippy-looking leather things. The sight stops him mid-movement. He sits back in the sofa. What the fuck happened last night. He can feel the skin of his left forearm start itching, as if a swarm of bugs underneath are crawling up and down from his elbow. He scratches hard, memories coming back in flashes.

He'd been drinking beers with the two foreigners. The bloke a wanker, the girl pretty enough. He'd been watching her, ignoring the bloke for the most part, but then she'd started yammering and yammering about their bloody car, as if it was his problem or something. He'd told them to fuck off, he just wanted some peace, wanted to get wasted. They'd gone, he thought they'd gone, he'd geared up, he remembers that, and then they were back, couldn't get their car started, their phones didn't work. None of it his fucken problem.

They'd started looking around the house. Could they use his radio? But the radio is fucked, they can't get a signal. He's been meaning to take it into town, replace it or get it fixed, but fuck it, most of the time he doesn't want anyone getting hold of him anyway. They'd been asking to use his car, yammering and yammering at him. He remembers now, feels his anger and anxiety, a kind of panic, growing again. They were trying to find his car keys, steal the vehicle. Fucken foreigners, come over here, act like they own the place, think they can take what they want.

Nervous energy drives him to his feet. Where did they go? What did they take? He looks around the room, searching for his phone, his keys, everything's a mess, can't find anything. He runs down the hall, out the screen door, sees his vehicle parked under the tree. At least they didn't take that, didn't get away with that.

The light is much too bright. He steps back under the shade of the awning. He needs a hit. Needs to get back in control. He's looking at the vehicle – there's a massive dark stain on the ground beside it. He can feel his heart beating out of his chest, the skin on both his arms crawling and itching.

They'd been trying to steal the car. That's what happened. They'd been trying to steal the car. He'd warned them. Told them to back the fuck away from the vehicle. He'd gone inside, found the rifle that he uses for hunting roos. The bloke had still been standing beside the car when he came back out, the girl already sitting inside. The fucken cheek. It was dark, the light from the veranda wasn't much to see by, but they were definitely trying to steal it.

He's back inside, on the sofa, hands shaking, lighting a pipe, waiting for the rush, feeling the release, feeling the power grow.

Reckon they can come out here and steal from him, but he's showed them.

As the drug hits, his mind clears. He remembers the bloke, talking, talking, talking. 'We just want to borrow it, mate, drive to Caloodie and then we'll bring it back. We just need to get a mechanic and get our car fixed.'

Fucken likely. The girl wouldn't get out of the car, he was screaming at her to get the fuck out of the car, and then the bloke started walking towards him, saying, 'It's OK, we're not taking the car' – telling a barefaced lie, thinks he's stupid or something. So he'd shot him. Pulled the trigger, bang. The bloke goes down. He lets out a laugh remembering it. He's dancing a little around the living room, holding a pretend gun. 'Reckon youse can fucken steal from me? Bang, bang,' he says. And the bloke goes down. Screaming and holding his leg.

The girl starts screaming too. Now she gets out of the car. Now she knows he's serious. He fires again but it's dark, too dark, and he misses. She's begging him, 'No, please, no', lying beside the car, her hands over her head. He grabs her by the hair, drags her into the shed and locks her in. She won't steal from him again. He'd left the bloke, hadn't he. Left him there. Where did he go?

He goes back outside. He's jumpy again but the drugs fire him up. He walks over to the vehicle, looks at the blood staining the earth black and sees the stain leading in a waving line towards the shed. Remembers. He'd dragged him into the shed with the girl. He looks over to the shed. It's gleaming bright in the sunshine and there's no sound from inside.

He goes back into the house, looks for the rifle. It's not in the bedroom, where he usually keeps it, in the wardrobe. Where the hell did he put it? He's kicking through the clothes on the floor – nothing. The living room is gloomy now the sun has moved overhead. He switches on the light and sees the dark gleam of the barrel beside the sofa. He'd kept it close by overnight. Good thinking. You can never be too sure. Can't trust these foreign types. He walks to the shed, taking the rifle with him. No telling what they'll be like, what he's gonna find when he opens the door. He'd like to sneak in, surprise them, but the lock is hot to the touch and the key is fiddly and he's cursing them loud for all the shit they've given him by the time he gets it open. He pushes the door with a jab from the barrel of the gun, showing them he means business. The shed is dark after the bright light outside. And it stinks to high heaven. Blood and piss and god knows what else. Disgusting.

When his eyes adjust to the gloom he can see the bloke, lying not far from the door, more or less where he'd left him. He's not moving but he's breathing, fitfully. As he stands there, the bloke gives a soft moan. There's a dark stain of blood in a big oval around him. The girl's in the far corner, crouched against the back wall, arms wrapped around her legs, her whole body shaking, crying sooky little whimpers. They got no guts, no sense, and still they come out here.

He stares at her. Her voice quivering, she says, 'Water. Please, we need water.'

Fucksake. 'I didn't invite youse, did I. But ya had to hang about, try to steal my car. What the fuck do I care if you want water.'

'Please help him,' she says, her voice shaking. 'He's lost so much blood. I can't make it stop. Please, please . . .'

'Shut up!' he shouts at her, waving the gun in her direction. She screams; his head reverberates. He needs to think. He can't focus with all her noise. He steps out, slamming the door shut behind him, biting his lip, scratching his arm.

He fills a bucket with water from the hose, pushes the door open just enough to slide it in, then slams it shut and locks it again. Double-checks that the lock is fast. He can't think straight and he's got barely enough meth for another hit. First things first. He'll toke up again and then he'll go into town, get hold of some more.

When he picks up his glass pipe from the coffee table his body keens in anticipation. Just holding it gives him a small rush, knowing that a hit is coming. He opens the bag of ice. It's almost empty but he brings it to his nose and inhales anyway. The bitter chemical scent is reassuring; it smells right and the colourless crystals like bits of broken glass look right too.

He pours the last of them into the pipe, tapping the stem gently to move it all into the bowl at the base, then fits the mouthpiece and flicks the lighter on. Holding the pipe halfway down the stem, he places the lighter beneath the bowl, not touching but near, and turns the bowl gently, keeping it moving so that the heat doesn't crack the glass. After a moment he sees the telltale vapour as the flame breaks down the crystals. He inhales slowly, savouring the moment, and exhales quickly. Holding the drug in doesn't add to the rush, it just burns. The pipe is hot – he puts it on the table, already pockmarked with a rash of burn marks, and feels the flash rush through him. He is breathing fast, his heart is beating faster, he is powerful, strong, full of energy. He can handle it all. Bring it on, fuckers. He dances around the room, he is invincible. After a few minutes the rush starts to fade, and he goes to repack the pipe.

Fuck, there's none left. He shakes the bag to one corner, wets his finger, picking up any powder that might be left, rubbing it on his gums. Looks around, sees the empty bottle. The fucken rum is gone too, and they drank all his beers. He feels a hatred for the pair rising in him. They fucken deserve it. Deserve all they get.

Tuesday

Three days missing

4

Walker loves the feeling of being in the water, the sense of weightlessness and power combined. Most days he gets up early to fit in an hour in the pool. Caloodie has a surprisingly professional set-up for a small country town: fifty metres in length, with lanes set apart for lapping, a lap timer and colourful flags hanging above the water to mark five metres before the turn.

He slept badly last night, dreaming vividly of being trapped in a dark place, the rusty taste of blood in his mouth, an ominous sense of doom, of waiting. When he woke he was sweating, the bed damp from his night terrors. He's spent so many years undercover, never relaxing, always waiting to be exposed, but only now, when he can finally sleep without fear, does he have these dark dreams night after night. He dozed for another hour, then as the dawn began to break gave up on sleep, arriving at the pool at 5.30. The first, and so far only, swimmer this morning, he's enjoying the unbroken water, the silence, the stillness.

He swims his usual forty laps, the last vestiges of disquiet disappearing, his mind stilling as he follows the black line through his goggles. His stroke is good; he was on the school swimming team and could have competed at a senior level if he'd had the dedication and single-mindedness to spend three or four hours in the pool each day. As it is, he's grateful he didn't. The enforced hours of lapping up and down would have killed his love for it. This way, he can still wake in the morning and enjoy the whole ritual, from the poolside freshness, his body shivering as it anticipates the initial chill, to the powerful feeling of scything through the water, his arms pulling strongly, his legs kicking. And the meditative, mind-emptying freedom of it. There are plenty of times he's found answers to whatever problems his mind has been working on as he laps up and down.

He glides in for his last touch and flips onto his back, pulling off his goggles, floating, his chest still heaving with the effort of his swim. The pool is fringed by palm trees, their green fronds in sharp relief against the blue sky above. A rosella parrot flies low over the water, flashing its red, yellow and lime-green plumage. The water, the palm trees, the pale concrete pavilion with its low 1950s-style changing rooms, brings to mind an art postcard that Ellen had pinned above the breakfast bar in her Sydney kitchen: a pool, a diving board, a blue sky. He can't remember the artist's name. He floats, thinking of Ellen. He needs to call her, can't keep ignoring her messages and emails. But he's realised that the longer he's away, the more certain he is that ending it was the right thing to do.

He backstrokes slowly for a couple of lengths, stretching, relaxing, revelling in the long slow movements, then pulls himself out and enjoys the sensation of drying off, the sun warm on his shoulders and legs.

Exercise always makes him hungry, so he drops in to the bakery to grab a strong coffee, two shots in the small cup, and a bacon-and-egg roll. They're good here, the soft flour-topped roll, the egg yolk runny when he bites into it, the bacon salty and crisp, and the whole sandwich tangy with brown sauce.

He decides he'll follow up the few leads Grogan has found. Rather than ask Grogan to show him the CCTV footage, he drives to the servo to see if they've still got a copy. He's in luck. He knows

Lucy who works there, and she plays back the tape for him, happy to chat and have a break from the routine of her day.

The two pull up at the pumps just after 11 a.m. on Saturday. The bloke, Berndt Meyer, looks like an obvious outsider, with his loose flowing trousers and long hair, filling the tank; the girl, slender with long dark hair pulled up into a loose bun, a halter top and cut-off denim shorts, the pockets visible at the tops of her thighs, going in to pay. Watching them, even on the servo's grainy CCTV feed, gives Walker a feeling for them, a sense of who they are, in a way that a still photograph never does.

Ali at the Federal remembers them too. At this time of year there aren't that many tourists, so the pair had stood out.

'Yeah,' she says, 'they were here. Stayed Friday night, had dinner. Left Saturday, mid-morning, I suppose.'

'Did they say where they were off to?'

'When they checked in, the bloke said they were on their way to jobs on a station out west of Smithton. Didn't look the type, to be honest. Reckon they'll have to toughen up a bit.'

So they'd still been talking about going to Glen Ines when they arrived here, at least.

'Anyone else in here that might have seen them?' asks Walker.

She thinks a moment. 'Yeah. The usual crowd were in. Paul Johnson, his drivers. Angus Jones. Hippy. Couple of others. Talk to Mike, he was at the bar more than I was. Friday is our busy night – I was helping in the kitchen and serving meals. There's a couple of young Telstra blokes working out here for a couple of weeks and staying here. They might have talked to them maybe. You could ask 'em – they're usually in for dinner around six.'

'Can I have a squiz at the guest register?' he asks.

She looks at him. 'Guess I'm supposed to ask for a warrant for that kind of thing.' She's half laughing, half serious. They've known each other since they were kids, in the same year at school. Ali the smallest in the class and yet, just like now, no one messed with her. He remembers playing some catch game at lunchtime and Ali eluding them all, slight and fast and giving no quarter.

'Help us out here, Ali,' he says. 'These kids could be in trouble. I just want to find them, nothing else.'

She bends down and pulls a black A4 diary from below the bar counter, flips through it, opens it to Friday, runs her finger down the names. 'There weren't many rooms taken that day – it's the off season now. Along with those two backpackers, the only other guests were the Telstra blokes.'

She pauses, then looks him in the eye.

'Angus Jones stayed the night too. He'd had a few so I talked him out of driving back to Landsdowne. He's not down here. We don't always bother registering them when we know the person. I'm only telling you this 'cause I know you're not going to dob us in to the taxman.'

'Righto,' says Walker with a smile. 'I'll keep shtum. Anyone else stay that night who's not on the list?'

'Nah, unless Mike gave someone a key while I was tidying up in the kitchen. But I don't reckon so, I'd have noticed when we were cleaning the rooms.'

Walker doesn't bother searching out Ali's husband, Mike. The bloke is the town gossip and you can never have a quick chat with him, he'll be talking for hours. 'That bloke makes ya ears bleed,' as Blair would say. Instead, he walks across to the café, buys a coffee and a Cherry Ripe and, on impulse, picks up a coffee for Grogan too. He's invading the man's territory, and he wants Grogan as an ally, not a rival. He'd guess Grogan is a good few years younger than he is, early thirties at most, and this remote posting is a way to fast-track promotion. Grogan would still be a constable in the city stations, one of many, but out here he's the chief. He'll spend a few years out bush and then head back to the city, perhaps a sergeant or a choice of specialism.

The thought of this life – the slow, local policing, as much about diplomacy as fighting crime, years out here killing time – makes Walker feel trapped and claustrophobic. He loves this place; it's where he spent most of his childhood, living with Grandma, attending the tiny country primary school, running free with Blair and the others, swimming in the creeks and billabongs, sleeping under the stars. He'll always consider it home, much more so than the big house with its landscaped gardens that his mum calls home in Boston. But still. To work here. To live here as an adult. The same day in day out, day in day out. That's not for him.

When he arrives at the station it's lunchtime and the front desk is unmanned, no sight of yesterday's receptionist. He rings the bell on the worktop and after a moment the door opens and Grogan comes out.

Walker holds one of his coffees out. 'I got you this. Not sure how you like it – it's white, no sugar.'

'Right.' Grogan takes the cup, sets it down on the worktop. 'You need something?'

'I called in some dashcam from a truck travelling on the Smithton road on Saturday and it passed their car, so those backpackers were definitely heading that way. Have you talked to all the cattle stations between here and Smithton? If they've broken down on the road, maybe they're staying at a homestead somewhere.'

'I got the teachers at School of the Air to put out a call. No one's seen them.'

'Righto,' says Walker. 'Is it worth paying a visit to the stations, anyone who hasn't got kids, maybe didn't hear the call-out?'

'The bush telegraph is pretty good out this way. They all talk to each other. If they were staying with someone, we'd know about it.'

Walker concedes this truth. The cattle stations are isolated but they stay in touch with their satellite phones or UHF radios and this would be news to share.

'Now that we know they headed to Smithton, is it worth getting a helicopter up to have a look for them? In case they went bush, broke down somewhere?'

'I still reckon they got to Smithton, saw the place and changed their minds,' says Grogan. 'Headed north and then east to the coast.'

He's probably right, the most likely case is that they've driven on somewhere. But the car was a bit of an old bomb so a breakdown isn't out of the question and Walker feels he has to do something. The conversation with the missing girl's sister is playing on his mind. It's unusual for youngsters to be out of touch for long. His own sister, Grace, who's nineteen, sleeps with her phone beside her.

'If they headed back to the coast, they should be picking up a signal by now,' he says. 'Even driving slowly, it shouldn't take three days to get there.'

Grogan nods. 'Alright. I'll speak to the misper unit in Brisbane. They're officially in charge of this. If they don't get a ping on the mobiles today, we can ask about getting a helicopter up tomorrow.'

'I thought I might set up a traffic stop on the highway too,' says Walker. 'Chat with the passing vehicles, maybe jog a few memories. Someone might remember seeing something.'

'Not much point, I'd say. It's not a busy road – you won't have much luck.'

Walker nods. 'I know the road, but I say it's worth trying. See if anything comes of it.'

'I can't stop you driving out there, but you can't just stop the traffic . . .'

'Look, mate,' says Walker. 'I'm trying to do this the right way, run things past you and all that, but I report to Foreign Affairs and I need to tell them, and the families involved, that I've done everything I can to trace these kids.'

Walker's not into pulling rank but if he has to he will.

After a moment Grogan looks up at the clock. 'I need to finish a couple of things. If you come back in half an hour we can drive out together and check it out.'

'No worries,' says Walker. 'I'll wait.'

'Suit yourself,' says Grogan, leaving the coffee on the counter as he goes back inside. Walker drinks it after he's finished his own.

It's closer to forty-five minutes before Grogan comes back. They drive to the highway, in silence, in the police cruiser. Grogan pulls up on the verge about ten minutes out of town and nods at Walker. 'All yours, DS,' he says, pushing his seat as far back as it goes and switching the radio to the cricket.

Walker sets up *SLOW* and *STOP* signs a couple of hundred metres in each direction, though on this straight road any driver will see the cruiser long before reaching it. The temperature is at its peak at this time of day, the tarmac radiating heat through the soles of his boots, the land towards the horizon distorted by the light and the hot air. He sits in the car with Grogan, the air conditioning on, listening to the cricket. They don't talk much, Grogan not a conversationalist or perhaps still not keen on this task. And Grogan is right, there's virtually no traffic. In the next two hours Walker only stops three ponderous road trains, which brake to a slow, noisy halt. None of the drivers came past in the last few days but they all agree to pass the details to their offices.

A white Toyota Hilux heading into town is the fourth vehicle Walker pulls over. The driver is late thirties, with russet-coloured hair, longer than is usual out here, falling in waves to almost his shoulders. He's slim, his shirt loose on his frame, his fingers drumming the steering wheel. He gives his name as Darryl Foley.

'You live out here, Mr Foley?'

'Yeah, got a place I use when I've got a few days off work.'

Walker doesn't know him and as they're not that far off in age, Foley probably hasn't been here that long.

'Righto. When did you last head out this way?' he asks.

'Ah, Saturday. Late morning, I reckon.'

'We've got a missing persons case, a young couple that were last seen on this road on Saturday sometime. They were driving a black Ford Fiesta. Do you remember seeing it when you came out this way?'

'Nah.'

Walker hears the door of the police car open behind him, turns to see Grogan ambling over.

'Alright, Darryl?' says Grogan.

The bloke nods. 'Alright, Dave. Listen, I gotta go. I'm on my way to work and Paul'll have me guts for garters if I'm late.'

'Fair enough,' says Grogan, slapping his hand lightly on the boot of the car, the way you would to set a horse in motion. As the white Toyota accelerates into the distance, Walker hears the engine misfiring a little, a beat out of time. 'Darryl Foley,' says Grogan. 'He drives a truck for Paul Johnson.'

Walker looks at him, not sure if Grogan is being deliberately unhelpful or just doesn't know much about policing. 'Would have been good to ask him a few more questions? He was out this way on Saturday.'

'To be honest, the bloke's full of bullshit. Any story you tell, he'll tell you he's done the same thing, only bigger and better. I wouldn't listen to a word he says.'

The next car that passes is a dusty white ute, not dissimilar to Walker's own, driven by an older man, his face toughened by a life on the land. He's thin too, a bag of bones, his skin nut-brown tinged with red, his face dotted with large freckles from the sun, his eyes half-closed in a permanent squint against the light. He's wearing a battered cowboy hat and a pale-blue shirt. When Grogan sees the car pull up, he gets out of the cruiser and walks over.

'G'day, Angus,' he says. 'Heading into town?'

The older man nods. 'Looks that way,' he says.

The air is still and the heat is almost unbearable. Walker can feel the sweat prickling along his back and chest.

'I'm DS Lucas Walker,' he says, wanting a full introduction and knowing Grogan isn't going to offer one.

The old bloke squints at him. 'Angus Jones,' he says eventually. 'What's this about?'

Walker notes the name – this is the one who slept at the hotel on Saturday night after drinking a few too many.

'We got a couple of missing backpackers, headed out on this road on Saturday,' says Grogan. 'Wondering if you might have seen them?'

Jones looks at Grogan; something unspoken travels between them. He takes his cowboy hat off and runs his hand over thinning hair. 'Can't help ya,' he says after a long moment. 'I wasn't on the road that day.'

Grogan nods and says, 'Righto. Thanks, mate. See you round, then.'

'You know each other?' asks Walker as the vehicle drives off.

'I know everyone round here. Part of the job. Angus has a property, Landsdowne, about fifty kilometres out west. Doing it tough right now. Missus left him a couple of years ago, drought's a shocker and he's losing money every day trying to keep his stock alive. He drives a truck for a Brisbane outfit once in a while, just trying to keep afloat. All the stress has turned him into a bit of a drinker.'

Walker files the information away and nods. 'Let's call it a day, then,' he says. There's no point doing this with Grogan here. Angus Jones was lying to them and he'd put money down that Grogan knows it. Jones was in the pub on Friday night and he stayed over at the hotel. He definitely saw the two missing kids at the bar and there's a good chance he was on the road home when they disappeared.

5

Rita is lying beside Berndt, holding his hand. She's lost count as to how long they've been in the shed. The heat is unremitting. With the sun pounding on the aluminium panels of the shed it's like lying inside an oven – dry, baking, parching. She can't move, just lies there waiting for it to end. The nights are cooler but the pitch-black makes it almost worse. The sounds of the shed creaking, the rustling and scratching of unknown animals and insects, the fear rising in her, a terrifying black tide of fear. She can't see Berndt, only touch him, talk to him.

She dips her shirt in the water, wiping his face, whispering to him, but he doesn't answer. She lies as close as she can, talking softly, encouraging him to get through this. Last night she'd crawled away to look for the water and it had taken her an age, a panicking, heart-stopping, terrifying age, to find him again in the darkness. Now she's moved the bucket beside them, won't leave his side.

Berndt hasn't spoken since that first night, when he'd been moaning in agony, begging her to help, and all she'd been able to do was bind his shirt around the terrible wound on his leg. The shirt was soon dark with blood. She'd ripped his trousers, tying them around his wound too, trying to staunch the blood, but it hadn't helped much.

Yesterday he'd been feverish, moaning, not making any sense.

She'd tried to keep him cool with the water the maniac had left for them. But it wasn't very much water and she needed to drink too. In the heat, her thirst is unquenchable.

Today the maniac had brought them another bucket of water and some bread. When she'd heard him coming, the screen door of the house opening and closing, his steps getting nearer, her bladder had emptied of its own volition and she'd scrambled to the far corner of the shed, away from the door. She'd left Berndt lying there, undefended, which made her ashamed but she was panicked. He'd had the gun before, he'd been waving it around, and she's terrified he's going to shoot them, shoot her, shoot Berndt again. But he hadn't done anything or said anything, just thrown in the loaf of bread and pushed a bucket of water through the door.

She eats the bread, she hasn't eaten for days and she's hungry, but it makes her mouth dry and she doesn't want to be more thirsty than she already is. She wants to save some water for Berndt, he'll be thirsty when he wakes up.

The heat is lessening slightly, the dim light in the shed getting softer. It's cooler but another dark night looms. She doesn't know how much longer she can stay here without going crazy. She needs Berndt to wake up, to get better, to hold her hand. When she hears the screen door open again, her heart freezes, her stomach cramps. She scuttles backwards, into the gloom, but this time he's not coming for them. She hears a car door open then slam shut, the engine starting and the car moving off. She goes to the door, shakes it, rattling it as loud as she can.

'No. No. Don't leave us! Help! Please, help.'

But there is nothing except the sound of the engine fading. Then, after a time, the shed creaks, the heat of the day retreats, and the space gets darker and darker. She's crying, hysterical. They're alone out here. What if he never comes back.

She goes back over to Berndt, tears streaming down her face, breathing heavily, her nose full of snot. His skin, which has been burning-hot to touch, is finally cooler. Maybe that's a good sign, she thinks, though his face is very pale, his eyes closed.

She needs him to wake up, they need to get out of here. She sits beside him, wets his face and lips with water. They're cool, pale, almost bloodless. She shakes him by the shoulder.

'Wake up, Berndt, you need to wake up. He's left us alone. We have to get away. Berndt' – she's shaking him harder – 'Berndt!'

But he doesn't respond.

Wednesday

Four days missing

6

Dave Grogan is standing by the French doors that open on to the back deck, looking over the garden, watching the early-morning sun play across the water of the pool. They'd built the pool last summer. It had made a huge difference, made the house feel cooler, more coastal somehow. The girls love it. Every evening when he gets home they're in the water in their matching pink togs. The eldest, Olivia, slim and tanned like her mum, usually floating on the inflatable flamingo; Amelia, the youngest, bouncing up and down or diving and holding her breath, showing him how long she can stay underwater. Amelia has his pale skin and chubby face. She is the sweeter of the two, but he wishes they'd both taken after Lisa when it comes to looks.

He can hear Lisa banging cupboard doors in the kitchen as she prepares the girls' brekky, making a point in the aftermath of their quarrel. The same old disagreements, about his job, about living in the middle of nowhere, about how this isn't what she signed up for. A circular argument that waxes and wanes but never entirely retreats. Earlier, lying in bed in the peace of the early morning, before the kids get up and the day's rush begins, he'd pulled her close, but she'd shaken him off, turned away.

'Get off me. It's too hot,' she'd said.

He'd rolled onto his back in a bit of a huff and lain there, quiet, relaxed. That had given her the breathing space to start up.

'You never assert yourself – you always let everyone else take over. Finally a case comes along that could get you noticed and you hang back, let that bloke from Sydney lord it around, acting like the boss.'

'He's a DS, what am I supposed to do . . .'

'You said when we came here that it would fast-track your promotion. Just a couple of years, you said, then we'll move back to the coast and we'll be set up. We've been here *five years*. Five years in this shithole where nothing happens and there's nothing to do and the girls are going to a crappy school. My friends are having fun, going to cool places. I've got nothing. No shops, no decent hairdressers, can't even get my nails done or eat at a nice restaurant.'

'You know it's because of cutbacks, love. They're not promoting anyone at the moment, there's no budget for it. If we go back to the coast now it'll mean all these years for nothing. I'll still be a conny on conny's pay. At least here we have a nice house, a big garden, a pool. We couldn't afford any of that on the coast, not on this money. Look, I'm due a long holiday at Christmas. We'll take four weeks at the coast, really live it up.'

'Four weeks! I don't want four bloody weeks. I want a life.'

He wants a life too. Doesn't want to spend the rest of his days handing out traffic notices on the dusty highway outside Caloodie, keeping an eye on the drunks at the RSL or the Federal. But there are no openings on the coast and there's no way he'll get Lisa to take another country post, even if it is a bigger town like Toowoomba. And he can't give her the life she wants, the life she deserves, on this salary.

His phone vibrates on the coffee table. He sees the number on the screen and feels his stomach contract. He picks it up, walks out of the living room, away from Lisa, before he answers.

'Yeah,' he says. 'Listen, I'm at home right now, I can't really talk.'

'What's the situation with these missing tourists?'

'What? What do you know about that? Is it something to do with you?'

'I pay you to answer questions, not ask them, Grogan.'

'I can't tell you much,' he says. 'A couple of missing German backpackers. There's a DS, a bloke called Walker, looking into it. Been appointed by the Foreign Affairs department because they're tourists or something.'

'Where'd you say he's from?'

'Dunno. He's not Queensland Police. He's a DS in Sydney, must have some links to Foreign Affairs. DS Lucas Walker.' Grogan pauses. He hadn't thought about it earlier, but this is a chance to get into their good books. 'Actually, I was gonna call you later - there's a helicopter going up this morning, having a look for their car. It might buzz over your place, in case you want to keep everyone out of sight. It'll be over by the end of the day.'

There's a pause. 'Alright. Listen, I want our guys kept out of this. Make sure you keep this DS away from them, it's nothing to do with them.'

'Shit. If you know something about this, if this is something to do with your operation . . . No, actually, don't tell me. I don't want to know about it. I don't want to be involved.'

'Keep him away from our places, that's all.'

The line goes dead and Grogan finds himself in the bedroom, sitting on the unmade bed with the white bedding that cost a bloody fortune, the ceiling fan rotating slowly above it, the air conditioner pumping cool air. He can hear the girls up and about, arguing about something, getting ready to leave for school. He lies back and exhales loudly.

The money is handy. He needs it. It paid for the pool, for Lisa's car, it's making a difference to their lives. And there's no real harm in giving them a tip-off once in a while or turning a blind eye to a bit of drug dealing. But if they know about these backpackers, then that's a whole other can of worms. He lies there thinking it through, working out his options. He doesn't really have a choice, can't walk away now. But if they are involved with these missing foreigners, if he's going to handle this kind of shit, he wants a whole lot more money. The thought cheers him slightly. If he can wangle an extra payment, they can take a five-star holiday to the coast. Lisa can show her mates that living out bush has its advantages. They'll stay in a bling hotel, go shopping, take the girls to Dreamworld.

He walks down the hallway and up behind Lisa, who's standing by the sink, looking out the back window. He puts his arms around her from behind and she jumps. 'Jesus, Dave, you frightened me. I was miles away.'

'Sorry, babe.' He keeps his arms around her, but she's stiff, doesn't relax into him. 'Look, you're right,' he says. 'I'm sorry that we're still stuck out here. Let me make it up to you. Let's book a really fancy hotel for our holiday. Somewhere that'll make all the girls jealous. We'll go shopping – I want to buy you an eternity ring, make up for the eternity we've been out here . . .'

She turns, pushes him back at arm's length, looks hard at him. 'Somewhere really fancy? I can choose?'

'You can choose, babe, anywhere you like.'

Her eyes soften; he sees the glimmer of a smile on her lips. It makes him rash. 'Next year will be our last year. I promise. I'll push them for a promotion and a coastal posting. I'm owed.'

The smile disappears. 'I'm going to hold you to that, Dave. You promised and I'm going to hold you to that.'

He nods. 'You can, I promise.'

This time the smile reaches her eyes. 'We can look at some houses while we're at the coast. See what we can afford.'

She drags him to the sofa, opens her iPad, starts looking at hotels and showing him houses. He sits with her for a while, but the cramps are back in his stomach and his heartburn too, and he's relieved when it's time to take the girls to school and go into work.

• • •

The morning passes slowly, his mind constantly veering to the missing backpackers and what it might mean for them and for him, if they're involved in this drugs operation. The helicopter is up, searching the bush along the highway between Caloodie and Smithton. He hopes they took his tip and keep the operation well hidden. By lunchtime his nerves are all over the place and he decides to head to the pub for a beer.

The bar is quiet, just Hippy and old Tom, who always comes in for something to eat at lunch; he's pretty sure Ali feeds him for free. Grogan nods at them but takes a seat on the other side of the bar, orders a beer and goes through the maths in his head: how much he needs to keep Lisa happy and still put a bit aside for when they move to the coast. Wondering how much they'll go for too, and how to play it. He needs the cash, but they need him more. What he really needs is a piece of information that will give him leverage. Something he can use to bargain with.

He's running through his options when Angus Jones slides onto the bar stool beside him, his face lined by the permanent frown and the downturned lips that are his trademark. The bloke's been having problems but so have a lot of people, and not all of them are as much of a misery to spend time with.

'Alright, Angus?' he says, picking up his beer and draining it. 'I'm just on my way out, mate.'

Angus catches the barman's eye and nods, the tiniest upward tilt of his chin. A moment later a schooner of beer, the outside wet with condensation, sits in front of him. Angus takes a dainty sip then turns slightly to face him. The man has the charisma of a lizard, thinks Grogan. Those still, unblinking eyes, the leathered skin, cold gaze.

'Did he call you?' asks Angus.

Grogan flinches and looks around the bar. Hippy and Tom are watching the horses on TV, paying them no attention.

'Yeah,' says Grogan, 'but I don't want to talk about it, especially not here.'

'That Sydney cop called me, says he wants to come out to my place for a visit, says it's routine. But that can't happen. I can't have him nosing around, it's not a good time. I can't have him coming out there.'

'Yeah, alright, I'm on it. But listen to me, Angus, this can't happen again. We don't talk like this. Never. You hear me? Never. I talk to him, that's it. You stay the fuck out of it. I'm not looking after you and I don't want to talk to you.'

Angus gives him a long stare, then picks up his beer and swivels back to face the bar. Grogan stands, pushing the stool back and dropping the money for his beer onto the bar. He nods goodbye to the group on the far side and leaves through the side door.

The conversation with Angus has soured his mood even further. Reptilian fucker, he thinks. It wouldn't surprise him if the bloke had something to do with those missing backpackers. The thought delivers a heavy rock of self-loathing to his stomach. He didn't sign up for this; this is a whole lot more than turning a blind eye to a bit of drug dealing.

7

Walker puts in a call to Rutherford, though there's nothing much to tell. 'There's a helicopter up having a look for them. The local bloke still seems to think they'll turn up back in Sydney or on the coast,' he says. 'But I don't know. There's something not quite right. That grazier, Jones, flat-out lied to me. I'm planning to go out and interview him, because why would he do that?'

Rutherford says: 'Have you looked into these kids' backgrounds? Is there any link to dealing recreational drugs, or drugs generally?'

Walker's internal radar gives a loud ping. Rutherford obviously does have a reason for involving him, beyond this Foreign Affairs bullshit. He has had a look at Meyer's life online. Helpfully transparent, with no privacy locks on his Instagram and plenty of traces on other sites, from gaming to community groups – he's a member of Extinction Rebellion and a sponsor of a dog rescue centre in Spain. His Instagram pictures are full of suntanned youngsters by pools, on beaches, on evenings out. The girls in short dresses with bare brown legs, the men like Meyer, with long hair, designer tattoos and a hipster vibe. Plenty of parties, so he could potentially be dealing recreational stuff. He's on the move a lot, so perhaps he could be moving it for bigger players too. Walker has checked the Federal Police database, but neither the Sydney hostel where the couple had been based nor the couple themselves are flagged with any drugs connections. There's nothing that rings any warning bells.

'There's nothing obvious,' he says to Rutherford. 'He might have thought he'd make some quick money bringing some stuff out this way. Maybe started dealing and crossed paths with someone who didn't like it.'

He's looked into the girlfriend's accounts too. Her online life is a little more private: he can't view her Instagram pictures, and there's no other obvious activity apart from a LinkedIn profile, quite sparsely completed. He checks her name on various search engines but only one picture comes up, the portrait shot she uses on LinkedIn.

'Are they on your radar?' he asks Rutherford.

'No.' Rutherford pauses again. Walker knows him well enough to know he's thinking about how much information to share. The biggest cases the team investigates are on a need-to-know basis only. Rutherford has a few undercover teams under his command and he doesn't disclose without good cause, knowing that a leak can compromise a cover. Walker has had cause to be grateful for this reticence in the past.

'There's an operation going on not too far from you,' says Rutherford eventually. 'There's nothing to link these kids to it, no reason to suppose this is anything other than a couple of kids gone walkabout, but I'd like to stay in the loop with what's happening. Keep an eye on it but keep a low profile. I don't want anyone linking you back to us.'

After the call, Walker sits for a while on the veranda thinking. The drug scene in these bush towns is surprisingly active, in particular a growing problem with meth addiction, which is supplanting alcohol and cannabis as the drug of choice. Powerful and highly addictive, the drug is weaving long tendrils of harm throughout the outback and coastal towns, places where jobs are disappearing and the future looks bleak and unpromising, and where the high that meth offers is so appealing that its downsides have little traction.

Not that long ago, drugs out this way were limited to a bit of weed that someone might grow in a quiet spot. Alcoholism was always a much bigger problem: the violence, the road accidents, the diseases associated with drinking too much. And maybe no wonder out in these harsh and remote parts, where a couple of years of drought or one big flood can ruin your life's work. The place is full of worn-down men whose entire lives revolve around work and spending any money they earn in the pub. Blokes drinking beers, what could be more fair-dinkum Aussie than that.

And then gambling came along, once the pubs cottoned on to the fact that betting was an even bigger earner than a few cold pints. Horse racing, keno, the pokies . . . Men and women alike lured in by the promise of mega-jackpots. And all legal too, even if the havoc it wreaks keeps cops as busy as some of the illegal stuff.

But in the last couple of decades, the face of addiction out here has changed. The older men with their red-veined faces and bulbous alcoholics' noses that Walker remembers from childhood, some frightening in their capacity for violence, others comical in their drunkenness, have been replaced by younger meth heads. There are even a few here in Caloodie – thin, sometimes to the point of skeletal, the worst with their faces covered in sores, their teeth brown and decaying.

But what this all has to do with the missing backpackers is less clear. He gets up from his favourite veranda chair and looks in on Grandma. She's sleeping, her skin pale, her breath horribly laboured. It hurts him to see her like this. She was always so full of verve and life. He's glad he has the distraction of this case; sitting here, watching her wasting away like this, is eating him up.

He ponders what Rutherford might define as keeping a low profile, then shrugs it off and calls up the drug-related incidents and violent assaults from the local region over the last five years on his laptop. It's not a big list but a couple of names repeat regularly. He notes them down: Donald Taylor, Todd Ford, Dawn Geddes. The names don't ring any bells but he knows the Ford and the Geddes clans. He can ask around. Looking at the list of their crimes – possession, shoplifting, breaking and entering – he doubts they're anything but desperate addicts. The big players, the serious dealers, aren't likely to be shoplifting to support a habit.

When his stomach lets him know it's dinnertime, he calls Blair. Blair is the cousin closest in age to him, more like a brother. They're quite different in some ways – Blair hasn't left Queensland, barely leaves Caloodie, and he's calm and quiet, an observer who sees everything but avoids being the centre of attention. Walker has lived with his mum in the United States, and his drive and a natural preference for action make him less cautious and reflective. But they share a love of the bush, a similar sense of humour and a belief in fairness and the importance of family.

'Fancy a bite at the Federal?' asks Walker. 'The parmi is on lunch special today.'

The pub's chicken parmigiana is, says Blair, the best he's ever eaten – a chicken schnitzel as big as a dinner plate, covered with melted cheese and served with chips. Walker thinks it's pretty good too, but on the drive to the pub he winds Blair up by listing a number of mythical places where the parmi is larger, tastier and all-round better. After they put their order in with Ali, they take a table in the dining room rather than sitting at the bar; Walker wants to talk without being overheard.

Blair knows all three of the drug users. 'Yeah,' he says, shaking his head. 'Total meth heads. All of them a lot younger than us too. I reckon Donnie Taylor is only eighteen or nineteen. His mum died a few years back, and his sisters can't stop him throwing his life away on that shit.'

'Any of them doing anything more serious?' asks Walker, outlining his theory that perhaps the missing backpackers had a drug connection.

'I don't know, mate,' says Blair. 'The dealing out here is pretty small-time; I can't see any of those meth heads doing something to a couple of backpackers passing through. And if they pissed off someone in Sydney, they'd have caught up with them before they hit the western suburbs. They wouldn't have tailed them all the way out here.'

If it wasn't for his conversation with Rutherford and all those years in the murky world of Sydney's organised crime groups, which has left him with a very real sense of both their power and reach, Walker would agree. He drops the subject and lets the topic drift to the dismal performance of the Queensland cricket team and Blair's ambitions to open an outback eco-tourism venture.

As they leave, he glances into the bar. Mike is serving and he sees Angus Jones sitting by the bar, his thin frame and lined face in profile as he talks to someone. Jones hasn't called him back and Walker decides he'll have a quick chat now, save him driving the fifty kilometres or so out to the bloke's property, but as he steps in he sees that Jones is talking to Grogan. Walker pauses, moving back behind the cover of the door. He doesn't want Grogan involved in this; his clumsy policing will be a hindrance, not a help. After a moment's thought he turns and leaves. If Jones doesn't call him back, he'll just go out and pay him a visit. Sometimes dropping in by surprise works out better anyway.

8

He's on his way home, loaded up with supplies. He'd run out of meth and out of ideas about what to do with the pair in his shed, so he'd left them there yesterday evening and driven into town. It had taken a few house calls, calling in favours, but he'd found some gear in the end and found a party too. He'd spent the night in town, toking up, drinking, slept in the car for a couple of hours, then had a beer at the pub, bought a couple of cartons and a bottle of rum to take away, and now he's back on the road.

But now they're back on his mind. Yesterday he'd thrown in half a loaf of bread and filled up another bucket of water. The girl still whimpering in the corner, the bloke just lying there, not even moaning anymore. He'd told himself that he'd sort it out, but he doesn't know how he's going to square this all up. He can't have them going around telling everyone that he's getting wasted and shooting at people. Even if he did have grounds, with them trying to steal his car, it doesn't look good. It's their word against his and there's two of them. He could handle the girl, would like to handle the girl. He cackles to himself at the thought. But the bloke. Shit. He needs to figure out what to do.

The scratching anxiety is back and the speedometer is north of 140 K. He feels as if someone is watching him, glances in the rear-view mirror and sees the bloke standing in the back of the tray, the one he shot, standing there with his leg full of holes, bleeding all over the back of his fucken vehicle. Horrified, he swings the car wildly to the other side of the road and back again, swerving from side to side, trying to dislodge him, but the bloke just stands there, surfing the curves.

He hits the brakes, skids to a stop. That bloke's got no right to be in his vehicle, that's what got them into this mess in the first place. He reaches behind him to the back seat, pulls out the rifle, jumps out ready to fire but there's no one there. The only movement is the tarp that's come loose, flapping in the wind. Perhaps he's hidden himself underneath. He cocks the gun and fires, one, two, three times into the tarp. The sound breaks the silence of the empty highway, flashing around his head in a ricochet of bangs. When the noise dies away, he pulls the tarp back. Nothing. The tray back is empty.

He folds over in relief, one arm on the vehicle for support, surrounded by silence and stillness, the heat radiating off the road and the car, no other vehicles in sight. He climbs back into the driver's seat, shuts the door and sits there for a moment, trying to calm his rising paranoia. This is a hallucination, a comedown. He's almost home. Just twenty minutes and he can gear up. The thought calms him enough to drive on.

It's late arvo before he checks on them. He's feeling much better – the meth and a few beers and he's back to strength. But when he opens the shed door the stink is horrendous. He turns to his left and spits, trying to get rid of the taste and smell. She's lying beside the bloke, just by the door, her head on his chest. Her lips are dry and cracked, he can hardly hear her when she speaks.

'Water,' she says.

He grabs the bucket, fills it from the hose and tips it over the two of them – maybe it'll stop the stink a bit. He goes out, fills it again and puts it at the far side of the shed. She drags herself up, crawls over to the bucket and dips her head in, almost fully submerged, drinking and drinking. He watches her in disgust.

While she's at the bucket, he takes a closer look at the bloke, prods him in the torso with his boot. He doesn't move. A host of flies are buzzing around the wound on the leg and on his lips and eyes. He looks more closely. The bloke's eyes are wide open, staring at nothing.

He leaves her drinking, locks the shed again, goes back inside. Fuck. The bloke's gone and died on him. He stinks already and it'll only get worse. He'll have to dump him somewhere. If someone comes out here, not that many do but you never know, they'll smell him for sure. He needs to get rid of her too, but he fancies taking his time with this one. They've given him so much trouble he might at least have some fun. He thinks of her throat, soft and pale and quivering under his hand as she tries to breathe, and feels a stir of pleasure at the thought.

First, though, he has to get rid of the bloke's body. He can't bear to touch it, he needs to wrap it up in something. He pulls the rug up from the living room floor and hunts in the kitchen for something to give her to eat. He needs to keep her alive, get her trusting him, so that he can do it right with her.

He tucks a cereal box under his arm, picks up the rifle and drags the rug behind him to the shed. When he opens the door, she's still sitting by the bucket, so he throws the box of cereal towards her. She watches it fall, doesn't move towards it, but when he bends down and grabs the bloke's feet, juggling his rifle with one hand, he sees her move, hears her cry, so he drops the feet and fires a shot into the tin wall beside her, the noise thunderous in the small space.

She cowers, screams.

'Stay back, bitch, or I'll shoot you too!' he shouts as he bends down again and drags the dead weight of the bloke, one-handed, the other holding the rifle, the few metres out the door. He drops the feet, closes the door of the shed and leans against it breathing hard. She's screaming again, it sounds like she's saying 'Burnt, burnt'.

'Shut up!' he roars, thumping the side of the shed. She stops. He can hear that she's still crying but at least she isn't screaming. He locks the door, then drags the bloke to the rug and rolls him up in it. It takes an age – the body is heavier than it looks and awkward to handle and stinks to high fucken heaven. He's grunting and heaving. 'Fucken nothing but trouble.'

It's disgusting work and all the time the girl is crying and calling out. He thumps the shed again to quieten her. By the time he's got him wrapped up, the head covered, the bare feet and skinny calves poking out one end, he's sweating like a pig and totally stressed. He kicks at the rug. 'Nothing but a pain in the fucken arse. Shoulda left ya both by the side of the fucken road.'

Getting the body up into the vehicle is worse. He manages it eventually, but the effort, the stench and the heat have him retching. He goes inside, drinks two beers, the ice-cold liquid refreshing.

He needs to find a place to dump the body, far enough away from the property so there's no link back to him, but at the same time he can't drive on the roads and risk discovery. In the end he opts for the bush at the back of his place, avoiding the highways completely. His property isn't big, but the paddocks of the adjacent place are unfenced and, except once in a while during the cattle muster, he's never seen anyone out there.

He drives for fifteen minutes at random across the paddocks before he finds a suitable spot: a rocky outcrop, the sandstone boulders taller than he is. There's no water or much vegetation to attract cattle, though perhaps they'll come here for shade in the heat of the day. He doesn't have a lot of options. The land here is featureless and it's better to be away from the trees that line the creek bed to the east. The cattle will hide among them when mustering time comes and that could mean someone spotting the body, even if most of the mustering is done by helicopter and motorbike these days.

He parks the vehicle and walks around the stones. The outcrop is almost three metres high, perhaps five metres in length. Halfway along, a triangular-shaped fissure, a gap between two of the huge stones, narrows to a point in the darkness beyond and is large enough to edge into if he goes in sideways, keeping his head bent. He drags the rug-wrapped body as far as he can, pulls and pushes it deep inside. Soon it's hidden from view unless you walk directly around the base of the outcrop. He hunts around collecting stones and small boulders and piles them in a pyramid as tall as his thighs in front of the fissure, high enough that it's almost impossible to see into the darkness beyond.

By the time he's finished, he's feeling good about the spot he found. It's smart. No one's gonna find this fucker. This is as deserted as the country around here comes. But he's exhausted too, the light of the day fading, the bush turning monochrome around him. He drives slowly home, his nerve ends tingling, his head pounding. Now he just has to decide what to do with the girl.

9

It's at least twenty-four hours since Barbara has slept. The flight is endless. First to Dubai, where men in white robes wander around the airport, talking on mobile phones. Then Singapore, a vast airport, a city in itself, complete with an indoor garden, palms and tropical plants and butterflies as big as her hand. There's a scent in the air that is different to home: jasmine and spice and something bordering on decay. She logs in to the airport Wi-Fi and checks her emails and texts but there's no news from Australia, only anxious messages from her parents, checking her progress, wanting updates already.

She'd talked it through with her parents and Carl Meyer and they'd all agreed: Rita and Berndt need at least one of them to be in Australia. It was her idea and with her police background it's clear that she's the best person to handle this.

She'd called Uli Fischer, the inspector she works with at LKA, explained the situation. It had been a struggle to get him to approve time off, they're understaffed already, but she'd known that if she had to, she would quit. Rita needs her and that is non-negotiable. This knowledge gave her a kind of confidence in the negotiation that she might not normally have had, and he'd relented and signed her off for two weeks.

He'd been kind, at the end, too. 'I hope you find her,' he'd said. 'I'm sure you will. You're a good cop. I'd like to have you looking for me if I was missing somewhere.'

She's grateful and she knows she owes him, so she spends her time on the flight putting together a long update on the Charlottenburg robberies and where her small team is with them. She knows her constable will keep ploughing through the CCTV footage but she makes a case for additional resources. He's hard-working but lacks imagination so it's possible the investigation will stall if they can't find a lead in the CCTV images; this perpetrator has the potential to be lethally dangerous sometime very soon.

Other than working, she thinks endlessly of Rita. Her light-hearted, easy-going little sister. Whether it's the advantage of being born later – nine years after Barbara – or just a personality trait, Rita has always been the carefree one. Even irresponsible at times. While Barbara studied hard, followed the rules, earned her grades and signed up for the police straight out of school, Rita was the one who climbed out of her bedroom window and went clubbing with the older kids when she was just sixteen, turning up at Barbara's apartment giggly and woozy at 3 a.m., with grinning boys in tow who Barbara had to send away with a flea in their ear.

Rita has been having a great time in Australia. Learning to surf, plenty of party nights, working in the flagship store of a big fashion chain to earn enough money to fund trips to New Zealand and Fiji. And she and Berndt seem to be head over heels in love. Barbara can't really see the appeal – the man bun, fisherman's trousers and arty tattoo vibe isn't really her thing. But to give him his due he seems kind-hearted and smitten with Rita, and after some of the tossers Rita has dated, Barbara is happy to take a decent guy, man bun and all.

After Singapore, the small map on her seatback screen shows the plane flying over Australia for what seems like hours. She pulls up the blind, looks at the land beneath, burnt red, flat and featureless, at least from this height. As the plane finally begins its descent, the countryside below seems marginally greener. A sea of houses, gardens with blue rectangular swimming pools, rooftops and buildings getting nearer and nearer, and then with a bump and a hiss of air she's pushed back in her seat as the plane skims along the runway, then slows, turns and stops.

As soon as she can she switches on her phone. Still no news about Rita, but she's here now and that brings with it a lift in mood, a sense of purpose. Being on the ground, closer to doing something, anything, she feels better. While she waits for her luggage, she texts Monika to let her know she's arrived safely. Monika hadn't been that supportive of her decision to come. Although she's a free spirit and all for Barbara taking time off and getting out more – would cheer loudly if it was Barbara who was quitting her job and going to Australia on a whim – she's never been that close to Rita. She thinks Rita is spoilt and that the whole family prioritises her needs and disregards Barbara's.

'Typical Rita,' she'd said. 'Getting herself into some kind of trouble and looking to everyone else to get her out of it. You've just been promoted and you're working this big case and now you're going to leave and run around looking for Rita, who's probably just having fun on a beach somewhere and not thinking of anyone else.'

It's true in a way. If there's ever a problem, Rita has no compunction about being bailed out by Babs, her parents, or whatever man she's with at the time. It comes from being the baby in the family, thinks Barbara, as she grabs her suitcase from the belt and gets into the customs queue.

She's overnighting in Brisbane as there's no connecting flight to the outback town where Rita was last seen until early the following morning. The taxi ride through foreign streets passes in a kind of blur. Palm trees, purple jacaranda, white-flowered frangipani and silvery-green eucalyptus trees decorate the front gardens of wooden houses set high above the ground and surrounded by shaded verandas. Then they cross a river and the high-rise buildings of a city emerge.

The hotel, an Ibis, has a bright and overlit reception that only serves to power up her exhaustion and anxiety. She feels the beginnings of a headache. The room itself is small but quiet and it's a relief to strip off her travelling clothes and shower. She stands under the hot water for a long time, trying to wash away her fear and apprehension and her sense of being in an utterly alien place. It's her first time out of Europe and she feels the nervousness of the unknown. Afterwards, wrapped in a towel, her hair damp, she stands at the window, looking over a curve of the river and the buildings of the city on the other bank. Night lights are coming on, the city twinkles and glitters with promise and modernity, but she's too wired and stressed to admire it.

She needs to rest, tomorrow will be another long day of travelling – she'll fly to a small town called Hopeville and hire a car there for the final leg to Caloodie – but her mind is racing, trapped in Berlin time, not ready for sleep.

She orders room service: a club sandwich and chips. The sandwich is generous, filled with chicken, salty bacon, mayonnaise and salad. She picks at it, too tired to be properly hungry, then mixes herself a strong vodka and tonic from the minibar, texts her parents and Berndt's father telling them she's arrived, and sends a text to the guy handling the case, DS Walker.

Good evening. Is there any news on Rita and Berndt? I am in Brisbane and will be arriving in Caloodie tomorrow. Barbara Guerra

The fact that she hasn't heard from him is worrying her. She knows that most missing persons are found within a few days or at least the first week, and it's been almost five days now since anyone saw Rita and Berndt. The longest five days of her life. Five days of not sleeping properly. Five days of anxiety, powerlessness, fear and a growing sense of danger. Five days that feel like they might change everything forever.

Thursday

Five days missing

10

Barbara is wide awake again at 4 a.m., her body confused by the time difference, exhausted but not sleepy. She checks her emails, sets up her out-of-office, then catches a cab to the airport. Fed up with the artificial air of airports and aeroplanes, she waits outside in the warmth of the tropical morning. Soon she is clammy with sweat. Barely 6 a.m. and it's already close to 30°C. She'd packed quickly, throwing in a summer dress or two and a couple of pairs of lighter trousers, but this morning she pulled on her jeans again, digging out a fresh t-shirt but not wanting to unpack and make decisions about what to wear.

The short flight passes in a blur. They soon bump back down – the countryside as they approach is parched and dry, pale grasslands, red earth, occasional stands of trees and shrubs. The town itself is there and gone in an instant as they fly over: she sees a few streets, wide gardens, and then the endless grasslands again. When the plane taxis to a stop, they disembark down external stairs. Stepping out of the cabin, the heat hits her like a furnace blast. The sky is such a deep blue that she feels you could dive into it, and the horizon stretches for miles in each direction. The airport is tiny, just one long low shed. The short walk across the tarmac has her sweating; this time the air-conditioned cool of the terminal is welcoming. There's no luggage belt; everyone waits inside the terminal until a little buggy appears, towing an open cart behind it carrying the handful of bags. Passengers mill around and drag their bags or backpacks off by hand. Most everyone else seems to know what they are doing, either being welcomed by friends and family or here on business. She sees two men shaking hands, one carrying a laptop bag and both wearing cowboy hats. In any other circumstance she would find it exciting to be somewhere so exotic, but today she's too exhausted and anxious.

She hires a car from the one small desk at the airport, asking for the cheapest and smallest they have; her budget isn't endless.

'Where are you off to?' asks the guy at the hire desk. He's young, no older than Rita, his face still dotted with acne.

'Caloodie and then towards Smithton.'

She makes a mess of the pronunciation again, and he corrects her. 'Ka-loo-*dee*. You'll need a bigger vehicle. I'm not trying to upsell you, love, but the roads aren't great out here and Smithton is in the middle of bloody nowhere. You'll be overtaking road trains and you need a bit of grunt for that. It'll be a lot more comfortable and safer in a four-wheel drive.'

She doesn't understand half of what he's saying; what he means by 'road trains' or 'grunt' is beyond her. But she thinks of Rita and Berndt disappearing while on the road and the vast empty distances she's flown over. 'OK. Give me whatever you think is best.'

The car is big and wide, a gleaming black four-wheel drive. Sitting in the driver's seat she feels incredibly high off the ground. She doesn't drive much in Berlin beyond the occasional crime scene for work. Otherwise her bike gets her around the city, and if she's going out of town she borrows her mum's little Peugeot 108, which she and Rita nickname The Roller Skate. This is a beast in comparison, and she's driving on the wrong side of the road too, but within a few minutes she's got the hang of it. It's not a challenging drive. The road is single-lane in each direction, straight as a die and there's no other traffic. She accelerates to 120 kilometres almost without noticing and has to pull back, slowing down to the 110 limit.

The car eats up the miles. To either side of her the vast plains of grass burnt white by the sun stretch to the horizon in every direction, the road a black river flowing between them. She's so tired that she feels slightly mesmerised by the flatness, the unchanging view, the unbending road. She tries the radio but picks up only static. She has to stretch in her seat, shake her head to stay awake. The sun is headache-inducingly bright; she'll need to buy a pair of sunglasses. Occasionally a huge truck thunders past from the opposite direction, leaving behind a swirl of air and dust that buffets the car in its wake. The air conditioning is blasting cool air on her hands and arms, but her dashboard says the outside temperature is 39°C and climbing. She tries not to think of Rita and Berndt, just focuses on driving, on arriving.

It's lunchtime before she reaches Caloodie. The town seems to be nothing more than half a dozen blocks of parallel roads, criss-crossed, all the streets incredibly wide, enough space for four cars side by side, though she doesn't see another vehicle on the move. The houses, too, are spaced far apart on blocks of pale dusty grass. The highway continues on – she sees a signpost saying *Smithton 203km* – but she turns left and drives into the town centre, which is compact and shaped like a cross, with a main street intersected at the top by another road. There are a handful of cars parked along the middle of the main street and a few on each side, clinging to whatever shade the awnings of the businesses that line the road provide.

The empty streets and the low shopfronts remind her of the set of a western movie. Her exhaustion and the long drive impart a dreamlike sense to her arrival. On Monday morning, just a few days ago, she'd been in Berlin, in the grey damp chill of autumn, wearing her coat and scarf, cycling into work, living her normal life. Today she's in a different world. A world of vivid white light, searing heat, where men wear cowboy hats and wide empty streets are lined by single-storey buildings with awnings. The biggest building is the hotel, two storeys high and covering most of one block. A shaded veranda runs the length of it. The date AD 1909 is written in cursive script above one door, and the hotel's name, *The Federal*, above the other. She pulls up in one of the empty parking spots outside the hotel, shuts off the engine and gets out, stretching her legs in pleasure after the hours spent sitting and driving.

The street is quiet. Somewhere in the distance she can hear the rumble of an engine, a truck on the highway perhaps, then it too disappears. There is no hum of traffic, no sound of voices, none of the usual noise of a city. The lazy caw-caw-caw of a single crow is all she can hear. She stands for a moment in the heat. Almost immediately she feels the top of her head burning, a trickle of sweat running down between her breasts, and her jeans sticking to her legs. She closes the car door, the metal hot to the touch. The ominous calm and the searing heat remind her again of a Hollywood western. She wouldn't be surprised to see an outlaw facing down a sheriff in the silence of the street.

When she pushes open the hotel doors, a welcome draught of cold air blows across her face and arms. She steps into a large square room with high ceilings and a bar running in a wide U-shape in the middle. The walls are painted pale blue and tiled to above shoulder height in a darker shade. The ceiling is a lemon colour with ornate cornicing and a ceiling rose, from which hangs a vintage light. The space is almost empty. Four men are sitting on high stools around the edge of the wooden-topped bar, each a prudent distance away from the next, all drinking glasses or bottles of beer. They turn their heads away from the TV on the wall above them when she enters, but she doesn't hold their interest long; the horse race on screen quickly draws their attention back.

'Sure thing, love,' says the woman behind the bar when Barbara asks about a room. 'We've got en suite rooms for eighty dollars a night.'

'OK, great, I will definitely need one for a few nights. But first I need to go to the police station. Can you tell me where it is?'

'Yeah. Go left out the door, walk down the street, take the first right and it's the second house on the right. You'll see the sign outside.'

Barbara thanks her but doesn't move. The cool air is so pleasant, she can't bear to step back into the heat outside. She's exhausted, wants to stop, doesn't want to face whatever news might be in store.

'Are you alright, love?' asks the woman. She's slim, no taller than Barbara, brown-skinned with dark hair pulled back in a ponytail. A series of tattoos runs up her right arm. She's wearing black shorts and a bright yellow t-shirt with *XXXX* written across the chest. Like four kisses, thinks Barbara, a little delirious with tiredness.

'Yes, thank you,' she says. 'I am a bit tired. I flew from Berlin and then Brisbane and then I drove from . . . I cannot remember the name, but it took a long time.'

'Berlin. Blimey. That's a bloody long way. You look like you need something to eat and drink before you do anything else. The cop shop will wait, they're probably at lunch now anyway. You have something to eat and a cold drink, and then we'll sort you out with a room for when you get back.'

Barbara hesitates. She *is* hungry and thirsty.

'Sit yourself down. How about a nice steak sandwich and chips?'

When it comes, the steak is still a little pink, topped with lettuce and tomato between two pieces of white bread, served with a side of chips, home-cut, thicker than her fingers, salty and hot. She orders a Coke; it's so cold it hurts her teeth. The sugar and the food revive her a little, although her mind is telling her that it's the middle of the night and she should really be asleep.

She thanks Ali, the woman behind the bar, as she pays. 'I really needed that,' she admits.

'No worries, love,' says Ali. 'You go visit the cops and I'll get that room ready for you.'

Barbara notices that the men around the bar are looking at her in a more interested way as she leaves. She gives them her 'nothing to see here' face and is happy to find it works as effectively here as it does on the streets of Berlin.

Outside, she's struck again by the quiet and empty streets. A woman and a girl wearing a pink-and-red school uniform and a large floppy hat are getting out of a car, the slam of its doors loud in the silence. They go into the pharmacy, which has a small screen outside displaying the temperature in large green digital letters: *38°C*. The heat is unbelievable. As Barbara pauses in the shade of the pub's awning, flies buzz around her face and eyes. She waves them away, moving off into the sun and down the street. By the time she turns the corner, her jeans are stuck to her legs, her t-shirt is damp and her face is flushed. The second house on the right sports a blue-and-white chequered logo above the word *Police* on a sign, but it's like no police station she's ever seen. A clapboard house sitting in a yard of burnt grass with a police cruiser in the driveway. It could be someone's home, a small, poor home at that, and her heart sinks at the thought that this is where the search for Rita and Berndt is based.

11

Walker's been digging around the local drugs scene. Blair had told him to try the RSL for Donnie Taylor, who works part-time there as a cleaner. The Returned & Services League was formed for Aussie veterans of the First World War and has become a fixture in almost every country town: a bar and dining room open to more or less all, and often extensive gambling areas filled with pokies – or one-armed bandits, as Grandma calls them.

He finds the kid – and he's only a kid, Grace's age or less, stick-thin and with a ruined face, meth sores dotted on his forehead and cheeks, burn marks around his lips – half-heartedly dragging a vacuum cleaner across the gaming lounge carpet.

'Donnie Taylor?' asks Walker.

Taylor shuts off the vacuum cleaner and leans on it, ready for a chat. 'That's me,' he says.

Walker flashes his ID and asks him about the missing kids. Donnie's relaxed vibe disappears at the sight of the badge. He scratches his face, hips jiggling from side to side.

'Nah, not seen any tourists, not for a while. Wrong time of year, mate.'

'You drink at the Federal on the weekends?'

'Nah, I'm barred from the Federal. Tried to pinch some booze from the bottle-o when I was fucked up and they don't let me in no more.'

The pub has a bottle shop at the back, with a drive-through service you can access from the car park, for those picking up cartons of beer or other big orders of takeaway booze.

'Where do you get your gear these days? Anyone new dealing in town?'

Donnie bites his lips. 'Dunno what you mean,' he says.

'I'm not trying to book you, Donnie. I don't care how much of that shit you smoke. I'm just interested to know if there are any new dealers in town.'

Donnie looks furtively around the room, whether checking for exits or to see if his boss is watching, Walker can't be sure.

'Nah,' says Donnie. 'Not that I know.'

'Who do you buy from, then?'

'Ah, ya know, here and there.'

'You got a car, Donnie? You ever drive out Smithton way?'

'Yeah, nah, don't have a car, don't even have a licence. Haven't been to Smithton, heard it's a right dump. Been to Hopeville a couple of times, but never been to Smithton.'

'Righto. Thanks, then,' says Walker, turning away. He can't see Donnie getting it together to waylay or somehow harm the two missing tourists.

'You got a durry, mate?' asks Donnie, calling him back.

Walker shakes his head. 'Don't smoke, mate,' he says, and Donnie nods his head in sad resignation, leaning more heavily on the vacuum cleaner as he watches Walker leave.

On his way home Walker stops and talks to Mrs Geddes, the mother of Dawn Geddes, another of the town's habitual meth users and a persistent petty criminal. The Geddes clan are not exactly neighbours but they live just round the corner from Grandma's place and he was friends with the older daughters when they were kids. Mrs Geddes is resigned, weary, when he asks her about Dawn.

'She's not dealing, she's too busy using. And she hasn't got any money. She steals. From us, from friends, from wherever she can. She did a stint in rehab in Toowoomba but soon as she got back she started using again. She's usually in Hopeville these days, that's where she collects the dole. Only comes back here when she's desperate. You'll be better off asking round down there.'

Hopeville is a bigger town, some 200 kilometres east. Back in his car, Walker is wondering if he knows anyone down that way who could help when his phone rings, number withheld. Probably Rutherford. He picks it up with a casual, 'Yeah, g'day.'

'Hello, this is Barbara Guerra. We spoke a few days ago. My sister Rita is missing.'

Shit. Should have let it go to voicemail.

'G'day, Miss Guerra. Sorry, but I don't have anything new to tell you.'

'I'm here, in Caloodie. Did you get my message? I have been to the police but they're saying that I need to talk with you. That you've been appointed to help the families?'

Walker's heart sinks. He hasn't seen the message; he barely checks his WhatsApp when he's out here, so far removed from Ellen, her friends, the rest of his Sydney life. Now this stupid story that Rutherford has concocted means he's about to become a family liaison officer for real.

'Well, yeah, kind of. I'm representing you, keeping an eye on the case and making sure the investigation is pursuing all possible leads.'

'Yes, good. Well, I am police also. Detective sergeant with the Berlin LKA, that's the CID, as I told you. And I want to help. To help find Rita. Can we meet? I'm staying at the Federal Hotel.'

Walker exhales loudly but finds himself agreeing. She's family. She's police. She's come a long way. He arranges to meet her in the dining room at the Federal; they'll have more privacy there.

She's waiting for him when he arrives, sitting at a table running her hand through her short dark hair. It's a messy but fashionable cut, the kind he'd see in Sydney rather than the practical 'I don't have much time or interest' haircuts you see out this way. Her hair stops above her ears and he can see three studs making a curving line in each lobe. She's wearing a short-sleeved red blouse and there's desperate worry written on her face.

'Rita would not be out of touch this long,' she says. 'She would find a way to send us a message.'

He notes the formal way she speaks. Her English is pretty good but she has a clipped accent that he likes for its foreignness.

He gives her a quick update. The brevity of it embarrasses him slightly. She's come all this way and there's really no news.

'What can I do to help? What do you need from me?' she asks.

'At the moment there isn't anything, really. Perhaps you could do a media call for information but that's handled out of Brisbane.'

'Have you seen that?' she says, pointing over his shoulder to a missing persons poster that hangs beside the door leading to reception. There are sixteen faces, a grid of four by four. 'Do you have a picture of Rita and Berndt? If not I can give you one. You can add it to the poster.'

'Ah, we got those, yeah. Mr Meyer sent us pictures already.'

She looks back at the poster behind him. 'That is a lot of missing persons. Are they all from around here?'

Walker stands and walks over, pulls the tacks free from the wall and examines the faces, looks at it properly for the first time. These are people who have been missing for more than six months, men and women, most of them young. The first half-dozen are from the last five years but others have been gone a long time, some missing since before he was born.

'These are actually cold cases, not current ones,' he tells her. 'And they're for the whole state, not just from around here.'

'Cold cases? So . . . long-term cases? None of these people have been found?'

'That's right.'

She looks at the poster in silence for a moment. 'Their families must be devastated,' she says. 'I mean, this woman is missing since 1973. And this man since 1988.' Her finger is pointing at the pictures, the poster lying on the table between them.

'Outback Queensland is a strange place,' he says. 'It's not like Berlin or Sydney. It's always attracted people who want to get lost and stay lost. It's huge. And people don't ask a lot of questions about where you're from or why you're out here. You can hide in plain sight if you want to. It's part of the history of the bush. There's even poems about it . . .' Slightly embarrassed, he finds himself quoting in the sing-song voice they used when reciting the poem at school: '*He's gone to Queensland droving and we don't know where he are* . . . We embrace it up here,' he goes on. 'That possibility of losing yourself in the great wide land. But the same great wide land means that it's possible to lose people too. If you die in the wrong place only the crows will find you.' He's thinking of the explorer Ludwig Leichhardt, lost for 175 years now. His remains and those of his expedition have never been found, despite extensive searches.

'So, Rita could be out there somewhere. Dead. Eaten by crows. And we will never find her.' Barbara's face is white, bloodless, with anger and grief.

Shit, man, he thinks, I am so not cut out for victim support. 'Nah. Not at all. That's not what I meant. I just meant . . .' His voice trails off. It's true, if these kids have gone off-track somewhere, they could struggle to find them. He remembers the statistics he'd heard in training: 38,000 people reported missing across Australia each year, 98 per cent of them found alive and well, usually within a week. But – he does the maths in his head quickly – that does mean 750 or so who disappear each year aren't found. And there are around 2,600 people long-term missing in the country. People like those on this poster, who have simply vanished.

'It's not always easy to find people who don't want to be found,' he says in the end.

He can see she's exhausted, dark circles curving under her eyes in wide half-moons, her face pale. She looks at the pictures for a long moment, studying them. He hears her sigh, sees her shoulders slump.

'I am going to be staying here for a while,' she says. 'I have a room here. I want to help any way I can. I have pictures, I can give media interviews, maybe get some information coming in for you.'

He thinks it through. 'You look pretty done in. Why don't you get a night's rest and tomorrow we can go to the station together. First thing in the morning – say seven-thirty? The local copper, Senior Constable Grogan, will be there and he can update us and see if there's anything you can help with.'

She nods. 'OK. Thank you.'

He watches her walk up the stairs to the rooms. As he turns to pin the missing persons poster back up, one face leaps out at him – an Aboriginal girl called Sheree Miller, who disappeared eighteen months ago from Hopeville. With Hopeville's drug connection still playing on his mind, he folds the poster and puts it in his pocket.

He doesn't remember hearing about her going missing but he's sure Blair or his aunt Michelle will have – it's near enough to Caloodie that maybe they'll know her or know her people.

12

When Walker arrives home, Ginger is delighted to see him, bending her body almost in half as she wags her tail, pushes against his legs and then rolls over in the dust, showing her belly, begging for a rub. He spends a few minutes sitting on the top step with her. 'I've only been gone a couple of hours, you ninny,' he says.

It's late afternoon, the sky tinged with pink, two clouds on the horizon backlit by the setting sun. A pair of rosellas flit past then settle out of sight in the poinciana tree in the front garden, hiding among its orange blossoms, readying for the night, cackling and cawing, as noisy as schoolchildren on playtime. He passes his hand over Ginger's head one last time and then stands. She stays tight by his legs as he walks to the door, and gives a small whine of disappointment when he leaves her sitting on the veranda.

He calls 'Hey' and hears an answering 'Hello' from his aunt Michelle in the kitchen. Grandma is lying in bed, propped up on her pillows, a light shawl around her shoulders despite the heat, her eyes shut. Her face has the same grey-green tinge it had this morning. The room is murky, the blinds closed against the light. The tall dark-wood headboard makes her seem even smaller and more fragile with its bulk. The nurse from the hospital must have been to see her. An oxygen tank stands beside the bed, the mask lying on the bedcovers beside her. The bed takes up most of the space in the room, but Michelle has wedged one of the dining chairs beside it for visitors to sit on. He's about to walk out, leave her resting, when she opens her eyes and smiles at him.

'Hello, Lucas,' she says. Her voice is thin and breathy. It stabs at his heart to see her like this. She's always been the strong one in the family, the one who holds them all together. The one everyone comes to for chats, advice, unconditional love. He walks over and sits on the edge of the bed and holds her hand. He can feel her palm, softer and less callused than usual, but she's so thin that her hand feels like only knuckles and veins.

'How're you doing, Grandma?'

'I'm OK, love. Just tired all the time. Michelle scared away the others to give me a bit of a rest but I'm glad you're here.'

'Sorry I haven't been around that much, I'm working a case. A couple of missing backpackers.' He doesn't go into details, but when she opens her eyes and looks at him, her gaze is as perceptive as ever.

'What do you feel?' she asks. 'Are they OK, will you find them?'

He's been so wrapped up in the facts, in the potential leads, in sorting through it all, that he hasn't listened to his intuition, hasn't tuned in to his gut feel. The older people say Grandma has a gift for it, a way of reading energies, of sensing things, that helps guide her to knowing things others can't know. They visit her to ask if their illness will get better, whether their daughter should marry this man, whether a son or grandchild, lost to city life, lost to addiction, lost to sadness, will find their way home. Endless questions. She always has an answer and they almost always listen to her advice.

She's always said that he's the one in the family who has a similar gift. He's not a believer in the spiritual sense, but he's seen how Grandma listens to undercurrents in what's being said, reading body language, absorbing the answers that are written everywhere if you know where to look. As a child he'd once found a toddler, lost for hours in the bush. He'd followed some taste of her on the air, some knowing where she might head, what might catch her eye, and there she'd been, curled up asleep atop a tree stump, no more than a couple of kilometres from her home.

He'd left Grandma's when he was eleven, after eight years of living there, attending the little primary school, feeling utterly at home in the remote bush community. His mum had finished her PhD at MIT and published the mathematical theory that made her famous. She'd married another professor, Richard Kline, and was taking time out to have a baby. There was finally space in her life for Lucas to join them.

His teenage years were consumed with the move to Boston, adapting to life with his mum and Richard and his baby sister, Grace, who he loved in a protective and unquestioning way that he'd never felt for anyone else before. And trying to blend in with the sophisticated American kids at his school – a life so entirely opposite to how he'd grown up. Everything about the city – from its centre of gleaming high-rise buildings to the sea sparkling in the sun and the clank of yachts as their masts shifted in the breeze in the harbour, the autumn colours and the snow that coated the roofs in winter – all of it was utterly foreign. It was beguiling and alienating at the same time.

The candle he carried in his heart for the stillness, the heat, the vast horizons and Grandma's small and love-filled home never wavered. He'd returned to Australia after university, pulled back by some invisible string of belonging, and his decision to stay was cemented when he found he loved his job with the Feds.

Now Grandma is watching him. He smiles. 'I've been too busy with work to dream,' he says.

She shakes her head at him. 'No one is too busy to dream. And

I can see that you fear something dark, something ugly,' she says. 'It's written in your eyes.'

It's true; meeting the girl's sister, talking about the missing who are never found, has brought the possibility of loss home to him. 'It's a hard country, Grandma,' he says.

She nods, then closes her eyes. He stays there holding her hand, lets himself stop thinking, tunes in to the sound of their breathing, hers laboured and thin, his smoother, longer, and the bangs and clatter of Michelle preparing dinner in the kitchen. He goes inside himself, but nothing rises to meet him, and after a few minutes he puts her hand gently on top of the covers. Still thinking of Boston, he pulls out his phone and sends Grace a text with a silly GIF that will make her smile.

He debates sending a message to his mum too, but he never knows what to say. She's so otherworldly, so wrapped up in her mathematics, in her teaching. They hadn't really managed to connect when he lived in Boston. He'd been a typical teenager, and after so many years apart they'd been virtual strangers to each other. It was only Grace that bound them together; the one place they'd connected was their shared love for her. In some ways he's closer to Richard, who's also bookish and quiet but worked harder than his mum to forge a bond with him. They'd gone sailing together on weekends, and perhaps because Walker had fewer expectations of the relationship they'd always enjoyed each other's company in a relaxed, men-of-few-words kind of way.

He finds a photo of the empty pool he took a couple of mornings ago, the blue sky and palm trees, and sends it to his mum and Richard. It'll be a nice contrast to the late-autumn weather in Boston. *No sailing here*, he writes, *but the pool is pretty good*. Then he adds: *Grandma not doing so well* and leaves it at that.

Richard texts him back: *Nice pool, has a modernist feel somehow*, which Walker files as something to look up. And: *Really sorry to hear about your grandmother. Love from us both.* Grace sends him a video of herself and her little fluffy white dog, whose ears she has seemingly dyed bright pink. He needs to FaceTime her soon; he misses her goofiness.

He stands slowly so as not to disturb Grandma and walks to the kitchen to chat with Michelle. She's sitting at the table when he comes in; he notices how tired she looks. Sometimes he forgets that he's losing a grandmother but she's losing her mum. And she's started shouldering the family's needs the way Grandma did before she was sick. Looking after Blair's kids, looking after Grandma, organising everything. He needs to make a bit more effort, he thinks, to give her a break too.

'Wanna cuppa?' he asks.

'I'm alright, love, ta. I'm just waiting for the rice to cook and then I'll take Mum her dinner.'

'I can do that for you,' he says. 'You can go home and rest a bit. You look pooped.'

'Thanks, love, but it's fine. I want to spend as much time with her as I can.'

He joins her at the table, pulls out the missing persons poster and shows it to her.

'Sheree . . . Yeah, course I remember when she disappeared,' she says. She looks at the poster again. 'Blimey, eighteen months ago already. Terrible. As far as I remember they found her car the other side of Hopeville, maybe fifty K out of town. Seems it ran out of petrol. She'd been seeing a bloke who was bad news – drug dealer, I think. It was his car they found but he said they'd had a fight and she'd taken it. The cops had an eye on him for a while, but they never found nothing.'

The mention of drugs piques Walker's interest. It's the second time today he's been directed to Hopeville in connection with drugs, and now there's another missing persons case too. Probably a coincidence but worth checking out.

'You don't reckon it's connected to this one here, ay?' asks Michelle.

'I don't know. Probably not. You know any of Sheree's family or friends? I might go and have a chat with them.'

'Not the boyfriend, no. I don't know his mob at all. But I know Sheree's mum – we were at high school together.' There's no high school in Caloodie so kids have to travel. Plenty of them board in Brisbane but Michelle had stayed with family in Hopeville and finished her Year 10 there, before coming back home. 'Her mum's still in Hopeville,' Michelle goes on. 'I could call her and see if she'll meet you?'

It's a start, thinks Walker. Something to look into.

13

Walker decides to commandeer the back room; he needs a space to work. It was a sewing room when Grandma had the inclination and energy, but it hasn't been used in a while. It's musty but neat, with a row of clear plastic boxes filled with colourful bits of fabric on one side and the table on the other, beside the window. He moves the covered sewing machine from the table to the top of the boxes and shakes the floral-patterned curtains, coughing as dust motes fill the air. Then he opens the window to the evening breeze. The sound of the birds roosting and calling in the mango tree outside drifts in. He places his laptop on the table, then puts in a call to Grogan, letting him know he'll be bringing Barbara Guerra in for an update tomorrow. Afterwards he calls the Hopeville police station.

'You need Senior Sergeant Sarah Jordan,' says the constable who answers. 'But she's gone home for the day.'

'I need to talk to her. Can you ask her to call me? Tell her it's urgent, regarding the mispers up here,' he says. 'I'll give you my number.'

While he waits for Jordan to call him, he sticks his map of Queensland on the wall above the table and tacks a picture of Rita and Berndt above Caloodie. The picture of Sheree Miller he pins by Hopeville.

He's barely finished when Jordan phones. He explains the

situation. 'I'd like to come down tomorrow morning and have a look at the files, talk to the investigating officers.'

'Righto,' she says. 'The investigating officers are based in Brisbane but I can get the files ready for you. Ask for me at the front desk when you arrive.'

Ginger has been sitting on the front veranda, whining a little; he's sure she can sense that Grandma isn't well. He opens the screen door and lets her in. Her first port of call is the bedroom, where she sniffs at the oxygen tank, and around the foot of the bed, resting her head on the mattress near Grandma's hand. Grandma is asleep and doesn't move to pet her, so Walker quietly calls Ginger to him and she follows him into the back room.

He looks again at the pictures on the board, the young faces of the two Germans. They look more or less the same age as Grace, who's nineteen. He's missed seeing her these last few years. He'd like to show her the bush, introduce her to his grandma, Michelle and Blair. She'd marvel at the wildlife and would love swimming in the billabong and eating ripe mangoes from the tree in the back yard. Maybe he should invite her to spend her summer holiday with him next year. It'll be winter out here, the best time to visit, when the days are pleasantly warm rather than this blazing heat.

At his feet Ginger, taking advantage of the new lax rules now that Grandma isn't chasing her out anymore, lets out a long sigh and turns onto her back, all four legs in the air. He leans down, rubs his hand on her soft stomach. She opens one eye, then closes it again and falls into contented sleep. He grabs his phone, films her snoring, sends it to Grace. *Miss you little sis*, he writes.

She texts him back a stream of emojis, love hearts and smiling faces and rainbows. His heart lifts as it always does when he thinks of her. He feels a burst of empathy for the German woman at the Federal. If something happened to Grace, if she was missing, he'd do anything and everything to find her.

Grandma is sleeping and Michelle is sitting with her, so he walks over to have dinner with Blair and Tracy and their kids. He's been home just over a week and he's seen the kids briefly at Grandma's, but this will be his first proper catch-up with them.

Night has fallen, the heat lessening a little with the departure of the sun. As he turns the corner onto Mission Road, the street on which Blair lives, he sees two small shadows start running down the street towards him. 'Uncle Lucas, Uncle Lucas!' he can hear them calling, giggling as they race each other to be the first to reach him. It's nine-year-old Zoe who triumphs. She's getting tall now, leaving behind early childhood, moving towards her pre-teens, but at times like these she still enjoys being picked up under the arms and swung into the air. Walker uses the momentum of her run to lift her high and swing her in a looping circle. Six-year-old Ruby is clamouring for her turn when he puts Zoe down. She's light enough to spin in the air a couple of times. Then he puts her on his shoulders and, holding Zoe's hand, the three of them walk down the street, the girls telling him stories of their day, of their new kitten, and still talking as he slides Ruby off his shoulders and smiles at Tracy, Blair's wife, who is standing at the gate.

'Righto, you two,' says Tracy, 'enough gabbing on. Inside, please. Wash your hands and set the table.'

The girls do as they're told, running up the stairs, giggling, pushing the screen door open and disappearing into the house.

'They're excited to see you,' says Tracy, reaching up and kissing his cheek. 'It's been too long, Lucas.'

'I'm happy to see you lot too,' he says. 'But it hasn't been that long.'

'More than a year,' she says.

He does the maths. She's right. He hasn't been here enough, caught up in work, life flying by.

'The girls are growing up fast,' he says, and she nods.

'They're good kids,' she says. 'Ruby worships Zoe and Zoe really looks after her.'

He follows her through the house – an old Queenslander with high ceilings and walls made of slatted wood. The living room, two bedrooms and a bathroom run off a long hallway, which ends in a wide kitchen and dining area that opens on to a raised deck overlooking the back garden – a stretch of grass with a trampoline in the middle and an unsteady-looking paddling pool under the mango tree on the left.

Blair is sitting on the deck, beer in hand. 'Grab yourself a coldie from the fridge, cuz,' he calls. Walker heads into the kitchen. A sea of lamb chops are frying in a large pan, emitting a delicious scent, potatoes bubbling in a pot beside them and a big salad already set on the table. He grabs a beer from the fridge and picks a cherry tomato from the salad on his way past the table.

'Tea smells bloody great, Tracy,' he says as she waves him past the table, telling him to leave the salad alone.

Out on the deck with Blair, they talk some more about Blair's plans for an eco-tourism business. Blair's spent years working out bush, on cattle stations across the region, but the drought has caused a lot of these jobs to dry up. It hasn't kept the tourists away, though, and Blair has partnered up with two friends, traditional owners of the land, to launch an eco-tourism adventure company. They want to show tourists a different perspective of the bush, show them how every single piece plays its part in keeping the country in balance. Blair's passion runs deep and Walker enjoys hearing him talk as he sits back, taking in the sounds of the girls and the garden, drinking his beer. Walker loves the bush too, but Blair has a different relationship with it. He feels connected to it in a way that Walker, now gone more than twenty years, has lost.

Dinner is a long, sociable affair. The girls, bored by talk of business, interrupt to tell him their stories, and the kitten takes centre stage, climbing first up the table legs, then up Walker's legs, and falling asleep on his lap. After the chops and mash, there's a big trifle for dessert. Then Ruby joins the kitten on Walker's lap and when Zoe's eyes are closing too, Tracy takes her to clean her teeth and he carries Ruby to her room. He kisses them both goodnight before joining Blair back on the veranda with another beer.

They sit in silence, Walker's thoughts turning to the two missing kids.

'You alright, cuz?' says Blair after a moment.

'Yeah. Just getting a bit worried about these missing kids. It's been almost a week. Their shitty car could have broken down – they won't have taken enough water with them. Y'know how it is.'

'Didn't they have a search helicopter out the other day, looking for 'em?'

'Yeah, it couldn't find any sign of them,' says Walker. He pauses. 'But she's a big country out there.'

Blair nods. 'I don't reckon they're out bush, but,' he says. 'Why would they turn off the main highway and go bush for no reason? Doesn't make sense.'

It doesn't make sense, thinks Walker, but then tourists don't always have a lot of sense. He says as much to Blair.

'I heard the call-out on the radio,' says Blair. 'Asking 'em to get in touch, asking if anyone's seen 'em. They'll hear it soon enough, they'll call in. And if they drove on past Smithton, they should be back in phone range pretty soon. I reckon you'll hear from them this weekend.'

'The other possibility is that they're staying with someone,' says Walker. 'But who wouldn't call it in? Unless they have something to hide . . .'

'You thinking drugs again?' asks Blair.

Walker nods. 'It makes more sense than two kids just disappearing.'

When Tracy joins them on the veranda, Blair changes the subject. They talk about their grandmother, tell stories about her from when they were kids, when Walker lived with her and Blair was always there too. Her formidable nature – 'Ya could never get nothing past her!' says Blair, laughing – and the way she cared for them.

'She fed the whole neighbourhood,' remembers Walker. 'Anyone who was around at dinnertime just stayed. Sometimes there'd be half a dozen kids chowing down.'

'She's the same with our kids; there's always a cake in the tin, or biscuits, and the fizzy drinks they're not allowed here,' says Tracy. 'The kids are gonna be devastated when she goes.'

Walker feels a jolt in his heart. He realises that he still doesn't believe she's really dying, a part of him still holding onto the hope that she's going to get better. 'She's tougher than she looks,' he says.

Blair and Tracy look at each other and something passes between them, but neither says anything. When Blair offers him another beer, Walker declines.

'Nah, thanks anyway. I better go home. Your mum's with Grandma and she needs to get some rest too.'

Back home he sits with Grandma after Michelle leaves. She's sleeping and her breathing is irregular, laboured. He holds her hand, the delicate papery skin. 'You can beat this, Grandma,' he says. 'We still need you.'

He leaves Ginger lying on the floor beside her bed. He knows she'll bark or whine if Grandma wakes or calls out or needs something. In the back room, distracting himself from thoughts of illness, he looks again at the map and the young faces he's pinned to the wall. He runs through his plans for the following morning – he wants to talk to Angus Jones. He's sure the man was lying to him and he wants to find out why. He's going to take a visit to Hopeville too. He needs to find a way into this case. Some kind of clue as to where the young Germans might have gone and why. He really doesn't want these two kids ending up on that cold cases poster, missing for decades.

Friday

Six days missing

14

It's the heat that wakes Barbara. For a few seconds the feelings of fear and the crushing anxiety of Rita's vanishing are displaced by confusion. The room's layout, its foreign smell, a mix of cleaning products and dust and the scent of cooking from a kitchen somewhere below, the noise of the wooden building creaking and shifting around her, are entirely alien and it takes time to orient herself. Then her mind clicks in. Rita is missing and she's in the middle of nowhere, in the heat and dust, looking for her.

Barbara lies back, trying to reclaim sleep, but her mind is on its anxious whirl and shutting her eyes only makes it worse. She couldn't get to sleep with the air conditioner on last night, the noise of it and the frigid air blowing on her body disturbed her, but now, only 6 a.m., the sun's just up and the room is already overly warm.

She looks around. It's a single but generously sized, with high ceilings, an antique wooden wardrobe and an incongruously modern en suite bathroom. The wood-clad walls are painted white, the bed has a white cotton bedspread and there's a pink patterned rug on the floor beside it. There are two doors. One opens to the high-ceilinged hotel corridor with its wooden floors polished to a high gleam, and the second, on the opposite wall, leads out to the hotel's wide veranda, shaded by a high awning.

She gets up and opens the veranda door, hoping for a breeze.

The low sun of early morning paints a broad swathe of light across the weathered floorboards. She walks three or four steps across the wooden planks, warm and rough under her bare feet, and leans on the railing. The veranda overlooks the main street and the stores that run along it. The street is, as it has been since she arrived yesterday, mostly empty. The stores that line the street must be family-owned – there's not a single chain store, not one brand name she recognises. The silence, the unfamiliarity, the stillness, the rising heat, all add to her sense of foreboding.

On the veranda directly outside her room are two bright-yellow plastic folding chairs and a small table. Last night after dinner she'd sat out here. The heat had dissipated but it was still warm enough to wear nothing more than the vest and boxer shorts, pale blue with red hearts and pilfered from an ex-boyfriend, that she wears to bed. It was barely 9 p.m. but the town had been as quiet and empty as if it were the middle of the night.

She'd talked to her parents and Berndt's father, explaining to them that she feels the police out here aren't taking this seriously enough, that they seem to think Rita and Berndt are on some extended jaunt somewhere. She'd proposed putting up a reward for more information and they'd come up with $10,000 between them. She'd put together a small poster with pictures of Berndt and Rita and asked Ali, the woman who runs the hotel, if she could print some copies and hang one in the bar. She'll distribute the rest around town and perhaps further afield today.

She thinks back to her meal last night. Apart from Ali who runs the place, she'd been the only woman in the bar. She'd ordered her meal, just a burger, something to eat quickly, and taken the chance to talk to Ali about Rita.

'She's your sister? The one who's missing? I'm sorry, love. That's terrible. Yeah, she was here, with her boyfriend. Just one night. They had dinner, left in the morning, nothing unusual about it.'

'Did she talk to anyone? Was there anyone they were drinking with?' She knows Rita; she loves to flirt and be the centre of attention. Maybe someone who spoke with them knows something about their plans or has some clue as to why they've disappeared.

'The police already asked all this,' says Ali. 'Constable Grogan and Lucas Walker. Like I told them, I don't remember exactly, I was cooking that night. But it was the usual crowd. Hippy, Paul Johnson and a couple of his drivers. Angus was here too.'

Ali looks around the bar. 'Hippy,' she calls out. A man a couple of stools further down looks away from the television screen. He's sporting an unusual look, with white-blond hair that falls, straight and gleaming, to his shoulders – even from a distance Barbara is almost certain he uses a straightener to achieve its curtain-like effect. Despite it being night-time, he's pushed a pair of black aviator sunglasses back on his head, holding the front strands away from his face.

'Ya remember that young girl and her boyfriend, the ones who're missing? Well, this is her sister. She's staying here, looking for them, and she wants to know if you talked to them, if they said anything about their plans.'

The rest of the bar quietens to an expectant hush. Hippy frowns. 'C'arn, Ali, you the police or something? I'm just trying to have a quiet beer and watch the races.'

'Come on yourself, Hippy. I'm only asking because this poor girl has a sister missing and maybe it'll help her feel better if you can remember anything they might have said.'

Hippy turns and looks at her. 'I remember 'em. Pretty girl. Bloke was a bit of a drongo. They were on their way to some station, wanted to play at being cowboys. Can't tell you much more – I was watchin' the horses, mindin' my own business. You wanna ask them Telstra boys, they had their eyes on her all night.'

Barbara feels a flicker of hope tinged with fear. Rita hasn't just disappeared. She was here. People remember her, they spoke with her. But they were watching her too, and maybe someone who was watching her has followed her or taken her somewhere. Barbara wants to keep talking to Hippy, wants to hear every last word Rita and Berndt said, but Hippy turns on his stool, angling it so that his back is facing her, and says something to the men around him. The group fall silent and two of them swivel their heads to look over at her.

Barbara looks at the room with new eyes. The men, and it's all men, are tough, watchful. They're men who work manually for a living, physically strong. Even Hippy has muscular arms above a protruding pot belly. From what she's seen of him in photos, Berndt would really have stood out here. Rita too. Young, soft, city types. They would have been vulnerable. She feels her own outsider status and decides to keep her counsel for tonight at least.

She eats her burger, committing the faces around the bar to memory. She notices that they watch her when they think she's not looking, sizing her up. To her tired mind, there's an undertone in the room. When she makes eye contact again with Hippy, he abruptly picks up his beer and downs it, puts the empty glass on the bar with a heavy thud, nods at Ali's husband Mike, who is serving behind the bar, and leaves. Mike had introduced himself to her when she sat down, curious for more information about Berndt and Rita, about her too. Barbara hadn't said much but had stayed friendly. She needs as many allies as she can get here.

'You off, Hippy?' calls Mike. 'That's a first, ain't it? You going while the beer's still pouring.'

In this morning's sunlight she knows she didn't handle it well last night. This is too personal, it's not a normal case; she can't be dispassionate and assess things. And she's so far from home, so far out of her comfort zone, that the place feels somehow menacing. Just thinking about the bar, the men in it, the unspoken undertone, puts her on edge. Everything about Caloodie feels threatening.

There are a few cars parked outside the bakery opposite the hotel, which doubles as the town's café and seems already to be open. She's not due to meet the Australian DS for an hour or so, so she walks over to get a coffee, noticing that the place opens at 5 a.m. Perhaps the early starts are to avoid the heat of the day. She doubts she'd get a coffee in Berlin at 5 a.m. unless it was in one of the all-night bars.

Inside the bakery there's a glass counter that displays cakes and pastries – very different to those she'd get at home, with pink-icing-topped buns and pastry horns filled with cream replacing the streusel cakes and pretzels you'd see in Berlin. The hot snacks are strange too – lots of pies and something called a sausage roll, which looks like meat covered in puff pastry. There must be a small kitchen out the back because they also serve breakfast. She can smell eggs, bacon, sausages, and her stomach rumbles, hungrier than she would usually be at this time of day because of the jet lag that is still confusing her body clock.

The women behind the counter, plain, doughy and red-cheeked, wearing bright-blue catering uniforms and hairnets, are friendly in a brusque way that reminds Barbara of home. Berlin is famous throughout Germany for the supposed rudeness of its inhabitants, but Barbara sees it more as an inability to tolerate fools, a trait she admires.

Most of the other customers at this hour are tradesmen or graziers, all in a kind of uniform that distinguishes them: the tradesmen in fluorescent workshirts, dark-coloured shorts, stout working boots and brightly coloured caps; the graziers in jeans or pale moleskins, brown leather boots, dusty cowboy hats. The tradesmen are almost always in pairs, the graziers alone. Occasionally a woman will pop in to buy bread or sweet buns to take away, presumably for a family breakfast, but she hasn't seen any women sitting here at this time of day.

She orders an egg-and-bacon sandwich with her coffee, which is surprisingly good, and takes a seat at one of the four aluminium tables in the side room, noticing that the Telstra workers, who are staying at the hotel, are sitting at another.

On impulse she goes over to them, introduces herself and hands them the flyer she's printed off. They look at the pictures.

'Yeah,' says the oldest one of the trio. 'We saw them, they were at the pub on Friday night. We'd heard they didn't turn up to their job, but I thought they just changed their minds, didn't like the look of Smithton.'

'Is that what they said to you?' Barbara's heart gives a leap of hope.

'Yeah, nah, we didn't really talk with them. They were mostly talking to a couple of other local blokes.'

'Why did you think they changed their minds?'

'That's what the local cop said the other night. They'd probably changed their minds, gone back to the coast. Can't say I blame 'em. We had a day in Smithton. Nothin' there. Just one street and a servo. Dusty and hot as hell. You wouldn't hang around if you didn't have to.'

Barbara's frustration with the local police rises. 'We're not sure they changed their minds and we are very worried because they haven't been in touch. Anything you can remember would be helpful.'

'Like I say, we didn't really talk to them, they spent most of the night talking to the bloke with the blond hair,' says the oldest again.

'Hippy,' says one of the others. 'That's who they were talking to. His name is Hippy.'

15

The Berlin copper is standing in front of the Federal when Walker arrives shortly after 7.30. She's wearing a green dress and white trainers and holding a manila folder in her hands. He parks outside the bakery and waves her over.

'Morning. Constable Grogan is going to meet us at eight a.m. at the station. We can have a coffee first if you like.'

'I have already had a coffee,' she says in her clipped accent.

'Fancy another?'

She shrugs acceptance. As he pushes open the door he sees a flyer stuck to the glass: pictures of the two backpackers, *MISSING* written in big letters, and *$10,000 reward*. He stops short. It's not an official police notice – there's a mobile number and contact details for Barbara Guerra.

He turns to her. 'You did this?'

She nods again, holds up the pink manila folder. 'I asked the hotel to print these out for me last night and the ladies here agreed to hang it up. My family and Mr Meyer are putting up the reward. I am posting these around the town and today I will drive to some of the other local towns and post them there too. I want to ask you to send them to other police stations in the area also and to local media.'

'You've been busy.' He's part impressed, part offended. She's taking these actions without checking in with him, as if she's running the show.

She doesn't say anything more until they've ordered their coffees and taken a seat at one of the tables in the side room. 'I have to be busy because nobody here is taking this seriously. You are telling everyone that Rita and Berndt changed their minds and went somewhere else but we don't know that is true and they have been missing almost a week now. You know and I know that the first week after a disappearance is the most important. That time has almost passed. And what has been done?'

'Look' – he's properly offended now – 'we've been talking to locals, we've followed up with dashcam footage of the highway, we've ascertained that they left Caloodie. We've had a helicopter up, and there's no broken-down car, there's no sightings of them. There's no reason to suggest they're missing. A lot of the mobile phone companies don't offer good coverage out here. Maybe they've decided to spend a bit of time somewhere with no network cover. There's every chance they're totally fine.'

'Have you tracked their mobile phones?' she asks.

'We can ask Constable Grogan that,' he says. 'I also have a question for you: are your sister or her boyfriend drug users?'

'Not that I know,' she says. 'Why?'

'One of the girls on the missing poster from yesterday, Sheree Miller, disappeared not far from here. She has links to a drug dealer. I want to make sure the two cases aren't connected.'

'As far as I know, Rita does not use drugs. I don't really know Berndt Meyer but Rita was not using drugs before she left Berlin. I lectured her about it when she was younger and I was first with the police. I was very insistent and I think she understood why.'

He finishes his coffee, and they walk the short distance to the police station in silence. The woman manning the front desk shows them through to the same small interview room. Walker sees it through Barbara's eyes – the three metal chairs arranged around the battered white Formica-topped table and the dusty venetian blinds at a window overlooking the overgrown side garden. There's an air-conditioning unit on the wall, cranking out slightly cooler air with a noisy, rattling hum. Walker sits, tips the chair back onto its hind legs, puts his hands behind his head and stretches his legs out in front of him. Barbara sits up straight, drumming her fingers restlessly on the table. He can see her irritation mounting as Grogan keeps them waiting for almost fifteen minutes.

'Sorry to keep you,' he says when he arrives. Grogan looks scrubbed clean this morning, his face paler where he's shaved, his hair fluffy as if just out of the shower. 'I was on the phone to our Brisbane missing persons department, getting an update on the case for you.'

'What can you tell me?' she asks.

'The helicopter search on Wednesday didn't turn up any sign of them locally so we're pretty certain they've left the area, driven on somewhere. HQ has put a call out to all Queensland Police to keep an eye out for them and they've also put an urgent message on local radio stations and the ABC, that's the national radio, asking your sister and Mr Meyer to get in touch or asking people to contact us if they've seen them. The message will be played regularly over the next few days. Our missing persons team in Brisbane HQ is pretty convinced that they've taken a detour. People don't just vanish into thin air, Miss Guerra. We believe they're just having a good time somewhere and not getting in touch.'

Walker sees a flash of anger cross her face. She's higher in rank than Grogan and he'd bet his badge that she's far more experienced too.

'I am also police,' she says. 'I work in Berlin CID so I know how it goes with missing persons cases and that sometimes people are voluntarily out of touch. But I also know my sister, and she is not the kind of person who just does not turn up for a job and then stays out of touch for almost a week. This is not who she is. And I know that if something has happened to them we are already far behind where we should be in tracking them down. It has been almost a week.'

'Miss Guerra, I understand you're very anxious. But please take it from me, our missing persons department in Brisbane is looking into every angle. They are taking this seriously and we will find your sister and Mr Meyer.'

'Have you run a check on their mobile phones?' asks Barbara.

'Yes. There's been no contact with them since Saturday morning, eleven-thirty a.m., which we think is the time they left here. That's not necessarily alarming as they're with a phone provider that has very bad coverage out this way. They wouldn't pick up a signal until they got to Longreach, if they were going north, or to Dubbo if they've headed south back to Sydney.'

'What about media interviews? I can give those.'

'Media interviews could be helpful, but all that type of thing is handled by our headquarters in Brisbane. Our press liaison team is based there and all the big media channels are too. If you want to be a part of the media operation, you'd be better off down there.'

'What about other cases?' asks Barbara. 'Are there other local missing persons cases that are similar?'

'Miss Guerra, believe me, I understand that being police yourself you're frustrated that we're making slow progress. But if you want my honest opinion, you'd be better off in Brisbane. You can see we're a small outfit here, it's just me, and I'm policing hundreds of kilometres. Brisbane has a specialist missing persons team and that's where your questions can best be answered. That's where you can have an influence. I can give you a contact at the missing persons team, and we can put you in touch with a family liaison officer down there too, and that's what I would suggest you do.'

She bites her lip. 'I understand what you are saying, but I'm sure you will also understand that right now I want to be as close to Rita as possible. This is the last place she was seen. I do not want to be a thousand kilometres away.'

He nods. 'I just don't know if I can help you much,' he says. 'Do you have any further questions?'

She reaches into the folder and gives him the flyer she's produced. 'I have a digital version too. Can you distribute it to other local police stations?'

'I'll need to check with Brisbane,' he says. 'We don't usually do rewards – it can just bring in a flurry of false information.'

'Better false information than none at all,' she says sharply.

He nods. 'That's true. I know this must be very difficult for you. But I'm not heading this investigation, so I can only tell you what I'm told from Brisbane. And like I said, I think it would be much better for you to be there rather than here.'

He puts his hand out and shakes Barbara's, nods at Walker and walks out.

Walker escorts Barbara to the door. 'I just need to talk to Constable Grogan,' he says. 'Can you give me five minutes?' She nods, and he turns and follows Grogan into the back office, a small room, just enough space for two desks, one covered in paperwork, Grogan sitting behind the other.

Grogan looks up, a flicker of irritation across his face that he tries to suppress.

Walker doesn't bother trying to play nice this time. 'I need to talk to Angus Jones,' he says. 'You know him, right?'

'Like I said, it's my job to know everyone.'

'I've left him a couple of messages and he hasn't called me back. He was in town the night those kids were here – he lied to us when we stopped him on the road. I want to speak with him, interview him properly. Tell him to come in to see me, will ya? I'll be back in Caloodie this arvo after five and I can talk to him then, or first thing tomorrow at the latest. If not I'll be driving out to his place to find him.'

Walker finds Barbara waiting for him in the shade of the front garden's lone tree. 'So what are we going to do now, then?' she asks him.

He looks at her. 'We?' he says.

'Yes. What are we going to do to find Rita and Berndt?'

'Maybe he's right and you should go to Brisbane, then you can hassle the blokes in charge instead of hassling me,' he says, smiling at her to take the sting from his words.

'I'm not going anywhere. You are meant to be looking after me – I represent Berndt and Rita. If there is any chance of finding Rita, it is out here. I do not think they have driven off somewhere for a bit of an extended holiday. She is in trouble and I'm staying to find her.'

Blimey, she's intense, thinks Walker. Intense and determined. But her sense of urgency is compelling. If this pair are missing, not just off somewhere, the search does need to ramp up. He might be on leave and only tasked with keeping a loose eye on things for Rutherford, but truth be told he's embarrassed at how little he's done so far.

'I'm going to drive to Hopeville today,' he says. 'I want to follow up on Sheree Miller, a woman who went missing last year. It probably isn't connected to your sister and Berndt Meyer but it's worth checking.'

'Good. I will come with you,' she says.

He looks at her for a moment. 'You don't need to come. I'll give you an update when I get back later.'

'My sister is in real trouble or maybe already dead, being eaten by crows, like you said, and you want me to sit around and wait for you to give me updates? I am a detective sergeant in the Berlin

Police. I am not just some civilian. I can help you with this.'

He holds his hands up in appeasement. 'OK, OK,' he says.

She breathes out. 'Sorry, I am tired and stressed and I'm not being polite. But you have to know, I will not sit around here waiting for you. I cannot.'

'It's fine, I understand; I have a little sister too. Come along if you want.'

He goes to the bakery first, to get some snacks for the journey. As he picks out a cold chocolate milk and a Mars bar, he berates himself. What the hell is he thinking, taking this woman to Hopeville, involving her in the investigation? He tells himself he's doing it just this once, to make it up to her for saddling her with that image of crows pecking her sister's body to pieces.

She follows him to the car and waits while he unlocks it and tries to tidy the interior, picking up Cherry Ripe wrappers and an empty can of Coke from the passenger footwell and brushing Ginger's hairs off the seat.

'Sorry, it's not very luxurious.'

'It is not a problem,' she says, then nothing more. Walker decides that silence is his best option. He turns right onto the highway and in less than two minutes they're out of town. It's just gone 9 a.m. He sticks to the speed limit until the *110km* sign comes into view and then pushes it a little bit over. It's slightly over a two-hour drive and he wants to be at the Hopeville police station before lunchtime if he can.

He loves the straight, empty road, the blue sky curving above the wide-open plains of pale grass. There's a deeply meditative feel to the emptiness and the endless horizon, and as they drive he feels his mind slow and his heart and breathing take over.

When she finally speaks, he's so deep in his own space that it gives him a start.

'Sorry,' he says, 'what did you say?'

'Is there any music we can listen to? A radio station or something?'

'Um, I doubt there'll be music. We'll get the ABC but it's usually news or talk shows or *Country Hour*. Will that do?'

She nods and he turns the radio on, pressing the Seek button to tune in to the ABC. The presenters are chatting about dealing with depression and the growing mental health problems that the drought is inflicting on rural communities. Hardly uplifting, thinks Walker, but she stares out the side window and doesn't complain, so he leaves it on.

'Australia is not what I thought it would be,' she says a few minutes later.

'No? What were you expecting?'

'I don't exactly know, but not this emptiness. It is so dry and dead. There is nothing for miles and miles. I think I was expecting bigger towns, houses with gardens and trees and swimming pools – you know, like *Heartbreak High* or something.'

He laughs. '*Heartbreak High*? You saw that in Germany?'

She looks a little sheepish, nods.

'Well, that's in Sydney, at the coast, and that's where most Aussies live,' he says. 'Plenty of pools and gardens and people down there. But it's not empty out here. It's full of wildlife. We're in a big drought so it's pretty dry at the moment, but I could show you waterholes with kangaroos and wallabies, goannas and lizards and so many birds.'

'Do you live in Caloodie?' she asks.

'Not anymore. My dad died in a car crash when I was a baby and my mum was offered a place at a university in the US, to do her masters and PhD. She didn't have time to look after me so she sent me here to live with my grandmother, my dad's people. I lived here till I was eleven. But I'm only on a visit now. I work in Sydney.'

'What do you do in Sydney?'

He pauses. He's so used to fudging the answer that he almost instinctively gives her the line about being an analyst that he always uses when asked. It's become such a habit – lying to everyone in his life. But since he's been back here, the uncomplicatedness of being himself, of being the same Lucas Walker that everyone's known since he was a pre-schooler, has been freeing. So he tells her the truth.

'I was undercover on drugs and organised crime ops.'

'That makes sense,' she says. 'You do not look like a local detective.' She pauses. 'That's why you were asking about drugs. Are you working on something undercover out here?' She sounds incredulous.

'No, I'm not undercover, I'm here on leave and they asked me to support Constable Grogan in the search for your sister and Mr Meyer. The drugs thing isn't anything official either – it's just a habit, I suppose. I've been working too long with organised crime; I think everything has a link to drugs.'

'So why are you out here?'

'My grandma is sick. I'm on leave, to spend some time with her.'

'I'm sorry to hear that,' she says, then pauses. 'I love my grandmother too. I miss her . . . She is Chilean – my parents came to Germany during the Pinochet times.' She exhales a deep breath. 'We haven't told her this news. About Rita. My parents can barely manage, I do not know how she would handle it. Family is everything in Chile. It is not like Germany, where people do not see their parents or grandparents for months on end. Rita and my parents and I, we have a family lunch every Sunday. Usually I will spend at least one night with my parents during the week as well. They live outside Berlin and it is too far to commute each day, otherwise they would want me to still live at home with them. Rita does. Did. Before she came on holiday. It was such a big thing for her to come away, on her own. She is more adventurous than me. We were all relieved when she met Berndt. We thought she would be safer.'

Her voice wobbles and breaks and she turns her head away to look out the window again. Walker looks at her profile for a moment. He knows how important family is, knows he'd turn over heaven and earth if anything happened to Grace. And he hopes that they're not too late to find her sister. Find her and get her out of whatever trouble she's gotten herself into.

16

Dave Grogan has been worrying over the DS's request to interview Angus Jones for the last couple of hours. Jones was never part of this deal. When he'd agreed to turn a blind eye to the dealing, it hadn't extended to covering the arse of anyone out here that might have a loose connection with the operation. He doesn't know what Angus's role is and he doesn't want to know, but he reckons he can use the situation to bargain for some extra cash. If he's going to cover extra arses, he deserves extra pay.

He puts in the call. 'They want to interview Angus Jones about these missing tourists.'

'No can do. Keep them away from him. It's not a good time.'

'I don't want to know what's going on, or if you or Angus have anything to do with these missing backpackers, but if you want me to cover his arse it's gonna cost ya. He's not part of the deal. You want me to cover for him, then I want double what I'm on.'

'You're in no position to bargain, Grogan. I've got your balls in my hand and if I squeeze them even a little bit you're out of a job and in the bin for corruption. So piss off, do what you're told, and stop calling me.'

Grogan digs in. 'Nah. You've got more to lose than I have,' he says, and it's true. If he doesn't get more cash out of these blokes, Lisa will leave him, and everything he's been working for is wasted.

Lisa deserves her holiday, and fuck it, so does he. 'I'm risking everything here, and now you want me to protect one of your shitty local dealers. It's not happening. You want extra, you pay extra.'

He's proud afterwards. Lisa would approve. He's finally standing up for himself.

• • •

'This is DS Barbara Guerra – she's over from the Berlin Police working with me on this case,' Walker says, introducing her to Senior Sergeant Sarah Jordan at the Hopeville police station.

Jordan's eyebrows go up. 'Bringing in the big guns?' she says.

'The missing persons are German,' is all Barbara says by way of explanation.

Jordan is solidly built – Walker's pretty sure he'd lose to her in an arm wrestle – with short blonde hair and grey-blue eyes. She's not only dug out the Sheree Miller files for him and spent the intervening hours reading them but has also called the investigating officer, who's based at the Brisbane HQ.

'I met him when he was here working on the case,' she says. 'He's convinced Sheree's boyfriend, Matt Monroe, killed her and dumped her body somewhere, but we could never pin it on him. Monroe's a meth dealer and has a history of violence towards women. But he had an alibi. His mum said he was at home all night, with her. Neighbours confirmed it. Monroe and his mum got into a fight and it got a bit ugly – lots of shouting and screaming and smashing things – late on, three a.m. or so. All the neighbours remembered hearing them. The investigating DS thinks maybe he killed the girl, drove out to dump her body and ran out of petrol. Called Mum, she picked him up and then went crazy when she heard what he'd done. For some reason they abandoned his car. But we never found a body, he had his alibi, and the theory is pretty flimsy so there wasn't enough to make anything stick. There's not much more but maybe you'll see something that links to your case.'

She leaves them with the files. A car was found abandoned just over fifty kilometres to the east of the town, early on a Monday morning by tourists, who reported it when they arrived in Hopeville. It belonged to a local – Matt Monroe. He was asleep at home when the police called, and claimed the car must have been stolen. Both he and his mum gave statements that Monroe had been home the night before and that the car had been in the driveway late into the night and that they hadn't noticed it missing. The car had run out of petrol and initially it was thought that whoever had stolen it had simply abandoned it, until police found a bag of Sheree's clothes in the boot. Sheree was the on–off girlfriend of Monroe. When police went to talk to her, Sheree's mum said she hadn't seen her since Sunday evening. She also said that, to her knowledge, Sheree hadn't had access to Monroe's car.

Monroe claimed he didn't know why Sheree's clothes were in the car: 'We had a blue on Friday and I haven't seen her since. She's fucking crazy. She could have taken the car, I wouldn't put it past her,' he'd said in his statement.

There's not much more. A few statements from witnesses confirming Monroe was at home on Sunday night, several having heard his argument with his mum.

Walker can see why the police wanted him for it; the bloke had a history of violence against this girl and others. It was his car, her clothes. And a pretty flimsy excuse to say the girl had stolen his car. But if he did kill her, why leave the car to be discovered with a bag of her clothes in the boot?

Barbara points out the names of the tourists who reported the abandoned car that first morning, right at the back of the file. It looks like they weren't called for a follow-up statement. She jots their details down.

'I will call them,' she says. 'Perhaps they will remember

129

something useful.'

They take the files back to the desk, thank Jordan and walk around the corner to a café for lunch. Walker orders a pie and chips, Barbara a chicken salad sandwich. While they're waiting she pulls out her folder of flyers and offers one to the woman behind the counter.

'These tourists are missing,' she says. 'We are trying to find them. Would you put this up in your window for us? Maybe someone will remember something.'

'Yeah, no worries,' says the woman, wiping her hand on her apron and reaching over for the flyer. She glances at it, then looks at it more closely.

'I remember them. They were here.'

A ripple of excitement travels through Barbara; Walker can feel her tense up.

'Really, you saw them? When? When was this?'

'Uhmm . . .' The woman thinks, pursing her lips. 'It was a few days ago. Last weekend. Saturday. Or maybe Friday. They had something to eat – it was just before we closed, around two-ish.'

'Can you remember which day?' Walker interjects. If Rita and Berndt passed through here on Saturday that could confirm the theory that they changed their minds and headed east or south, not west to Smithton.

The woman behind the counter looks at them. 'I think it was Friday,' she says eventually.

'How sure are you?' asks Barbara. 'It is very important. Because if they came through on Saturday, we are looking for them in the wrong place.'

'It was Friday,' says the woman more definitively. 'I was working with Caro and she doesn't work weekends. I remember we commented on the fact that you don't see many tourists at this time of year.'

They take their food to the table. 'This is good, right?' Barbara says to Walker. 'We know they were here on Friday.'

He nods. 'Yeah. I guess they stopped for a break on their way to Caloodie.'

'We can trace them to Caloodie but then no further. It's as if they've vanished into the air.'

'It doesn't mean they didn't come back this way on Saturday,' says Walker. 'They'd have been coming through here after two p.m. and she said they close at two.'

Barbara takes one bite of her sandwich, then pushes the sandwich round her plate, breaking off tiny pieces but leaving most of it.

'You should eat,' he says to her.

'I am not hungry, thank you.'

'It'll make you feel better.'

'Who are you, my mother?'

He shrugs, it's a fair point, but before they leave he grabs two chocolate milks from the fridge. Ice-cold and sweet, they're his favourite pick-me-up. He offers her one. She sighs, takes it with bad grace, half snatching it out of his hand. But he notices she drinks it all.

'They're pretty good, ay?' he says, dropping his carton into the bin.

'Yes, they are. I don't usually like drinks this sweet.'

'You need something in your tank, you're running on empty. If we're going to pick up ideas or find anything new, we need to be thinking straight. Can't do that on an empty stomach.'

Despite his slim build, he's always had a sweet tooth and a big appetite. He's not one of those coppers that can go all day on a couple of cans of Coke and a packet of cigarettes; he likes to eat and eat well.

'*Mein Gott*, it is like being at work with my mother,' she says, but her tone has lost its angry edge. 'Are you sure you're not half Chilean? You literally cannot go an hour over there without someone force-feeding you.'

'Sounds like my kind of place,' he says.

She smiles, and in that instant her face changes. The lines on her forehead and around her mouth disappear, her eyes light up and she looks much younger. He hadn't thought about her age but now he realises she's probably younger than he is.

'The food is really good in Chile. Perhaps better than here.' She's smiling as she says it, and he finds himself smiling back.

'No way. You can't beat our meat pies or parmies.'

The car has been sitting in the sun and the inside is sweltering, the seats hot to the touch. He opens both windows, turns up the air conditioner.

'I thought we'd see if we can have a chat with Monroe and then talk to Sheree's mum. I told her I'd be there around two-ish. She's on the way out of town so we can head back to Caloodie afterwards.'

Monroe lives in a small, low-built house. The front yard is overgrown and uncared for, the grass brown, the trees wilting. Two cars, one old battered red Holden sedan, the other a brand-new Toyota Hilux, a metallic, shimmery blue with a distinctive racing trim, sit on the dusty driveway. A tricycle and a bright-yellow plastic tractor are lying in the dirt in front of the two low steps that lead up to the veranda and front door. Barbara stands back as he walks up the steps. A frantic barking starts inside; two dogs, by the sound of it.

Walker knocks on the door and the barking intensifies; they hear a man's voice shouting, 'Shut the fuck up' from further inside. Walker knocks again, sending the dogs into a frenzy. They hear a heavy tread, some growled curses and then one of the dogs yelps and the noise abates as the door opens.

The man inside is tall and well built, his chest and arms the product of many hours of lifting weights, well-defined muscles visible underneath a tight black t-shirt decorated with a large red V being cleaved by an axe. Walker notes his tattoos, which cover the length of his arms and emerge from the neck of his t-shirt to climb his throat. One, newer than the others, has the same axe-and-V symbol as the t-shirt, with *Vandals* inked in red above it. Bikie gang, thinks Walker. The Vandals are one of the most powerful gangs in the country, though Monroe's short hair with shaved tracks, and his black tracksuit bottoms and expensive-looking sneakers, don't make him look much like a traditional bikie recruit.

'Yeah. Whaddaya want?' he says.

'We're looking for Matt Monroe.' Walker flashes his police ID. 'Police.'

'That's me.' He's bored, unbothered by their presence.

'We want to talk to you about Sheree Miller.'

His face twitches in a grimace. 'What? Not this shit again. Bro, that was ages ago. I never did nothing to her, I don't know where she is. I don't know why she took my car and left it by the side of the fucking road.'

'We've got some new leads. Can we come in?'

'Nah. What for? I got nothing to tell ya.'

'When did you get the Hilux, Matt?' says Walker, conversationally.

'Why do you wanna know?'

'Just answer the question.' Walker is already sick of the bloke's shitty attitude.

'Alright, alright – relax, mate. I bought it in June, didn't I.'

'And where'd you get the money for that?'

'Me mum lent it me.'

Walker makes a show of pulling out his notebook and writing it down.

'Where's your mum living these days?'

'She's out Caloodie way now.'

That gives Walker pause. 'Is she. When did you last visit her?'

'I dunno. Last week, week before. I go an' see her regular, like.'

'Last weekend? Maybe you were heading that way then?'

Monroe pauses. 'Can't remember. Why d'ya wanna know?'

'But you might have been in the Caloodie area last weekend?' asks Barbara.

'What? Nah, I dunno. Nah, I wasn't.'

A young woman appears behind Monroe. She's slender with long blonde hair, wearing a tight cream-and-gold dress that finishes above her knees. Her legs are tanned and she's wearing gold sandals and holding a baby girl in her arms. The baby is dressed in a bright-pink sequin-covered dress and has tiny diamond studs in her earlobes.

'Where was I last weekend, Kelly?' Monroe asks her, brusque.

'I dunno, Matty. We were here, I think.' Her voice is as tremulous as the breeze, light, barely there.

'Not good enough, Matt,' says Walker. 'Tell us where you were or we're hauling you in. There's another girl gone missing and we've got our eye on you for it.'

'What the fuck. No way.' He turns to the girl. 'Get my phone.'

She scurries away down the hallway. 'I didn't do nothing to no girl.' His voice has an edge to it and his eyes are bright with anger.

The girl returns and Monroe snatches the phone from her hand. He looks at it, scrolls through, pauses for a moment, then shuts the screen off with a touch of his thumb. 'I was here,' he says, looking over their heads at the yard behind them. 'Here with Kelly and then later I had a few drinks with the boys.'

He thrusts the phone back at the girl and says, 'Fuck off, Kelly,' in an undertone. Walker watches her disappear, phone in hand, and thinks he wouldn't mind seeing what Monroe was looking at on it.

'Got any proof of that?' he asks.

'Kelly was here, you heard her. And some of the boys came round in the arvo, you can ask 'em.'

Walker knows Monroe's friends will back his alibi and the frustration drives him to lie. 'We've got evidence this time and we're getting forensics. When we get all that together, we'll be back and you'll be going down for both of 'em.'

They turn and walk away. 'Fuck you!' shouts Monroe from the porch. 'I didn't do nothing to no girl. You got nothing on me.'

• • •

'What do you think?' Barbara asks as they drive back through the town to Sheree's mum's place.

'He's trouble. I recognise the symbol on his t-shirt and his tattoos – he's part of the Vandals, one of the outlaw motorcycle gangs. They're not just bike gangs anymore, they're organised crime. Mostly drugs. And something on that phone made him pause. I'm pretty sure he was in Caloodie last weekend . . .' He lets it hang.

'You think Berndt and Rita have something to do with organised crime?' Her voice is incredulous. 'Rita is a total innocent, she would not be involved in something like that.'

'How well did you know Berndt?'

Barbara has to admit she doesn't know him at all. But the pictures she's seen, the stories Rita told her . . . 'I do not think he was that kind of guy. He seemed a bit of a hipster.'

Walker's hoping this is nothing to do with these kids. He's remembering his Sydney life, the Middle Eastern gangs, the extreme violence they'll inflict on those who cross them. It seems incongruous out here, in these sleepy outback towns, but he knows the tendrils of these organisations are far-reaching.

Their route to Sheree's mum's place takes them along wide empty streets. Each house sits on a big block, though the houses themselves vary in size and age, from old Queenslanders, wooden and raised off the ground like Grandma's, to more modern brick places. The Millers' house is a small wooden place on a side road running off Boundary Road, the old edge of town.

That figures, thinks Walker. Back in the day, Aboriginal people weren't allowed to live within the boundaries of towns and cities, their communities relegated to the scrub that encircled it. Despite being the original owners of the country, they were corralled on the edges, often far from the rivers and lands that had previously sustained them. Whenever he sees a Boundary Road in a city or town, he feels a flicker of anger inside him at the treatment of the land's original people.

As they park the car in front of the house, Walker's phone rings, a Caloodie number he doesn't recognise.

'Lucas Walker, g'day?'

'Yeah, g'day, DS, this is Dave Grogan. I, um, I spoke to Angus Jones this morning. Interviewed him for ya, like ya asked.'

Walker feels a surge of annoyance. He wants to talk to Jones himself, doesn't trust Grogan to do a thorough job of it. It's difficult in a small, isolated town like Caloodie for a sole policeman to keep some distance between himself and the rest of the population, a distance that's sometimes needed for clear-headed policing. Grogan seems to be hamstrung by his inbuilt perceptions of the people he polices, or perhaps by his relationships with them. But this is Grogan's turf so there's not much Walker can say.

'What did he say, then?' he asks.

'Yeah, so Angus was in town on Friday night. He says he might have seen the missing youngsters in the pub but he was pretty blotto and doesn't remember much. He stayed at the pub overnight and left early Saturday morning. He didn't go home because he had a job on later that day. Mike at the Federal confirms it. He remembers because Angus wanted to take a couple of slabs away with him and the bottle-o was still closed, so he must have left before ten a.m.'

'What job?' asks Walker. 'I thought he's a grazier?'

'Yeah, nah, well.' Grogan seems momentarily confused. 'I heard he's doing it tough on his place right now. With the drought an' all. Like I said the other day, he takes a drive now and then for some extra cash.'

Walker remembers Grogan mentioning it. 'Who'd you say he works for again?'

'Ah, um, yeah – some Brisbane outfit,' says Grogan.

'Righto, good one. Thanks for letting me know,' says Walker, and hangs up. Jones's alibi fits with what Ali told him but he'd bet that Grogan hasn't dug too deep into the story. The time Jones left the pub isn't that important. He could have gone home before he went to this job, whatever it was. Most country people use a trip into town to pick up supplies and run errands so there's still a chance that he could have been heading along the road at the same time as these backpackers. But Grogan seems confident. And maybe he's underrating the constable. Grogan did everything right when he first heard the two were missing, so perhaps he's wrong to assume the bloke hasn't asked Jones some hard questions too.

They walk up the driveway to Sheree's mum's home and knock on the door. The woman who opens it is tiny, almost as thin as Grandma, though younger, perhaps in her fifties. Despite the heat, she's wearing a black-and-white-striped long-sleeved t-shirt and three-quarter-length black trousers. Her hair is braided close to her head, two slim tracks running down on either side of her face.

She shows them into the living room and then says, 'I'll just get youse a drink', and disappears.

The living room has an oversize sofa and two large armchairs in brown velveteen, all genuflecting towards a flat-screen TV that takes up most of the wall in front of them. There's a wicker cabinet on the left near the window. It has a large framed photograph of Sheree on the top shelf, and a host of sporting trophies crammed in on the shelves below.

Sheree's mum reappears, balancing a tray with three glasses of fizzy orange drink and a plate of Custard Cream biscuits. She hands them around and he's relieved to see that Barbara takes both without question; it would be rude not to sit and chat for a while before getting down to the business of their meeting.

They exchange news of family. Sheree's mum asks after Grandma and he tells her about Blair's kids. He lets her dictate the pace. When she stops asking questions and takes a sip of the orangeade and passes the biscuits around again, he says: 'Did Aunty Michelle tell you I'm with the police now?'

Sheree's mum nods. 'Never would have taken you for a copper from the look of you, though. You need a haircut.'

Self-conscious, he runs his hands through his curls. 'That's the style now, Mrs Miller,' he says. 'We wear it longer like this.'

She gives an unconvinced 'Hmmpf' for an answer.

'This is Barbara, she's from Berlin. Her sister, Rita, is missing. She and her boyfriend went missing on the Smithton Highway last week. There's been no sightings of them and of course we're worried about them.'

Her lips tighten. 'Like my Sheree.'

'That's why we're here, Mrs Miller, to see if you have any information that might help us.'

She looks at him for a minute, then shakes her head. 'Where were you when Sheree went missing? Why wasn't there more police here asking questions and digging around then? It's been eighteen months. And apart from chasing after that Monroe boy, no one's done a thing. And no one knows where my Sheree is. But now there's a white girl from Germany missing, and whaddaya know, now you're interested again.'

Beside him Barbara speaks. 'I am so sorry for what you're going through,' she says. 'I cannot imagine it, eighteen months without any news. It has only been a week and I feel destroyed. I am so sorry.' She leans forward and puts her hand over Sheree's mum's thin fingers where they rest on the arm of the chair.

For a long moment no one speaks, then Sheree's mum sighs. 'I hope to god you find your sister. No one should go through this.' She stands and goes over to the wicker cabinet, picks up the photo and slowly runs her hand over the girl's face, then gives it to Barbara.

'She was only nineteen when she left and she's a good kid. Played netball for years, won all these trophies. When she finished school she was looking for a job but there was nothing around. She was working at the IGA supermarket part-time when she met that Monroe boy. He was pure trouble. Into drugs, drinking, fighting. She started using drugs too. Staying out late, not coming home, not looking after herself properly. He beat her up a few times, she'd come back here crying for a day or two, then go off with him again. The weekend before she disappeared, she was back here. Said she was leaving him. Wanted to make a new start, wanted to go to Brisbane or Toowoomba, try to find work there. She'd said it before, so I didn't pay that much attention. When I woke up on Monday morning she wasn't here. I didn't worry straight away – like I said, she'd gone back to him before. But then the cops came round. They'd found her clothes and things in a bag in the boot of that bastard's car, by the side of the road, on the Monday morning. He said she musta taken the car but we never heard from her again. The cops thought he killed her, hid her body somewhere. But they never proved nothing.'

She runs out of steam, going inside herself, her memories overtaking her voice.

'What do you reckon, Mrs Miller?' Walker prompts her.

'He coulda done it, he's a nasty piece of work. Then again, maybe she took his car, decided to go to Brisbane or Toowoomba after all. She didn't know much about driving so she wouldna thought about the fuel, and when it ran out she mighta changed her mind. Maybe hitched a ride somewhere? If that's what happened I reckon she must have been coming back here, back to town. The only reason she woulda left her bag behind is that she was coming home and didn't need it. But the police never looked into that, really. They were convinced it was that Monroe. When they couldn't prove he done it, they said there's nothing more they can do, but they'll keep watching him.'

She pauses for a moment. When she speaks again Walker can hear the edge of tears in her voice.

'He's still here, still selling drugs and wasting space, and she's gone and never came back. Sometimes I reckon maybe she started a new life somewhere, but she's never used her phone or claimed her benefits or took any of her clothes, so how could she be living somewhere else? And I know my Sheree. She wouldn't disappear like that. She'd call me. She knows I'd stand by her no matter what.'

There's a long moment of quiet. Barbara is looking down at Sheree's picture. She says: 'It is the same as my sister and her boyfriend. They were on an empty highway too, and they just vanished. And I know Rita would contact us, she would find a way to let us know where she is, if she could.'

She hands the picture back to Sheree's mum. Her face is grim but determined.

'I am going to find them,' she says. 'I am going to find Rita. And I am going to find out what happened to your daughter. To Sheree.'

17

Rita can't think straight. Berndt has gone. The maniac took Berndt away. Maybe he took him to hospital. Berndt needed a doctor, so that's good. As soon as he's well again, Berndt is going to come and rescue her. As soon as he gets better, he'll tell them where she is, and he'll come and get her. But how long will it take? She's been here forever, for an endless number of hours and days, and the heat, the dark, the thirst, the terror, is never-ending.

She knows this is all her fault. If she hadn't insisted that they drive on, if they'd stayed another night or two, none of this would have happened. She feels the shame of having let everyone down, of not being responsible enough. This would never happen to Barbara. It's Berndt that she's let down the most. Where is he, where is he, where is he.

Sometimes her guilt transmutes to rage at him for leaving her. She beats her hands on the wall of the shed, crying his name, asking him to help her, to get her out of here. '*Wie kannst du mich so allein lassen?*' she screams at him.

When the anger fades, the terror returns, her chest tight, her stomach cramping, her mind a fog of confusion. How long has she been here, what does this maniac want with her, when will he let her go? She's cried so much she has no tears left. Her throat is raw and her eyes are swollen. And always the heat.

The unbearable, unending heat.

As time passes, she feels more and more that this is a dream, a nightmare. She's not actually in the shed. She's watching from afar, dreamlike, removed, as if she's watching a movie, seeing a terrified girl lying below her, all alone.

He comes to the shed once or twice. He hasn't brought the gun since the day he took Berndt away. He brings buckets of water and usually some food – dry cereal, a lukewarm pizza, the crust still frozen in the centre, bread. She has no appetite, just thirst. She ate a little of the pizza but it made her stomach cramp and gave her diarrhoea and there's nowhere to go in the shed. She'd used one of the buckets. The next time, he took one look and then left, coming back with a roll of toilet paper and a dirty scrap of soap, hard, cracked, grey.

'You stink,' he'd said. 'Clean yourself up. You're disgusting. If you clean yourself, you can come inside and have a beer with me.'

Pressed as far back as she can against the wall of the shed, she avoids making eye contact with him. She doesn't use the soap, doesn't touch it or pick it up, horrified at the threat of being close to him, having to sit with him. She can't smell herself anyway. She's not really here. This is just a dream.

• • •

He's been in town, showing his face, buying food and booze and picking up more meth too. He's been using more than usual and he can feel it. He's wired as fuck. Can't calm down. His arms are itching, he's scratched a couple of raw patches. They're scabbed and obvious. He needs to stop for a day or two, take a break, but this bitch in the shed is making him jittery and he needs the hit to deal with her. He opens a can of beer, sits on the couch. He'd had a message from the boss while he was in town:

Got a run for you if you want it, need you here by 8am tomorrow.

Fucken bad timing. He'd thought of the girl in the shed – not good timing at all. But in the end he'd sent a quick message:

yeah, good one, see u tomorrow.

It's a hassle but he doesn't have much choice. He needs the money and he doesn't have a good reason for turning it down. They'll only start asking questions he can't answer if he doesn't show up.

So now he lies on the couch and decides against a hit, better to be sober when he turns up for work. But the meth binge he's been on means he can't sleep, he's hyper all night, watching porn on his phone, thinking about the girl in the shed. She's too disgusting to touch at the moment but he fantasises about cleaning her up and enjoying her properly.

When the sun rises he takes a shower, standing under the cold water until he feels calmer, then dries himself off and loads a couple of sticks of gum in to freshen up his breath as he tucks his shirt into his jeans. Wears a long-sleeved shirt to cover up the scabs on his arm. Looks in the mirror, relaxes a little. He looks OK, smells OK.

In town, he pulls up at the bakery, orders a coffee and a cream bun. He's not hungry but he knows he needs to eat. Drinks a second coffee. Goes into the gents, pukes it all back up and afterwards feels momentarily better. What he really needs is a hit but it's going to have to wait. He throws water on his face, slicks his hair back, jams his hat on.

The girl plays on his mind. He wants her but only if she pulls herself together a bit. Maybe a day on her own will do her good. She might start to appreciate how well he's been treating her. The more he thinks of her, the angrier it makes him. Women are all the same. Nothing but stress and fucken hassle. He makes up his mind. He's had enough of trying to win her over. When he gets back he's going to finish the job, and he'll enjoy it too.

Saturday

One week missing

18

It's a week since Rita disappeared. Barbara is in the bakery, a sweet bun on the plate in front of her, untouched. The all-consuming worry about Rita has taken away her appetite. She drinks a coffee, plans her day. She wants to drive out to Smithton, hand out some flyers. Maybe, just maybe, she'll find some trace of Rita there.

She's almost finished her breakfast when Walker appears. He's wearing the pale moleskins and light-blue shirt that's a kind of uniform among the men out here, but he still stands out. Perhaps it's his curly hair, backlit by the sun into a pale halo, or his physique, which is leaner than most of the others'. The men here are large – tall with strong arms and solid legs – but most have bellies that spill over their waistbands and faces that are pudgy and red-cheeked from too much drink.

Walker is tall, 190 centimetres, she'd guess, strong and broad-shouldered, with long limbs and well-defined muscles but without being bulky. His curly hair is light brown, going blond at the tips from the sun. Looking at him, she realises he's handsome, especially when he smiles and his eyes light up. She wonders what his girlfriend or wife is like and whether he has children. Wrapped up in her fears for Rita, she hasn't had any of the usual introductory conversations she'd have with colleagues.

He places his order, takes the numbered wooden spoon that's

the bakery's marker of who gets what, and glances around the room for a seat. She raises her hand and he smiles and walks towards her.

'You're up early,' he says.

'I'm still not used to the heat.'

He nods. 'Yeah, she's a scorcher today. Do you swim? You should come to the pool in the morning. There's no one there early on and the water's refreshing.'

'You're a swimmer?' she says, thinking to herself that this explains his physique.

'Yeah. It's my way of getting my head into the day. Swim up and down for half an hour, clear the mind.'

'I don't have anything to swim in,' she says. 'I was not planning on swimming when I packed.'

'Try Harris's, the store on the corner. They have some togs in the sports section.'

A swim could be nice, she thinks, a way to cool off at the end of the day, float in the water, wash away her fears.

'I have been planning my day,' she says, watching his smile fade slightly. Before he can interrupt or put her off, she ploughs on. She doesn't want to be sidelined. Work is always a balm and being involved in looking for her sister, even a little, is the only thing that's making this bearable.

'I'm going to drive out to Smithton. I know the helicopter has been looking and Constable Grogan has already driven along it, but I might see things differently, more like Rita and Berndt. I might see a place that could have tempted them to turn off. And I want to hand out some flyers in Smithton, see if anyone can remember seeing them. I'm also going to call the tourists who reported Sheree's car missing,' she adds. 'I want to see if they remember anything that might help.'

'Have you had any calls from the flyer?' he asks.

She shakes her head. She had one text message but when she

called back it was a child that answered, laughed, said something she didn't totally understand and then hung up.

Walker looks at her for a moment; she can see him mentally running through options. 'I don't want to rain on your parade but you do know that you can't act in an official capacity here,' he says. 'You need to leave the official investigation to us. I am taking it seriously, I promise you.'

She nods. 'I know. But I promised my parents I would look for Rita, and I also promised Sheree's mother that I would look into her daughter's disappearance. I intend to keep both promises. There are things I can do here that the team in Brisbane is not doing. And it can only help.'

In the end he capitulates. 'I can come with you to Smithton if you like, but I've been thinking about Matt Monroe. I'd like to chat to his mum, see if I can place him here on the day that Berndt and your sister disappeared.'

'I'm fine,' says Barbara. She doesn't need hand-holding.

'Please don't take any turn-offs – just make a note of the mile marker if you see anything, and we can check it together later. If you turn off and disappear too, you'll be no help to anyone. Also, take plenty of water with you. At least half a dozen big bottles. And if the car breaks down or you have any problems, don't leave the vehicle. Just sit tight and someone will drive past. At the very worst, if you're not back by eight tonight, I'll drive out and find you.'

She's grateful for his advice. She'd never have taken so much water and might have panicked if something had happened with the car. Now she knows he'll come and find her, she can wait if necessary.

They agree to meet at the end of the day for an update and Barbara goes back to the hotel, sits on the bed. She needs to call her parents but she's dreading the conversation. There's nothing good to report and she knows they'll be devastated. She can't face it right now. She texts a brief update to Berndt's father and sends a message to her parents, saying she'll call tomorrow. On impulse she calls Monika. It's late in Berlin, almost midnight, but Monika will be awake, she's a night owl; she's never asleep before 2 a.m.

'Babs, how are you? I'm so glad you called. I've been worried about you.'

Hearing Monika's voice, the familiarity of it, makes her instantly homesick. She wants to find Rita and get out of this hot, dusty hell. She wants to go home. Speaking in German, too, is such a relief. She doesn't have to think about what she wants to say or how to say it, or listen with every fibre of her being to try to understand.

'Sorry I haven't answered your messages, it's all a bit crazy out here.'

'Don't worry. No problem. Are you OK? Any news on Rita?'

'No. Nothing. Not a word from either of them.'

Monika is silent for a moment, then she says: 'Oh, Babs, hon, I'm sorry. That's not good. But it is good that you're out there. If anyone can find her, you can. You're a shit-hot detective.'

'You don't know what it's like out here. You can't imagine.' She describes the town, the countryside, the heat.

'Are you on your own? What about the police?'

'There's a missing persons unit that's meant to be working on it and a couple of local guys too, but, Mon, this country – it's huge and empty. The police station is in a tiny old wooden house, there's just one cop out here, and the others are thousands of miles away and I don't know if they really are taking it seriously. I'm scared that we're never going to find her.' She's breathing fast, her chest tight.

'You'll find her, hon. You will. Get those organising and bossing-around skills of yours into play. You'll have them on the job in no time.'

'It's different here, Mon. It's not like at home. I don't know if I can do this.' Her voice is shaking, tremulous, so she changes the subject. She needs to think about something else, even just for a minute or two. 'What's happening with you, anyway? Talk to me about something else.'

They talk for a few minutes more, Monika rambling on about a night out, some guy she met at the bar who hasn't called her back, Anika and Olaf's pizza night. Day-to-day things that come to her from such a distance it feels as if she might be on a different planet, in a different lifetime.

After she ends the call, she lies on her bed for a few moments then shakes herself into action. She digs out her notes from yesterday. The couple that reported Sheree's abandoned car are from Western Australia. Along with the address there are two phone numbers. The first one she tries is no longer in use. The second rings and rings and she's about to give up when a woman answers, a little breathless.

'Hello. This is Detective Sergeant Barbara Guerra, from—' She's about to say Berlin LKA as usual and has to pause and correct herself. 'I am calling from Caloodie in Queensland. I am helping the Queensland Police with a missing persons case and I wanted to talk with you about the car you spotted outside of Hopeville last year.'

'Well, that's taken you a while, hasn't it?'

'Yes, well,' says Barbara, a little surprised by the reply. 'We have another missing persons case and there are some similarities. That is why we are calling now.'

'You don't sound much like a Queenslander,' says the voice at the other end.

'No. I am from Germany, from Berlin. I am helping on the new case.'

'Hmmpf.' The woman sounds unimpressed. 'I always wondered why the police hadn't called us back then. It seemed strange we never heard.'

'Why is that?' says Barbara.

'Well, we'd already left Queensland by the time we heard that a girl was missing in Hopeville. I said to Brad, maybe it was that broken-down car we reported. But he said if it was, the police would have been in touch asking us for more information. We never heard but I always wondered.'

'Do you have some more information for us?'

'I don't know. It's quite a while ago now.' The woman lets out a deep breath. 'I don't remember much but I always said to Brad, we should have told the police about the truck. We saw a truck ahead of us, you see. You know what the roads are like out there, so straight that you can see for miles. I thought it had stopped next to the car and was pulling away, but Brad wasn't sure, he said maybe the driver only slowed down for a look. We weren't in a hurry, just pootling along, so when we saw the car parked there, we stopped too, to be on the safe side and make sure that there wasn't someone hurt or whatever. They say you should always stop when you're that remote – it's a rule of the road, isn't it? But the car was empty. No one around. And then, because we were towing the caravan and we don't drive that fast, the truck stayed ahead of us the whole way into town. We were close enough to see that he passed straight through Hopeville, didn't stop to report the car, which is why we dropped in at the police. Afterwards I thought, what if he picked up the girl, the one that was missing? But Brad said you'd call us if it was connected, and also we don't know that the truck did pick anyone up. Probably passed by and saw that the car was abandoned, like we did.'

Barbara feels a surge of something close to excitement. This is what she loves most about policing, the moments of breakthrough, when a lead, however small, opens a door into a new possibility. And this seems like a big lead in Sheree's disappearance. How could it have been missed? Even if the truck driver wasn't involved, it seems strange that he wouldn't report the empty car. Walker had said that if Rita and Berndt had broken down, everyone who passed would have stopped to help. It could mean the difference between life and death in remote areas in this heat.

'Can you give me any information about the truck?' asks Barbara.

'It was almost two years ago, love, and we were behind him and not thinking anything of it. The only thing I know is it wasn't a livestock truck because those are terrible things and I would have remembered that.'

'Did you take down the registration number?'

'Oh, no – I mean, it wasn't that we were suspicious of him or anything. It was only afterwards that I wondered.'

'What about your husband? Maybe he might remember some other details?'

There's a slight pause. 'Brad died in the winter. Cancer.'

'I am sorry,' says Barbara, though she isn't sorry, she's angry. Angry that no one spoke to these people when Sheree went missing. It's the worst kind of incompetence. Maybe this truck driver picked her up. At the very least he needs to be ruled out as a possible suspect.

'You know, we might have some dashcam footage somewhere,' says the woman. 'We were always recording, in case there was an accident or something. You never know, do you? Normally we didn't keep it but maybe Brad saved it from that day. He was good at thinking ahead like that.'

'That would be very helpful,' says Barbara, her hopes lifting. 'Could you check?'

'I'll have to go and see if I can find it. It might take a while. I'm not much with computers. But I can ask my son to have a look.'

'Yes, please can you do that,' says Barbara. 'Can you let me know later today?'

'Not today, no. My son, Jack, he's working today, but he'll

probably pop in tomorrow. I'll ask him then.'

'It's quite urgent,' says Barbara.

The woman gives a loud 'Tsk'. 'It's almost two years ago, love, it can't be that urgent.'

'There is another girl gone missing and the information could be very helpful,' says Barbara. 'You could be saving a life.'

19

Barbara decides she'll pay a visit to the local trucking firm, to see if they had anyone in the area when Sheree disappeared. She's already called Sarah Jordan in Hopeville, who has taken the information and promised to follow up with the big national companies, but perhaps a face-to-face with the local firm here won't hurt. She always prefers face-to-face interviews; there's so much more you can read and pick up when you're talking with someone in person.

She googles them and finds the address. They're open until 12 noon on Saturday so she'll do it now and then drive out to Smithton afterwards. She grabs her bag, checks she has her phone and notebook and heads downstairs. Outside, the heat hits her like a blast, searing and dry. The temperature on the pharmacy screen reads 39°C.

In deference to the heat, she pops back into the bakery and buys a bottle of cold water, then goes into the store on the corner, Harris's, to look for a hat. All the men and most of the women here wear their hats all day, usually a felt cowboy style but they're expensive and she'd feel like the worst kind of tourist walking around in a cowboy hat. Instead she chooses a straw panama, with a black-and-white chequered ribbon around its brim. She looks stupid in hats, has never liked the way they sit on her, but the heat here demands protection. On impulse, she picks up a bright-red swimsuit too. Perhaps a swim later on will help drown out the noise in her mind, the fear for Rita that is looping and looping and looping, all day and all night.

Her walking route to the trucking company takes her to the west of town, past the local hardware store and the butcher's. Two or three cars are parked diagonally in front of the awnings of the shops but otherwise the streets are quiet and still. Once she leaves the shade of the awnings, the pavement is so hot that she can feel it burning her feet through the soles of her sandals, and the heat of the sun stings her arms. She's naturally olive-skinned and tans easily but the strength of the sun out here is unlike anywhere she's been. Even though she applied sunscreen at the hotel, she can feel the skin on her arms burning.

A block further on, the footpath peters out and she's walking on dusty verges. Long dry blades of grass scratch her ankles and calves. There's no one about; the houses look deserted and the paint on the wooden exteriors, weathered by the unending sunshine, is pale, brittle and peeling in places. One or two have green lawns as their front gardens, but most are untended and neglected, with thirsty-looking brown grass.

She's beginning to understand why she never sees anyone on the streets or in their gardens during the day. The heat is overwhelming and enervating. It reflects from the ground, beats down from the sky, blows against you in the wind and saps the will to do anything other than lie in air-conditioned coolness. She pauses for a break from the heat in the shade of a large tree in front of a pale-blue cottage. The garden is neat and tidy, grass mown and green, with a water sprinkler ticking back and forth across it and a flock of grey-and-pink birds rootling around on the moist ground.

'You lookin' for me?' says a voice behind her, causing her to start. Hippy, hair as neat as ever, is standing at the garden fence, looking at her. He's wearing his aviator shades, a blue vest and a pair of very short blue shorts.

'Actually, no, but I am glad I found you,' says Barbara. She's been wanting to ask him more about Rita and Berndt. The Telstra guys said he was the one who spoke with them.

'Come on in, then,' he says, opening a wire gate. 'Too bloody hot to stand out here, and what will the neighbours say when they see me chatting to a cop. Don't want to be the talk of the town.'

She looks down the empty streets and back at him.

'Sarcasm, love,' he says. 'Don't they have it where you come from?'

'My English is not so good – sometimes I do not understand a joke.'

'Yeah, nah, it's probably not your English. It was a pretty piss-poor joke, to tell the truth.'

She follows him inside, where they sit on an emerald-coloured velvet sofa in a white living room.

'Thanks for talking with me,' she says.

'Yeah, well, look – I don't know nothing. But it's better you ask me your questions here and not in the pub when everyone else is earwiggin' and spreading bullshit afterwards.'

Barbara nods. It's probably not easy, she reflects, to be an eccentric in a small town like this. 'I know you talked to Rita and Berndt and you are the only person I have found who did. I just want to know what they said to you, that is all. Anything you can remember could be really helpful.'

'I can't really remember, I had a few drinks on me. Your sister didn't say much. I was mostly talking to him, taking the piss out of his trousers. He was saying they were going to work on a station out past Smithton for a couple of months. The backpacker visa extension thing. We get a few youngsters out this way, working in the pub in the tourist season, doing the same thing. But not usually at this time of year when the heat is bad. It's not the right time for people who don't know the bush.'

'Did they sound like they were having doubts? Like they might have changed their minds?'

'Nah, not to me. Seemed they thought it was a bit of a lark. Well, him at least. Like I said, she didn't say much, your sister, but I don't think she was as keen on the idea as he was. She didn't look that impressed. I don't think he had much of a clue what he was letting himself in for. He's got muscles like a chook's instep, reckon he'd be done in after a couple of hours of hard yakka. But he didn't say anything about not going.'

She pauses for a moment, trying to decipher what he's saying, then, joining the dots best as she can, presses on. 'Was anyone else interested in them? Anyone taking any special notice?'

'Your sister was wearing pretty short shorts, love, so I'd say all the blokes took a bit of special notice. Even old Angus perked up a bit . . .' He laughs.

Barbara feels herself tense. Don't talk about Rita like this, she thinks. Perhaps he notices. 'No one was paying any special notice,' he says. 'Nothing unusual. They were just as busy checking out the bloke and his stupid dacks.'

She leaves it at that. She doesn't want to know that the men out here were assessing her sister, laughing at Berndt.

'Can I use your bathroom?' she asks, just to have a quick look around.

He nods. 'Down the hall,' he says, pointing.

She walks down the short hallway, glancing surreptitiously into the other rooms. The whole place is neat as a pin. She sees curtains with pale-green and white stripes at a kitchen window, reflecting the colour of the tiles that run in a line above pale-wood kitchen units. Hippy must be in his late forties, if not older, and he's clearly a drinker – and yet his house has the feel of a suburban housewife's. It reflects the man's obsession with his hair, Barbara decides, standing in the bathroom with its matching hand towels, neatly arranged.

'Is there a Mrs Hippy?' she asks as she goes to leave.

He gives another bark of laughter. 'No, love, there's no Mrs Hippy.' She can hear him chuckling to himself as he closes the door behind her.

After the air-conditioned cool, walking outside feels like being in a sauna, the wind blowing, the dry, burning heat almost a physical thing. It's only five minutes but feels much longer before she turns left into the small industrial cul-de-sac on which Johnson's Transport is based. There are warehouses on the left with businesses including farm-supplies merchants and what looks like a small used-car dealership and mechanic. Johnson's is on the right, taking up most of the block.

By the time she arrives at the gate to the compound she's sweating in places she didn't know she could sweat: her neck, her back, behind her knees, the bottoms of her feet are all damp with heat. She pauses under the limited shade of a spindly tree, its orange blossoms carpeting the dust beneath her feet, to catch her breath. Her small bottle of water is empty already and she remembers Walker's advice to buy plenty of large bottles for the drive to Smithton.

The Johnson's Transport property is ringed by a high-wire fence, inside of which are a large gravel parking space and a warehouse. To the left of the warehouse is a low Portakabin office with the company's name written in red and white across the top. The gravel outdoor space is virtually empty, just three cars parked beside the office and the front end of a truck, bonnet up, visible just inside the warehouse.

The office is blissfully cool, the air conditioner pumping out icy air. She pauses at the water cooler beside the door, a large inverted bottle that burbles invitingly, and drinks. The liquid is so cold it makes her teeth hurt and she can feel it running down her throat and into her stomach, cooling her from the inside out. Ahead of her is a reception desk, unmanned, and a door that seems to lead to a larger space behind, the details concealed by slim grey venetian blinds.

She rings a bell on the reception desk and hears it buzz in the far distance, helps herself to another cup of cold water while she waits, and stands in front of the air conditioner vent, shivering as the sweat coating her body cools in the frigid air.

The internal door opens and a young woman emerges. She has light-brown hair, pulled back tight from her round face into a ponytail, a broad nose and fleshy cheeks. She's wearing three-quarter-length trousers and an oversize t-shirt, in a bid, thinks Barbara, to conceal her body shape.

Her eyes run over Barbara and she can sense the quick calculation: not a local, not a client, not a prospective driver. 'Yeah? Can I help you?' the girl asks, wheeling out an office chair from below the counter and dropping onto it. The chair squeaks a little as it gives under her weight.

'I'm DS Barbara Guerra, on secondment to Queensland Police from the Berlin Police,' she says, opting for the white lie and showing her Berlin ID to the woman, who takes it in her hand and scrutinises it before nodding and returning it. 'I'm investigating the disappearance of two young Germans here last week and the disappearance of a woman in Hopeville last year.' Barbara takes one of her flyers out of her bag and passes it over.

The girl looks at it and nods. 'Yeah, I seen these posters in town. We can put one up here if you want.'

'Thank you. But I also want some information. We have reason to believe a truck driver might be able to help us with our enquiries.'

'One of our blokes?'

'We're not sure, but I'd like to talk to someone in charge about it.'

The woman considers her for a moment. 'You can talk to me. I'm Terri Johnson – this is my dad's company and I run it day-to-day.' She says it without pride, a bald and phlegmatic statement of fact.

'We are looking for the names of your drivers who were on the Warrego Highway outside Hopeville in the early morning of Monday the tenth of May 2021, and on the road between here and Smithton last Saturday, the fifth of November. Perhaps they might have seen something, anything at all could be useful. If we could see any dashcam footage they might have, that would be helpful.'

'Yeah, Constable Grogan asked us already about the Smithton road. We didn't have anyone out that way.'

Barbara nods. 'OK. What about Hopeville last year?'

The girl picks up a pen and peels off a bright-pink Post-it note from a multicoloured stack. 'Hopeville, tenth of May 2021 . . .' she repeats back as she writes, looking up for Barbara's confirmatory nod.

'It'll take a while, I need to check the records. If you give me your number, I'll call you back.'

'I will come back in,' says Barbara. 'What time is best?'

'We shut at lunchtime today, so Monday morning would be best.'

'You cannot do it any quicker than that?' asks Barbara.

'Nah, sorry. We don't keep computerised records, so I'll have to check it manually.'

Sheree's case is eighteen months old – another day probably won't hurt, thinks Barbara as she thanks her and leaves.

• • •

Terri Johnson is going through the files, pulling out the transport lists for the dates the policewoman asked her about. She hadn't looked much like a cop. Too small, to start with, and with the earrings and the stylish haircut she looks more like a singer in a band. Even her top, a red blouse with white buttons, was kind of plain but it stood out.

She finds the records for 10 May 2021: Steve Burnett was on a Hopeville cattle run and Darryl Foley had the refrigerated unit from Brisbane back to Caloodie, so he'd have passed through Hopeville too. She flicks the pages of the manifests with her finger as she thinks. Burnett's been with the company five or six years, and her dad really likes him. He always goes for a drink with Burnett after work and keeps saying how good it is to work with a bloke he trusts. And Foley, well, she's always liked Foley. He's older but he's handsome and this morning he finally asked her out.

She turns the moment over in her mind, replaying it like a movie scene. She wants to savour it, Technicolor it, so that later, in the years to come, she'll be able to say, 'Remember the first time you asked me out?' and delight in the retelling of it.

He'd been in, picking up the manifest for his drive. He hadn't said much to her, just 'G'day' like normal, but then, just as he'd turned to go, something must have given him courage.

'Listen, love,' he'd said. 'Would ya like to have a drink with me sometime? Or maybe dinner at the pub or something?'

She'd felt her face flush red, a curtain of colour rising from her throat to her forehead.

'Um . . .' She'd been speechless. She cringes a little at the memory – she'd barely been able to respond.

'Ah, OK, no worries,' he'd said. 'I shouldna asked . . .'

'Nah, nah' – she'd been talking fast. 'I mean, yeah. Yeah, defo. That'd be good. A drink or dinner.'

She can feel her face is puce.

'Righto, beaut,' he'd said, smiling. 'We'll do that when I get back, then', and he'd winked at her as he left.

She hasn't had a boyfriend since high school and now she's finally going on a proper date. Hidden away in here, with her dad always keeping an eye on her, the drivers don't usually pay her any attention. She really wants a boyfriend, wants to move out of home, get married, have kids, the whole shebang. She can't stop thinking about him and about how the date will go. If he'll kiss her. Her stomach is filled with butterflies. She can barely eat with excitement, which is no bad thing as she needs to lose a few kilos, really.

She hasn't decided what to wear but she's been online this morning and ordered a pink skirt and a matching blouse with a check pattern from the Katies website. The outfit looked dead good on the girl in the picture. She's got a pair of silver shoes that she's never worn that might work with it. Or maybe that's taking it too far. It's just a drink. She wishes it could be tonight, but she can wait: she'll make sure he gets another drive next week and then they can make the arrangements.

Meanwhile, this copper is a nuisance. She's pretty sure none of their drivers would know anything about a missing girl, and what could they tell the police all this time later anyway? They won't still have dashcam footage and the drivers won't remember what they saw a year or more ago. It seems a bit suspicious to her. She watches enough crime shows on Netflix, and most likely the police are trying to set someone up for this because they can't find who really did it.

The truth is, the company doesn't need bad publicity right now. The competition from the nationals is already killing them because they don't have the logistics to manage things the way the big companies do, using drivers as economically as possible by setting up deliveries in both directions. And then the solo drivers, with no admin costs or overheads and probably not declaring half their runs to the taxman, undercut them too. The business is struggling to survive; they're already giving their drivers fewer runs than they were six months or a year ago. They might have to lose someone in the next couple of months, and she knows Foley is in the firing line. Her dad's never really liked him and he's always half looking for a reason to let him go.

She sits at her desk and looks at the manifest again. She needs to decide what she should tell this cop. Perhaps she could conveniently lose the files. She'd set up the system when she started here a couple of years ago. Before that it was chaos: Dad couldn't have told you who was where last week, let alone last year. It's feasible that they wouldn't have records ... It's best not to involve her dad in this either, she decides. She doesn't want him letting Foley or anyone else go and then ending up on the road himself again. The stress of it, the long hours, the not sleeping, the shitty diet – it would kill him.

No, she decides, Dad doesn't need the stress. Whatever happened to that couple on the way out of town, it was nothing to do with them: they had no one on the road that day. And half the drivers in the state pass through Hopeville on a run from north to south or east to west. Let the cops find who they want without wasting time digging through their drivers' histories and maybe ruining the company in the process.

20

Walker is sitting in his makeshift office, thinking about Monroe and his fancy car. If he's a dealer, he's a clever one. The best dealers, the ones who profit from it, don't use themselves, or at least not to the point of heavy addiction. Monroe didn't have the look of an addict – too bulky and healthy-looking – and his girlfriend didn't have the telltale skinny frame or marked face either.

He calls Jordan, the senior sergeant at Hopeville, partly as a courtesy but also to see if she has more information on Monroe and his family.

'You lot are busy up there,' she says as she answers the phone.

'Yeah?' He's not sure what she means.

'I was talking with your colleague, the German copper. She's passed on a lead on the Sheree Miller case. A truck that might have been in the vicinity. I'm following it up with the big trucking companies.'

Walker mentally salutes Barbara but feels a twinge of embarrassment too. She shouldn't be unearthing their leads. 'How come that didn't get picked up last year, then?' he asks.

'I think we were so focused on Matt Monroe that it got missed, but it's worth a follow-up now, I'd say.'

Walker knows it's possible to get blinded by a theory and miss leads that point in a different direction, but it's still sloppy policing.

Saying that, he fancies Monroe for it himself – he's far and away the most likely suspect. He hasn't personally had much to do with the bikie gangs, which are handled by a special squad, and he'd thought Caloodie too small and too far west for a gang presence, but it makes sense that there'd be a local connection for drug distribution. And if Monroe was up this way last week, there might even be a link to the missing Germans.

He asks Jordan about Monroe. She suspects he's still dealing meth and other drugs, but he hasn't been nicked for it recently. 'After Sheree went missing the team searched his place, but they found nothing, not even for personal use,' she says. 'We had our eye on him for a while, but he was keeping his head down and we don't have the resources to keep track of him full-time.'

Walker makes a note to ask Grogan if Monroe has come to his attention. If he's out this way regularly to visit his mum, he might be dealing out here too. Meanwhile, he decides he'll go and have a chat with Tina Monroe. It's not strictly within his remit, but he always operates on the policy that it's easier to apologise for innocently overstepping the mark than to ask and be denied permission. He looks up her address: she lives on a farm a fifteen-minute drive out of town. He checks the online property register to see how long she's been living there and discovers that the property belongs to Angus Jones. Curiouser and curiouser, he thinks.

He misses the turn-off the first time and has to swing round, keeping an eye on the mileage markers to find the gravel road that leads to her property. It's been recently graded and the car rattles easily across it. He likes this part of the country; it's as bucolic as it gets out here. The grass is pale now from the long drought but seemingly there's still enough of it to feed the small herd of caramel-brown cattle that dot the paddock, some grazing, others resting in the shade of large eucalyptus trees. A kangaroo inside the fence, close to the road, takes a few lazy hops into the shade, where it vanishes, camouflaged in the dappled light.

A few kilometres along, Walker reaches an open gate and the GPS instructs him to turn right, down a dirt track with grass growing high between clearly marked grooves, worn smooth from use, which curve through a large open paddock towards a house, a low modern place made of brick. Walker parks the car alongside a waist-high wire fence that demarcates the garden around the house from the paddocks surrounding it. The garden is being well looked after, the pale-green grass a verdant rectangle, a pool to the left glimmering in the sunshine and flanked by white loungers and a yellow-and-white-striped umbrella combo that looks more Coogee than Caloodie. Set behind the house are three large farm buildings, gleaming and well maintained, with a neat gravelled area in front.

The air is hot and still, and he can hear a dog barking as the gate shuts behind him with a clang. There are no cars in the drive, but a large black Harley-Davidson is parked in the shade of the carport, its gleaming chassis in vivid contrast to the dusty surrounds.

Bingo, thinks Walker, memorising the Harley's registration plate. He's cutting across the grass to the house when the front door opens and a huge man steps onto the porch. He's tall, six-six at least, and his physique makes Matt Monroe look like a scrawny teenager. His chest is as wide as the doorframe, his biceps are ham-sized, his hands like shovels. He's bald, covered in tattoos and there's a genuine sense of threat emanating from him. Walker has no doubt he's capable of, and experienced at, dishing out serious violence. He's holding a dog on a leash, a dark-brown pit bull, all chest and muscle, its ears small triangles, a growl emerging from somewhere deep in its throat. It's not a small dog, but beside this giant of a man it looks diminished, though no less ferocious for it.

'Police,' says Walker, reaching into his back pocket for his ID. 'I want to talk with Tina Monroe.'

The bloke looks him up and down and casts a sideways glance at the battered white ute. 'If you're a cop, show us a warrant, otherwise we ain't talking to ya. No warrant? Then fuck off. If you're not off my place in five minutes I'll set the dog on ya.'

He turns and goes inside, the dog growling once more, before the door closes with a thud behind the two of them.

Not a total waste of time, thinks Walker, as he bumps away down the dirt track. The Harley and the conversation have further confirmed that Matt Monroe is closely linked to the Vandals. Monroe deals drugs, and if he was here last weekend, the same day that Rita and Berndt disappeared, there is a better-than-average chance that drugs, the Vandals and Monroe himself have something to do with their disappearance.

21

Walker adds a picture of Matt Monroe to his board. He can't find a picture of Tina Monroe's meaty boyfriend, so he uses one of a gleaming Harley. He adds Angus Jones's name above the property too as he snacks on a Cherry Ripe and tries to find a pattern among it all.

He's run a registration search on the Harley and come up with a name, Brian Burgess. He does a few searches but, surprisingly, the bloke's not on any police database. He types the name into Google and a load of faces appear, none of whom even slightly resemble the man built like a human refrigerator that he'd met at the farm.

He tries a different tack, searching instead for Tina Monroe. She has a decent list of minor convictions - shoplifting, drunk and disorderly, possession - but these all come to a halt more than two years ago. It looks as if she's cleaned her act up. Maybe this Brian Burgess is having a good influence, thinks Walker, though somehow he doubts it.

He checks out social media and sees she's active on Instagram. She looks younger than he expected, late thirties at most, so would have been just a teenager when her son was born. Her hair is long and blonde, her skin tanned, and she's happy to display her curvaceous, possibly surgically enhanced body in the pictures she posts. There are plenty of pictures of herself and Burgess - sunning themselves by a pool, swinging designer-label shopping bags, drinking cocktails in Bali. He reads the captions and notes that she refers to the man as Stefan, not Brian. Walker makes a note. Perhaps the bike is stolen.

Matt Monroe appears in a few of the pictures, his girlfriend too. They're all living a good life, plenty of designer kit and holidays. Walker searches the police database. Matt Monroe has a caution for holding drugs for personal use, but nothing else. Walker reflects on the limitations of these records. He knows from Jordan that Matt Monroe had a couple of assault charges by ex-girlfriends that were eventually dropped – he can only imagine the pressure the girls came under – and regular domestic disturbance call-outs. None of these made it to court and he was never convicted, so his record is much cleaner than it should be.

He takes a screen grab of a couple of the images of Tina Monroe with the big bloke, and another of Matt Monroe with his girlfriend, plus details of the bike, and fires off a brief email to update Rutherford.

It's less than ten minutes before a response appears. The speed surprises him; Rutherford isn't the kind of boss who sits around waiting for emails to appear in his inbox. He's up to his eyeballs in running a big team.

The email is as brief as it is quick in arriving:

Until further notice please desist with any investigation of Stefan Markovich and his associates and please advise immediately how he has come to your attention.

Walker leans back in his chair. He remembers hearing that Rutherford was part of the biker task force, Morpheus, for a while. Morpheus was formed a few years ago, a pooling of intelligence between state and national law enforcement agencies, with a focus on all OMCGs, outlaw motorcycle gangs. Maybe this is stepping on Morpheus territory.

Rutherford has, perhaps unwittingly, given him the name of the big man: Stefan Markovich. And it's a name that Walker knows. Markovich is the Vandals' head honcho. Walker hasn't had much to do with OMCGs in his work and he's never met Markovich or seen him – he'd have remembered the man, the size of him alone – but he's heard the name plenty. He also knows that, with more than fifteen hundred members across Queensland and New South Wales, the Vandals are one of the biggest OMCGs in Australia. A bikie called Pedro Silva had founded the group and headed it up for decades, until he went to prison in 2015, found guilty of murdering a policeman. At the time, Walker had only recently gone undercover on his previous op, and the word on the street was that Silva had been set up by someone in the gang, aided by corrupt cops. The evidence around the murder was a bit circumstantial but Silva's bikie connections – he'd worn his Vandals colours in court – helped lead to a conviction. Since Silva's been in jail, Markovich has more or less taken over.

What a big player like him would be doing out here, in the middle of nowhere in outback Queensland, isn't so clear. Walker searches for Markovich in the database and it comes up with a flag: *Contact Morpheus* and an email address. He searches for the Vandals instead, and finds plenty: members, nominees and associates reported or arrested on more than fourteen hundred charges including serious assault, stalking, kidnapping, firearms and drugs offences.

He does a little more digging in Matt Monroe's social media. He's friends with plenty of blokes with a similar look: young and muscled and tattooed. But the style is far from the bikies of old. It fits with what he's heard on the streets. The younger members, so-called Nike-bikers, are ditching bikes and turning instead to fashionable clothes – by the look of the pictures, red Nikes are a favourite – expensive jewellery and luxury cars as a way to flash their cash. He remembers Monroe's car: out this way, a top-of-the-range brand-new Hilux is definitely a status buy. The younger members still use tattoos to mark out their affiliation but also as an aesthetic statement. They're less loyal than the older blokes too, patching over to other gangs if the opportunity seems to be better.

Matt Monroe's connection to the gang seems simple enough – he's a dealer so the Vandals are his conduit to the drug. Presumably his mum's boyfriend helped set him up. But what, Walker wonders, do Berndt Meyer and Rita Guerra have to do with all this? There are no obvious links and Berndt Meyer's tattoos and fashion sense, his long fisherman's trousers and Birkenstocks, don't square with the street-style leisurewear vibe of the likes of Monroe. He decides Rutherford is most likely to know, picks up the phone and dials his number, the direct line listed at the bottom of his email.

'Alright, Walker,' says Rutherford. 'You saw my email? You're calling to let me know that you've dropped everything related to Markovich . . .'

Walker explains the situation: Sheree Miller, Berndt Meyer and Rita Guerra possibly linked to Matt Monroe to Tina Monroe to Stefan Markovich.

'Right,' says Rutherford again. 'Well, you have to drop it. You know Markovich, right?'

'I've heard of him,' says Walker.

'He's the leader of the Vandal chapters in Queensland and the brains behind the whole Australian operation since Pedro Silva's been in prison. He moved up to Queensland because some of Silva's mates think he helped set Silva up in order to take control of the organisation. Feels safer on home ground, I suppose.'

'Who's Brian Burgess? He comes up as the owner of the bike I saw.'

'Their lawyer. Based in Brisbane. He must have bought the bike. Markovich probably wants to keep his name off the radar.'

'And how does Tina Monroe fit into it?'

'Bit player. Been Markovich's girlfriend, or one of them, for a couple of years. But you need to stop digging into this. Right now. We have an operation linked to Markovich. You don't need to know all the details, DS. I'm ordering you: stay away from him.'

'Sir, I'm up here in the middle of this misper investigation that you asked me to be part of,' says Walker. 'Markovich looks like he's connected, so I'm investigating it. I'm not trying to mess things up for your other op but the less I know, the more likely I am to step on toes as I take my investigation forward.'

It's the truth – he can't avoid what he doesn't know about. Rutherford seems to see the logic of his argument. After a long pause he says: 'You know The Company?'

Walker does. The Company is an Asian drug syndicate, perhaps the most powerful methamphetamine distributor in the world. The syndicate has targeted Australia, importing and distributing large amounts of illicit narcotics into the country over the last decade. It's believed to be responsible for as much as 70 per cent of the illegal drugs that reach Australia.

'Well, they've been taking a hit lately. Law enforcement is onto them worldwide. In 2020 they got busted in Myanmar – the cops there found 200 million meth tablets and five hundred kilos of crystal.'

'Yeah, I remember,' says Walker. 'It was a hell of a lot of drugs.'

'Exactly. It caused supply issues out here for a while. And then Interpol arrested the head honcho, Tse Chi Lop, in Amsterdam.'

Like everyone else, Walker has heard of Tse's arrest and the attempt to extradite him to Australia: it's the Australian equivalent of nailing Pablo Escobar or El Chapo Guzmán.

'Right,' he says. 'I knew that. But what's that got to do with Markovich?'

'All this action against The Company has impacted the Vandal supply quite badly and we think Markovich has decided to take out the middle man, turn the Vandals into producers as well as distributors. We think they're trying to set up a manufacturing site out your way, a nice long way from anywhere. So far, we don't have any evidence. We can't get near Markovich, he only works with a couple of his closest lieutenants, but we've got someone who's building trust and working his way up. We're getting closer. And that investigation has priority over anything else. You can't go near Markovich or the Vandals – I don't want him getting a sniff of us on his radar.'

'Might be too late for that,' confesses Walker. 'I paid a visit out there today, trying to talk to Tina Monroe.'

Rutherford curses long and loud. 'Anyone up there know you're Federal Police?' he says eventually.

'No,' says Walker. 'I told them I was a DS in Sydney, working on this misper case.'

'Well, let's hope they buy it. Don't go near him again. Stay well away from Markovich. I want him feeling safe and secure for a while longer, so that we can get together the evidence we need.'

Rutherford hangs up. The silence rings in Walker's ear. He knows Rutherford is right. The big cases, the ones that make a difference to disrupting major organised crime, have to take precedence. They can take a whole cohort of dangerous criminals off the streets, not to mention significantly depleting the drugs supply line. But he thinks of Barbara, and the way that Rita's disappearance is diminishing her. Sheree Miller's mum and the pain she's been through. These aren't irrelevances, these are people and families who have a right to answers. With Matt Monroe and Angus Jones linked to Markovich, even if tenuously, both his key suspects for these missing backpackers have connections to the Vandals. He has to figure out a way to keep looking into it without disrupting Rutherford's operation.

He's tapping his pen against his teeth, thinking, thinking, thinking, when his phone rings – it's Grogan. Walker is half tempted to let it go to voicemail. He picks it up. 'DS Walker' – hoping his rank will put the bloke off any bullshit.

'Yeah, hello, DS. Are you trying to arrange an interview with Tina Monroe? She's called in, saying someone wants to talk to her?'

'Yeah,' he says, 'that was me.'

'Is it in relation to this case?'

Walker sits up a little. It's highly unlikely that Grogan would know anything about Rutherford's investigation, but why else would he be asking. 'What else would it be?'

'Ah, right, yeah, of course.' Grogan seems flustered. 'But what's her connection?'

'Her son, Matt Monroe, was linked to the disappearance of a girl in Hopeville eighteen months ago. Similar MO. Just wanted to check if he was in the area the day this couple disappeared.' Walker wants to be sure to make the connection only with regard to missing persons, doesn't mention drugs, doesn't mention the Vandals. He's respecting Rutherford's need for secrecy but it's more than that. Something about these questions from Grogan doesn't sit quite right with him.

'Righto.' There's a pause. 'Well, she's coming into the station, if you want to interview her.'

22

Tina Monroe is seething. Life has been going great the last few years. Stefan moving out this way is the best thing that's ever happened to her. She'd met him in a bar in Hopeville, when he was passing through with a gang of bikies on a weekend ride out bush. She hadn't known then he was checking things out, thinking about moving some operation up here. She'd just liked the look of him; she always goes for the bad-boy type, with muscles and tats and a bit of attitude. He'd liked the look of her too, she'd found out that night. Had invited her down to Surfers a couple of times, shown her a good time and then asked her to put this rental in her name and moved her in with him. He takes care of her. No one gives her grief when he's standing beside her. He's happy to splash the cash, they go on holidays, he buys her expensive things, they've got this nice house and life is good. Until the police turned up uninvited and had Stefan throwing a fit.

'Have you been using or stealing again?' He'd grabbed her by the arm, pushed her against the wall the second she'd walked in the door. Still standing in the hallway, the grocery bags in one hand, keys in the other. She remembers it now, him squeezing her upper arm so hard it hurts, and he's never done that before. She's seen what he can do and he's at least three times her size, so she's scared, can feel her heart beating, but doesn't let it show.

'What are you doing? You're hurting me. Let go, for fuck's sake.'

His grip tightens. 'A cop was here, asking for you. Less than an hour ago. Wanting to talk to you.'

That gives her a shock. Maybe he sees it in her eyes because he loosens his grip and lets her arm fall. She rubs it and thinks about crying, but decides against it.

'I haven't done nothing, babe. Not even a traffic ticket. I'm not an idiot. I know how important this is. I've been clean since you said – more than two years. I don't know what they want.'

She can see him thinking, putting two and two together and making six. 'Fucking Matty,' he says. 'If this is down to him, I'll beat the shit out of him.'

She puts her hand on his arm. He shrugs it off, glowers at her.

'You don't know that it's anything to do with Matty. It could be anything.'

'Such as?'

She shakes her head. 'What do I know?' She thinks about it. 'I thought that Grogan was on our side. Isn't he bought off?'

'Weren't him.' He hits his fist against the wall, one, two, three times. She feels a pent-up desire for violence emanating from him and a prickle of fear rises in her. He looks hard at her again. 'Find out what's going on. Call Matty now and find out if he knows what this is about.'

She stands looking at him, still wondering why the fuck the cops would have come here.

'Ya waiting for a printed fucking invitation?' he roars. 'Call Matty now!'

She doesn't argue, defers to his rage but pushes past him, playing indignant, and walks down the hallway.

'Orright, let me put these down and then I'll call him.'

'You better sort this out. This is too big to lose just because your idiot kid is too stupid to stay under the radar.'

She walks into the kitchen, dumps her groceries on a countertop and fishes out her phone and ciggies from her bag. Her hand is shaking slightly as she lights up, but she feels calmer after a couple of puffs, here in the oasis of her kitchen, one of her favourite places in the house. She's had it done up. She saw something like it in some magazine but she's added a bit of colour, not all the acres of bloody white that the magazines seem to like. She's chosen nice pale-pink finishes for the cupboards, a black granite top polished to a high shine, the best appliances. She walks over to the kettle, decides against a tea and goes to the fridge instead. Opens a bottle of white wine, pours a big glass, taps her nails against the worktop, thinking.

Living with Stefan isn't easy. She's seen him bash the shit out of prospects, even members if they fuck up. And heard that he's done worse than administer a bashing, though she keeps her nose well out of the business. He's always paranoid that someone is out to get him. If it's not the cops, it's one of Pedro's old mates who blames him for Pedro going down. He doesn't trust anyone, but over the last two years he's come to trust her. And she's done nothing, not even a speeding ticket. Because even when he scares her, this is the best life she's had and no way is she ruining it – it's way better than anything she'd ever hoped for. She'll calm Stefan down, get him in bed, fuck his brains out. He's probably right. This will be Matty up to something.

Stefan's never had much time for Matty but she managed to get him a bigger role, get him promoted to membership. Trouble with Matty is he's impatient and not fucking smart enough. Doesn't know when to keep his mouth shut, always giving lip, no respect. Looking around the kitchen, at what there is to lose, she decides that, if she has to, she'll sell Matty down the river, ungrateful brat. She's not going back to where she was. Push comes to shove, even though Matty's her son, she's not losing

Stefan and the life he gives her.

She takes her wine to the living room and sinks into the sofa. Stefan is nowhere in sight – he must have gone across to the warehouse. She digs out her mobile and dials Matty's number.

'What the fuck have you been doing?' she says when he answers. 'I've had the cops out here.'

'Yeah, hello, nice to talk to you too,' he says.

Cheeky prick. He's too stupid to see where this is gonna land him.

'I'm serious, Matty,' she says. 'Stefan is raging.'

That pulls him up. 'I ain't done nothing,' he says. 'The pigs were here too yesterday. Some girl gone missing up your way and they reckon I did it because of Sheree and because you're living up that way.'

'What girl? That German tourist that's missing?'

'I dunno. I dunno nothing about it. Told 'em that.' He pauses. 'But it happened the day I was up your way, collecting the gear. I didn't tell 'em that, obviously.'

'How did they know I was living up this way?'

'I told 'em. Told 'em you'd be able to put me in the clear. That you'd say I wasn't around your way on the day they said. That I didn't do it.'

'You selfish little shit. You gave them this fucking address? You know how important this is to Stefan. To everyone. This is much bigger than some girl, much bigger than you doin' a bit of time for something stupid. Stefan is gonna kill you.'

She hangs up. Let him think on Stefan being angry as fuck for a while. She didn't think he could be such an idiot. Too stupid and selfish to see the bigger picture. She sips her wine and when Stefan comes back in she plasters a smile on her face.

'You talk to Matty?' he asks, not smiling back.

'He didn't do nothing. Cops were asking him about some girl that disappeared up this way. Trying to pin it on him because of that ex-girlfriend of his that did a runner last year. It's nothing to do with us.'

'Why were they here, then?'

'I guess they figured they'd ask me, see if I was stupid enough to give them Matty on a plate.'

Stefan thinks for a long moment. 'What girl up here? You mean those backpackers?'

She nods. 'Reckon it must be.'

'Matty have something to do with that?'

She gives him an injured look. 'Course not. He's not like that. They got it in for him, that's all.'

'Right, then. Well, you better go in and see the pigs, clear this up, make sure they don't come back out here. Find out who that cop is and what he wants. If he comes back out here, sniffing around, we'll have to shut this whole thing down. That happens, I'll go, this house'll go, and you'll be back dossing with Matty.'

And with that he turns on his heel and walks out, the back door slamming shut behind him.

So now here she is, at the cop shop, smiling and making nice and fucking seething inside. The bloke she's talking to doesn't look like a cop, curly hair that's a bit wild, jeans and boots. He's introduced himself, a detective, DS Walker, taken her into a little interview room, a table and couple of chairs, him with his notebook, her sitting there while he asks all the old questions about Sheree and Matt. She tries not to get arsey about it – she needs to clear this up, make sure they don't come back out to Stefan's place, make sure they think Matt is in the clear.

'I heard you came out to see me. Is there some kind of problem?' she asks.

'No, no. I just wanted to have a chat with you about your son and Sheree Miller, the girl who disappeared last year.'

'Jesus. Not that again. He didn't do it. They tried to stitch him up when it happened, but he was with me all night.'

'Could I take a statement from you? We've found some new evidence and it'd be very helpful to rule Matt out.'

She goes through the whole story. 'So there ya go: I was at his place that night – all night,' she finishes. 'We had a few drinks and had a big blue. The neighbours were banging on the door telling us to shut the fuck up, so you could ask them about it. He didn't have nothing to do with that girl disappearing.'

'What were you blueing about?'

This was before Stefan was living up here full-time, when they'd just had a casual thing going. Matty wanted her to whisper sweet nothings, get him a bigger role in the whole business, wasn't happy with being a nobody. Thought nobody gave him enough respect. She'd told him to grow the fuck up. Bide his time. There was plenty of money and respect coming his way.

'Nothing,' she says. 'Nothing I remember. Reckon I didn't like the way he talked to me – he didn't have no respect.' That much is true. He'd started calling her names and she'd lost it. 'It kicked off 'cause we were drinking. Wasn't nothing, but proves he wasn't out killing no girl.'

'When's the last time you saw Matt?' he asks.

She's got her answer ready. Stays clear of the date Matty was here last but not so far out that she can't change her mind later, if she needs to. 'He comes out regular – he's got a shack at the back of our place, comes for the weekend sometimes. I reckon the last time was two weekends ago. He came up on the Friday and left on the Sunday.'

The cop brings up the calendar on his phone, counts back the weeks. 'So that was Friday twenty-eighth to Sunday thirtieth October.'

She looks at the phone. 'Yeah, that must be right.'

'Did he bring his girlfriend?' he asks.

'Nah. That stupid bint doesn't like the bush. Never leaves Hopeville unless he's taking her to Brisso or the coast.' She doesn't like Kelly, never has. She hasn't got a brain cell to her name. Matt doesn't tell the girl anything about the business, just as well, and he never brings her out this way, doesn't want her getting wind of things.

'You didn't see him the weekend of the fifth and sixth of November?'

She takes her phone out, makes a show of looking at the dates. 'Nah. He wasn't here then.'

The cop writes it all down, then says, 'Thanks for coming in, Ms Monroe. Appreciate it.'

She looks at him, pretty sure he's taking the piss, but he looks innocent enough. 'Can I have a ciggie?' she asks.

He nods. 'Sure. But we're done now, so you're OK to go.'

She pulls one out anyway, lights up, takes a drag.

'I just need a quick one, always makes me nervous talking to you lot.' She exhales. 'Why are you asking us about all this again? And where're you from, anyway? You're not from round here, are ya?'

She's pushing it, asking questions like this, but Stefan wants information and she wants to get back in his good books.

The cop opposite gives a half-smile. 'You the cop now, is that it?' he says. Then he leans back and answers her anyway: 'You probably heard about that couple went missing on the Smithton road? I've been sent to help out with that case. We're just ruling Matt out, that's all.'

It's what she thought. Nothing to do with Stefan. 'And you got all you need? Are you good now? You gonna leave me alone? Gonna leave Matty alone?'

'Yes, thanks, that's great. All cleared up. We're dotting the i's, you know how it is.'

Back in the car, she gives Stefan a call. 'Some cop, not from round here, looking into that missing couple, like I said. They thought Matt might have had something to do with it. But he's in the clear. I told them he wasn't here. It's nothing to do with you.'

'What's his name?'

'Who?'

'The cop you talked to?'

'He's a detective, his name's Walker.'

'Righto.'

'You want me to bring some pies from the bakery for tea?'

'Yeah, yeah, sure. I gotta go.'

After hanging up, Markovich stays sitting in the big leather chair in his office. It's been going pretty smoothly. They make everything here, move small batches at a time to a storage warehouse on Jones's other place near the highway, and handle the big distribution, the weekly trucks, from out there, where there's no one to connect anything back here. But that cop . . . Something about him smells wrong. He didn't get to where he is today without knowing when something doesn't smell right. He puts in a call to Nick, his number two, gets him chasing down the background on this Walker bloke. They pay off enough cops – time for some of them to get useful.

23

Barbara's unease, her sense that she might never find Rita, grows stronger during the drive to Smithton. A two-hour drive in a straight line, through featureless countryside, plains of dry grasslands, the light so bright that even the sky is washed of blue. Nothing to see, literally nothing, and nowhere that might have tempted Rita and Berndt to turn off. She thinks of them driving out this way, to a job in this unremitting heat, and wonders if perhaps Grogan isn't right. They gave up, turned round and went somewhere else after all.

Smithton only reinforces that feeling. The village, if you can call it that, is nothing more than a service station and a handful of dilapidated houses on a dirt track perpendicular to it. Everything looks run-down, verging on derelict. There are no lawns, no trees, no paved streets. One house has the rusting carcasses of a handful of cars outside it, like so many skeletons of civilisation. It reminds her of the *Mad Max* movie she'd streamed a few years ago and its desolate post-civilisation vibe.

She reapplies sunscreen before she gets out of the coolness of the air-conditioned car. Her skin normally tans easily, but here it's no match for the ferocity of the sun; this morning's short walk has burnt her arms and her face. She catches the smell of the cream as she applies it, a scent that has always reminded her of summer and beaches and good times, but which will now be forever associated with this heat, this fear, this foreign and unappealing country.

She could be on another planet, that's how alien this is to her. The searing heat, the unbearably bright light, the endless horizon, the untamed countryside, the bush, as Walker calls it, pushing right up to the backs of the houses. And not a person in sight. No movement or sound, just a handful of flies buzzing around her face, persistent even as she waves them away.

The silence is as heavy as a blanket. Oppressive. She turns towards the service station. The door emits a squawking buzz and as she steps inside she can hear a radio blaring in a room out the back. There's a makeshift general store to one side, its shelves dusty and virtually empty, only a few items of canned food, some biscuits, UHT milk, bottles of soft drink. A cash register sits in front of her at one end of a long glass counter under which lie a few unappetising pies; she can see a fly crawling around on one of them. There are two aluminium tables in front of the counter, stained with ring marks from cups and spots of grease. The place smells of oil fried too many times.

Barbara calls, 'Hello?' and a moment later a woman emerges from a back room, pushing through the curtain of colourful plastic strips that cover the door. She's hugely overweight, wearing a sleeveless dress of faded blue, her clothing, face and hair all damp with sweat.

She shakes her head when Barbara shows her the picture of Rita and Berndt.

'Nah, haven't seen 'em,' she says. 'Been no tourists through this week. Wrong time of year.'

Barbara leaves her a flyer for the window, but she feels Smithton is a dead end. There is no way Rita would stay out here to work. Not even for one day. She thinks again that Grogan is probably right – perhaps they did just take one look and carry on, drive through to somewhere, anywhere, better than this. But where could they have gone and why haven't they been in touch?

When she arrives back at the hotel in Caloodie, her room is baking hot. There's a message on her phone, a response to the reward. She feels a surge of hope. Other than the prank call yesterday, she hasn't had any responses, and they need a lead so badly.

She calls back, hands shaking a little. A woman answers.

'Ah, yeah, yeah, I saw 'em, them two on the poster. Well, pretty sure it was them. Coupla tourists. They was at a barbecue at Mitch's place. He met 'em at the pub, invited 'em over. We tied one on and it got a bit out of hand – everyone was pissed, Mitch got lairy, calling 'em stupid bastards 'cause they didn't have a clue, really. Was only a bit of fun but the bloke got all offended, started throwing punches . . .'

Barbara's heart is in her mouth, she can barely breathe. They're alive. They went somewhere else. They are off partying. That's all this is.

'Where was this?' she asks. 'And when did you see them?'

'Told ya, didn't I, they was at Mitch's place,' the woman says. 'Musta been three weeks ago now. It was Mitch's birthday, October the nineteenth.'

As quickly as that the flame of hope goes out – that was weeks before Rita and Berndt left Sydney. Some other couple, drinking and arguing.

She sits on the bed, trying to manage her disappointment. She tells herself it could still be that Rita and Berndt are off partying somewhere. That Smithton horrified them the way it did her, and they've just driven on somewhere, passing a few days without phone signal, enjoying the adventure, and this is all just a panic over nothing. She goes over the scenario in her mind again and again, hoping, wishing, she could believe it was as simple as that.

She takes a shower to try to cool down but it doesn't revive her at all. The water from the artesian springs far beneath the ground is still warm when it reaches the pipes. It's a rust-coloured brown, not dirty but heavy in minerals. She longs for the jet of clear, cool water that her shower in Berlin would emit. Afterwards, still feeling hot and with the metallic scent of the water on her skin, she switches both the fan and the air conditioner on high and lies on her bed, trying to cool down. The heat is unending, day and night, no break. She couldn't bear to live out here, with no respite for months upon months and the vast dry emptiness all around her.

She has a visceral longing to be back home, back in the everyday normality of her life. She wants to be in the office, wrapped up in the details of a case or out with one of the team, interviewing suspects. She misses the team, misses the banter and the irritations, misses the routine. She doesn't want Rita to be lost. She doesn't want to be stuck in this strange cowboy town in the middle of this vast, empty, hot country. She wants to go home with every fibre of her being. To wake up in her own bed, in her own place. To shiver a little as she gets in the shower because the heating hasn't quite cut through the November chill, to drink a strong coffee for breakfast, wrap a scarf around her neck, sink her hands deep in her coat pockets and debate about whether to take the bike or, if the light drizzle warrants, braving the crush of other commuters on the S-Bahn. She wants to complain about the cold, meet friends for a beer and go home to watch a movie in bed. But she can't. She can't leave Rita alone in this alien and inhospitable landscape. She has to stay, find her little sister and bring her home.

She needs to call her parents again. She's been putting it off. Her father had been firm in his belief that her arrival in Caloodie would deliver Rita back to them and last time she'd spoken with him he'd been angry, frustrated, tormented. 'How can it be that they don't know where she is? This is killing us. It's killing your mother, it's killing me, it's killing our family.' Seeing her strongman father crying and disconsolate is more than Barbara can bear.

The phone rings and rings. She's about to hang up when her mother answers, 'Hola', the Spanish greeting she still sometimes unconsciously uses.

'Mama, it's me.'

'Have you found her? Is she OK?' Barbara hears a sudden hope in her mother's voice, and she wishes with every cell in her being that she could say, 'Yes, she's here!' and have all of them laughing and crying and talking at the same time.

'No, Mama, no news yet. But don't worry, I will find her.'

'I know you will, *mi amor*. I know you will. How are you doing, *querida* – are you OK? Are they looking after you?'

Barbara's eyes fill with tears. She wants her mother's love, but it might just crack her thin veneer of coping if she opens up and lets it in. 'It's hard, Mama, but I'm OK. There is a local detective here who's working on it. But it's so far from home, it's so different. And I feel like I'm letting you down, letting Papa down.'

'No, *querida*, no. You are our shining light, our biggest hope. I know you're doing more than anyone else could and so does your father. It's just ... well, this is bringing back terrible memories for us.'

There's a long pause, Barbara trying to suppress her tears.

Her mother starts talking again. 'When we were in Chile, we were just Rita's age when the killings, the disappearances, began. Everyone was so scared, so helpless, just like this.'

Barbara knows the story. Her family had been supporters of the left-wing Allende government in the 1970s. When the military coup brought General Pinochet to power, the arrests, killings and disappearances began. It was only because of some loose connection to Clodomiro Almeyda, the former foreign minister, that her parents managed to escape. They'd made it to safety in East Germany, the GDR, a leftist bolthole. But others weren't so lucky. Her father's brother, Raúl, was arrested and never seen again. Her mother's cousins, Victor and Maria, were both tortured and executed; their mother Rosa died of a broken heart.

Her mother is still talking. 'And now the same thing with Rita. Her missing like this – ah, *querida*, it's killing him.'

Barbara's heart clenches in pain for her father, who has lost so much already. And she knows she's failing them by not finding Rita. She wishes she could impart to her mother the sheer size of this country. The hundreds upon hundreds of miles of emptiness and nothingness. The roads that run straight for days on end. Where strangers lift their hand to you in greeting as cars pass on the highway, in the relief of finally seeing another human being. Where people go missing and are never found.

Now Rita and Berndt have joined the legions of the disappeared. She wonders how many families are feeling the same despair as she is, not knowing what has happened to someone they love. She thinks of the missing men and women on the poster. From one day to the next, they simply vanish. They climb onto a bus heading west. Perhaps they surface for a time in a remote town, a ripple of their presence discernible to those who search for them later, but then they're gone, the way a breath of air is lost in a tornado, without so much as a whisper or a trace.

24

Walker watches Tina Monroe stalk out of the office and down the path, head high. She'd told him a pretty good story, sticking to the version she'd told back when Sheree disappeared. But she was too sure about the dates on which Matt had visited her recently, so no doubt he'd primed her on that. Walker would bet his life savings, if he had any, that she's not being entirely honest.

And the fact that she's turned up to give him a statement, just a couple of hours after he visited Markovich, is a big red-alert bell as far as Walker's concerned. Avoiding cops is an innate skill for the likes of Markovich, so this is probably Tina Monroe's idea, which means maybe Matt Monroe does have something to hide . . . and Walker still has a gut feeling it could involve Rita and Berndt. If Monroe was up this way the weekend of their disappearance, it's just too much of a coincidence. He has form. He got away with it once before with Sheree – he might try his arm again.

Walker hopes his acting was up to hers, and that she buys his assurance that Monroe is off the hook and that he has no interest in Markovich. As she struts downs the path, she seems pretty confident. Hopefully she'll pass that info on to Markovich, and Rutherford's investigation will stay in the clear.

He goes back to chat with Grogan. He wants to sound him out, find out what, if anything, he knows about Rutherford's operation.

'You reckon her son had something to do with these missing backpackers?' asks Grogan.

'I don't know,' says Walker truthfully. 'There's a good chance he was up this way the weekend they disappeared and he's in the frame for his missing ex-girlfriend, so he's a strong possibility. His mum's given him an alibi, but she did that the last time too. You know Matt Monroe, right? Have you had any run-ins with him?' he asks.

'No, none at all,' says Grogan. 'He has a little shack in the back paddock at Tina's place and he comes and goes quite regularly. I've seen him in the pub from time to time. Bit of a poser but I never had any problems with him. I don't see him round as often anymore – I don't reckon Tina's boyfriend likes him.'

'Did you see him here the weekend the backpackers went missing?'

'No, but I wasn't at the pub that night.'

'And what's the story with his mum, then?'

'I know her fairly well. Quite often has a drink with Lisa, my wife. Lisa says she's a bit rough around the edges, had a hard life, but seems to have put it behind her since she moved out here a couple of years ago.'

Walker works to keep the surprise off his face. He's not sure that Grogan's wife should be chummy with the girlfriend of the leader of an outlaw motorcycle gang.

'Why did she move up this way, then?' he asks.

Grogan pauses, looks at Walker, who reads indecision in his eyes. 'I reckon she moved in with her boyfriend,' he says after a moment.

'Who's he? The boyfriend, I mean.' Walker is digging, wondering again if Grogan knows about the Morpheus op.

'I wouldn't know him from a bar of soap,' says Grogan. 'Never even talked to him.'

This time Walker can't hide his surprise. Grogan is proud of knowing all the locals, of being the man with his finger on the pulse, but he hasn't clocked a bikie living on the town's outskirts? It seems inconceivable that he doesn't know who Markovich is, but even if he doesn't, the bloke's size, his demeanour and appearance would ring bells for any cop.

'I thought you knew all the locals,' says Walker.

Grogan looks flustered. 'He doesn't come into town. Tina says he doesn't drink, so he doesn't come to the pub, and he works away a lot. He's down the coast most weeks. I've never seen him around. But it seems a pretty solid relationship. Lisa says the bloke looks after Tina.'

Walker's alarm bells are ringing loud. Grogan would be unlikely to miss Markovich. There's just no way in a small town like Caloodie that Markovich would stay invisible. Maybe Grogan is being professionally discreet, protecting the bigger operation that's going on. But Walker doubts very much that Rutherford would include a constable in an outback town, even an outback town that might be a site for a meth lab, in the details of any operation. Grogan is more likely protecting someone in town. Probably his wife and her friendship with Tina Monroe, a clear liability given who Markovich is. He was right to worry that the constable is too chummy with the locals to do any proper policing.

After he leaves the station, he sits in the car, thinking. He's learnt two interesting things. Monroe has a place out this way that he uses regularly, and Grogan has some very dubious connections. There's no way Grogan can be linked to Rutherford's op. He's too inexperienced, and a bit shoddy. Rutherford has higher standards.

Walker starts the engine and drives to the pub. He wants to check on Barbara, that her trip to Smithton went OK. As he drives he decides he needs to go and take a look at Markovich's place again, and check out Monroe's shack too. Just to make sure the missing backpackers aren't being held there. But he needs to do it on the quiet – he doesn't want to mess up Rutherford's operation by giving Markovich any reason to think he's under investigation.

When he arrives, the bar is still quiet; Ali is stacking bottles of soft drink into the fridge. She straightens up and smiles at him.

'You looking for Barbara, love?' she asks.

Walker nods.

Ali looks at him, remembering the exhaustion on Barbara's face the day she arrived, her desperation to find answers on her first night. The blokes in town are always happy to see a new woman, someone to add a bit of interest to the routine. And Barbara, with those big brown eyes, the red lipstick and the curves that are almost more alluring because she conceals them, had definitely got a bit of blood flowing.

But then she'd started asking everyone in the bar if they'd seen or talked to the missing pair, and that had put the wind up most of them, none of them really that comfortable with a cop in their midst. Ali'd had to offer a couple of them a beer on the house to settle them down, convince them Barbara was just a woman desperate to find her sister. She'd let the thought run through her mind that it would be better if Barbara could stay somewhere else, but there is nowhere else and, poor girl, Christ, what a terrible thing to have to go through.

Still, she's noticed that the others skirt a wide berth, especially Paul Johnson. He's done time so he's more wary of the cops than the rest of them. And even Hippy, who will usually banter with anyone, has been keeping clear. Walker is the only one who's really helping her out with this.

'I'm glad you're looking after her,' she says to him. 'I reckon it really helps that she's working with you.'

A cloud passes across his eyes. 'We're not exactly working together,' he says, but Ali notices that his smile is warm when Barbara appears.

Barbara invites him upstairs, sits down at the desk and pulls a notebook from her bag.

'Driving to Smithton was a waste of time. They did not see Rita and Berndt.' She looks at him. 'That place ...' she says. 'It's horrible.'

Smithton is one of the least lovely towns in the area. 'That's why Grogan reckons they might have turned round or driven on,' says Walker.

'Yes,' she says. 'I understand now.' She pauses. 'I have also been looking into the Sheree Miller case.'

Walker nods. 'Yeah, I heard. I spoke with Senior Sergeant Jordan earlier and she told me there was a truck driving away from the scene. Good work on your part and not great policing on theirs that this was missed.'

Barbara nods. 'The truck driver did not stop in Hopeville to report the abandoned car. That's strange, no? Everyone has been telling me about the unwritten law of the road, about always stopping if someone is in trouble or they could die. If the truck driver had nothing to hide he would have stopped to report it ...'

Walker concedes it's unusual, but he doesn't think it's a smoking gun. 'Maybe he saw the caravanners stop and figured they'd report it,' he says.

He can see she doesn't agree but she doesn't push the point. He updates her on his interview with Tina Monroe but doesn't mention Markovich or what he plans to do tonight – that's all best kept off her radar.

'I still think Matt Monroe is a strong suspect,' he says. 'It could be really helpful if you would do some research. I need to know whether Meyer and your sister have links to the drugs scene, and if so how they were involved. You know your sister, and you can contact her friends, dig into that, find out more.'

'Rita was not a drug user back in Germany.' Her tone is sharp, frustrated. 'She lives at home with my parents, and they are old-school, they have strict rules. And her friends are not this type either. They drink beers at the local bar or hang out by the lake in the summer, house parties in the winter. Maybe she smokes a joint or two but nothing more than that – her friends just are not that type of crowd. She doesn't hang with the clubbing crowd, the ones who use harder drugs.' She pulls up a picture of Rita and Berndt, taken in Sydney, on her phone. 'Look at this. Rita is not trafficking drugs. She was working at a fashion shop, Berndt was a barista in some trendy café.' She walks over, thrusts the picture at him. 'Have you even looked at the pictures of them? They are kids on holiday, they are not dealers.'

'When I worked undercover in Sydney, lots of people who are dealing look exactly like your sister and Meyer. They sell to their friends, it's easy money, they get drawn in, they don't realise the dangers.' He pauses. 'I know it's hard to accept but this is the best lead we have. People change, circumstances change. You don't know anything about Berndt – maybe you need to put in a call to his father, ask some hard questions. Could he have been dealing, got them mixed up in something terrible?'

'You think you are still undercover in Sydney. You see everything the way it was down there and you are not looking at the facts of this case. Rita and Berndt were on their way to a farming job in an old car. They are not drug dealers.'

She's small, barely up to his shoulders in height, but, standing there with her arms crossed and sparks of anger in her eyes, she's formidable. She reminds him of Grandma. There's a core of strength; you can see it in the way she stands, with her back straight and chin up. Like she's on parade, he thinks, suppressing a smile.

She's right too: he's still in Sydney, still among the career criminals. His visit here hasn't shaken the world view that he's assimilated over the last three years, but having Markovich down the road confirms he's right to think that their reach is long, and it is deadly.

The disagreement hovers between them as he takes his leave. She doesn't invite him to dinner and he's relieved he doesn't have to turn her down and reveal that he has plans of his own.

As he leaves the pub he glances into the bar, busier already than when he'd arrived. The usual suspects are all there: Hippy, Johnson and one of his drivers, Tina Monroe too. She has her back to him but he recognises the top she was wearing when he spoke with her. She's talking to another woman. Grogan, who has changed out of his uniform, is standing beside them, laughing at something the two women are saying. A young girl, seven or eight maybe, is leaning against Grogan's legs and calling, 'Daddy, Daddy,' to attract his attention.

The scene fills him with a kind of claustrophobia. This community harbours secrets – drugs, organised crime, missing tourists – and Grogan sits here, drinking beers, playing happy families and making friends with the likes of Tina Monroe. He turns on his heel and leaves; he doesn't want any part of it.

25

Barbara stands on the veranda outside her room, watching Walker's ute drive off down the road. It's over a week since Rita and Berndt were last seen – here, on Friday night, at the hotel. The fact that the only lead they've come up with connects them to a drug dealer horrifies her.

She's certain that Rita wasn't a drug user, let alone dealer, but she does need to check with Berndt's father. Still, it seems far-fetched. She thinks about Sheree Miller's mother and the endless months without news, the truck that the caravanners saw pulling away from Sheree's car playing on her mind. What if the truck driver has some information that could help find Sheree? And what if the two cases are linked? They're not totally similar; Sheree was alone, her car was left by the side of the road, but both disappearances happened just out of town, on a quiet and isolated road. She knows it's tenuous but she's desperate to find something, anything, to get her closer to her sister.

She wishes now that she'd invited Walker to eat with her. She's not in the mood to sit alone and she knows the hotel menu by heart; there's nothing on it that appeals. It's heavy on meat dishes – steaks, schnitzel, burgers – or some kind of pasta with chicken, bacon, avocado and cream that looks like someone threw up on the plate. She thinks nostalgically of her local Vietnamese restaurant at home. The spicy papaya salad with peanuts and lime juice and big pieces of red chilli floating in the dressing. Her favourite breakfast spot, with its focaccia filled with omelette and melted cheese, and the local Turkish place, where the hummus is homemade and delicious but so garlicky that she only dares eat it when she has a few days off work.

The street below her is quiet. No one in sight, just a handful of cars parked, nose into the gutter, outside the hotel. She thinks again of Berlin, its vibrant streets, the little bars, the crowds that spill onto the pavement with their beer or Aperol spritz glowing bright orange, the drink of summer. She misses the parks filled with big Turkish families having picnics and barbecues and the guy who wheels his old piano onto the canal side on sunny weekend afternoons and gives impromptu concerts. She misses home.

She goes back into her room, changes into a cool dress and heads down to eat. The bar is fuller than usual, a buzz of noise emanating from the open door, and she chooses the first empty stool she sees, hoping to make herself inconspicuous. She's still not entirely used to sitting at the bar on her own, aware of the glances of curious strangers, most of them men, sliding over her.

Ali looks harassed. Her husband, Mike, is standing in the far corner, leaning against the bar with a beer in front of him, deep in conversation, for all the world as if he were a drinker, not the publican. Ali is serving beers and taking dinner orders. Barbara steels herself to sit and wait. Her phone is charging upstairs and with nothing for her hands to play with, nothing to drink or eat, she feels as self-conscious as a teenager.

'Orright?'

She finds she's sitting beside Hippy, who nods at her.

She smiles back, noting again his overstyled hair, thinking of his neat-as-a-pin house. He's an oddball and she's not sure she entirely trusts him. She's saved from small talk by Mike's arrival.

Both he and Ali are wearing Hawaiian-style shirts. Ali's is a relatively safe option, black with a large neon-yellow pineapple pattern, but Mike's is printed with a photorealistic tropical beach scene – white sand fringed with palm trees abutting vividly blue water and an equally blue sky.

'That is a very bright shirt,' she says.

'Enough to make ya eyeballs bleed,' says Hippy.

'We wear 'em every Saturday,' says Mike. 'Party night.'

The print stretches across his stomach, weirdly elongating and distorting the beach and sea view, and Barbara decides it's best to focus on the palm trees, which by dint of positioning higher on his chest remain true to life. She orders the daily meal special, a chilli con carne, and a lemon-lime and bitters, a mix of lemonade, lime cordial and a splash of Angostura bitters, the combination of sugar and citrus refreshing and reviving.

'Bloody ladies' drink,' says Hippy in disgust beside her.

'There'll be a meat and chook raffle at eight o'clock,' says Mike when he brings the drink back, nodding at Hippy, who has four strips of brightly coloured numbers lined up on the bar in front of his beer.

She buys a couple of tickets, just to be part of the crowd. 'You can have my meat if I win, Hippy.'

He chokes on his beer, giving a spluttering laugh. 'God, love, if you knew what you just said. It's lucky you're German or I might have taken that the wrong way.'

Barbara doesn't get the joke, but she smiles as she nurses her drink, with half an ear on the local gossip, the banter about Hippy's legendary losses on the horses, someone else's golfing prowess or lack thereof. She's thinking of Rita and Berndt here, over a week ago. Time is running on and they're getting nowhere. She knows Hippy doesn't like talking to her in public, but if someone knows something, perhaps they are here, now, drinking.

'It seems busier tonight,' she says. 'Is this normal for a Saturday?'

He looks round the bar. 'Well, it's a lot busier in the tourist season, plenty of people passing through, or when we have picnic races or a band at the racecourse – then the place is packed. But at this time of year, this is about it.'

'Was it like this last week? Was anyone else here that is not normally here?' she asks.

Hippy picks up his beer, takes a long gulp. He keeps his eyes ahead, looking across the bar, not making eye contact. 'Couldn't say,' he says. 'Wasn't paying that much attention.'

He takes another gulp of beer, puts the glass down and turns towards her, his gaze harder than she's seen it. 'Look, love, like I said the other day, I know she's your sister and you're worried and all that, but you can't keep coming in here asking questions, acting like someone here did something to them, accusing people who didn't have anything to do with it. They were here and then they left. End of. Nothing to do with anyone in this town.'

'I am not accusing anyone,' she says. 'I am just desperate.'

Hippy looks back over the bar, the conversation over. He's wearing his usual outfit of short navy shorts, flip-flops and a red Australia Post shirt.

'Are you a postman?' she says, to fill the silence, get him talking to her again.

'Nah, I'm not a postie, love, but the shirts are bloody good quality and I get 'em for a good price at the disposals store.'

'So what do you do?' she asks.

'I drive a truck. Got me own rig. Park it at Johnson's. Pick up a load for them or anyone else who needs it when I'm in the mood or need some dosh.'

'There are a lot of truck drivers out here,' she says.

He thinks about it. 'I guess so. Paul Johnson's got a couple of blokes working for him. Steve Burnett' – he nods vaguely at a group of men opposite – 'Darryl Foley. I reckon Angus Jones is back driving again too – they say he's doing it pretty tough at his place.'

Back upstairs, the meat and beans sitting heavy in her stomach, the noise of the bar still thrumming beneath the floorboards, Barbara writes the names in her notebook, realising she's never heard Hippy's real name.

26

'I don't know, cuz,' says Blair. 'I don't need aggro from the cops right now. Got the kids to think about. Tracy will go mental.'

'There won't be any aggro from the cops,' says Walker. 'I *am* the cops.'

Blair looks disbelieving. 'So why do you wanna go out there at night, not get seen, sneak around?'

'Cops do that shit too. We don't want him to know we're suspicious. Come on, mate, there's two youngsters missing – it could mean saving their lives.'

They're standing in Grandma's yard. The sun has set, the light from the kitchen window illuminating a small patch of the back patio. The smoke from Blair's cigarette swirls and disappears into the night air and a mozzie buzzes loud in Walker's ear. He reaches back, swats at his head. He doesn't want to get Blair involved, really, but he needs Blair to show him the best way across the paddocks at night and to stay with the car, and, in the worst-case scenario, to alert Grogan in case it goes pear-shaped and he doesn't come back.

Blair shakes his head. 'Man, this better not get me into trouble.'

'It won't, I promise,' says Walker. 'I'll pick you up around one a.m., we'll be back by three latest. Tracy doesn't need to know.'

'I can tell you ain't never been married,' says Blair, dropping his cigarette butt and grinding it under the heel of his boot.

• • •

When he pulls up at Blair's just before one, the lights are all out. Walker curses silently. He's debating whether to knock on the door, risk Tracy's wrath, when the passenger door of the ute opens. Walker turns with a start as Blair climbs in.

'Christ, mate, what are you doing hanging around here in the dark?'

'I didn't want you knocking on the door, wakin' everyone up. The missus's got the shits with me already.'

'Happy birthday, by the way,' says Walker. It's gone midnight; Blair turns thirty-four today.

Blair snorts. 'Yeah, right,' he says. 'This ain't the way I usually choose to celebrate.'

They drive the rest of the way in silence. Walker knows Blair is doing him a huge favour. He's downplayed the danger, and he's not planning to let Blair get near the house or take any risks, but Blair has every right to be angry with him for being asked to help out. He parks the car a kilometre or so before the turn-off to the house. Blair directs him to a spot beside a stand of trees, where the car can be less conspicuous, a little off the road. It takes a moment for their eyes to adjust to the night light. The moon has moved beyond a crescent, almost at half, and the blanket of stars, so copious out here compared to the night sky of the city, gives them just barely enough light to see.

Blair walks with him to the fence. 'If we cross here at a diagonal, we should come up behind the farm. You want the back of the place, yeah?'

'Yeah, perfect,' says Walker. 'You stay here. If I'm not back in an hour, go home, call the number I gave you.'

'Right,' says Blair. 'As if.' He pushes down the top wire of the fence and steps across it in a fluid motion.

'Blair!' Walker hisses a whisper at him. 'I mean it. You don't need this shit, like you said.' Blair moves quietly onwards and after a second Walker follows. When he catches him, he grabs Blair by the shoulder. 'I'm serious. I need you to wait here. They might be armed, it's too dangerous.'

'You shoulda thought about that before you got me into this. You go on your own, you'll wake the whole place up, stumbling around in the dark.'

'For fuck's sake . . .'

But Blair is moving again, Walker behind him, cursing under his breath. Sure-footed and silent, Blair knows the land here intimately. Walker stumbles at first and struggles to keep up but after a few minutes he's found his night vision, his rhythm. When they reach the second fence, the one that marks out Markovich's home paddock, they can see a light behind the house, a bright circle in the dark night lighting up the gravel drive in front of the sheds. Walker looks at his phone – almost 2 a.m.

They follow the fence until they are approaching the house from behind and against the night breeze. The backs of the sheds are clearly visible now. Everything is in darkness, just the light in the yard. There's no movement. A dog barks in the distance. Once. Twice. Then settles. They crouch and wait to see if there is any movement, anyone keeping an eye on the place. But the farm is silent. Walker is disappointed. It makes it easier, but it also implies that they'll find nothing here. If they had a couple of kids locked up or anything similar, the place would be guarded.

'I'll look in the sheds,' he says. 'Can you see if there's another place further out back? There should be a shack. Most likely it's empty but have a look round if you can. We'll meet back here in fifteen minutes.'

Blair nods and disappears into the night. Walker climbs over the fence, keeping low to the ground and away from the pool of light. He approaches the largest shed first, easing around from the dark side into the circle of light, feeling horribly exposed, keeping as close to the wall as he can. When he gets to the door, it is bolted but not locked. He slides the bolt, slowly, quietly, pushes the door open and slips inside. The darkness is complete. In the distance, he hears the dog bark a couple of times in succession, then stop again. Walker remembers the pit bull straining on the lead at Markovich's side. He wouldn't like to meet it out here with only his bare hands to defend himself with. He stands silently, listening, his heart beating loud in his ears. There's no more barking, no other noise. He pulls his small torch from his pocket and switches it on, directs the beam of light around the space.

It's no farm shed. Pristine-clean, a series of metal tables run in two lines in the middle of the space, the sides and back wall covered in warehouse-style shelving. Cartons line the higher shelves, box after box of cold and flu tablets, the packaging familiar but marked in a different language – Thai perhaps. On the lower shelves are plastic bottles, unmarked, filled with liquid. There's a smell too, acrid, chemical, pungent. He flicks the torch back towards the tables; the burners and chemical flasks confirm it. Rutherford is right: the Vandals have a major meth-making operation out here.

He switches off the torch, slips out the door and slides the bolt shut, marvelling at the lack of security. They're obviously assuming they're too far from anywhere to need guards.

But this is a whole other level of operation than he'd expected and he's suddenly certain that if Rita and Berndt are involved in this, they're dead. If they messed up at this level, or accidentally came across something at this level, they're both dead. Their car might still be here, though.

The next shed, the smallest, is a garage. He flicks the torch around as quickly as possible. The lax security suggests that this outfit isn't expecting any trouble but he doesn't want to wake them and test their response times. The thin beam highlights a van and two motorbikes; no sign of Berndt Meyer's vehicle.

The third shed is different from the others. It's a Portakabin, with windows and an air-conditioning unit, which is thrumming and gurgling, loud in the silent night. The door is closed. Walker circles the cabin, listening closely. There's no noise. He climbs the three stairs to the door, feels the handle move as he pulls slowly down on it. Not locked. The door opens towards him. He stands behind it, using it for cover, and lets it swing open naturally, as if caught by the wind. Every cell in his body is listening for movement but he hears only sonorous breathing. As slowly as a cat stalking a mouse, he walks back down the stairs, still using the door as cover, so that he's not a visible target if someone is aiming for the open door. At the bottom he steps quickly across the stairs, passing in front of the open door and onto the ground, then edges close up to the side of the cabin. The hairs on his neck are standing up and he has to fight all his instincts as he puts himself in the firing line and looks inside. Directly in front of him is a small living area, a sofa and an armchair, and beyond are two sets of bunk beds. All the beds seem to be full but it's too dark to make out the occupants. He steps back out of sight to consider his next move. As he does, he stumbles against a cinder block on the ground and falls, backwards, into the side of the cabin, which emits a loud metallic clang.

The crash of his fall reverberates around the yard. The dog starts barking, he hears a voice calling from inside the cabin and then he's up and running, around the back and behind the sheds, staying as close to them as he can for cover.

Voices shout behind him as he sprints across the home paddock. He can see the fence ahead of him and Blair jumping over, off to his left. A sudden shot of illumination behind him turns night into day. They've turned on another spotlight. He finds a burst of speed – the country beyond the fence, still in darkness, offers safety.

He takes the fence as fast as he can, hurdling it in one smooth leap. The barbed wire catches his trousers, tearing a gash in the material, but he's over. Blair is already moving across the paddock in the direction of the road and the car. Bent over, keeping low to the ground, Walker follows, trusting Blair to find a path, both of them running fast now. The lights behind them, flooding the night, help their escape. No one in the brightly lit yard will see a thing in the night beyond. He can hear voices shouting, confusion. The other sheds are all closed, he's left them as he found them. But the Portakabin door was open. Shit. That dashes his hope that they'll write it off as a possum or kangaroo crashing through the yard in the night. The barking dog sounds closer – perhaps they've let it loose.

They scramble over the fence at the edge of the road. They're both breathing hard as they reach the car, Walker searching in his pocket for the keys, fumbling to unlock the doors. He starts the engine, drives off, the ute sliding on the dirt road as he takes the corners at speed, lights off, keeping an eye on the rear-view mirror for anyone following them.

'You find anything?' he asks Blair.

'There's a place out back, small shack, no one there. Bedroom at the back was empty and I could only see a sofa and a bit of a mess, beer cans and whatnot, in the main room.'

So Monroe has been here recently, thinks Walker.

'They're in a vehicle,' says Blair, looking out the passenger window across the paddocks behind them. 'I can see the headlights.'

Walker accelerates hard. They have at best a couple of kilometres' advantage on their pursuers. When they reach the highway, he turns towards town, picking up speed, lights still off. The road is straight for miles but there's a slight incline ahead. If he can get over the top of it, they might not be visible from the turn-off.

His mind is racing. This is a huge discovery: it confirms

Rutherford's inside intel, and the operation is bigger than he'd believed would be possible in a small town like Caloodie. His eyes flick back to the rear-view mirror but the car that's tailing them isn't in sight.

Sunday

Eight days missing

27

Barbara is sitting in the pub dining room, flicking through her notebook. The bakery isn't open on Sunday, so she's eating breakfast in the pub, a disheartening affair with miniature boxes of cereal, lukewarm milk and instant coffee. She's feeling frustrated. They have nothing to go on. There's no sign of Rita and Berndt, no sign of their car, no clue as to where or with whom they might be. All she's got to follow up is the truck driver from Sheree's disappearance.

Staring vaguely round the room, she notices the four tacks still in the spot where Walker had taken the missing persons poster off the wall. She tries to visualise the poster. Maybe there's a clue there that will give her some kind of lead – anything. She's aware she's clutching at straws but there's nothing else.

She scrolls through the photos on her phone and, sure enough, she'd taken a shot of the poster the first day she arrived. She reads through each description. The one that upsets her the most is a young redhead with full lips and big blue eyes, her hair blow-dried in a sixties style. Lilian Stone. She disappeared in November 1973, almost fifty years ago. Never found. Born in 1955, she'd be an old woman now. The thought that she might spend the next fifty years searching for Rita is too much to bear.

She reads through the more recent listings. There are no couples missing but there are two young women who've disappeared in the last five years. One in 2018, from Gympie, which she finds is a town close to the coast, some 900 kilometres to the south-east; the second in 2019, from Barcaldine, 500 kilometres north. She looks up the numbers of the local police stations for both and picks up her phone.

The Gympie number is answered by a bored-sounding PC.

'It's DS Barbara Guerra here, calling from Caloodie,' she says, bending the truth. 'I'm looking into one of your missing persons cases that has some similarities with a case we're working on out here.' She gives him the details. 'I just want to know the status of the case, if you have any updates?'

She hears his fingers clicking on a keyboard, his breath in her ear. 'Still missing, presumed dead,' he says eventually. 'If you want more details, you'll have to send an email to CID and they'll get back to you.' He gives her the email address and rings off. She'll have to ask Walker to send them a message.

She has more joy in Barcaldine. The senior constable who answers the phone is in a helpful mood.

'I do remember Tanya,' he says. 'Hang on a minute and I'll get the file.'

She waits for a few minutes, listening to tinny repetitive hold music that pushes her patience more than silence would have. Eventually he comes back on the line, his strong Australian accent, a calming drawl, a welcome relief from the music.

'Righto,' he says. 'Tanya Bowen, twenty-nine, pretty chaotic life, meth user and sometime prostitute. She'd occasionally hitch a lift to her mum's place in Rockie, so when she wasn't around for a few days her sister thought she'd gone there. It was a week or so before she spoke with her mum and realised Tanya hadn't showed up. Tanya's phone was off and she never turned up to collect the dole. It was winter, tourist season, and we put out an alert, but no one came back to say they'd seen her hitching. Her sister said she sometimes went to the truck park on the edge of town, to turn a trick or hitch a lift, but no truckers came forward to say they'd seen her either. The last time people remembered seeing her was in the pub on the Saturday night, a week earlier. It was after a race day and there were a lot of people in town so the pub was chockers. No one remembered anything unusual. She just disappeared.'

The hairs on the back of Barbara's neck are standing to attention. Another woman hitching. Another link to truck drivers. They could be looking at a serial killer.

• • •

Walker is swimming off another dream. He'd had a vision of being in the bush at night, stars flowing like a river of light above him. It was calm, peaceful, and he was not walking but somehow floating high in the sky when he saw Rita Guerra, as small as an ant, lying in the shade of a tall gum below him. As he moved closer, he saw that she was swaddled in a pale-blue sheet, binding her arms to her sides and covering her body to above her breasts, only her shoulders bare and exposed. Her eyes were closed, her long hair fanning out in a triangle behind her head, dark and glossy. The scene was peaceful until he was directly above her, looking down at her, when her eyes flicked wide open – dark brown, filled with confusion and pain, flashing in the dark night. She'd opened her mouth and screamed, 'Help me!' long and piercing, directly into his face and at the night sky beyond.

He'd woken with a start, and lain under the slow-moving fan, calming his breathing. Light was filtering in past the curtains. Just gone 7 a.m. He'd only had a few hours' sleep after last night's scouting of the Markovich place, but he was wired and knew he wouldn't sleep again, so he got up and drove over to the pool.

Now he swims, the water as soft as velvet around him, until

he can feel an ache in his arms and his chest is tight from lack of breath. He pulls himself out of the pool and stands, holding his towel to his chest, water running off his legs and pooling at his feet. The hard swim and bright morning sunshine have done little to dispel the dark mood he brought with him. He didn't find anything linking Markovich to the missing couple. Rita and Berndt are no nearer to being found and he can only hope his night-time excursion hasn't impacted Rutherford's bigger operation. Though he knows he couldn't have lived with himself if he hadn't checked to make sure the missing kids weren't out there, it was a huge risk to take and one that hasn't paid off.

When he gets home, Ginger jumps up and rests her front paws on the gate, tongue lolling in a wide grin. She gives a series of small barks of pleasure on seeing him, and as he walks up the stairs she pushes between his legs, eager always to be the first on the veranda.

He hears the screen door creak and Grandma's voice: 'Is that you, Lucas?'

Ginger bounds over, delighted to see her up and about, and nuzzles her hand. Grandma rests a hand on the dog's head and he notices she's leaning heavily on the door, her frail frame hidden in a dress with a floral pattern that seems several sizes too big. She'd been a big woman when he was young. Strong arms, big chest; he remembers being hugged by her, enveloped in a wave of warmth and softness. Now her skin hangs loose, her veins and bones visible underneath, though on good days her eyes are as bright and perceptive as they've always been.

'Grandma, should you be out of bed?' He's at her side, holding her arm, bending down to give her a kiss, her cheek still soft, but her scent, baby powder and Pears soap, is now tinged with base notes of illness. He can smell the drugs she takes for pain seeping through her skin, sulphurous.

'Stop fussing,' she says. 'I'm fine. I'm waiting to go to church.'

For Grandma, Sunday morning is synonymous with church. He wouldn't usually go, hasn't a shred of belief in him in the Christian sense, but he is starting to fear that he doesn't have long left with her. She's fading away – he'd never understood the expression until now. Her skin is translucent, her face pale, her lips almost bloodless.

'I'll take you, Grandma,' he says, and the smile on her face more than makes up for the prospect of an hour sitting on a hard pew.

After brekky, he helps her into the car and drives slowly to church. The route takes him past the small school that's barely changed since he was a boy. Two wooden buildings on the high stilts that are typical of the older constructions round here, built this way to let air circulate and help keep them cool. In the dusty playground, the big jacaranda trees with benches beneath them are still the same. Only the school sign is new, brightly painted and with an updated motto – *Think, Connect, Innovate, Celebrate* – which sounds like something dreamt up by a consultant a thousand miles away. He turns right at the servo with its bright-red awning and yellow-painted facade before pulling up outside the church.

Attendance has been dropping for years. Grandma's generation are still engaged, indoctrinated perhaps, but his aunts and uncles and their kids don't have any time for it. Last year the vicar had organised a working bee to paint the church and Grandma had guilted Blair and a few of the others into helping out. The vicar had chosen a pale purple for the building and painted the windows and doors and the small peaked belltower in cream. Tommy Simpson, a local artist, had donated two stained-glass windows in a simple abstract pattern. Walker thinks it looks pretty good from the outside, but he's not sure it's translated into any great increase in the number of people turning up on Sundays.

For his part he prefers the two huge mango trees that frame it. They must be fifty years old, perhaps more, taller than the church, with deep-green foliage and a huge crop of mangoes that are sweeter and more succulent than any he's eaten elsewhere. The mangoes aren't ripe yet – another few weeks, they'll be perfect in time for Christmas – but the tree is filled with a flock of parrots, and as he helps Grandma out of the car and bangs the door shut with his foot the birds take flight, chattering and calling, their green and red and blue foliage flashing bright. Grandma leans on his arm, catching her breath, watching them wheel away and settle in another tree a short distance down the road behind them.

He lets the sermon, the prayers, the hymns, wash over him, holding onto this time with Grandma, wanting to stretch and elongate the moment and the feeling of love he gets simply from sitting beside her. When they get back home, he sees Barbara waiting outside. She's leaning over the gate, patting Ginger. He feels a prick of pleasure, a smile on his lips.

He pulls up and gets out.

'Morning,' he says, his smile growing. 'I see you've met Ginger.'

She smiles back, but it doesn't quite reach her eyes. She looks worn out.

He helps Grandma from the car. 'This is Barbara,' he says. 'She's over from Berlin, helping out on a case.'

As Barbara smiles and says, 'Hello. Pleased to meet you', he sees Grandma take her in. She seems to like what she sees; she reaches out a hand to touch Barbara's arm in welcome.

'You should have told me you were inviting a guest,' she chides, as Walker helps her back inside, his arm around her waist. She's as frail and weightless as an autumn leaf. She sits at the kitchen table while he makes them all tea and hunts in the cupboard for a pack of biscuits. He finds some chocolate-coated Tim Tams and puts a handful on a plate on the table, grabbing one to fortify himself while he fills the teapot and digs out cups and saucers.

He eats another couple of biscuits as he drinks his tea, watching

Barbara chat to Grandma, noticing the seam of nervous energy underneath her smile.

Afterwards, he helps Grandma back to her room and she lies on top of the bed. Her breathing is laboured and he can see the excursion has exhausted her. He makes her comfortable, covers her with a light bedspread, and she's asleep by the time he leaves the room. Barbara is still at the table where he left her, chasing crumbs around her plate with her finger.

'Is she OK?' she asks. 'I'm sorry to intrude on your Sunday. I can leave if you need to look after her.'

'She's sleeping,' he says. 'It's no intrusion.'

She pulls her notebook from her bag. 'I think I have found another case. Another girl who disappeared hitching,' she says, and outlines the details. 'So now we have two missing girls with a similar MO: Sheree and Tanya Bowen. Barcaldine is not that far away. Tanya Bowen had a history of hitching from the truck stop. Perhaps this could be a serial murderer. Maybe a truck driver looking for girls.'

Walker is conscious that he's disappointed she's here to talk about work, though he has to concede that Barcaldine is pretty local, as distances out here go.

'It might be worth looking into, but I reckon it's a bit of a stretch,' he says. 'I'm not sure we can connect these cases. Rita and Berndt especially. They had a vehicle – where would that be?'

'I think it is worth looking into,' she says. 'Rita and Berndt – it's true there are two of them with a car, but they've also disappeared on a deserted road. If we extend our search, find some other cases that are similar, other girls hitch-hiking or people who went missing on isolated roads, maybe we can see a pattern.'

Walker invites her into the back room, where he stands in front of the map. He runs his finger along the main highway that traverses north–south across the state. 'Where do you want to start? If you want to look at trucking routes, you'd have to go from Winton and Longreach to Toowoomba, even Stanthorpe. And on this route' – he runs his finger east to west – 'Townsville, Mount Isa, maybe even Tennant Creek in the Territory. There's the mining loop around Emerald too, and some of the big coastal stops.' His finger jabs at the towns of Rockhampton, Townsville and Cairns.

Barbara looks at the distances he's marked out. Queensland is a huge state, almost five times the size of Germany. She pushes the thought away. 'You do not think this is strange? Three girls missing, in this area, in a few years.'

'Rita wasn't on her own,' he points out. 'She was with Berndt, so that doesn't fit.'

'Why are you being so negative? I think this is a good lead.'

'The fact that Rita and Berndt's car is missing means that this isn't some opportunistic pick-up from the side of the road. What would a truck driver do with their car?'

She nods. 'I thought about that too. What if he got them to go with him for some reason? They were looking for an adventure, they wanted to meet new people. Maybe he told them to follow him somewhere.'

'I don't know. I reckon we need to focus on Monroe and the people he's linked to. Angus Jones owns the house where Tina Monroe lives. He was on the road the day Rita and Berndt went missing. Constable Grogan interviewed him but . . .' Walker leaves the sentence unfinished. He doesn't entirely trust Grogan but he doesn't want to denigrate the bloke in front of Barbara – it feels unprofessional.

'I know that Rita was not using drugs,' she says. 'Not at home, anyway. And I spoke with Berndt's father last night and he said that Berndt is really anti-drugs. One of his friends took a bad pill at a festival and died when he was sixteen, and Berndt never took anything after that. He does not sound like the kind of person who would suddenly start dealing.'

'People can change, if they need money or find themselves in with a different crowd.' Walker is aware he sounds defensive. There really is nothing to indicate that Rita and Berndt were dealing for the Vandals. But he can't imagine why or how the pair would disappear otherwise. He's worked for so many years around these gangs and he knows that all types can get drawn in. 'A truck driver, a serial killer. It sounds less likely than a drugs connection to me,' he says.

'Please,' says Barbara. 'I really do not want to forget this trucking connection without checking first. Could you call some of the bigger towns, just to see if there's any other cases similar to this? I cannot really call them, like you said, I'm not officially on the case. I could follow up the trucking companies, see if I can get some names of drivers in the areas of these three disappearances. Maybe I can find a driver who was there around the time of the disappearances, maybe that will lead to something.'

She's standing there, dark circles under her eyes, her face pale, and he notices that she's biting her nails. He feels a rush of sympathy for her. He can't imagine how it must feel to think that a serial killer might have lured your sister and her boyfriend to their deaths. Perhaps she's just trying to rule this theory out, to still a worry inside herself that Rita and Berndt might not make it out of this alive.

'OK,' he says. 'I'll put in a few calls to some of the big regional police stations, see if there are any other cases with profiles like these.'

28

After Barbara leaves, Walker takes the picture of Rita down from his board and looks at it more closely. He sees the resemblance to Barbara, the same eyes, the face shape. He realises that he now thinks they won't find the pair alive. Failing to find any trace of them last night means he's operating on the assumption that some kind of link to the Vandals has gotten them killed.

Their list of suspects is thin. Barbara has added Hippy, Paul Johnson and his two regular truck drivers, Steve Burnett and Darryl Foley. Angus Jones is up there, too, alongside Matt Monroe and Stefan Markovich. The fact that Jones is renting a property to Markovich needs more investigating. Walker starts by searching the police database. Nothing. Jones doesn't even have a speeding fine. And, as expected, he also has literally zero online presence, not even a Facebook account. On a hunch, Walker runs a national property search under Jones's name. All the talk in town is that Jones is flat broke, doing it tough, but if he's renting out one property perhaps he has others too. And sure enough, the register reveals that Jones owns half a dozen properties in Caloodie, Hopeville and two in Surfers Paradise.

Bingo, thinks Walker. It's definitely time to pay the man a visit, as he'd intended to on Thursday. Grogan has more or less ruled Jones out for last Saturday, but given Walker's doubts about Grogan's personal links to Tina Monroe and his general inability to see past his local friendships, he's less and less inclined to take the constable's reading on any situation.

In his mind Walker can hear Barbara insisting that Rita and Berndt don't have any links to drug dealing. He remembers his first chief drumming it into him to keep an open mind. 'Assumptions make an ass of you and me,' the chief used to say, butchering the proverb till it barely made sense, which is maybe why Walker has always remembered it. Thinking on it, Walker admits Barbara might have a point – he's in danger of being blinded by the Vandals link. What if he is barking up the wrong tree? He looks again at the map. This vast, empty, desolate country means that for a killer who's abducting women – someone devious enough to choose victims whose disappearance doesn't create a massive outcry, and with a bit of knowledge of the bush – hiding their bodies wouldn't be difficult. Without a lead it'll be virtually impossible to find a body in this vast expanse, except by pure chance.

He starts dialling, calling CID teams in Toowoomba, Townsville, Bundaberg, Longreach, Roma. But it's not until he calls Mount Isa in the far north that he finds anything interesting.

'We might have a similar case,' says the DS he speaks with. 'Sylvia Stevens. Local woman, nurse at the hospital. Not missing but murdered, five years ago now. Her body was found about sixty K out of town, in the bush, not far off the highway. She was last seen in a pub called the Overlander. It's not a truck stop but quite a few truckies use it – it's on the edge of town and easy enough to park a rig there. She was a regular and staff remember seeing her the weekend before she disappeared. She spent the night chatting with a bloke: white, thin, tall, anywhere from mid-thirties to mid-forties, dark hair.'

Too old for Monroe, too young to be Angus Jones, thinks Walker.

'We've got a bloke we're looking at down here,' he says. 'Much younger, early twenties, big build, lots of tattoos. Anyone like that come up in the description?'

'Nah. The only thing they all agreed on was that he was white, thin and a bit older.'

'Right,' says Walker. 'Any links to drug use? Meth especially?'

'Nope. She liked a drink but nothing else, as far as I remember.'

Stevens is not as young as the others – she was thirty-six when she was killed. That and her regular lifestyle, the lack of drug use, make her case a bit different, but something in Walker's gut gives a twinge. Given her links to the truck stop and the place where her body was found, off the highway, on the way out of town, there could be a connection here.

'Can you send me the details?' he asks.

When the files appear in his inbox, there's an e-fit of the suspect too. It could resemble any number of men but it's definitely not Matt Monroe or Stefan Markovich: one too young, the other too well built. It doesn't really look like Angus Jones either, thinks Walker. But e-fits are not the most reliable of identifiers, and it was five years ago; it could, perhaps at a push, be the older man. He pins Sylvia Stevens and the e-fit above Mount Isa on the map.

This could be a link to the Sheree Miller case, but he's not entirely convinced it fits with Rita and Berndt: there's two of them and the car. To help himself think, he makes a ham sandwich with sharp English mustard that makes his eyes water, then calls a few more regional stations. No one else has anything for him that matches. 'I'll ask them to check at Emerald and Blackwater,' says the Rockhampton sergeant. 'I'll give you a call back tomorrow.'

He calls Barbara to see how she's getting on, but her phone goes to voicemail. On impulse, he decides to drive to the hotel and find her. He wants to head out for a quick swim at the billabong; maybe she'll come along. They're having a family barbecue later for Blair's birthday and Michelle and Tracy are already here preparing things, so Grandma is being looked after, and he hasn't been out to the billabong yet this visit. A bit of distance, a swim, spending time in the bush, might just help him find clarity on the case too.

. . .

Barbara puts her phone down, rubs her right earlobe, trying to bring some feeling back into it. She's been on the phone all morning, calling trucking companies across the state, and the phone is hot in her hand.

The big national distributors have been helpful; their records are extensive and they can easily let her know who was in the Hopeville, Gympie and Barcaldine areas on those dates. They've agreed to run reports and send the information within a day. The smaller ones mostly aren't open on a Sunday, though some of them divert to mobile numbers, owners taking calls at home. The few she speaks with are pleasant enough but they don't keep the kind of records that will help.

'I don't reckon I can help you,' says one woman. 'We don't keep track by route, we track the pick-up and the destination and the cargo. So I could tell you if we'd had a pick-up or drop-off in Gympie or Barcaldine but not if the drivers passed through there on their way somewhere.'

She calls in what she can but soon realises it won't be anywhere near definitive – poor record-keeping aside, a large majority of drivers are self-employed – those like Hippy, who pick up loads on an ad hoc basis. There's no way of putting together a comprehensive list.

After a few hours of frustrating work, with nothing of use presenting itself, Barbara feels the need to get out and do something. She's standing on the veranda, stretching in the sun, looking at the empty street below her, when she sees Walker's ute pull up in front of the hotel.

She leans over the balcony and waves at him as he gets out of the car, Ginger, tail swishing, beside him. He waves back and disappears from sight under the awning. She walks into the room, checks her appearance in the mirror. Tries to smooth down her sticking-up hair, decides against applying lipstick; it's just too hot somehow.

The two of them come to her room. She sits on the bed, Walker perching on the side of the desk and Ginger lying down on the floor beside him, her tail brushing the floor. They fill the small room with energy.

'Found another case that's a bit similar, up north in Mount Isa,' he says, giving her the details. 'I'm waiting on callbacks from a couple of other stations but maybe there is something bigger going on here.'

She feels a pulse of excitement tempered with fear. They could be on the trail of something important, and finding an answer for Sheree's mother would be satisfying, but if she thinks too much about what it might mean for Rita and Berndt she'll go crazy. Still, it's something at least, after all these days of nothing. 'I'm waiting for the trucking companies to send me information but it won't be till tomorrow and it won't be comprehensive,' she says, frustrated.

'Yeah, well, I'm going for a swim now – there's a waterhole just out of town, it's a lovely spot. Why don't you come along?'

'I'm not sure,' she says. 'I . . .'

'Come on. You need a break – you won't get any of the reports back this arvo. Get your togs and we'll go for a swim. I'll have you back in town by sundown.'

She looks at him. 'OK,' she says, 'let me put my swimsuit on.'

'Bring your sunnies and a hat, I've got the towels.'

Walker is standing by the ute, whistling tunelessly, when she comes outside a few minutes later.

'Like your thongs,' he says.

'Sorry?' She's confused.

'Those.' He nods at her feet. 'Hard to miss in that neon pink.'

'Flip-flops. What did you call them?'

'Thongs. Or Queensland safety boots,' he laughs. 'Not bloody "flip-flops".'

She shakes her head. 'A thong, I thought – well, is it a woman's underpants?'

'Not here, it's not. Well, maybe it is as well. But here, when we say "thongs", we mean those. What kind of colour is that, anyway?'

'It is the only colour they had in the store,' she says. 'It seems they like things to be bright out here.' She pulls the strap of her dress to one side, exposing the bright-red strap of her swimmers. 'The swimsuit is colourful too.'

He drives them out of town, not the highway but one of the smaller roads that leads to a handful of local cattle stations. The size of each station, some as big as a small German state, means the road runs for well over a hundred kilometres, with small turn-offs signposted by metal barrels with names hand-painted on them – *Milton Downs, Hawksmoore* – demarcating the change of ownership.

There's no traffic but at one point Walker slows for a drover and a herd of cattle. The cattle, deep brown and rangy, are ambling slowly along the side of the road. A woman on a horse, wearing the same moleskin trousers and battered cowboy hat as the men but with a long-sleeved pink shirt, is riding alongside, about halfway along the half-mile-long column of beasts. She sits low and loose in the saddle, carrying but not using a long leather whip, and nods, a low barely-there nod, at the car as they pass.

'I did not know you had cowboys in Australia – or cowgirls, rather,' says Barbara.

'She's droving cattle, moving them from one paddock to another,' he tells her. 'Used to always be done by horseback but you don't see it so much these days. For the big musters they use motorbikes or helicopters now. She's only moving a few head and probably not far.'

Thirty minutes out of town, he slows and leaves the road, turning right down an unmarked dirt track. The earth here is red and as the ute bumps and rattles, it trails a cloud of rust-coloured dust behind them. A whirlwind blows up ahead on the side of the track, twirling and stirring up the red earth like a spirit dancing. He sees her watching it.

'That's a willy-willy,' he says. 'Well, that's what we call it. I think the weatherman says "dust devil". Sometimes they can reach a hundred metres high or more.'

'It's like another planet out here,' she says. 'How do you know where you're going? It all looks the same to me.'

'I've been coming here since I was a kid. You get to know the bush. There are plenty of markers when you know what to look for.' He shows her a thicket of trees ahead and the line of trees running west from them. 'That's the creek and the waterhole,' he says. 'Not what you were expecting?'

'Not really. I was expecting to see more green. I have never been anywhere like this. So red. So empty.'

Walker looks at the land and sees the gum trees and their silvery leaves; the grass, spiky and white but hiding a world of life, from ants and lizards to spiders and birds. There are kangaroos standing in the coolness of the shade under the trees, still and silent, blending invisibly into the grass until you get close enough to disturb them into movement. Goannas lying on rocks, birds resting in trees; he can find all these things for her. But first he has to help her see the beauty here in this wide-open space, the horizon stretching for miles, the red earth, the sky intensely blue, a vast inverted bowl above them.

He parks the car in the shade of one of the gum trees and leads her down the sandy bank. In this particular curve of the creek, the water always catches. No matter how dry the rest of the country, no matter how dry the creek is up- or downstream, there's always been a swimmable pool here. It's low today; the years without rain have drained it to less than half of its fullest depth. He can see the cracked earth running down from the high-water mark some two metres above the current waterline. If this drought continues there's a chance even this waterhole might dry up. In the stories of this land's First Peoples, this water has always been here. For the last fifty thousand years, people, birds and animals have found succour here. Since being back, Walker has noted how dry the land is, that there are fewer insects, not as many birds. But it's this waterhole that really brings it home to him, a clear warning note as to how much the climate has altered the bush he loves.

29

The waterhole is a muddy brown. For some reason Barbara had expected a lake like those that surround Berlin: blue water, small beaches fringed by grass – something cooling. Instead, dry cracked mud leads down to a caramel-coloured pool of water about twenty metres across at its widest point.

The sense of being in a foreign land, an utterly different country and culture, gives her a moment of anxiety. She knows Walker's made an effort to bring her out here, to distract her a little bit from the endless fear of where Rita is, what she might be going through. She's grateful and resentful at the same time. She should have stayed in town; she could be doing something, anything, more useful than this.

Walker lays out a blanket and a couple of towels and turns away to strip off his t-shirt. He's surprisingly coy about his body. This is the first time she's seen him with bare legs and even now his board shorts are long, almost to the knee.

She admires his back, broad and toned and brown; his muscles ripple as he lifts his arms and pulls the t-shirt over his head. She has an urge to reach out and stroke his skin with her fingers. He drops the t-shirt on the towel and turns to her. Her eyes are drawn to his chest and shoulders but she forces them up to meet his, feeling her face flush slightly.

He's smiling. 'Ready for a swim?'

He doesn't wait for an answer but turns and runs down the bank, taking two or three long steps then diving and disappearing under the brown water. Ginger follows him down the slope and into the water, barking with pleasure. Barbara sits on the rug and takes off her dress, feeling a little awkward and exposed in the red swimmers, and watches Walker strike out across the water with long, strong strokes. Almost at the other side, he turns and floats on his back. Ginger stays closer to the edge, standing, the water up to her chest.

'Come on in!' calls Walker, his voice travelling across the water. 'The water's beaut.'

She walks down the bank, leaving her flip-flops on for as long as possible. As she enters the water the ground feels a little slimy underfoot and the thought of what else might be in there with her brings her up short. She doesn't like to swim when she can't see the bottom.

He swims over to her and stands, holding out his hand. 'Come on, it's fine. I'll swim with you.'

The water is running across his chest and flat stomach, small streams shimmering on his skin. She puts her hand in his, feels his strength, his fingers cool in hers, and lets him guide her in. Once her feet are off the bottom and she's floating, suspended and free, she feels better. He pulls her along beside him, lets her hand go when they're almost in the centre of the pool, and flips onto his back. She does too, spreading her arms wide, floating. They lie there, not speaking, the sky deep blue above them, the dappled shade from the leaves of the tall eucalyptus trees on the bank flickering across her face. At first the stillness seems absolute, but slowly she hears the bush sounds: the caw of a parrot, the hum of cicadas, an unidentifiable birdsong. The calmness of it, the cool of the water . . . Something in her unwinds; a coil unknots.

She's the first to emerge from the water, maybe fifteen minutes later, her fingers wrinkled and prune-like, her body pale against the red bathers, her feet coloured rust from the mud. She picks up one of the towels and sits on it, in the light shade of the trees that ring the teardrop-shaped waterhole, watching Walker float and dive and swim. She lets herself dry naturally, enjoying the slight coolness of her damp skin in the heat of the day. Ginger jumps in and out after the sticks and pebbles that she throws for her, and scratches and digs in the mud. The dog stays active and alert until Walker emerges from the water, then drops with pleasurable exhaustion beside him, half on his towel, half off, emitting a damp doggy scent, tongue out, breath heavy.

He's put together a light picnic: water, crunchy apples, hunks of cheese between salty crackers, a couple of the Cherry Ripe bars he seems to live on, and they sit on the rug snacking, not really talking, the torpid heat keeping them still and silent. Barbara lies back, relaxed. Occasionally he points out birds in the tree above, naming them. The hum of cicadas grows louder.

She watches a neat line of ants marching up the grey bark of the eucalyptus above her, drowsy and at peace. She can feel the nearness of his body, hear his calm breathing, and she fantasises about rolling over towards him, pressing herself against him, feeling his arms around her. Flustered, she sits up.

'You OK?' he asks.

'Yes, fine. I'm hot. Maybe I'll take another swim.'

He raises himself up to his elbows and looks over the water, then touches her leg gently. She flinches a little at his touch.

'Sorry,' he says. 'I wanted to show you . . .' He points across the water and she sees a lizard as long and thick as a man's leg, still and grey and prehistoric, sunning itself on the opposite bank. He laughs at her horrified expression.

'It's a goanna. He's more scared of you than you are of him. He won't come near us,' he says, but she surreptitiously pulls her legs onto the towel.

'I think I'll forget the swim,' she says, but in the end the heat, and Walker's encouragement, lure her back. And at the end of the afternoon she finds herself cooler, calmer and more relaxed than she's been since she arrived. The constant fear, the worry about Rita, is still there, but it's a low murmur, not a full-throated shout.

On the way back to the car he leads her on a short detour towards a clump of high grass at the far end of the pool. She's wearing her hat but she can feel the sun hot on the back of her neck and shoulders and the grass sharp and prickly against her bare legs, her feet dusty red. He stops so suddenly that she almost walks into him, has to put her hand on his back to stop herself. He half turns and pulls her gently forward, putting a finger to his lips. Seemingly out of nowhere, three kangaroos emerge from the grass to her left and hop, languidly yet with surprising speed, out onto the plain ahead of them. They're bigger than she'd expected, almost to her shoulder in height, their pelt a sandy reddish-brown. Their movement, so incongruous yet elegant somehow, startles her into a laugh. This most Australian of icons, here in the wild, right in front of her. It makes the whole afternoon feel simultaneously more and less real. That she is here, now, watching this, seems like a dream. Walker holds Ginger beside him with a command, but her tail has stopped its constant swish and her ears and eyes stay focused on the kangaroos long after Barbara has lost sight of them among the grass.

Back in the car, Walker turns to her with a smile. 'We're having a barbie this arvo for Blair's birthday and I'm under orders to bring you back with me.'

She's not sure she's up for it but Walker won't take no for an answer.

'Whenever you want to head off, just tell me and I'll take you back to the hotel,' he says.

• • •

By the time they get back to Grandma's, the place is full of people. In the back garden a barbecue is burning with high flames, and a semicircle of white plastic outdoor chairs is set out on the grass under the shade of the mango tree. The garden is narrow, only as wide as the house, but long. The grass runs for some twenty-five metres, then there's a big vegetable patch, more fruit trees and a chicken coop right at the back. A sagging line of chicken wire marks the end of the garden, and beyond it are the white grass plains and spindly trees of the bush. There are no neighbours on the left, but on the right a row of citrus trees and the same chicken-wire fence mark the start of another block, though there is not a garden as such, simply an extension of the bush, which runs almost to the back door, kept at bay only by a slim concrete patio, buckled from the sun and dotted with weeds.

'This is a lovely big garden,' she says.

'My grandad bought this house from a Chinese bloke,' says Walker. 'He was a legend in these parts, used to grow vegetables and sell them, and the eggs from the chooks, in town. My grandad did it too. But since he passed, my grandmother has turned most of it back to grass and now Michelle just keeps the back bit going.'

She wants to ask him more about his family but Blair, whose birthday is being celebrated, calls him over. Blair, wearing very short navy shorts and a faded navy cotton vest, is guarding the flames, holding a cold beer. Walker joins him and the women pull her into their circle. She's introduced to a rush of them, their names blurring into each other as Walker's aunt Michelle finds her a chair, deposing a rangy teenager from his seat. When Barbara protests, the teenager gives a shy smile, shakes his head. 'No worries,' he says.

Plastic bowls of chips are passed around before being abducted by children aged from toddlers to teenagers, who appear and disappear so rapidly that she can't quite distinguish how many there are. There seem constantly to be new faces, saying shy hellos, making requests and appeals to various adults. Walker has introduced her as a colleague and no further explanation seems necessary. Conversation flows and whirls around her, assuming an inbuilt knowledge of family topics and somehow including her without any demands. She feels enveloped and welcomed and it reminds her of Chilean family gatherings – noisy, inclusive, relaxed.

Although it's Blair's birthday, it's Walker's grandmother who's the centre of attention. She's frail with illness, as thin and tiny as a sparrow, but she's still a commanding presence, a force of nature who draws adults and children alike in constant eddies around her.

When the flames subside enough for cooking, a group heads inside, Barbara carried along in the flow. The kitchen table is piled high with dishes of food covered in plastic wrap, condensation forming underneath. Salads of pasta, rice, potatoes and coleslaw, all creamy in rich mayonnaise dressings. Bread rolls, squashed flat and misshapen by some accident of transportation. Plates with steaks sitting in bloody pools, burgers, sausages, chicken wings ready to be cooked. A huge bottle of tomato sauce. Bottles of cola, lemonade and a vivid-orange ginger ale are piled on the counter beside the fridge, which is filled with more of the same and a carton of white wine with a small tap at the front. An old bathtub outside by the back door is filled with ice, the tops of beer cans emerging like circular mountains from a sea of white.

She sips a beer, icy and refreshing, and becomes part of the tide of chat and banter that surges in waves around the circle. Walker catches her eye from time to time, checking on her from a distance, Ginger taking turns to sit by him and Grandma.

The smell of meat cooking makes her hungry, hungrier than she's been for days, and she eats a burger, then a couple of sausages, piles her plate high with salads. She finds herself sitting beside Grandma. Blair comes over with a plate. 'Here you go, Grandma,' he says. 'A snag sanger for ya!'

She takes the plate, which has a sausage sandwiched between white bread and a small portion of potato salad, and smiles at Barbara. 'I'm not hungry these days but it makes them feel better if it looks like I'm eating. The cancer has taken all my appetite,' she says matter-of-factly. 'I really like a lemonade, though, it helps with the nausea.' Her eyes, bright and clear, search Barbara's face. 'It's good that you're eating, love, you need to keep up your strength. It won't be easy, these coming weeks, but you'll get through it. Follow your gut and your heart. Lucas will help you. And you'll help him.' She reaches out and pats Barbara's hand. 'You'll get through this,' she says.

Barbara can feel tears threatening. She doesn't want to cry, doesn't want to give in to it. Not now, not ever. She forces a smile at Grandma, then looks away. Around her, everyone is eating, and the garden is stiller than it's been all afternoon, the buzz of conversation reduced to a low hum. The birds calling from the trees quieten as the sun slips lower behind the horizon. A pair of fruit bats flutter overhead and she slaps at the mosquitoes that appear as it darkens.

The children disappear into the living room, entwined on the floor in front of the TV like puppies. The adults are getting louder, laughing and talking, opening another carton of wine, putting more beers on ice. One of the men brings out a guitar and starts to play a low accompaniment to the conversation. She can't identify the tune; it's slow and a little mournful, and it tweaks at her heart. Rita, where are you, my sister.

She hasn't thought enough about Rita all afternoon and now she's overwhelmed with guilt. While she's sitting here, enjoying life, Rita is alone somewhere, terrified, perhaps hurt, waiting for her big sister to find her, to help her.

All her life she's been the one who's had Rita's back. The one who stood over the bullies who teased Rita for being a 'dago', the one who convinced her parents that it was alright for Rita to go out to the movies with a boy when she was fourteen, the one who was there when that same boy broke her heart. The one who listened and kept her secrets as Rita got older, and who fought the battles that needed to be fought so that Rita could sail through life, the family's golden girl. Rita, who would talk and talk and talk and talk. About anything and nothing, sweet and silly and lovely. Now, when she thinks of Rita, she hears only silence in her mind. Rita is missing. Rita is gone. Perhaps she'll never again hear her voice, see her smile, tease her, reminisce with her, talk to her. Perhaps it's already too late. Perhaps Rita is already dead.

Abruptly she stands. She can't be thinking like this. She needs to be doing something; she needs to find Rita and make this alright. She's standing, marooned in the dark of the garden, outside the semicircle of chairs.

Walker appears at her side. 'Everything OK?'

'I need to go,' she says. Her breath is coming in short, rapid bursts, her heart is beating fast, too fast, and she can feel her hands shaking and legs trembling, as unsteady as jelly.

He puts his hand to the small of her back and leads her away from the circle of people and light, towards the left of the house, where an old sofa has been pushed up against the back wall. She sits, off balance, struggling to catch a breath, and he sits beside her.

'Take a couple of deep breaths,' he says. 'Breathe in.' He pauses. 'Breathe out.'

She follows his voice, he coaches her breath back to a normal pace, and she feels her heart slow.

'I need to go,' she says again. 'I shouldn't have done this. I've spent hours without doing anything to find Rita. She's out there alone, scared, hurt, and I'm here drinking beer and, and . . . having fun.'

She's thankful that he doesn't give her trite words about needing a rest or taking a break. He simply nods. 'I'll drive you back now,' he says, and leads her away from the crowd to the front of the house.

'Wait here a minute,' he says, 'I'll get the keys.'

She sits on the stairs and Ginger appears beside her and rests her head on Barbara's knee. She runs her hand over the dog's head and ears, warm and soft, and down the muscles of her flank, and hears Ginger's tail beating time against the stair. When Walker returns with Michelle beside him, she's feeling calmer.

She stands. 'I'm sorry to leave early,' she says to Michelle. 'I'm not feeling too good.'

Michelle walks down the stairs and enfolds her in a hug – not the kind of half-hug you might give a new friend but a firm, comforting hug, the kind a mother or sister will give. Barbara resists for a second, then leans into it and a moment later finds herself crying.

'I've let her down,' she says. 'She always counts on me to help her, to get her out of trouble, and now when she needs me the most I can't find her.' Head still on Michelle's shoulder, her voice is muffled. 'And I'm so angry at her. It's typical of her that she's got herself into this situation. She's always so careless. She lets this kind of thing happen. Sometimes I just want to go home and leave her to sort out her own mess for once.'

Her tears build into sobs. Flowing and flowing, out comes the fear and horror and anger and guilt that's been building up since Rita disappeared. She doesn't know how long she cries. Michelle keeps her arms around her, and Ginger sits beside them. Walker disappears and returns with a glass of lemonade and a handful of tissues and sits on the step above them. She cries until she runs out of tears, wipes her eyes, sips the lemonade.

The sugary drink revives her and, taking a deep breath, she looks up at Walker, asks the question that has been haunting her for days. 'Is she still alive? If something's happened to them, if they're in trouble, not just off travelling somewhere, can they still be alive? It's so hot here, so dry . . .'

He takes a long moment to answer. 'If they have water, if they have shade, they can survive. Even without much food, as long as they have water and somewhere to shelter from the worst of the sun, they'll live. People can last a month without food. They have each other too, that will help.'

It's a small consolation. She wills herself to believe that Rita and Berndt are lost, not in danger from some unidentified killer. That they brought water with them, had thought through the dangers of driving into the unknown.

'I'm sorry,' she says when he drops her off outside the hotel. 'Thank you for inviting me tonight.'

'No problem.' He puts his hand out, touches her arm.

The feeling of it sends a tingle through her. She turns to look at him, remembers the strength of his chest and his arms, the warmth of him lying beside her on the blanket and notices for the first time that his eyes are golden-brown. A silence hangs between them but after a long moment he drops his hand and says, 'Goodnight. Try to get some sleep.'

Monday

Nine days missing

30

He's been gone longer than he'd planned. He'd finished the job and found a party in Hopeville on the way back. It had run all night. He'd crashed at some point, on a stranger's living room floor, and woken early this morning feeling lousy and ready to go home. As he'd passed through Caloodie, he'd stopped at the supermarket to pick up some food. He'd been angsty, tired, coming down, when he saw the poster on the supermarket noticeboard: pictures of the girl and the bloke and a big reward: $10,000.

He'd felt his heart beat fast and a sweat break out and had to wipe his face surreptitiously as he walked away from it. What if someone saw him looking at the poster, put two and two together. He'd glanced around, over his shoulder, but the place was virtually empty, no one looking his way.

He doesn't usually buy anything more than toilet paper or shower gel, but he needs to feed the girl. She'll be hungry – he's been gone a couple of days now and he only left her a box of cereal. But what the fuck, he's not a hotel, is he.

He'd rehearsed a kind of story as he walked round the supermarket picking things out – 'Got family visiting . . .' – in case anyone asked him why he was stocking up, but no one paid him any attention, the bored kid at the checkout counter passing the groceries across the scanner in a kind of daze, only opening his mouth to ask for money.

The tension is subsiding now that he's closer to home. When he gets back, he's going to warm her up a bit. She'll need a shower. Maybe he can get her to take a toke, something to relax her. He wants to finish her off by hand. It's more rewarding that way. He didn't want to touch the bloke, a horrible thought, but he loves the feel of a woman's neck, the softness, the smallness in his hands, the muscles straining for air.

The first woman he'd killed hadn't been planned. He'd stopped for something to eat at a pub on the outskirts of Mount Isa, halfway through a trip from the Territory, on his way back to Caloodie. She'd been around his age, mid-length blonde hair, tight jeans, teeth a bit crooked when she smiled. She'd talked to him at the bar, drunk the beers he'd bought her and afterwards had come to the truck with him for a drunken fumble, nothing good about it except the release. After they'd had sex, still pulling her t-shirt down over her tits, she laughed. Said she'd barely known he'd started before he'd finished.

Something inside him clicked. He'd punched her hard, that had been satisfying, then straddled her with his legs, pinning her arms to her sides, grabbed her round the throat. 'Let's see you laugh now, bitch.' As he'd tightened his grip the look in her eyes had turned to fear, then desperation, then absolute terror. He'd held on, tightening his grip, his anger giving him strength he never knew he had, until he saw the life go out of her. Afterwards, he realised he'd never felt so powerful, so in control.

The feeling didn't leave him for weeks. He only had to recall the way she looked at him in those last seconds, the power he'd felt at the moment of her death, and it was better than any hit, any drug, he'd ever tried. He dumped her body off the highway, among the iron-red hills that surround the town, and he's only been through Isa a couple of times in the intervening years and hasn't pulled back in at that pub anytime since.

He'd known he'd do it again – the buzz was so good, and he's taken the chances he's had. But he's been careful. He can spot them now, the women who live on the margins, who don't have a man watching over them or kids or family in town. The ones who take drugs and pay for the habit by selling themselves. People don't notice if they're gone. Or, if they notice, they don't care. There'd been one other close call, a sudden decision he'd made with the girl just outside Hopeville beside the broken-down car. Young and beautiful, she'd been flirtatious until he drove through town without stopping and he'd had to knock her out to stop her jumping out of the cab. She'd begged and pleaded and cried more than the others and he'd let her carry on until he got bored. He'd hidden her body well, they won't find her, but he'd been worried for a while. Bit too close to home. This one is even closer. Too close. If he hadn't been wasted and gone and shot the bloke, he'd have never done it. But what's done is done and he might as well enjoy it now.

He's got skilled at hiding the bodies. He pays attention on his drives to places that would suit, hidden gullies, empty land, tracks leading to nowhere. Only takes a few weeks before the bodies are skin and bone. No one will ever find them. Even if anyone was looking, which mostly they're not, the country is too big and the cops are too useless. He reminds himself of this. They won't find the bloke's body, let alone pin anything on him.

He needs to figure out a way to dispose of her afterwards too. It'd be safest if he dumps her far away but driving around with a body is too much risk and he doesn't think he'll have a chance to drive his rig out this way. He'll have to scout for another place nearby.

When he pulls up in front of the house, switches the engine off and breathes out, his shoulders slump with relief. He hasn't realised how anxious he's been, how much he's been wanting to get back here. That poster at the supermarket has really given him the heebie-jeebies.

His urge to see her is bigger than his need for a hit. He tucks a pack of cereal and a loaf of bread under his arm and fills a blue bucket with water from the hose. There's no noise from the shed. She's obviously given up crying, screaming for help.

It gives him a rush of pleasure, the fact that she's given in. He's in charge. He's the boss. He decides who lives and who dies. He brings her food and water; he holds the key to her life. Without him she's nothing. Still, he needs her to trust him, to let him get close enough to touch her. He puts the water on the ground, finds the key to the lock on his keyring. It's a small key and an awkward lock and it takes him a few seconds of rattling away to get it undone, the cereal box clamped under his left arm. Finally it clicks free and drops onto the ground at his feet. He picks it up, keeping his weight against the door in case she tries to make some kind of silly escape attempt, but there's no sound or movement inside.

He pushes the door to open it and feels it sticking; she's pushed something up against it to try to keep him out. He laughs. 'You won't keep me out,' he says, pushing with his shoulder to open it. It barely budges.

He runs through his mind what she could possibly have used – the shed was more or less empty, she must be holding it closed herself. Stupid cow, she's no match for him. He puts the cereal on the ground and, using both arms and all his force, manages to shove the door open by a foot or two, enough for him to squeeze sideways through.

He turns round, picks up the food and throws the cereal inside ahead of him. 'Got ya some tucker,' he calls out, thinking she might be hungry enough after a few days to make a run for the food, but she doesn't move. There's no sound at all from inside.

Cautiously he slides fully in, thinking he should have brought the rifle with him, though a small woman like that is no match for him. It takes a few moments for his eyes to adjust to the gloom; then he sees that she's lying in front of the door. As he thought, she was using her own weight to try to block his entrance. She's obviously dispirited by her failure, lying face down, her body still crumpled into a strange shape by the movement of the door. She doesn't move, doesn't acknowledge his presence. He turns, grabs the bucket of water and throws a good splash of it over her. She stays motionless.

He steps towards her, kicks her in the guts. Her body moves from the force; her head slaps onto the metal sheeting of the wall. Not a sound from her, nothing. Slowly he realises from her stillness, the unnatural shape of her body, the way she's lying, that she's not ignoring him. She's dead. There's no life left in her at all.

He feels his face flush red, his stomach cramp, a mixture of disappointment and shock shot through with anger. He stumbles out of the shed into the sunshine, legs shaking, breathing heavily, sits on the steps leading up to the veranda.

How did she fucken die? She wouldn't starve to death over a weekend. He goes back inside. Her body lies where he left it, contorted against the outside wall. He notices the other buckets of water he'd left her, one lying on its side at the back of the shed, the other also empty. Runs his fingers along the inside: dry. She knocked one over, perhaps, or simply miscalculated how long he'd be, how much she could drink. The shed is hot, the metal no match for the power of the sun. He was gone too long, and she had no water. He kicks at the side of the shed in frustration. It gives a metallic thump and the wall rattles.

He has to find a place to dump her body. But not now, not now. He's sweating and exhausted, his nerve ends tingling, his head pounding from the bright light, from a night without sleep. He needs sustenance, he needs another hit. It can wait. Later on he'll take a drive, find somewhere, sort it out.

• • •

Rita has been in some halfway world for endless hours. A world of arid heat, unbearable pain, visions and nightmares. A place between the real world and the plane of death. She sees Berndt, not the beautiful man she loved, but some creature, leg swollen and black, crusted with blood, his face crazed with fear and pain. She screams at him to run, run, run. But he stays, filling the space with horror and death, and no matter how hard she tries, she can't help him or save him. He stays, exuding agony.

The heat builds and builds, the light bright and sharp, until she can barely breathe, the air dry and burning around her. All the while she has a terrible thirst. Her tongue swollen in her mouth, her lips huge and cracked. The bucket is dry, nothing left, she's licked it in the search for any liquid, but it tastes only of dirt. She hears the car arrive and the sound gives her hope and enough energy to crawl to the door, every movement torturous. Just some water, all she wants is just a gulp of water. She puts her mouth to the tiny gap between the door and the ground, a place where she'd scrabbled, pointlessly, trying to dig her way to freedom, a long time ago, a lifetime ago. To make it here, to crawl and move, has taken every last ounce of her strength, and all that emerges is a whisper, a croak, hardly a sound. Then everything goes black.

She dreams of water, a cooling refreshing rush of liquid, her lips open. In her dream she is drinking, a glimmering stream of water running endlessly into her open mouth, but never quenching her unbearable thirst. She hears a sound from a distance, someone speaking to her, and an instinctive rush of fear pushes her near consciousness until there is a jolt of agony in her stomach, her head, and all goes black again.

When she wakes the shed is hotter than ever, fire is running through her body. Her mouth is cracked and dry but her hair is damp and her t-shirt, too, feels moist. By some instinct, hardly conscious, she grabs a handful of her hair, sucking on the ends, extracting the liquid, the delicious wetness of it. Another handful of hair, more liquid, precious water. She tries to sit but the pain is too sharp. She pulls her t-shirt up, rubs it across her face, her lips, sucks it. Wanting more, greedy for more.

She hears Berndt call her name, opens her eyes, sees him standing in the shadows at her feet. He's smiling, his hair long and loose the way she likes it, blowing in the breeze. He's not wearing a shirt – she can see his chest, tanned and strong. She tries to call to him, 'Bring me water, please, babe, bring me water.' He calls her name again. She notices that he's standing by a bucket, a blue bucket. Water. Her thirst overrides the pain that burns through her. She crawls, on her stomach, towards Berndt, towards water.

31

The board is filling up but there isn't a clear picture emerging. Walker lets his eyes run across it, not overthinking it, to see if anything tweaks his interest. Anything he might have missed, anything that might give him a way in.

He hears the screen door open and recognises Barbara's soft tread in the hall outside. She looks rested but as if she's been crying again, her eyes red and a little puffy. She nods at him and puts her bag on the table.

'You OK?' he asks.

'I talked with Berndt's father and my parents,' she says. 'Berndt's father is flying out. He thinks he needs to be here. It cannot hurt. He can add extra pressure. But my parents are not coping. My dad especially is not coping and I cannot give him answers. I'm not getting closer to finding Rita and I'm not there with them. They need me but I also cannot abandon Rita. I just cannot leave her here alone.'

He feels for her. Her parents must be devastated. But he also knows that if it were Grace he would stay, and he would turn over every rock between here and Tennant Creek if that's what it took to find her.

He resists the urge to walk over and put his arms around her. She's wearing cropped black trousers, a white t-shirt with red polka dots and flat red leather sandals. Her short hair is even messier than usual. She couldn't be more different from Ellen in Sydney, with her blow-dry and blonde streaks, the half-hour-long make-up routine, diamond earrings, Rolex watch and vast walk-in wardrobe. His girlfriends have all been glamorous. They seem drawn to his understated style and the bad-boy appeal of an undercover cop. He shakes himself from these thoughts. Barbara's a colleague, or, more accurately, family of the victim, nothing more.

She joins him in front of the board, stares at it for a moment and then summarises where they're at: 'We have five missing or murdered. Along with Berndt and Rita, there's Sheree Miller, who disappeared from a broken-down car last year. Tanya Bowen, last seen in the pub in Barcaldine three years ago and Sylvia Stevens, killed five years ago, last seen in a pub in Mount Isa.'

'If these are all linked,' says Walker, looking at the cluster of names around the drugs op, 'it's harder to pin it on Matt Monroe or Markovich. Markovich was in Sydney until fairly recently and Monroe would only have been seventeen when Sylvia Stevens died. Neither of them matches the description for Mount Isa either.'

'Does the e-fit remind you of anyone?' asks Barbara. 'It definitely doesn't look much like Monroe. But how about Hippy?'

Walker thinks of the barfly, his dyed hair and dark sunnies. Hair is easily changed, but still. 'Nah,' he says. 'They'd have noticed his hair for sure, it's always been long and blond.'

They stare at the board for a while, willing answers to come from it.

'Do you really still not think that we are looking for the same person on all of these?' asks Barbara. She doesn't wait for him to reply. 'When Sheree disappeared, the caravanners saw a truck ahead of them that might have stopped to pick her up. Tanya Bowen was also known to have contact with truckers. Sylvia Stevens was last seen in a pub frequented by truckers and her body was found beside the highway. And Berndt and Rita went missing on an isolated road that's mostly used by trucks.' She points at the names beside Johnson's. 'I still think we should be looking more closely at the trucking connection.'

Walker doesn't say anything. Despite media myth-making, serial killers are vanishingly rare. Even the FBI estimates that in the US they make up less than 1 per cent of murders, and here in outback Queensland – well, they're far from likely. Still, this serial-killer-trucker thing has been nagging at him; there are enough similarities in the cases of the three missing women that they could be linked.

But Rita and Berndt don't fit the profile, and it seems to Walker that the most likely scenario is a connection to the Markovich operation, even though this means the pair are likely dead. Then again, if this is a random abduction, a random killer, they're also likely dead and he has less chance of finding them in this vast country, with the few thin leads they've managed to drum up so far. There's no good news anywhere, so he keeps all these thoughts from Barbara.

'I think we need to bring in a bigger team,' says Barbara. 'If this is all the same man, he's a serial killer. He's killed three women in five years, even if he didn't abduct Berndt and Rita.'

She turns to him, arms out in supplication.

'Please. It is worth investigating, even if just to rule it out. Could you make a call to the Brisbane team?'

Walker knows that Rutherford will be delighted to have the spotlight pointing away from Markovich, and if Rutherford drops the intel to Queensland Police they're more likely to follow it up.

'I'll make a call,' he says. 'Let's see what they say.'

'I'll go to Johnson's, get them to add the Barcaldine and Mount Isa dates to their search,' says Barbara after a moment. 'It would be a good start to rule out drivers in this area. If this is the same guy, he made a big mistake when he picked up Rita and Berndt. If they disappeared between here and Smithton, it has to be someone local. Their car hasn't turned up, so he's had to hide it somewhere.'

On this last point Walker agrees. Rita and Berndt weren't at Markovich's place, so he's going to pay a visit to Angus Jones today. He shouldn't have let Grogan do the interview; his trust in the constable is diminishing every day. Taking a closer look at Jones's place makes sense.

He taps his finger on the map, fifty kilometres or so west: Landsdowne, Jones's property. 'I'm going to visit Angus Jones. He owns the place that Tina Monroe is renting. Grogan already spoke to him, but I want to take a look around myself.'

'Right, great idea.' She stands, throws her bag over her shoulder. 'I'll come with you.'

'Hang on, hang on, hold your horses.' Walker decides he needs to rein this in. 'Look, you're not a cop out here. You're family. I know how important this is to you. I get it, I'd be the same if it was the other way around, but I can't take you out to interview Angus Jones. I can't involve you in the investigation like this.'

'Why not? You just said you would get involved if it was you.'

He doesn't really have an answer. Just knows he prefers to work alone, that he doesn't need to be distracted by looking out for her.

'It's against all the rules,' he says. 'And I operate better alone. You need to talk to Johnson's anyway. I'll go out and talk to Angus now, and I'll come and meet you at the hotel later and update you.'

She glares at him. He can see her thinking about arguing. Instead, she turns on her heel and leaves, slamming the door of the office shut behind her. The small house reverberates with the noise. He listens to her footsteps down the hall and then the front screen opens and closes, more quietly. When he walks into the hallway, he sees Grandma standing by the door of her room.

'Did we wake you up? Sorry, Grandma.' He goes to her, to help her back into bed, but she shakes her head.

'I'm fine – I feel like sitting up for a while. I'm sick of lying in bed like an invalid. Who was that?'

'Barbara. She's annoyed because she wants to be more involved in finding her sister, but I've told her she can't be.'

'Why not?'

'It's against the rules. She's the missing girl's sister; she's not police.'

'As if you've always been a stickler for regulations. If it was Grace that was missing, what would you do?'

'Grandma . . .' he appeals to her – doesn't want another woman angry at him. 'I'm looking out for her. I want her to stay safe.'

'Hmm.' She sits at the table, trembling slightly from the exertion of the walk down the hallway. He puts the kettle on for a cup of tea, finds a pack of biscuits, the plain and sugary ones that the whole family calls Grandma Biscuits. He puts them on a plate, the way she likes, then goes for her shawl, a pale-blue knitted thing that she's taken to wearing even in the heat of the summer, drapes it over her shoulders and sits opposite her while she sips her tea and eats a biscuit, dipping it in the hot drink to soften it.

'Lucas, I know you had a difficult childhood' – she puts up her hand to stop him disclaiming. 'Yes, it was. Your dad dying and your mum having to leave you here with us. Then going to Boston when you were in high school. You never really found a place where you fit but you always did so well. It made you independent, and that's a good thing, but sometimes you have to let people in. You'll be happier if you let yourself become part of something bigger. You'll find you don't always need to have all the answers yourself.'

. . .

Walker thinks about her words on the drive out to Angus Jones's place. He's always valued her advice and her wisdom, but right now he thinks she's wrong. Other than Grandma herself, relying on others has never really worked for him; they're liable to let you down just when you need them most.

32

Walker's ute jitters over the dirt road that leads to Angus Jones's place. The track is in good condition, graded and relatively smooth, but otherwise Jones's farm is doing it tough, thinks Walker. The paddocks are nothing but dirt and dust, the grass long gone, eaten out of existence by cattle desperate for fodder. It's been more than seven years since some of these properties have had rain. It's always been dry out this way but the last decade has been the worst in living memory.

Some properties north-east of town had a shot of luck, a deluge and run-off from the Diamantina River at the end of last summer that watered the grass and added a couple of vital inches to the dams. But those further west, like Angus, missed out, as the dead land for miles around testifies. Walker hasn't seen any cattle on his approach, and even here, close to the homestead, there's no stock in the paddock. The creek that marks the turn-off to the place is dry but perhaps the animals are sheltering in the shade of the trees that still line its banks.

Jones's property, too, looks dusty and unloved. The garden is dead and besieged by the bush, the paint on the house peeling and faded. Walker hopes the man takes better care of his rental properties or he has a short future as a landlord. There are a few farm sheds to the right of the house, with a concrete yard in front of them. Walker notes one, shiny and new, the aluminium sides gleaming in the sun, which speaks of a recent investment. The rest of the place has a forlorn feeling.

Jones is home – Walker can see his car parked in front of the new shed. He pulls his ute in behind and cuts the engine. When he opens the door the heat of the afternoon surges in and the paddock, where it meets the main road in the far distance, shimmers enticingly, the heat providing a mirage of water. He hears a crow cawing, a slow lazy heat-addled aaaah-aaaaaah, and a bird of prey, a goshawk perhaps, floats in circles high above on an invisible thermal current. Otherwise the air is still.

He walks over to the house and up the stairs to the veranda. The front door is open, the screen door unlocked. 'Alright, Mr Jones?' calls Walker through the mesh, which partially obscures a gloomy hallway. 'It's DS Walker here.'

The noise of his voice travels through the house and Walker is certain the place is empty. It emits the kind of silence, a stillness, that a busy house never does. He walks back down the stairs and as he rounds the corner he sees Jones emerging from the shed opposite, shutting the metal door behind him with a clang and pushing a bolt home. He locks the shed, notes Walker, but not the house. Thinking of Markovich's place the other night and the poor security there, he wonders if perhaps the operation is taking extra precautions in light of his late-night incursion.

Jones wipes his hands on his trousers, tilts his hat back and runs his arm over his forehead as he walks over.

'G'day,' says Walker.

Jones nods, looking at Walker, his eyes squinting against the light. 'Help you?' he asks.

'I've come to have a chat with you about these missing backpackers,' says Walker.

'I already talked to Grogan,' says Jones. 'It's got nothing to do with me.'

'Right,' says Walker. He turns and looks around, across the garden towards the home paddock. 'Drought's pretty bad out here, ay.'

'Drought's pretty bad everywhere.'

'You still got cattle on this land? Looks like there's not much feed left in it.'

'Haven't had any feed on these paddocks for over a year.' The man's voice is low and bitter. 'Was hand-feedin' 'em till I ran out of money. Still waitin' for the government's emergency cheque to arrive. Doesn't come soon, won't be no fuckin' emergency – it'll all be over.'

'How many head you got left, then?'

'Barely none. A few yearlings in the far paddocks, the ones that can scrabble to stay alive . . .' His voice trails off. 'You didn't come out here to talk about farmin'.'

'No,' agrees Walker, turning to look at him again. For the first time he notices the defeat that is written all over the grazier, his thin frame, lined face. A coiled spring of anger, tightly wound, is all that's holding the bloke together. If he's working with Markovich, it's probably what's keeping him from going under.

'Thing is, you were in Caloodie on Friday the fourth, when those backpackers were there.' Walker doesn't bother messing around.

'So?'

'You told me you weren't on the road on the Saturday they disappeared, but I heard you stayed at the pub the night before.'

Jones looks at him. 'I told Grogan this already. I wasn't on that road. I was working. I take a trucking job now and then to make a bit of money.'

'For Paul Johnson?' asks Walker.

'Once in a while. Drive for some other outfits too.'

'Where'd you go that Saturday, then?'

'Took a load to the coast. Surfers Paradise.'

'Who for?'

'Look, mate, unless you wanna arrest me or something, I don't need to answer these questions. It's my business who I work for. I got people who can vouch for me. Grogan knows 'em – you go check with him.'

'Can I take a quick look around?' asks Walker. 'Round the sheds, that sort of thing? Just so's I can tell the boss that I did it, that we crossed all the t's, you know how it is . . .'

Jones's face hardens. 'No. You can't. This ain't nothing to do with me. You want to look around, you better come back with some kind of warrant.'

He pushes past Walker and up the stairs to the house. The screen door closes with a clang behind him.

Walker heads towards his car. He looks over his shoulder: Jones has disappeared inside, so he walks past the car and behind Jones's vehicle, which is directly in front of the shed door. The shed is new, well built, clean. As he'd thought, it's locked, and the heavy brass lock is also new, still shining, not yet tarnished by weather, hanging on the eye of a thick bolt. He gives the door a shake, rattles it a little. It's solid construction, barely moves, but by the sound of it, the way it fails to reverberate, the shed isn't empty.

On impulse he calls out quietly: 'Rita? Berndt? Can you hear me?'

There's no answer. He walks quickly over to look in each of the other sheds. An old Toyota, dusty and covered in spiderwebs, sits in one. It's nothing like the car that Meyer owns but Walker snaps a quick picture on his phone anyway. The other shed is empty. It smells faintly of animals and leads out to a holding pen.

He goes back to the car via the shiny new shed, rattling the door again. Calls out, 'Hello, anyone there?' Listens, ear pressed to the tin wall, to see if he can hear anything – a tiny scrabble, or muted cry. Nothing. Silence and stillness.

As he gets into the car he sees Jones watching him from one of the side windows. When he realises Walker has spotted him, he lets the curtain drop back into place.

Walker thinks about the locked shed the whole drive back into town. He wants to get a search warrant, have a proper look round the place. Jones makes out he's broke but he has a heap of rental properties, one of which he's renting to Tina Monroe, which gives him a strong link to Markovich. And the locked shed, this far out of town – it's a red flag. People out this way don't lock up their sheds; there's simply no need, no risk. Unless of course they have something to hide.

He won't ask Grogan to organise it – he's as likely to call Jones in advance to check it's OK. Walker can run this by Rutherford. If they organise the warrant under the guise of searching for Rita and Berndt, it might get Rutherford a look into what Jones's links are to Markovich's operation. He thinks about driving to the hotel to debrief Barbara but decides to wait until he's got something more concrete to tell her. He wants to give her good news for once. He'll go and see her when he can let her know that they've got approval for a proper search of Angus Jones's place.

33

He's toked up again. He wanted to calm his nerves, but instead it's made him jittery and anxious. He knows he needs to do something about the bitch in the shed and do it fast. Can't have her body lying there. But he doesn't know where to dump her yet. He's been thinking about it, making a mental recce of possible places, but nowhere feels right.

He grabs his phone, maybe he can find a place using the map, and sees a heap of missed messages on the Johnson's drivers' group. Fuck, he hasn't checked his phone for hours. They must have come in when he was in town. The first is from Terri. He has to read it twice before it sinks in:

> Cops are asking questions about some missing women and 2 backpackers. If they contact u, call me please.

Then responses from the other drivers:

> WTF? Why they asking us?

> We got nothing to do with this.

His heart stops. The cops have worked it out. He looks again at the messages, his hand shaking. Fuck. This is too close to home. He needs to find a place to dump her, fast. He drops the phone on the table, goes outside in a rush. He'll bury her now.

He's halfway to the shed when a thought pulls him up. He needs to answer the messages. He's the only one who hasn't replied – that looks strange. He thinks it through. Decides he'd better show his face at the depot. Make out he's shocked and horrified and what can he do to help. The dead girl can wait. He needs to knock this on the head with Johnson's first and foremost.

When he arrives in town, he starts by taking the car to the carwash at the servo. You can never be too sure – the bloke was in the back, he doesn't want any evidence of him there.

'You're taking pretty good care of that vehicle,' says the woman who hands him the tokens. 'That's twice in a week you've been through.'

She's got short hair, tattoos that run all the way up her tanned and muscular arms. She's half bloke, he thinks, and he isn't in the mood to play nice.

'Got fuck all to do with you,' he says, taking the token and turning on his heel. He can see her reflected in the plate-glass windows and she flicks him the bird as he walks away. A flame of rage ignites in his stomach and he's tempted to go back and throttle the bitch for her fucken attitude. But there's another car on the forecourt and a woman walking towards the doors, ready to pay for her petrol. He walks on, barging past the woman, who says, 'Mind yourself,' in a bossy tone.

In his head he imagines gunning her down with his rifle, boom, boom, boom, then walking into the shop and taking that other bitch by the throat, looking her in the eyes so she knows who's the boss around here.

He sits in the car as it passes through the automatic wash, the suds running down the windows, the brushes drumming on the roof and across the tray back behind him. His stomach is in knots. He's sweating. This is too close to home. He's glad it's Terri not Paul that sent the message, she's an easier touch.

The car gleaming in the sun, he drives over to the depot. The gate is locked, the yard empty. He glances at the clock on the dashboard. Fucksake, it's gone 5 p.m., he's too late. He spins the car round and drives over to the pub. Paul's usually there – he can have a word with him, set him straight on this. He needs to get a feel of how much the cops know, find out what the fuck is going on.

The pub is quiet when he gets there. Paul's not in. He orders a beer, looks round and sees the poster hanging above the bar. The pictures of the two backpackers, the big reward. He feels the tremor of fear return. He needs to get away. He needs to leave town. He's turning to go when Mike puts the beer he's ordered in front of him on the bar. The glass is cold, dripping condensation, the beer amber and inviting. He drinks it fast, orders another, forces himself to sip this one. He needs to think. His eye is constantly drawn back to the poster. He has a sense that the girl is about to step out of it and point at him: 'He did it.' The whole set-up is giving him the heebie-jeebies, his arms itching, his mind racing, and he's just about to leave when Paul comes in with Steve Burnett and pulls up a stool at the other end of the bar.

The two of them order their beers, acknowledge him with nods, and he stands and takes his beer over. He needs to sort this out with Paul. Put himself in the clear. But Paul and Burnett are mid-conversation and don't stop talking when he arrives, so he stands beside them, feeling like a tool. That's when he sees her.

For a moment he thinks he's hallucinating but when he closes his eyes and opens them again she's still there, smiling at Ali behind the bar. She's older and her hair is different, much shorter. The clothes, too, are more conservative, rather than the tiny shorts and fitted halter top she'd worn when she was younger. But her face, the big brown eyes, dark lashes that sweep onto her cheeks, and those full lips – he'd recognise her anywhere.

He's sweating a little, his heart is beating faster than it should be. Maybe it's just another hallucination, but if not he should get up and walk out. She'll point at him when she sees him, 'There's the bloke who killed me', and he won't have an answer. He looks at his hands, half expecting to see them covered in her blood. He picks up his pint to finish it, the glass shaking. Tries to stay calm, tells himself he's hallucinating again.

At that moment she glances over the bar at him. She looks straight into his eyes. His hand still trembling, he puts the pint down on the bar, preparing to back out, to run if he has to. She looks at him for a moment, then Hippy says something to her, and she turns away.

She's real. She's talking to Hippy. His heartbeat doesn't slow its frantic pace. He keeps his eyes on her and moves behind Johnson and Burnett for cover. He turns his back on the bar, facing the mirror above the shelf, where he can see her in the reflection without being observed, watches her, listens to her. She has the same accent as the other girl, but her voice is deeper, huskier. When Hippy gets up to play a game of keno, Ali goes over. He ceases breathing, holds himself in utter stillness so that he can hear their conversation over the low chatter and the hum of the television.

'How you doing, love? Any news on your sister?'

Sister. She's the sister. He feels a kind of relief. She can't know anything.

'We've got some leads,' says the woman, and she looks over at him while she says it, stares right at him, he can see her eyes in the mirror. She knows. She knows. 'We're going to get some more detectives from Brisbane up here, a proper team, and then we'll find them.'

'Ah, beaut, that's good news,' says Ali.

He bites his lip. A team of cops is coming. He's brought this too close to home. He needs to head off, go west. But the cops aren't here yet. So far, it's only her that's seen him. If he can take her out, if he can get rid of her, maybe they won't find him. He'll have a head start on them at least, and that should be enough. He'll go west, he'll disappear.

He finishes his beer. While she's eating, not staring at him anymore, he walks to the far end of the bar, stands slightly out of sight behind a pillar and orders another beer from Mike.

'Who's the sheila over there?' he says, nodding his head in her direction, real casual like.

'You interested, mate? I don't reckon you're her type. She's always with that Lucas Walker – you know, Lucille's grandson?'

He doesn't know and he doesn't care, just wants the intel on the woman. 'I'm not interested in her, mate. Got plenty of sheilas chasing me round. More trouble than they're worth. Just wondered who she is.'

'Course you have. Where's all these women, then? I never saw you with no one.'

'I don't bring 'em here, do I.' He picks up his beer. 'I guess you don't know nothing about her, then.'

Mike loves being the one in the know, needs to think he's the centre of the town's universe.

Sure enough, stung, Mike gives him the whole story. 'Course I know her. She's staying here, isn't she. She's a cop, from Berlin, she's trying to find her sister and the boyfriend, the ones that have gone missing. Have you been under a rock or something? It's been all over the news.'

When Mike stops talking, he says, 'Yeah, course I heard.' He shakes his head. 'Terrible business. Don't expect that kind of thing around here. What is the world coming to, ay?'

Ha fucken ha.

Drinks his beer, thinks it through. It's like he thought: she's on her own, the cops from Brisbane aren't here yet. If he can get rid of her, he'll buy himself some time. Time to get away. And now that he knows she's staying here, he has an idea.

He's stayed at the pub a few times himself, when he's been too wasted to drive, and he knows there's a way in through the side door at the top of the fire escape stairs. It's designed so that guests can leave before the pub opens or come in late at night if they're back after closing. It's meant to be locked but it never is.

He drains his beer in one and says a loud 'See ya' to Mike, who's more or less ignored him since telling him the story. Mike barely nods as he leaves, arrogant fucker. He'll take your money, make nice while you're drinking at the bar, but wouldn't give you the time of day otherwise. Makes it even sweeter to do it this way.

He heads out as if he's leaving but in the corridor he turns left and takes the stairs to the guest rooms on the first floor, with a snigger at the feeble *Guests Only* sign. There's a landing at the top of the stairs with comfy chairs. Sit in one of those and you get a good look down the corridor at all the rooms. He jams his hat low over his eyes and pretends to sleep.

Time passes. He's jittery, his knees bouncing, his feet tapping, scratching at his arms beneath his shirt. When he finally hears her tread on the stairs, he forces himself to relax into a sleepy pose. His heart is beating fast. If she's onto him, if she tries to arrest him, he'll grab her now, he can if he has to. He watches her from under his hat, ready to move. She glances at him but it's cursory and she turns left down the corridor and opens the door to her room. He gives it a few minutes, the whole time keeping his eye on the door she opened. Then he walks down the corridor and straight past her room, noting the number, 12. He hears other voices and footsteps coming up the stairs, speeds up a little and makes it out the exit door at the end of the corridor without being seen.

Outside on the fire escape he takes some deep breaths, shaking a little with fear and excitement. He waits until the men in the corridor go into their rooms, then leans back inside and puts the door on its catch. He hopes that Mike and Ali won't check it and lock it before they go to bed. Usually they don't. There's not much reason to worry about security out here.

34

He drives home like a man possessed. Once back he lights a pipe, smokes just enough to feel the surge and the burst of energy, to fire himself up for the night ahead. He has a target and a plan. He can get away with this, if he plays it right.

He'll bring her out here. He'll get rid of her out here. He can get rid of the two of them at the same time. They'll never find the bodies. Won't know where to find him either. He can head west, keep his head down for a while.

He's not in the mood for sleep. He's pacing around the living room, full of energy, has a couple of beers on the sofa and then another hit before he drives back into town, opening the windows wide and shouting 'Yeaaaahhhh!' into the blackness as he rides the high. He's too clever for these country hick cops. He knows what he's doing.

In town, he cruises slowly. The roads are empty, windows dark, no one about. He pulls into the alley behind the pub that's used by the garbos to collect the bins from the local shops once a week. There are no windows overlooking the alley, only the wall of the drive-through bottle shop on one side and the wall of the butcher's on the other. He has to move the bins to get the car in, and when he pulls them back into place it's almost impossible to see the vehicle. He waits a while in the alley, sitting quietly in the dark, making sure no one has seen him parking here.

The alley is open at both ends so that the bin truck can drive through without reversing. The other end opens to the road that leads out of town. The shop directly opposite that entrance is abandoned. It used to be an employment agency but the drought and the recession and whatever else has put an end to that. No work out here these days. With the bins at one end and the empty shop on the other, he can operate more or less unseen and he's not planning to hang about long once she's in the car.

He picks up the wrench he's chosen and puts it in the pocket of the driver's-side door. It's easily heavy enough to knock her out.

The stairs creak as he walks up them, the noise loud in the quiet of the pre-dawn street. He stops at the top, breathing as softly as he can. There's no sound or movement. He turns the door handle. Sure enough, it's still unlocked. He pumps his fist in pleasure. Gotcha.

It's too early to wake her, so he walks quietly along the corridor and sits in the same chair he was in last night. By 5.30 he can't stand it anymore. Dawn has broken and he can hear the occasional car on the street outside. The bakery will be open by now and it might be that one of the men staying here is a worker who likes to start early. He needs to get going.

Along with en suite rooms, the pub still offers the old-style cheaper rooms with shared bathrooms at the end of the corridor. He goes into the men's, uses the loo, throws some water on his face, then heads along to the guest kitchen and boils the kettle for a cup of tea. The rattle of the electric jug as it boils the water is loud, but he wants the noise, wants it to seem that the day has begun and that guests are up and about. He hears a door open in the corridor and his heart stops. The steps are too heavy to be hers, so he turns, opening the fridge, leaning in as if picking something out of it. The person walks past the kitchen without stopping and goes into the men's bathroom. Now he really has to move quickly. He pours the water into the cup and grabs it, teabag still floating, no time to mess about, then walks to room 12 and knocks on the door.

. . .

Barbara's awake early, well before 6 a.m. She looks at her phone to see the time, wonders if it's worth trying to get back to sleep. Her thoughts turn to Rita, to the possibility of a serial killer. She won't sleep and if she lies here she'll tear herself to bits with her spiralling thoughts and endless fears, so she starts her daily routine, opening the veranda door and looking across the rooftops opposite at the pale morning sky.

It's already warm. She's only wearing her short pyjamas, her feet bare, her shoulders bare too in her vest top, and the veranda is still in shade, but the sun is slanting in a bright triangle across the awnings of the shops on the other side of the street.

She hopes that maybe they're getting close to a breakthrough. She'd talked with the girl at the local trucking firm again yesterday and been promised a list of any drivers who might have been in the areas they're looking at by this morning. She'd spent the rest of yesterday beginning to go through the lists of drivers from the big trucking companies, seeing if there were any who'd been in more than one of the towns on the dates the girls disappeared. It's slow work and so far no leads, but hopefully Walker will hear back from Brisbane today, to see if a team is available to help them sift through the information.

She sees a car pull up outside the bakery opposite, a door slamming loud in the peaceful early morning. She decides to go over, get a coffee and some breakfast. Maybe Walker will be there too, and they can push forward.

She's dressed, trying to smooth down her hair, when she hears a knock on the door. Walker's come to get me, she thinks, opening the door with a smile on her face, which fades when she sees a man she doesn't know standing there, holding a cup of tea. He's thin, his eyes are dark and he has long hair and the beginnings of a ginger beard. He smiles awkwardly at her. She places him: he was in the bar last night, she remembers his intense stare. She closes the door a little, keeping just the side of her body visible.

'Sorry to bother ya,' he says. 'I saw ya last night and Mike told me that you're staying here because your sister went missing, out on the road to Smithton.'

'Yes, that is right,' she says.

'I reckon I saw her,' he says. 'Well, them. She was with a bloke, a long-haired bloke, beside a small car.'

Barbara's heart leaps into her mouth. She opens the door slightly wider. 'Really. When? What happened? What did you see?'

He saw Rita. He saw Berndt. Oh god, let this be the breakthrough they need.

'Yeah, I live out that way and I was driving home. I woulda stopped but there was already someone with 'em so I drove past.'

'Who was with them? What did you see?'

He pauses, shifts the tea to his other hand. 'Sorry, this is a bit hot. I'll just put it down ...' He bends to put it on the floor and she says, 'Come in, here, put it on the table', opens the door to him, invites him in.

She's impatient, wants to shake him, wants to scream 'Tell me now!' as he places the cup on the table. She closes the door behind him.

'Tell me what you saw.'

'Well, the thing is, I don't want to get someone into trouble. I'm not sure that it's important ...'

He's playing with her, she feels it. Looks into his eyes. He's enjoying the power of the moment; he doesn't know anything.

'Tell me what you know or please leave.' She's back at the door, opening it. Why is he here in her bedroom at 6 a.m.? He could have just called the number on the poster if he wanted to taunt her.

'It was Angus Jones,' he says. 'Angus was standing there, looking at the car with 'em. His vehicle was pulled over, so I thought they'd be alright.'

Barbara feels a rush of adrenaline, a huge surge of energy. Angus Jones. Rita is right here. Rita's been here all this time.

'Why did you not tell us earlier? Why have you only come forward now?' She's close to shouting.

'I only just heard they're missing. I haven't been around. I'm a truckie, I've been on the road, and I heard last night that they were missing and, well, I don't want to get in no trouble. I didn't know any earlier, did I . . .'

She turns on her heel, grabs her bag from the chair, cursing to herself at his reluctance, his absence. Please let it not be too late. 'I understand. Of course. You are not in trouble,' she says. 'But we need to go to the police. DS Walker is handling this. We need to talk to him right now.'

As she pulls her phone out of her bag to call Walker, she sees that he's biting his cheek, his hands twitching, obviously nervous at getting involved.

'You do not know how thankful I am that you've told me this now, it really is not too late.' She's trying to be reassuring, wants him to be relaxed, needs to get him in front of Walker, hopes against hope it isn't too late, that they can find Rita and Berndt. 'Look, let's walk over to the station. It's not far. I'll call DS Walker, he will meet us there. You are not in any trouble. In fact, there is a ten-thousand-dollar reward if we find my sister.'

He nods. Perhaps the reward has convinced him. 'My car's parked at the back of the pub. If ya like I can drive us over.'

He seems jumpy, anxious, and she doesn't want him to change

his mind. She'll call Walker from the car, she decides, dropping the phone back in her bag. 'Thank you, yes,' she says.

She leads him to the fire exit, the front of the pub still closed. He walks down the stairs ahead of her and she shuts the door behind her, clicking the lock on as she leaves. It's often unlocked but her Berlin copper instincts can't leave a door open, it doesn't feel secure enough. She can't remember if she checked it last night before she went to bed or if someone has already left this morning and not locked it behind them. She makes a note to mention it to Ali later. It's not a good system.

The man, still jumpy, leads her behind the pub to an alleyway she didn't know existed. His car is parked there, a white tray-back, the kind everyone here drives. He presses the key fob and the doors unlock with a quiet click. She gets inside. The car is pristinely clean; she can smell detergent and a fake pine scent emanates from a tree-shaped air freshener that's hanging on the rear-view mirror. He climbs in and turns to close the door behind him. She drops her bag on the floor and is looking over her shoulder for the seatbelt when some instinct, some premonition of danger, makes her turn back towards him. He's in his seat, facing her, and is swinging his arm towards her, a heavy metal tool in his hand. She tries to duck away from the impact but she's too late. Her head explodes with pain, a burst of vivid light, and then everything turns black.

Tuesday

Ten days missing

35

He's worried at first that he's killed her. He wants to have a bit of fun with her – after the last one died, he's owed that. But she'd moved at the last minute and he hadn't been able to adjust his swing. The wrench had caught her full on the side of the head. He hadn't swung hard at all, just wanted to knock her out, but her eyes rolled back and she's completely white.

He forces himself into action. Can't worry about all this now. Leans over and pushes her off the seat and down into the footwell, her body crumpling. Lucky she's small, she'll be invisible under the blanket, even if someone looks in. He pushes her as far down as he can and then reaches behind him and grabs the duct tape and blanket from behind her seat. He tapes her hands together and then ties them to her legs, hitches her up the way you would a calf, then throws the blanket over her. She's out of sight.

He starts the engine and drives slowly out of the alley, turns left onto the road and out of town. The road is empty; no one sees him leave the pub. Once he's out of the town's speed limit he floors it, but when he sees a car coming towards him he slows back down. The car belongs to Angus Jones, who raises his forefinger in salute. He's not sure if Angus recognised him – he probably acknowledges everyone he passes, old-school country style. But it would have been better if he hadn't been seen at all. He doesn't want to attract any attention. Mr Invisible, that's him.

Fifteen minutes later the woman in the footwell groans, tries to move and then throws up. The stench of her vomit fouling the car.

'Dirty bitch.'

He can't do much about it, has another fifteen minutes' or more drive ahead of him; opens the windows to let in some fresh air, hot as it is already. He leans over and pulls her up so that her head is leaning against the door. She tries to open her eyes, groans again and passes out. Her face is covered with vomit, her clothes too. Disgusting. He throws the blanket back over her, covering everything except her face, to dampen the smell.

By the time they reach the turn-off for his place, she's groggily awake. When she tries to move, he picks up the wrench. 'Stay still or I'll fucken kill you this time,' he says. She cowers back into the door, her body bent into an unnatural shape by the way he's tied her. She keeps her eyes on him but doesn't move.

When they arrive, he parks the car and gets out, walks around to her side and opens the door. She's been leaning against it and falls into him as he opens it. He steps back and lets her fall to the ground. She groans and passes out again, which suits him. He drags her along the ground to the shed, takes the tape from her legs.

Now that he has her here, he's not sure exactly what his plan is. He likes to kill them with his bare hands. The soft skin at the throat, the pulse as they pull for air, the look of terror and submission in their eyes: all of it gives him strength, power, pleasure. But usually they're cuddling up to him, want him close, they're not fighting him. And he has a feeling this one will put up a fight. On impulse he goes out and rummages around the other shed. There's a length of chain in there somewhere, he'd used it to tie down a load when he first moved out here.

He finds it. It's not too heavy, mid-size links, but it'll keep her quiet while he has a hit, thinks about how to handle this. He goes back, fixing the chain tightly around her ankle and then locking it around the leg of the workbench.

She's covered in vomit, it's disgusting – she'll have to clean herself up before he has his fun. He thinks about throwing some water over her but decides against it. Fills a bucket and leaves it within reach. Let her sort it out.

On his way out he sees the other body in the far corner. Goes over, drags it into the centre of the shed, almost within reach when she wakes up. 'Told you I knew where she was,' he says, laughing.

He locks the door to the shed as he leaves, shaking it hard to make sure it holds. Now he has time to treat himself to a pipe or two. She needs to come round, wake up properly, build up some fear, then he'll be in control.

Inside, he flops down on the couch and exhales in satisfaction. His plan worked. He opens the bag of meth and as he lights the pipe he warms through with pleasure. He's done it. He's gotten rid of the cop. He's safe. No one else knows.

· · ·

Barbara wakes in agony. Every bone in her body hurts but it's her head that incapacitates her. When she opens her eyes, the light slices in as sharp and cutting as a knife. Her skull feels as if it has been split, jolts of agony running down along her hair parting, into her forehead and behind her eyes in sharp, lightning-like bursts. The pain is so bad that she throws up, and then everything goes black again.

When she comes to, her head is still throbbing. This time she doesn't open her eyes fully, just squints a little. The room is swelteringly hot and her mouth is dry, her tongue swollen with thirst. She is lying on a dusty floor, a platoon of tiny black ants walking over her left wrist and inner arm. She blows at them, shakes her arm, noticing with shock that her hands are bound in front of her with some kind of tape. A few of the ants disappear, the majority march onwards, so she turns slightly and smears the arm against her torso and the tickling feel of them disappears. Her head aches and for a moment she can't remember where she is or why, but her rapidly rising fear drives her into action.

She starts to move, to manoeuvre slowly into a sitting position, and discovers there's also a chain around her leg. It takes her a long time, panting, her head in agony, before she's upright and leaning against the wall behind her. There's a bucket beside her filled with water.

She cups her hands as best she can, drinks four, five handfuls before she feels nauseous again and forces herself to stop. The water is warm, hot almost, and tastes of plastic, but it revives her. She throws a couple of handfuls over her face to cool down and wash away some of the vomit and to ease the throbbing, thrumming ache in her head.

She looks around and tries to understand where she is. Some kind of outbuilding, perhaps a shed. She's sitting on a dusty paved floor. The walls are corrugated aluminium, warm to touch. She moves her wrists back and forth, loosening the tape marginally, to give herself a bit more manoeuvrability. Panic rises within her – she's in trouble here but she doesn't know why, or even where she is. It hurts to think and she can't remember much. She wants to cry out, scream for help, but forces herself to take a deep breath. And then another. Calms herself and tries to remember.

She's in Australia. Rita is missing. The heat, the dust. Caloodie. Walker. Her head throbs. She was at the pub, having dinner. She breathes in. She went to bed and this morning she woke up and then . . . ? No matter how hard she tries, she draws a blank. She remembers getting out of bed, standing on the veranda, but nothing more.

The smell of her vomit is strong in the heat and she retches. There's nothing to throw up except bile that burns her throat. Afterwards she drinks again and clumsily wipes her face with her forearm, constrained by the way her hands are tied.

'Pull yourself together, Guerra,' she says out loud. She can't indulge her fear right now. She needs to figure out where she is and how – if – she can get away.

She tries to call out, 'Help. Help me,' but her voice is croaky and the sound is low and hoarse and next to useless. Anyway, it seems there's no one around outside. She listens intently and all she can hear is the lazy squawk of a crow, a rustle of leaves in a breeze and the occasional creak as the shed contracts or expands in the heat.

She looks around, trying to get a better sense of where she might be. The space is gloomy, not quite dark but it's difficult to see clearly. There are no windows, just traces of light that filter in under the walls, which begin a centimetre or so above the ground. The shed is quite large, wide enough to park two or three cars side by side. A tangled lace of cobwebs hangs between ceiling and walls.

The chain runs to her right, tethered to what looks like a large metal workbench. Her head is still throbbing and any movement rocks her equilibrium. Standing upright takes a long time. She leans against the wall breathing heavily, her eyes closed, letting the pounding in her head subside. She has to move very slowly, shuffling forward, one step at a time. The chain is nowhere near long enough to reach the doors, giving her perhaps a metre of movement at most. She walks slowly towards the workbench, stubbing her toe sharply on a raised paving stone, happy to be able to lean for support on the solid surface of the bench when she reaches it. Up close she can see that it has a wooden top, a series of drawers beneath it and square metal legs, as sturdy as a man's thighs. The top of the workbench is scarred and gouged from years of use and marked with oil and dabs of paint, but there are no tools visible. She tries the drawers; they're all locked.

As her eyes adjust to the gloom, she spots a bundle on the floor, between herself and the doors. She crawls in that direction, walking is too much for her head, and as she moves closer she sees that it's a body. There's no movement, the person lying completely still. She can see bare feet, black with dirt, ankles swollen, covered in bites, scabs and scratches. A pair of shorts, a striped top. Barbara stops still. Feels her hands and arms start to shake, feels her body quivering in fear. Rita. It's Rita. The moment the thought registers, she's scrabbling forward again, fast as she can, until the chain brings her up short, pulling hard at her ankle, Rita still out of reach.

'Rita! Rita! It's me, it's Barbara. Rita!' She's reaching out, calling out. 'Rita!'

36

Walker's grandmother is sitting up in bed, drinking tea and nibbling at a piece of cake for brekky, when Blair and the girls pop round on their way to school.

'You look like a queen, Granny,' says Ruby, Blair's youngest, which makes her laugh till she coughs, her eyes streaming.

Walker is worried about her. She's even paler than usual and her breathing is irregular. She'd taken a turn for the worse yesterday afternoon and it was bad enough last night that he and Michelle had called the doctor, who'd tried to talk her into going back to hospital. When she'd refused, he'd given her a morphine drip. Walker notices that she's pushing the button for another dose regularly. She's nearing the end, he senses it, but pushes the thought away. He's not ready to lose her.

After the others leave, she calls him into her room. She pats the side of the bed and he sits beside her. 'When I go, Lucas, make sure you still come back here from time to time. This is your home. This place is a part of you. It's important that you find your way back here. I'm going to leave the house to Michelle but if he was still alive it would have been half your dad's too. Michelle knows that. This will always be your home. You'll always be welcome here.'

'Ah, now, Grandma, don't talk like that.' He doesn't want to have this conversation, doesn't want to have to face it.

She grips his hand more tightly. 'I'm going, Lucas, and I'll go in peace if I know that you'll still come back here.'

'Of course I will, Grandma. This is home. You know that.' He pauses. 'I don't want you to go. Hold on a little longer? I still need you around.'

The saying of it makes his heart hurt. A dull throb. She's been more of a mother to him than anyone. She taught him everything that he values, everything that makes him the man he is. How to carry himself with honour, to stand up for himself, be gentle, be strong. Do no harm but take no shit. Even when he was far away, when he went to live with his mother and Richard, she was his lodestar. He looks at her lying there, and his heart aches.

'I'll be here in your heart,' she says, touching his chest gently. 'Always. Wherever you go. And in the meantime I'm still here in this bed. Can you get me a lemonade, I'm parched. And maybe another piece of that cake. Best thing about getting old – you can eat as much cake and drink as much lemonade as you want and no one can say one damn thing about it.' She cackles and coughs and he squeezes her hand, then fetches her the cake and drink. She sips at the lemonade but waves the cake aside. He puts it on the bedside table for later.

'You better go to work now,' she says, shooing him out of her room. 'I'll see you later.'

As he's driving to the hotel to see Barbara, he's wondering if he should be staying with Grandma instead, making the most of these last days. But he also wants to help Barbara. He'd texted her to let her know he'd be late this morning, but she hasn't replied. He's got good news for her. Rutherford is open to the idea of searching Jones's property. It should happen later today, once some details are ironed out with Queensland Police.

When he pulls up outside the hotel he looks at his phone again: still no answer from Barbara. The pub isn't open yet, it's only mid-morning and they're still cleaning, but Ali lets him in and he goes upstairs and knocks on the door of her room. There's no reply.

Ali hasn't seen her. 'She's usually up at sparrow's fart and gone before we open,' she says.

He goes to the bakery to see if she's there. No luck. He has a coffee, an egg-and-bacon sandwich to see him through the morning, and brings some lamingtons back to the house for Grandma, who's sleeping, her breathing fitful. He's staring at the board, worrying about Grandma, thinking of Barbara, failing entirely to concentrate on the case, when his phone rings.

'Oh, hello, this is Mary Wilson. Could I speak with DS Barbara Guerra?'

'She's not here right now,' he says. He doesn't recognise the name. 'This is DS Walker – can I help?'

'Um, yes, well, I spoke with your colleague on Saturday. We reported the abandoned car and she was asking me about the girl who disappeared near Hopeville.'

'Yeah?'

'Well, my son came to visit yesterday. I'm sorry it wasn't sooner but he's very busy in his new job and this really was the earliest he could do. I mean, it's been well over a year, so I don't think it's fair to ask him to upend his life.'

Walker is leaning back on his chair, looking out the window, listening with half an ear, waiting for her to get to the point. He doesn't have a clue what she's talking about. He says, 'Righto.'

'Oh. OK. Well, he found the dashcam video your colleague was looking for and she told me to call this number when we had it. If you give me an email address I can send it through.'

Walker sends his chair legs to the floor with a thump. He gives her his email and she sends it promptly; it's in his inbox a few minutes later. He watches the footage on fast-forward. Far in the distance he sees a white refrigerated truck by the side of the road and then pulling away. A moment later Matt Monroe's old red Holden comes into view, parked on the side of the road. The video shows the driver's car slowing and stopping and the truck disappearing from view up ahead. Once the car starts up, Walker uses fast-forward again – lots of the long, straight, empty road, no traffic in either direction until ten minutes later the truck becomes visible, still some way in front. Too far to read the registration but it's clearly a white refrigerated unit. The outskirts of Hopeville appear, then the main street. The car slows but the truck drives through, pulling away and out of sight, as the car turns right and stops in front of the police station.

Maybe with some image enhancement they might get the details of the registration. He rootles round in his mind for the name of the technician who has helped him with video enhancement in the past. Susie Cheever. Another woman who likes red lipstick. Happily married and delighted to flirt. She might do him a favour on this. He sends her a quick email:

> Hey Suse! Working on a case up north and the truck in this footage might be involved in the abduction and murder of a young woman. Any chance you can read the rego? Ta muchly, Lucas

He wants to show this to Barbara. He tries her number again but it's out of reach. He messages her:

> call me when you get this. got a new lead.

'Where the hell is she?' he says out loud.

He puts the phone to one side and goes to check on Grandma. She's still asleep, her skin a sickly green hue against the pink pillowcase. It hurts him to look at her. He walks back to the desk. He hasn't heard from Rutherford, but he's still hoping he'll sort out permission for this search today.

It's almost 2 p.m. He tries Barbara's phone again but it's still switched off. It's not like her not to be in touch. When a yellow Post-it with *Johnson's Transport* written on it in her handwriting flutters to the floor from the board on the wall, he picks it up and, for want of any better ideas, drives over to Johnson's. Perhaps she's there going through their files. If not, he'll ask them about Mount Isa and Barcaldine.

He parks beside two other cars in the haulage company's yard and heads into the Portakabin office. He recognises one of Paul's daughters sitting behind the reception desk but can't remember her name. 'G'day,' he says. 'Paul around?'

She nods. 'Yeah. Sorry, I don't know your name . . .'

'Walker. Lucas Walker.' He pulls out his ID and shows it to her.

She disappears through a frosted-glass door and a minute later Paul comes out, the girl in tow behind him.

'Orright, mate?' says Johnson.

'Just wondering if my colleague Barbara, the German one, has been in today.'

It's the girl that shakes her head. 'Nah,' she says.

'Right,' he says. His consternation grows; he'd been expecting to find Barbara here. Where the hell is she? Johnson and his daughter are looking at him. 'We were just after some information,' says Walker, 'wondering if one of your drivers might be able to help.'

'Yeah, your German cop was in at the weekend. Terri here's been looking into it. We ain't got much,' he says. 'Tell him, Terri.'

'Uh, yeah, well, here's the list.' She thrusts a piece of paper towards him. There are two names on it. 'No one was driving on the Smithton road last weekend when those backpackers went missing. Steve Burnett was picking up cattle in Hopeville on the day in 2021 that she asked me about and Darryl Foley might have passed through – he was on a run back from Brisbane.'

'Thanks,' says Walker. 'Barbara didn't tell you that we have some new information? We're looking at some dates in Mount Isa and Barcaldine.'

'Yeah,' says the girl. 'Well, she asked about the dates yesterday but it's a long while ago. I'm still looking for the information.'

Walker taps the piece of paper she's given him. 'Either of these two drive a refrigerated truck?'

'Nah,' says the girl, a slight flush creeping up her neck.

Johnson looks at her, shakes his head. 'Yeah, they bloody do. Christ, Terri, get with it. Foley, Darryl Foley, he drives our refrigerated unit.'

Walker looks at the sheet of paper; Foley could have been in the Hopeville area when Sheree disappeared. 'It's not that he's a suspect, but he might be able to give us information. Could you check the Mount Isa and Barcaldine dates for us too?'

'Gonna take me a couple more hours,' she says.

'Any chance I could get them quicker?'

'Go and have another look now, Terri,' says Johnson. 'I reckon you can find them pretty fast in that new system of yours.'

When the girl disappears Johnson looks at him, his eyes hard and angry. 'You picking on us because of who I am? Because I did time back in the day? I paid my dues, mate. I'm clean. Got my girls, got this business. We keep things straight down the line now.'

'It's nothing to do with you – I didn't even know you had form,' says Walker. 'We've got three girls missing in five years. We need to find out who's taking them. A truckie might be able to help us, that's all it is. If we've got someone like this out there, your girls aren't safe either. Think of it that way.'

As he's speaking, saying the words out loud, he's berating himself inside. His obsession with Markovich and the Vandals has stopped him following this up earlier. There's something ugly going on here, and he didn't listen to Barbara or read the signs properly.

. . .

Terri calls up the new dates on her system, starting with Barcaldine. She's crossing her fingers that there'll be no one, but Darryl's is the first name she sees. He'd been through Barcaldine twice around the dates she's got. She types in the Mount Isa dates and her stomach contracts when she sees Foley's name again. She can feel her face getting hot. She could just not tell them . . . But what if it's him? What if he's hurting these girls? Nah. He's not that kind of bloke. She thinks of the look on his face when he asked her out, the smile he gave her afterwards. He's not that kind of bloke. But she needs to talk to him. Needs to ask him for his side of the story.

She closes down the system and sits for a moment, rehearsing her words, then walks back out front. Her dad is in his office again, and she breathes a sigh of relief as she walks past. It's easy enough to lie to a cop, harder to get one past her dad.

The cop is waiting, sitting on one of the plastic chairs under the window, his legs stretched out long in front of him. He smiles at her when she opens the door. He has a mop of curly blond-brown hair, a good tan and a muscled chest and arms, visible under the pale-blue shirt he's wearing. He's slim and strong, not the bulky muscles of her dad. If he wasn't a cop, he'd be good-looking.

'Sorry,' she says. 'Those dates are too far back to be on our new system. I'm gonna have to dig out the paperwork. It'll take a while. Tomorrow arvo maybe.'

'OK, thanks,' he says, 'appreciate your help. But it's pretty urgent so better if you can get it to us quick as possible. Give me a call as soon as you can, yeah?'

She nods and watches him leave, can feel her face flushed and hot, her armpits sweaty; she was never much good at telling fibs. Gets herself a drink of cold water from the cooler in reception, gulps it down then crumples the plastic cup into the bin. She needs to talk to Foley today.

Her dad calls out to her as she walks back to her desk.

'Hey, Terri, whatcha tell 'im?'

'Nothin', Dad,' she calls back, not going into his office. 'Those dates are too far back. I need to check the paperwork – I'll do it soon as.'

She grabs her phone, scrolls down to find Foley's number. She's messaged him a few times since he asked her out on Saturday. He usually replies. Sometimes with a smile emoji, sometimes longer, more garbled messages that she tries and fails to decode. But he likes her, she knows it. She reads through his messages, feeling her heart flutter. She really wants to go out with him. There's no way he's got anything to do with this. She decides to call him instead of messaging and feels butterflies in her stomach. Maybe they can arrange a time for their drink too. When the phone goes to voicemail she feels equal parts relief and disappointment.

She walks to the far back of the office to make sure her dad can't hear, to leave a message. 'Hi, Darryl, this is Terri,' she says. 'Uhmm, can you call me please. We just had the cops here and I need to ask you something. It's kinda urgent. Umm, call me, not Dad. OK, bye.'

37

'We've got a problem,' says Markovich. He's standing in the shade in front of the main shed, holding the phone with his shoulder while he rolls a cigarette. He's talking to Tony Chisholm, a chief superintendent in Queensland Police. Big head honcho down in Brisbane, fingers in every pie. He costs them a shitload but he keeps the operation safe, even out here. 'There was someone snooping round out here over the weekend. The blokes woke up, the door to their room was open, noise outside, the dog barking like crazy. I sent a couple of 'em for a drive just to check. They thought they saw a vehicle . . .'

'I thought you had the place secure.'

'Yeah, well, I can't secure a thousand miles of bush.' No point telling him the idiots hadn't locked the shed, just bolted it shut. Fuckwits. Getting complacent out here, middle of nowhere. 'I told ya it was more difficult out here,' he says. 'Everyone knows everyone's business, they all want to come around, chat and nosy about. It's safer in a city.'

'You think this was someone local?'

Markovich looks down at the pale-cream piece of material he's holding; one of the blokes had found it fluttering on the barbed-wire fence of the home paddock.

'Reckon it might be that other copper. The Sydney one that

was sniffing around here. He paid a visit to Jones's place yesterday too. We had to bring forward the collection, pick it up last night, couple of days early, just in case he came back with a warrant. Jones doesn't want us storing stuff at his place for the foreseeable and I agree. We need to back away.'

'Walker's a problem. I can't find out who he's reporting to. I'm checking if he's from major crimes. Morpheus, even.'

'Yeah, I'm looking into it too. But we're gonna pack it up here anyways. If people are getting nosy, we need to move on. The truck is on its way back today – we'll be gone before morning.'

'Gone where?'

Markovich toys with not telling him. He's never liked working with the pigs. Greedy fuckers always have their noses deeper in the trough than anyone else. But he needs them. Needs them here, needs them at the coast.

'Down Surfers way. We got a few warehouses down there and a big chapter. No one will pay us any attention. Just need you to handle the local cops.'

'Yeah, leave that to me. Is this going to affect your supply?'

You mean is this gonna affect your pay packet, thinks Markovich. 'Nah. Like I said, last load's just gone, and we'll get set up pretty quick down there.'

'OK. Good. We'll talk later, then.'

Markovich calls Nick, his number two. 'That copper I asked you about – any updates?'

'Yeah, came through this morning. Looks like he's some kind of financial analyst for the Feds. Handles money laundering, fraud, dodgy corporates, that kind of thing. Spreadsheets and accounts, not on the streets.'

'He didn't look like no accountant to me,' says Markovich.

'Maybe it's not the same bloke. Hang on, I'll send you his file pic.'

The phone pings and Markovich opens the image. It's the same bloke alright. Few years younger, hair shorter and neater, wearing a suit and a tie.

'Yeah,' he says to Nick. 'That's him. What's he doing up here, then?'

'He's on sabbatical, family leave or something. Our man at the Feds says he's been given clearance from Foreign Affairs to act as family liaison for a pair of missing tourists out your way.'

'What are they putting an accountant on that case for? Doesn't make sense.'

'Yeah, nah, I don't know,' says Nick. 'But my bloke said it looked legit, a PR exercise – got a fall guy up there, just in case there's an international stink later on.'

Markovich ends the call, puts the roll-up between his lips. It all ties in with what the cop had told Tina. But still, he doesn't like it. Too neat. Maybe this bloke is just a pen-pusher and it was someone different paying them a midnight visit. Could be coincidence, but he doesn't believe in coincidence. Leaving now is the right move.

He calls Jason over. 'Get them others goin'. Start getting the stuff packed up. Truck's back this arvo, we're movin' out.'

'Righto, boss.'

He turns and walks towards the house. He's got one more call to make and he needs privacy for this one.

'Where we goin', boss?' Jason calls after him.

Markovich looks back over his shoulder. 'Back to fuckin' civilisation. Tell the others: tomorrow we'll be drinking in Surfers.'

• • •

Grogan's heartburn has been killing him. The whole last week he's been chewing pink Pepto-Bismol squares like an addict but his chest is still burning and his stomach pain isn't going away either. When he sees the number come up on his phone, the pain in his chest gets worse.

He decides to ignore the call. He's busy, working; maybe he can't pick up. When the phone stops ringing he feels a pleasurable surge of power. That'll show 'em. They need him. They rely on him.

The phone starts up again. Shit, shit, shit. He picks it up.

'Yeah, hello?' – as if he doesn't know who it is.

'Don't ignore my phone calls, I need you to pick up when I call.'

'I was just . . .'

'We've got a problem. Someone might be onto our little operation. Someone was snooping around at the sheds over the weekend. That Sydney DS, most likely. He was out at Angus's place too. What the fuck is going on? We're paying you to keep him away from our places.'

'He's a DS, I can't just tell him what to do.'

'Well, he's not just a DS and he's not from Sydney. He's from the Feds. You know what that means, right?'

'No?'

'It means most likely he's not here looking for these kids. It's a pretext. To get him close to our operation. Maybe they already know about us. About you.'

Grogan feels himself flush hot, then icy-cold. A trickle of sweat rolls down from his armpit. 'What do you mean? How can they know?' Grogan can hear the pitch of fear in his voice and doesn't like it.

'I don't know. But we're all fucked if they've worked it out.'

'But he can't be. He's a local bloke, he's here visiting his grandmother. That's legit – everyone knows him.'

'Of course he is. They'd need someone who wouldn't be suspicious. Can't send some hotshot Federal cop up with no business being here.'

'Fuck. Fuck. I knew there was something off about him. About this whole thing. I've never heard of oversight from Foreign Affairs before.'

'You need to tidy this up. If you still want a career, if you don't want to end up in the bin, you need to sort this out.'

There's a pause. 'Righto,' Grogan hears himself saying.

'Sort it and I might have some good news for you too.'

'Yeah?'

'There's a posting coming up down Surfers way. I need someone loyal there. You fix this, you make sure nothing goes wrong, that this Walker bloke isn't onto us, and the job's yours.'

The line goes dead.

Surfers Paradise. The answer to his prayers. Lisa will be over the moon. The girls too. This is why he does this shit. This is why. Surfers Paradise. A house by the canal. Days at the beach. Taking Lisa to the casino, the girls to Dreamworld. For the first time in days his stomach isn't hurting and his chest isn't burning.

He picks up his phone and dials Walker's number. The phone rings a couple of times and goes to voicemail. He leaves the office and gets in the car, drives around the corner to the bakery.

'You seen Walker today?' he asks Ann, one of the women who works in the bakery. 'You know, Lucille's grandson . . .'

'Yeah, he was in earlier. Just before lunchtime.'

He goes over to the pub. No sign of Walker. Asks Mike the same question.

'Yeah, he was in earlier, looking for Barbara.'

'Righto. Did he say where he was going?'

'Nah, mate, no matter how many times I've asked him, he doesn't keep me updated on his schedule.'

Grogan doesn't bother twisting his mouth into a smile. 'Let him know I'm looking for him if he comes back in, yeah?'

Mike nods. 'What's he done, then?' he asks.

This time Grogan forces himself to smile. 'Just get him to call me, yeah?'

38

Walker folds the piece of paper with the two drivers' names on it and puts it in his pocket. He's pretty sure the girl was lying to him; her face was flushed red and she looked nervous. He unlocks the ute and sits in the driver's seat, keys in hand. Something about the names on the list is bugging him. He pulls the paper out again and looks at them: *Stephen Burnett, Darryl Foley*. He closes his eyes, lets his mind drift, the names turning over. There's something he's forgotten, something he's overlooked. Both names are on the board, but there's something else. He thinks a moment longer, gives up, puts the keys in the ignition and looks over his shoulder before reversing. A white Hilux, parked in front of the hardware store on the opposite side of the road, sparks his memory and it comes to him in a fast moment. Foley.

He'd stopped the bloke on the highway, the day after Rita and Berndt disappeared. He turns off the engine, flicks through his notebook, finds it. Darryl Foley. It was a white Hilux – he's written the registration in his book too. Shit. How had he forgotten about Foley? Barbara had written his name on the board but it hadn't triggered anything.

But his first priority right now is to find Barbara. He needs to set his mind at rest about not being able to contact her. Then they can look into this Foley bloke.

At the pub, Mike is behind the bar and sends him in search of Ali, who is surrounded by paperwork in a back office.

'Could you go up and check on Barbara for me? She still hasn't surfaced today and she's not answering her phone and I'm worried about her.'

'Sure thing, love,' says Ali. 'But I don't reckon she's here. The girls cleaned the room already and I'm pretty sure they'd have told me if she was sick or something.'

They walk up the winding wooden stairs together. Ali and Mike have done a good job with this pub. The stairs are sanded and glossy and there's a pleasant smell of wax and furniture polish in the air. A pale-pink runner up the middle is worn but spotlessly clean. On the landing a pair of original doors hide the guest area from public view. The doors have been restored, the colourful decorative stained-glass panels glinting in the sunlight. Ali pushes them open and they walk into a small lounge area with three easy chairs surrounding a coffee table and a bookshelf with a selection of paperbacks up against the far wall. The wooden floors of the corridor are as glossy as the stairs and the lights are vintage-looking with decorative white glass curving over the bulbs. Ali stops outside room 12 and knocks on the door.

'Hello, Barbara, are you in there?' she calls.

There's no answer. She knocks again, then pulls out a chain of keys, finds the right one and opens the door.

Barbara's room is spotless. Walker looks quickly around. The bed has been made, the t-shirt and trousers she'd been wearing yesterday are draped over her grey suitcase at the end of the bed, a pair of trainers sitting beside it. Her iPad is on the desk, but her bag and notebook aren't there.

'Did she say anything to you about what she was planning to do today?' he asks.

'Nah, nothing. She was in the bar last night. She seemed better.

Said there were some Brisbane coppers getting involved? She was chatting with Hippy and Paul Johnson, mostly.'

Ali closes and locks the door and nods hello to another guest, a young bloke, perhaps mid-twenties, wearing a bright-blue t-shirt branded *Queensland Water*, who is opening the door to the room next to Barbara's.

'You haven't seen Barbara, the woman who's staying here today, have you?' asks Walker.

The young bloke shakes his head. 'Nah, I heard her talking to a bloke quite early this morning, but. Must have been around six a.m. – I was getting ready for work. They left shortly after. I was still getting dressed.'

'You're sure?' says Walker, pushing back a pang of something like jealousy. As far as he knows there's no one else Barbara would invite to her room.

'Yeah, pretty sure. I heard him knocking. It woke me up, I thought it was my door. They were talking for a few minutes, then I heard the door close and them walking down the corridor.' He nods his head in the direction of a door at the far end.

'Early-morning exit,' says Ali, seeing the question on Walker's face. 'When the pub's closed guests can leave that way.'

'Did you hear what they were talking about?' asks Walker.

'Nah,' says the Queensland Water bloke, shaking his head.

Walker goes down the corridor to the exit door. It opens on to an external staircase leading to the side car park and the back of the bottle shop.

'Is this door always open?' he asks Ali.

'Pretty much,' she says. 'There's a lock on it but we leave it open in case someone is coming back late or leaving early . . .'

'So someone could come in here, someone who wasn't a guest?'

'If they knew about it, I guess they could. But they can't get down into the pub or anything, those doors are locked, so why would they?'

Walker has a bad feeling. Someone woke Barbara early in the morning, she's gone with him, without a call or a message, and now her phone is off or out of range.

He walks back to room 10, bangs on the door. The bloke pulls it half-open; he's taken off his clothes, standing there in his underpants and socks, using the door as cover.

'Did you see the man who she left with?' asks Walker. 'Or recognise his voice?'

The bloke shakes his head. 'Nah. I don't know anyone out here anyway. I'm not from round here – I'm only here a couple of days for work.'

'Can I get your name, the name of your boss and where you were working today?'

'What for?'

'Standard procedure,' says Walker, his eyes over the man's shoulder into the room beyond. It's identical to Barbara's, with the bed on the opposite side of the room. Ali is restless beside him, shifting from foot to foot.

'Yeah, OK, whatever. Billy French. I was working out at the Lightfoot Dam all day, checking the wall. You can check with Matthew Simpson at head office. I've been sending in readings and talking with him all day.'

Walker writes down the names. 'Thanks,' he says.

'Thanks, Billy, and sorry to bother you,' says Ali. 'Have a beer on me when you come down to the bar later, alright?'

Billy nods and shuts the door fractionally harder than he needs to.

Ali turns and glares at Walker. 'Look, I know you're worried, but you can't go interrogating our guests like that. They haven't done nothing.'

'How do you know?' says Walker. 'Barbara is missing and could be in trouble. And whoever she's with, it's either a guest or someone who gained entry to the pub because your security is next to useless.'

He strides down the corridor away from her, taking the stairs at a half-run, turning right into the bar. Hippy is there, a beer in front of him, watching the keno numbers on the screen opposite with the concentration of a Zen master.

'Hippy,' he says loudly, breaking the spell. 'You talked to Barbara last night. Did she tell you what she was up to today?'

Hippy swivels his gaze away from the screen, towards Walker. 'Nah, mate, we don't talk business anymore. I'm trying to keep the poor girl's chin up, stop her thinking about it all for a little while.'

Walker calls to Mike, who's pouring a beer, his back to them. 'Mike, did you talk to Barbara? Any idea where she might be today?'

Mike finishes the pour with a deft flick of his wrist, turns and shakes his head. 'Maybe try Paul Johnson? She was talking with him before she left last night.'

Another possibility occurs to Walker.

'You got any CCTV at the back of the hotel there, by those exit stairs?'

Mike delivers the beer to a burly bloke that Walker doesn't know, wipes his hands on a bar towel and comes over to stand in front of him.

'The bottle-o cameras cover some of the car park. Not the stairs but the car park.'

'Does the camera run all night? Or only when you're open?'

'Yeah, we leave it on. Had a few fools trying to break the shutters in the past so we leave it on now.'

'Can I have a look at this morning's footage? Around six a.m.?'

'Knock yourself out, mate, but I can't leave the bar right now. You'll need to ask Ali.'

As Walker goes, Mike calls after him, loud enough to make sure the rest of the bar can hear: 'Dave Grogan was in earlier, looking for you. Urgent, he says.'

Walker wonders if Grogan might know where Barbara is. He needs to call him directly and find out. First things first. He finds Ali back in the pub's office. He tells her what he needs. 'If they walk across the car park, maybe we can see who she left with.'

Ali rolls her chair to the desk with the computer on it. She boots it up, switches on the screen and they watch the start-up process flicker across it.

'You really reckon she's in trouble?' He can hear concern in her voice.

'I hope not but it's not like her to be out of touch. And she doesn't know anyone to leave with, does she?'

'Only Hippy, and I don't reckon he's a morning kind of person,' says Ali as she pulls up the CCTV on screen. 'Six a.m., right?'

They watch from 5.30 until well after 6. There's no sign of Barbara.

'Start a bit earlier – see if we can see someone coming in,' says Walker.

The camera captures the drive-through bottle shop; bright-yellow XXXX-branded shutters and a triangular slice of the car park, including the rear wall. The stairs aren't visible. The car park is gloomy, the night lights barely illuminating it. But as the early light of dawn rises, a man walks through at the far edge of the screen.

'Stop there,' says Walker, and Ali hits the pause button. It's a fleeting glimpse: three strides and he's gone. They run through frame by frame. His legs and some of his torso are visible but his face never comes into shot. He walks through the far corner of the screen and disappears from sight.

'He's come out of the back lane,' says Ali.

'What's back there?'

'Nothing, really. It's where we keep our bins.'

Walker replays the frames. There's nothing particularly distinctive about the bloke: lean frame, skinny legs in a pair of jeans, a black t-shirt. 'You recognise him?' he asks Ali.

She shakes her head. 'Nah. Not much to see, is there? Let me ask Mike.'

She leaves the office and a minute later Mike comes in. Walker plays the frames a couple of times.

Mike purses his lips. 'I couldn't say a hundred per cent, probably not even eighty per cent, but it might be Darryl Foley. He's tall and skinny and he was in last night wearing a black t-shirt like that.'

39

Barbara keeps calling Rita's name, first loudly, then more quietly, but Rita doesn't respond. She wants to reach out, wants to hold her, but she's just short. She pulls at the chain in frustration.

She can't give up. Rita is here. She's noticing more details now that her eyes have adjusted to the gloom. The pain in her head is down to a dull throb. The floor of the shed is covered in dried blood, huge patches of it, opposite the workbench and in the centre of the room and a trail of it leading to the door. It reminds her of an abattoir. The image comes unbidden and she suppresses it quickly.

The shed is unbearably hot, and there's no way to cool down, no breeze, no respite. It's rank with the smell of vomit, of urine, faeces and blood. Her nausea rises. She spies the bucket of water and crawls over and drinks the warm, plastic-tainted liquid, then splashes some more over her face.

She sits as near as she can to Rita, calling her name softly, she's not sure for how long, when she notices a change to the noise outside. The birdsong has stopped and a second later she hears footsteps and then a rattling at the door. Instinctively she scoots back, as far away from the doorway as it's possible to get, her back against the tin wall. The door opens and the long barrel of a gun pokes in.

'Stand back, bitch, or I'll shoot.' As she hears his voice, the memories of this morning return. The man in her room, telling her he knew where Rita was, leaving with him, walking down the wobbly stairs at the back of the pub. Though his voice has a different timbre from this morning – more excited, higher-pitched.

The metal door of the shed clangs wide open and he's a black outline, silhouetted against the bright light of the outside. She winces, squinting her eyes against the brightness.

He's holding a rifle, keeping the barrel trained on her. 'I see ya found the pressie I left for ya,' he says, and laughs. 'Told ya I knew where she was.'

'Please,' she begs, 'please, let me hold her. Just for a minute.'

His smile dies. 'What for? Stupid bitch went and died on me, didn't she. Couldn't wait for me to get back.'

The nausea in Barbara's stomach turns to a cramping, twisting pain. Rita is dead. The shock of it distracts her from the man at the door, her eyes drawn to Rita's body on the floor in front of her. She's dead. Her little sister is dead.

She wants to scream, to cry. Rita is dead. Her greatest fear. She'd maybe even known for a while, suspected that it must be so, not to have any news, or any sightings, but she'd pushed the thought away. Now, to hear it from him, to know the horror Rita must have faced, it's all she can do not to throw herself at him, beat him to death with her bare hands.

His voice, his shouting, penetrates slowly. She looks back at him. He's jabbing the gun at her, his face angry and twisted. His eyes look huge and his feet are moving in a silent dance. Barbara can feel the hot tin of the wall at her back as she pushes herself as far from him as possible. He's manic, high on something.

After a moment his face relaxes a little and the twisted smile returns.

'Yeah, I'm going to have some fun with you. You're not as pretty as she was but you're a pig, and that makes up for it.'

He looks at her as if he's waiting for a reaction, but she stays quiet. A frown appears between his eyes. 'Not scared, hey, pig? Reckon I didn't mean it?' He steps suddenly forward, pointing the rifle in her direction, and she pulls back, the wall behind her shuddering and clanging as her weight hits it. He fires, the bullet puncturing the tin wall above her, the sound exploding in the shed, and she cowers, putting her bound arms in front of her face as the noise rises and travels and spreads in the space.

'That's the ticket. Now you're scared, pig, now you're scared.'

She's trying to think of the best way to defend herself, how to survive if he starts shooting, her mind racing, adrenaline surging through her, wondering if she can make it to the workbench, take cover there. He watches her cower, laughing with a rising hysteria, pointing the rifle at her. Then the laughter stops. Cut off as if by a switch.

'You cops think youse are so clever but you ain't. I'll get rid of ya, the way I got rid of him, and no one will ever find ya.'

She's shivering now, fear making her ice-cold, despite the heat. He's crazy, he's high. She can see it in his eyes. She cowers lower. There's nowhere to hide but the instinct to make herself small is overriding.

'That's it, pig, now you're scared,' he says again. 'She was too – pissed herself every time she saw me. Especially after that wanker she was with died. Then she knew I was serious. And now ya know what's coming. Now it's your turn.' His voice is low; he rubs his left hand hard up and down his right arm. Without warning, he steps back and pulls the door shut with a violent clang behind him. She hears a bolt and a lock click and then his footsteps recede.

In the aftermath her body is riven with shock. She's shaking and shivering, crying. Rita was with this man, alone with him for days. He killed Berndt, killed Rita and now he means to kill her.

She drags herself back to the water, drinks again, rationing herself to a couple of mouthfuls, then inspects the chain around her leg more closely. It has heavy links and is tied tight, digging into the skin around her ankle. She tries to move it down, hoping to pull her foot out, but it's too tight. It barely moves. She succeeds only in tearing the skin of her ankle; a thin roll of it peels over before the chain sticks again. She follows it to the other end and finds that it's locked, looped around one leg of the workbench, not fixed to the wall. The lock is new, heavy, and she has nothing that might help her pick it. She looks more closely at the bench. Perhaps if she can lift it an inch or so, she can pull the chain from under it and free herself that way. She bends her knees, leaning her shoulder under the worktop, and pushes with all her might. The bench doesn't move. Not even a shudder runs through it. She tries again and again and again, until she has to sit, shaking and exhausted.

He's tied her to it for good reason. The metal bench, its wide drawers probably filled with tools, weighs a ton. She tries one more time, putting her legs straight behind her, her shoulder under the lip of the bench, and pushing with all her weight up against it. She feels it shiver slightly but nothing more. She won't lift it. Panic threatens; she can feel her heart beating fast and she's sweating. If she can't move this, if she can't get free, he'll kill her too.

She forces herself to sit and think, to breathe deeply. Imagine this is a training session. Just a routine training session. There is a solution to the problem, Guerra, she hears the instructor saying. You need to calm down and think.

She's sitting there, assessing her options, when she hears a sound. A low moan, an exhalation from behind her. Barbara swings her head round, fear coursing through her like ice. Someone's here.

But there's no one, just Rita. As she listens, she hears it again. A soft, low moan. It's Rita. Rita's alive. Joy, hope, excitement wash through her. Rita's not dead. She's not too late. She needs to comfort her. She crawls forward, calling, 'Rita, Rita, I'm here', but Rita doesn't respond. She reaches the end of her chain, strains forward, calling Rita's name.

She has to get free. She needs to hold Rita, touch her, make her better. But the solid immovability of the bench taunts her. She goes closer, inspects it and the paving stones on which it sits, and an idea comes to her. The pavers are brick-sized and probably three centimetres or so thick, laid in a herringbone pattern. Perhaps moving the two stones in front of the one on which the leg rests will help her pull that one out too, despite the weight of the bench. And if she can do that, she'll be able to slip the chain under and off. Moving the stone under just one leg hopefully won't cause the bench to tilt into the small gap beneath.

She sits beside one slightly raised paver, the one she stubbed her toe on, and runs her fingers in the dirt around it. The dirt is not compacted and she can clear a reasonable depth but not quite enough to lever it out. She needs a stone or a tool of some kind to dig deeper, to dig under. Taking it slowly, she begins a search of the shed, crawling as far as the chain allows, looking for something, anything, that might help save her life. Right at the edge, where the walls finish just above the ground, she sees a small triangular piece of glass.

She lies down, uses her fingers like chopsticks, and pulling and pushing and twisting as best as she can tries to bring it inside. With her hands still tied together, it's difficult to grab it. Twice she has it and twice she drops it. Beads of sweat are running down her forehead, falling in her eyes. She pulls her arms back, wipes her face on her shoulder and tries again. This time, when she gets hold of it, she works slowly, centimetre by centimetre, turning and pulling it inwards. It catches on the edge of a paving stone but she holds firm, twists it again and brings it up. It's small, shorter than her thumb and not much wider, but it's something.

She tries using it to cut through the tape round her wrists but the way he's tied them gives her no leverage, so she has to awkwardly scrape the glass back and forth around the four sides of the paver, using her bound hands. She moves as fast as she can, digging deeper on each side until she feels the stone move slightly. She angles the glass under one corner and the paver tips a little. She jams her fingers under, rocks and pushes it as best as she can. With her hands taped together she struggles to free it but finally one short side breaks loose and slowly she's able to pull it out. One more to go before she gets to the one on which the leg of the workbench is standing.

She takes a break, gets as close as she can to Rita, calls her quietly: 'Rita! I'm here, Rita. It's Barbara.' But Rita doesn't move or respond. She's wondering if she dreamt that exhalation, that moan. No. Rita is alive. She has to get free. Rita is here, just out of reach. And she doesn't have much time. He'll come back. And he'll hurt them, she's sure of it.

40

He's had a great day, a successful day, one of the best days of his life. Picking up the pig had been easier than he'd thought. They think they're so clever but they're no match for him.

He lies on the sofa, toking up, planning. He spends so much time here that he's made a permanent curve in the brown velour, which cradles him, warming him like the arms of a lover.

He needs to kill her and he's not sure he can do it by hand. There's something about her he doesn't like, doesn't want to touch. He'll put a bullet in her, that makes more sense. Then he needs to get rid of them both and take off. Head west. Or maybe he should hang around for a week or two before he goes. It'll look suspicious if he just ups and leaves. But he's feeling stronger than he ever has and he knows he can get away with this, no problem. He's way ahead of the cops, he's way ahead of them all. He's in charge now.

He'd been three years old when his father walked out the door and never came back. After that, his mum turned to one man after another and it was always his fault when they left. The first time, he'd probably been five or six, asleep in the back bedroom when he was woken by raised voices, heard the crash of things being thrown against the wall, her voice screaming abuse as the man left the house, slamming the door, his car coughing into life and revving away round the corner in an angry roar. He'd gone into the kitchen to find her. She was standing at the back door, screaming angry curses into the dark night, holding a bottle of Bundaberg Rum by the neck. The floor was covered in broken crockery and glass.

'Mum?' He was crying with the shock of it all.

She'd picked up the bottle, tipped it up into her mouth, and finding it empty had thrown it with all her force onto the floor, where it shattered, brown shards of glass cutting his feet, his legs, his arms and face. He'd screamed in horror and she'd walked over and grabbed his pyjama top and shoved him into the hallway.

'It's all your fault, you useless piece of shit. Always hanging around the house, whining, crying, needing something. You drove your dad away, now you've driven my chance at happiness away too. Get out of my sight, you little turd. I wish you'd never been born.'

Her tirades were worse when it was just the two of them, when there was no one else for her to direct her anger at, so he was always thankful when another man appeared, even when those men cuffed him in the head, or took their belts to his back. He could always walk away from a beating, but her voice, her taunts, her hatred, still reverberate in his skull on bad days.

He'd been almost sixteen, tall and lanky for his age, the last time one of her men had tried to hit him. He'd had no real technique, but the force of his anger was so powerful, the release of years of disgust and hatred so intense, that he'd pummelled the bloke, some drunkard as usual, until he was lying prone and silent in the living room, his face a bloody mess.

He'd bent down, pulled the bloke's wallet out of his back pocket. She'd flown at him - it was his taking the money, not the beating, that had angered her, of course - but he'd downed her too with a swing of his right arm. She'd fallen, whimpering, holding her face. It had given him less satisfaction than he'd hoped for. He'd gone to his room, thrown a couple of t-shirts in his sports bag and left the rickety wooden cottage on the outskirts of Charters Towers, and never gone back.

He'd worked as a labourer on building sites in Townsville for a few years, then landed a job in the mines out west. They'd trained him to drive the heavy mining vehicles and he was making plenty of money until he turned up drunk one day, dropped a load, almost killed a supervisor. He was fired and broke, all the money gone on drink and good times. He'd hitched south, no clear destination in mind, and a truckie had talked him into driving for a living.

'Free and easy, mate,' he'd said. 'No boss, just the wide-open road in front of you. Save up for your own truck and you'll earn plenty enough cash to live a good life.'

He'd found work with Paul Johnson, driving the refrigerated rig, but he'd never managed to save any dosh. He'd found meth here too and it relieved him of both the cash and the need for a future. Planning for the next pipe was enough.

The first woman he'd killed had been an accident, but the power of it was intoxicating. He'd killed her and it had silenced his mother's voice too, all in one simple, pleasurable moment. Whenever he's had the chance he's done it again, and he's never come close to getting caught.

It's risky taking the pig, he knows that. Likely to cause a very big stir and so close to home too. They'll be looking all over for her. He's always been careful until now, and the pigs couldn't find a fucken tree in a forest, if they even bothered looking. But this is different. He's coming down a little, and the reality of what he's done, abducting a cop, killing a cop, is growing on him.

He thinks back to the messages from Terri Johnson and the drivers' group yesterday evening. Perhaps the pigs are already onto him. On their way here. He leans over, picks up his phone from the coffee table, but there's no bloody signal, of course. And his radio is still out of order. Fuck. Fuck. What if they're coming for him? Anxiety courses through him. He kicks out at the table in a flash of anger; the pipe, the empty tinnies, the rest of the shit on top of it, clatter across the living room floor.

Terri Johnson. It comes to him in a flash. She's a soft touch, she fancies him, and he's been stringing her along, even invited her for a drink. Silly bitch. It's as much to get at Paul as anything else. He's tried to be a mate to Paul, but Paul's not interested, has always liked Steve Burnett better. Gives Burnett more drives, invites Burnett for beers and barbies. So getting under Terri's skin is an easy way to give a big fuck-you finger to Paul. And now she'll come in handy. She'll know what's up.

He needs to talk to her. He usually picks up a few bars of signal about twenty K from town, a half-hour drive, no more. Grabs his keys. Gonna sort this out. Get a heads-up.

First he checks the shed is properly locked. Rattles the door. It's solid, she's not getting out. Then drives, fast, towards town. He's panicking the whole time about what the cops might know, thinking he should be driving west, getting the fuck out of here. His arms itching, his heart beating too fast. He realises he's got a signal when his phone buzzes on the passenger seat. A moment later it buzzes again, vibrating across the seat and dropping to the floor. Fuck, fuck, fuck. They're onto him for sure. He slams on the brakes, the car skidding as he pulls onto the gravel verge. Leans over, picks up the phone, sees a missed call and messages from Terri. The last message leaps out at him:

Need 2 talk 2 u urgent, pigs here.

Fuck. Presses his thumb on the unlock button and opens the message app.

Hey Darryl! can u call me pls

Need 2 talk 2 u urgent, pigs here. Call me dont call dad.

Hands shaking, he dials her number.

'Hey Darryl,' she answers. He can almost see her blushing at the other end of the phone.

'Hey Terri, my love.' He forces a smile into his voice. 'You in some kind of trouble with the pigs?'

'Nah, nah, it's not me. They were here asking about . . . asking about our drivers. Some girls got themselves killed in Hopeville, Barcaldine and the Isa and they want us to check if any of our drivers was around. I checked and, uhm, well, on the dates they're looking for you were there, at all of them places.'

He feels cold, as if a flow of icy water has been injected into his veins. His stomach turns to stone.

'What are ya saying, Terri? You think I killed some girls? How can ya say that? I thought we were mates.'

'Nah, course not. I know you didn't do it. I know it wasn't you. Course not. That's why I called. But they want us to tell 'em who we got and, well, I dunno what to tell 'em.'

He is breathing as calmly as he can. 'What does Paul reckon?'

'He doesn't know how to work the system – I'm the only one who knows how to use it and I haven't told him. You know how he is sometimes. He'll start thinkin' the worst and even if it's nothin', well, he'll have you out . . .'

'Righto. Thanks, Terri. I mean, I didn't do nothin' but it wouldn't look good, you're right.' He pauses again. He needs to stall her. Needs time to get the fuck out of here. Needs her not to say anything to Paul, to the pigs. 'Look, love, do ya want to meet for that bevvie maybe? I can tell you where I was on them dates – for sure it's a mix-up. I've been looking forward to you and me getting together, so maybe we can do it tonight. I mean, if ya got time . . .'

'Nah, yeah, Darryl, that'd be great. Yeah, defo.'

'How about a bit later on. I'll pick ya up around seven.'

'OK.' She sounds a bit breathless. 'OK. Listen, it's better not to pick me up at the house. Better not to tell Dad yet that we're going out' – she pauses – 'well, for a drink, ya know. Can ya pick me up outside the school? The main gate. It's just down the road.'

313

'Sure I can, love, sure I can.'

He throws the phone down on the seat beside him. They know about the other girls. He breaks out in a sweat, cold and icy; the ants inside his skin are back, crawling and itching. Pulls the car in a tight circle on the road, steps on the accelerator, heading away from town. He needs to get out now, go west, out to the Pilbara or somewhere where they need drivers and aren't too fussy about where you came from as long as you've got your licence.

He scratches at his arm until the skin tears and bleeds. The sting of it, the bite of the scratch, calms him a little. They haven't asked for him. They don't know about him. Only Terri has his name and she won't say nothing. That's the good thing about fat bitches, they're grateful for any attention, if you smile and play nice you don't even need to fuck 'em to get them onside. He has some time.

And he's still got the pig and her sister at his place. What to do? He could leave them in the shed, just fuck off. But he's owed. The dead bitch and that fucken hippy, they're the cause of all this shit. And he wants another hit before he leaves. Wants to terrorise the pig a little too, have some fucken fun. Better not to leave any evidence for the Brisbane pigs to find anyway. He'll have his fun, kill the pig, then head west, take both their bodies with him, dump them somewhere on the way. They'll never find them.

He pulls up in front of the house, driving too fast, hitting the brakes late, the back sliding. Goes straight inside and to the sofa, finds the pipe and the bag in the mess on the floor and tokes up. The ritual of filling and heating the pipe, the smell of it, the taste of it: he's calm and then he's on fire. Goes to the kitchen, finds the knife he uses to skin roos after he's been hunting, the one with the long sharp blade. He weighs it in his hand: that'll do nicely. He wants her clothes off. Wants to check out her body in the flesh and to show her how it feels when you can't fight back, when you're powerless. Yes, that'll do nicely as a starter before the main course.

41

'You're sure?' asks Walker. 'This is Foley?'

'Nah, like I said, not that sure,' says Mike. 'I mean, all I can see is his jeans and t-shirt, could be a lot of people.'

'But Foley was wearing something like this? It could be Foley?'

'It could be Foley,' agrees Ali. 'He's skinny like that.'

Walker looks again at the screen, trying to remember the bloke. He was sitting in a car and all Walker can visualise is a ginger beard, longish hair. But he's now heard Foley's name twice in twenty minutes and he'd been on the road where Rita Guerra and Berndt Meyer had disappeared. That's a lot of coincidence.

He pauses, not really wanting to share anything with Mike and Ali but needing answers. 'Where's Foley live, do you know?'

Mike shakes his head. 'Can't help ya, mate. I don't reckon he lives in town. He sometimes stays here when he has a few too many.'

'Did he stay here last night?'

'Nah, not last night,' says Ali. 'Actually, now I think of it, he left pretty early last night, so probably this isn't him' – she gestures with her head towards the screen. 'He'd have no reason to be back here early in the morning.'

No reason, thinks Walker, unless he was looking for Barbara. He leaves the pub at a half-run, drives back to the house, speeding through the mostly empty streets, hand on the horn as he runs a stop sign. He pulls up in front of the house, slams the car door and takes the three steps up to the veranda in one leap. Michelle is in the kitchen but he doesn't pause, goes straight into the back room and powers up his laptop, cursing as he waits for the system to load, the AFP logo slowly spinning as its various firewalls and security systems do their thing.

'Come on . . .' He slaps at the desk in frustration, and beside him Ginger gives a quick bark in support. He drops his hand and strokes the soft curves of her head.

The system loads and he types in Foley's name, looking for an address, any information, any previous. There's no mention of him on the system. Not even a speeding ticket to his name.

He flips through his notebook and finds Foley's registration number, enters it into the Austroads database. An Emerald address comes up, dated some six years ago.

Paul Johnson must have an address for his employee. Walker stands and strides out the door, back to the car. He opens the driver's-side door and Ginger whines in supplication. 'Come on, then,' he says, slapping the seat in invitation. She's up and into the cab in an instant, moving over to the passenger seat, sitting up proudly beside him. He drives to the truck depot but it's already closed. He checks his phone: almost 5 p.m., perhaps he's just missed them. He digs in his pocket for the business card he'd picked up from the front desk earlier and dials the mobile phone contact listed.

The phone rings and rings. He holds on. He'll dial the number every minute all night until he gets an answer if need be.

'Johnson's,' says a man, irritation in his voice.

'This is DS Walker, we met earlier today. I urgently need to talk to Darryl Foley and I'm looking for a home address.' There's no time for pleasantries. If Foley is the man they're looking for, he's had Barbara since this morning. Walker forces his thoughts away from speculation. He needs to take action, not think about ifs and maybes.

'Is this to do with them women gone missing? Terri said we don't have anyone in those areas on them dates.'

'No. My partner, Barbara Guerra, is missing and she was last seen early this morning with someone resembling Foley. I need to talk to him. I'm worried about her safety.'

There's a short silence at the other end of the phone. 'The bloke's a wanker but I don't reckon he'd go in for hurting a cop or whatever else,' says Johnson. 'Hasn't got it in him. Full of bullshit and hot air.'

'Fair enough, but I still need to rule him out. I just need to pay him a quick visit and it'll be done.'

'I'm at home. All that information is at the office. Can we do this in the morning?'

'No, we can't. A woman is missing and it's possible your employee is involved in her disappearance. We need to resolve this right now.'

'Righto, mate, righto. I'll meet you down there in ten minutes.' Johnson hangs up.

Walker drums his hand on the steering wheel, willing him to arrive. He tries Barbara's phone again but it's still off or out of range. When Johnson arrives, the girl, Terri, is on the passenger seat beside him. Her eyes and nose are red, and she looks at Walker with undisguised dislike.

'Terri'll find the information for you,' says Johnson, pulling a huge wad of keys from a clip on his belt and opening the door. 'Get a move on, girl – your mum'll have dinner on the table for us at five-thirty.'

Terri sniffles and disappears into the back office.

Johnson shakes his head at her back. 'She's got a crush on that idiot,' he says to Walker. 'She didn't want to give you his address, says you're picking on him, that he hasn't done nothing. I don't like the bloke much, never have, but I reckon she's right. He's all hot air. Got no ticker.'

Walker's not interested in discussing the case, but he says: 'If he's involved, he's extremely dangerous. We're looking into the deaths of three women. You should keep her well away from him.'

Johnson fixes a steely eye on him. 'He won't go near my girl. He's not that much of an idiot.'

They fall into silence, the only sound the occasional gurgle of the water cooler on its pedestal beside the door. The room is hot and stuffy with the air conditioner off. Johnson stands by the reception desk, Walker pacing back and forth, trying to hold his frustration at bay. After a couple of minutes they hear the sound of a filing door slam shut and the girl's footsteps coming back up the corridor.

'About bloody time,' says Johnson. The girl ignores him, fixing a glare on Walker as she thrusts a piece of paper at him. Walker looks at the address: it's a property out of town, by the sixty-five-kilometre mark.

'This up to date?' he asks, not wanting to drive all that way on a wild goose chase.

She shrugs. 'It's all we got.'

Johnson looks hard at her. 'You know where he lives, Terri?'

She is close to tears. 'No, I don't. I know he lives out of town, that's all, so this must be it. Why do you want him, anyway? He hasn't done nothin'.'

'Just ruling him out,' says Walker. 'Not accusing him of anything.'

'He wouldn't have hurt them girls, he's not like that,' she says. 'It's a coincidence ...'

'What's a coincidence?' says Johnson. 'Terri, what are you talking about?'

'Nothin',' she says, but she's flushing, her face bright pink.

'He was in those towns on the dates those girls went missing, wasn't he?' Walker says.

'It's a coincidence!' She's shouting. 'He's a good bloke, you all pick on him but he's nice to me, he's always nice to me. You haven't seen what he's really like.'

'For fuck's sake, Terri, what are you talking about?' Paul Johnson walks over to his daughter and grabs her arms. 'Was Foley in those towns where them girls disappeared?'

She twists away. 'Let go of me.'

'Answer me, Terri – answer me now.'

'Not all of them, not all of them. Not the two from near here.' She's crying, her face red and twisted.

Johnson lets her go and his hands fall to his side. He shakes his head. 'Foley. Fuck me sideways. I don't believe it.' He turns to Walker. 'I'll come with you to his place.'

'Dad, no, he didn't do anything,' she wails.

Johnson ignores her and walks to the door.

'I don't need you to come with me,' says Walker, following him. 'Take her home, make sure she doesn't call him and warn him that I'm coming. I can handle this.' He turns to the girl and puts his face close to hers. 'Don't call him,' he says. 'If he's innocent he's not in any trouble. If he's done this, if he's killed other women, he'll kill Barbara too if he finds out that I'm coming. If he hurts Barbara, I will see to it that you go to jail for a long, long time.'

She's crying openly, her face bright red, her nose running.

'I'll handle it,' says Johnson, pulling him away by his arm, pushing him out the door. 'Leave her out of this. You do your thing. I'll handle her.'

Walker drives out of town, onto the highway. It'll take him at least forty-five minutes to make it to Foley's place. He doesn't know if Johnson will take his advice and keep the girl from calling him. He doesn't even know for certain if Foley's the man they're looking for. But what makes him really anxious is that, if Foley does have Barbara, he's had her for twelve hours. What is he doing with her, and is she still alive?

42

Barbara is digging and scratching, a haste born of desperation. Rita is alive. Now that she has one paver out, it's easier to dig under and pull out the second one. The next will be the most difficult. It's sitting fully under the weight of the workbench.

She needs her hands free; she wants to be able to wiggle both sides of the paver, try to loosen it. She stands the loose paver on its end and, kneeling beside it, rubs the tape that binds her hands rapidly back and forth along the edge of its chipped side. It scratches and scrapes but doesn't cut through. In frustration she leans her full weight down into the tape and moves her hands back and forth again. The edge catches and her weight does the rest, puncturing into the tape and finally tearing through. The move slices a long scratch into her inside arm but her hands are free. She rotates her wrists, getting feeling back into them, and wriggles her fingers, then tears the tape off, pulling hair and skin with it in her haste.

She's so absorbed in her task that she doesn't hear him coming until the lock on the door rattles. She freezes, her heartbeat loud in her ears. He's coming to kill her. But after a moment she hears his steps fade away and then the car starts up and drives off, the sound of the engine slowly disappearing. The close call increases her sense of urgency. If he comes back he will kill her, and she'll never be able to save Rita. And if he's leaving for good, she needs to get free or they will die in this shed. The heat is rising by the minute and he hasn't left them much water.

Now that she has full use of her hands, she scrapes more quickly under the stone in front of her, digging out as much dirt as she can from beneath it. First tiny amounts and then, as it gets easier, small handfuls at a time. After a few minutes the paver drops fractionally. The workbench stays still, resting on its three other legs, immovable. The gap isn't quite large enough for the chain to come under, so she keeps wiggling and digging. She lowers the paver fractionally but it's still not low enough for the chain to slide out. Grunting with frustration and effort, she digs further, her fingernails torn, the tops of her fingers bleeding, and the next time she lowers the stone the chain slides across the gap above it. She has to pull, wriggle it, scraping slowly along the top of the paver, until finally it makes one last loud scratching noise and comes free.

She sits on the floor with a thump, her heart beating fast with the exertion, her head still throbbing. Then she pushes herself to her feet and scrambles, half at a run, the chain dragging behind her, to where Rita is lying.

Rita is curled up like a child sleeping but her face is dry and pale, her lips cracked and bleeding, and her clothes are covered in blood, the halter top and front of her shorts dark and stiff with dried bloody patches. There's a wound on her upper thigh, purple and green and thick with the scent of decay. Her bare legs and feet are stained with blood and there's a terrible stench, blood mixed with faeces and urine. Barbara can hardly bear to look. This is her fault; she wasn't working hard enough or fast enough. She can't let herself think of what her sister went through, alone, terrified.

'Oh, Rita – oh, my poor love.' She leans forward, strokes her sister's hair, touches her face. She's crying, sobs loud in the stillness. 'Rita, Rita, I'm so sorry.'

She touches her sister's face again, stroking it. Rita's face is hot, burning hot. Barbara picks up her wrist, checks her pulse. It's erratic, barely there. Rita is very ill, perhaps close to death. She's burning with fever. Unconscious. The wound on her leg is festering and badly infected. Barbara pulls off her t-shirt, dips it in the bucket, wipes Rita's face as gently as possible, cools her neck, her torso. Wets Rita's lips, tries to get her to drink but she's unresponsive, unmoving. She wets her t-shirt again and, trying to cool the burning skin, leaves it damp across Rita's forehead.

She has to figure a way out of the shed. She has to find a way to get Rita to safety. She can't lose her now she's managed to find her. She wraps the chain in loose circles around her lower left arm and wrist. It's still attached to her leg but, heavy and bulky as it is, she can carry it as she walks.

She walks around the entire space searching for possible exits. He's locked and bolted the door from the outside. She shakes it hard but there's not much give; it's locked fast.

She kneels down and runs her hand along the base of the wall where there's a small gap, about as wide as a finger. Perhaps she can dig a hole, dig under and out. With her bare hands in the dry dirt, she tries for a minute then gives it up. Digging under the pavers has taken her a long time and she only gained a few centimetres. She doesn't think she's got the time to dig a hole large enough to squeeze under.

Periodically she goes back to the bucket, wets her t-shirt again, gently cools Rita's face and body, wets her lips, talking all the time, telling her, 'It's Babs, honey, I'm here, you're safe, you're OK.' She keeps her eye out for signs of recognition, of consciousness, but Rita doesn't move.

She takes another drink of water herself. The level is very low now and the grit of dust and dirt fills her mouth along with the taste of plastic. She spits, licks her lips to feel more hydrated. She has to find a way out.

Bar the workbench, he's cleared the shed out. The bench, its immovable heft, is useless to her. It provides next to no cover; she can't shift it away from the wall, which means she can't get behind it.

She doesn't think they're in town. She's listened but there is no human sound: no distant rumble of cars, no voices, no buzz of air conditioners, nothing. Just rustling grass, leaves and branches moving in a breeze, the creak of the shed, birds calling. She shouts for help a few times but she's certain there's no one around to hear her.

In desperation she begins digging again, trying to make a hole under the wall of the shed, but she makes virtually no progress. Her fingers are bleeding and the hole is tiny, not even a cat could crawl through it, but it seems to be their only chance. She's still scratching fruitlessly when she hears the sound of an engine coming closer and then wheels skidding to a stop, a car door opening and slamming shut, the sound of a screen door clanking closed. He's back. He's coming to kill her.

She looks around for something, anything, to help her. The piece of glass is too small to be useful as a weapon. She'd need to be right on top of him and all the scratching has worn it down to a tiny smooth nub. She goes to the workbench, trying the drawers, wondering if there's a way to unlock them. Perhaps there's a tool in there that she can use. She's pushing, pulling, getting nowhere, when she hears the door of the house banging again and then his footsteps.

He's coming. She freezes in horror. She has nothing, nothing. She looks over and sees Rita, her damaged body, the agony he's caused. The sight of her sister acts like kindling to a fire of rage that burns out any fear. This man has hurt her sister and she is going to make him pay. She unwraps the chain from around her arm until she has a loose length of the heavy metal links in her hand, and stumbles towards the door. She can hear him approaching. She jumps in shock as he slaps the tin of the shed, fear rising again, mingling with her rage. An adrenaline surge pushes her into hyper-readiness; she can see the dust motes, hear his breathing.

'Hey, little piggy, ready to play?' he calls as he begins to unbolt the door.

The door swings inwards to the left so Barbara stands to the right. Perhaps she can dart outside, draw him away, when it opens. He pushes it and she freezes, holding her breath, unmoving. She needs the element of surprise in her favour. As the door opens, a vivid band of light moves in front of her feet and grows into a large triangle, spreading across the floor. It doesn't reach as far as the workbench. She's counting on the fact that he'll be struggling to adjust his eyes to the gloom after the vivid light of day.

He steps forward, calling, 'Here, piggy-piggy . . .' Somewhere in the distant recesses of her awareness she sees that he's holding a knife with a blade as long as her hand. One more step, she wills him, one more step . . . She wants him past her so that she can come from behind.

But he stops. His eyes have seen through the gloom, she's not where he expects. More quickly than she expected him to move, he turns and pushes the door hard against the wall.

In that instant, his back towards her, she pulls her arm behind her and swings the loose piece of chain at his head with all the strength she has. Luck is with her. As the door slams against the wall, he turns his head back round and the chain connects with his ear and jaw. He gives a startled grunt and stumbles, half falls backwards, hitting the metal door with a heavy clang, slashing at her with the knife, a sharp tear of pain across her cheek as he goes down. She steps forward and kicks him hard in the crotch and again in the stomach. He gives a muted scream of pain as he chokes for air. She's onto him, using her chain-wrapped hand to punch him as hard as she can. She's no fighter, but she has learnt self-defence techniques on the job and she's stronger and fitter than her small frame suggests. Her fury and fear give her added focus; she keeps hitting as hard as she can until his face is covered in blood and he's not moving.

She clambers up, away from him. Rita is lying horribly still. Barbara doesn't want to leave her alone again but she needs to get help, has to get out of the shed and find help. She turns and runs out the door, stopping for a second to get her bearings. There's a run-down house to her left and his car is parked outside another shed. In front of her is scrubby bush, the red earth covered with clumps of tall pale grass and, a couple of hundred metres to the right, a thin stand of trees. She runs to the car, it's not locked, pulls open the driver's door. The keys aren't in the ignition. She rummages in the glovebox, looks behind the sun visor, but they're not there. Her heart is beating fast, her cheek is throbbing. She can taste blood where he's cut her. She runs into the house.

The house is dark, blinds drawn against the light, and it stinks. Rank and foul, a mix of human perspiration and rotting food undercut with a vaguely medical smell. She's in a short corridor that ends in a living room and kitchen, the stench stronger here. There's mess everywhere, clothes on the floor and sofa, a half-eaten pizza going green on a plate, a coffee table in front of the sofa turned over, spilling more junk onto the floor.

The car is her best bet. She needs to get Rita away and his keys must be somewhere. She has a vision of him opening the shed door, a bundle of keys in his hand. He has them. She runs back to the front of the house. As she reaches the door, she hears the clang of the metal shed door. She peers through the screen, sees him back on his feet, knife in hand. Leaning against the door for support. She can't fight him without the element of surprise. He's too tall, too strong.

She runs to the back of the house through the kitchen. Thank god, a back door. She twists the handle. It's unlocked. She's out and running across the scrubby grass and red earth at the back of the house, heading across the paddock towards the stand of trees. They will give her some cover. She can hide there. She's leaving Rita behind, leaving her alone again, but at least he believes that Rita is dead. She wants him focused on chasing her, not thinking about Rita. Everything else fades as she runs. She focuses on the stand of trees, breathing hard, running as fast as she can, the chain around her leg slowing her down, making her clumsy. With a jolt of horror she remembers the gun he'd had earlier. If she'd been thinking more clearly in the house she could have looked for that, not the keys. Now as she's running she's fearing all the while that he'll come out the kitchen door behind her, that he'll shoot at her back. Her fear tightens her chest, sends tremors through her legs. The trees are too far. She won't make it. The chain around her leg, the weight of it on her arm, makes her ungainly. She stumbles on a high clump of grass, sharp and spiky, and falls hard, stones and grass cutting her hands and her knees. She's breathing ragged burning breaths, her lungs on fire, her head pounding. The sun is beating down; she is sweating and shivering at the same time. The grass gives some cover. She lies as flat as she can, low on the hot red earth, facing the house, tries to quieten her breathing, to be still, be invisible.

The silence flows in a wave around her. She's two hundred metres from the house, no more, and she doesn't know if he'll be able to see her. She doesn't know if running makes more sense than hiding and she's about to gather herself up, to run again, when she hears him shouting, indistinct, and then a shot from the gun. Rita. Please god, not Rita. She stifles a sob, flattens herself back into the earth. There's a moment's silence, then he starts shouting again and she can see him this time, standing at the back door, waving the rifle in his hands. She presses herself into the ground, as flat and as still as she can be. Trying to make herself invisible. He stops shouting and the fear rushes back. He's seen her. She's trembling, shaking all over, but forces herself to raise her head, to see if he's coming for her. She can't see anything, just clumps of grass leading to the back of the house and the back of the shed. He's gone.

She looks behind her. The trees are still too far but a dozen metres or so away is a red termite mound. It's as tall as she is and as wide as a telephone box and is surrounded by more clumps of grass. That will give her better cover. Staying on her stomach, her eyes on the house, she starts to crawl backwards, the chain dragging in the dirt, catching on stones, the metal clank of it horribly loud to her ears. She moves slowly, slowly, slowly, a short push at a time. She's only gone a few metres when she hears an engine start up. He's in the car. She pulls herself up, half crouching, half running, reaches the termite mound, diving behind it as the car comes at speed around the side of the shed, bumping and jolting over the rough ground. He drives directly towards her. He's seen her. She's crouching, frozen with indecision, with fear, when the car skews suddenly left, towards the treeline.

She edges around the mound to keep herself hidden from view. The car bounces and swerves; he's driving erratically, heading away from her. When the car reaches the treeline he cuts the engine and she can hear his voice, indistinct shouting floating back to her on the silent afternoon. He's looking for her among the trees. How long until he realises I didn't make it that far, thinks Barbara. Then he's going to come back.

She needs to get Rita out of the shed – she needs to get them both away. The shadows are getting longer but she can't wait for darkness to fall. She has to get back to Rita. She can't leave her alone, not now, not again.

43

Walker is pushing the ute harder than it's been driven in the ten years he's owned it. The speedo hasn't dropped below 140 the entire trip. Ginger is alert and restless, alternating between sitting on the seat and resting in the footwell. Normally she's calm on car journeys; she must be picking up on his anxiety.

It's almost 6 p.m. The shadows are lengthening and the heat is slowly going out of the sun as it drops towards the western horizon. He's trying to block out thoughts of Barbara. She's been missing for twelve hours now. That's too long. Anything could have happened. And if she's not there, if Foley isn't the bloke they're looking for, then he hasn't got a single idea where to find her. He brushes the thought away. Foley fits the bill. She has to be there. She has to be OK.

About thirty kilometres out of town he thinks of Grogan. Maybe he knows where Barbara is – that's why he's been chasing him around town.

'Where are you, DS?' is the first thing Grogan says.

'You haven't seen Barbara Guerra, have you?' Walker asks by way of answer. 'Is she with you?' Hoping still that there's a better explanation for all this.

'No, I haven't seen her. Where are you? What are you doing?'

Walker wonders at the urgency in Grogan's voice; he hasn't

been interested until now. But he brings him up to speed. 'I reckon Darryl Foley's taken her. I've got his address. I'm on my way to his place.'

'Fuck, Walker, you can't be heading out there alone, fronting up to Foley. If he's abducted her, he's dangerous.'

Walker knows this. It's been running through his mind on the drive, giving him a new appreciation of the challenges of outback policing. In Sydney he can get a back-up team with him, even a specialist team, in no time at all. Out here? Well, it's impossible. Brisbane is more than an hour's flight away. Add in the time to get a team approved and the helicopter out, and you're looking at three hours, probably more. Barbara has been missing too long already, there's no way they can wait.

'You want to call HQ? Bring in a SWAT team? Get some back-up? Do it. Please. But if he's got Barbara, he's had her twelve hours. I need to get out there now. It can't wait.'

Grogan exhales loudly. 'We can't call a SWAT team in on a hunch. You don't even know he's got her for sure. Look. I'll come with you. I'm leaving now. Wait for me – don't go in there half-cocked.'

Walker hangs up without answering. Grogan is at least twenty minutes behind him, probably more unless he's pushing the cruiser the way Walker is pushing the ute.

A few moments later his phone pings with another message. Michelle this time.

Grandma having a bad turn she's asking for u its not looking good, dont reckon she has much longer

Walker lifts his foot from the accelerator, bites his lip. Shit. He wants to see Grandma, doesn't want her to go without saying a last goodbye. But she was eating cake and drinking lemonade this morning. Laughing with Blair's girls. She can't have turned so bad. Probably she's going to need another dose of morphine and tomorrow she'll be better again. Grandma won't die. He wills it so. And Barbara is in danger. Right now. He floors the accelerator again.

As he comes up to the turn-off to Foley's place, Walker slows the car a touch so that he doesn't drive past it. He slows his mind too, putting thoughts of Grandma and Barbara to the back, focusing simply on the job at hand. Grogan is right: if Foley has abducted Barbara, he's dangerous and he could be armed. He needs to figure out a way to get in there without Foley knowing about it. Find out if he's got Barbara and get her protected before Grogan comes in with his siren roaring.

The GPS announces the turn-off is 600 metres ahead. Walker slows down and cruises to a stop just past the dirt road that leads to Foley's property. He parks the ute in the long grass at the edge of the road. It will act as a signal to Grogan. He opens the door and gets out, Ginger following him.

There's a line of trees running the other side of the track along a dry creek bed. They will give him the cover he needs. He jogs slowly along the sandy bed, Ginger loping easily along beside him. He forces himself to run steadily; he needs to pace himself and be as quiet as possible. According to the GPS the house is some two kilometres off the road, but he's run less than that, perhaps a kilometre at most, when he hears a vehicle crashing through the bush ahead of him. It can't be Grogan, he won't have made this much time.

Walker darts to the far side of the creek, taking cover behind a broad paperbark gum. He gives a hand signal to Ginger, who lies down in the grass beside him, her pale dappled coat offering the perfect camouflage.

A white Hilux is driving erratically on the opposite bank. It comes to a stop and a man emerges. Walker recognises Foley's russet-coloured hair and notes that he's wearing jeans and a black t-shirt. He's holding a gun, a long-barrelled bolt-action .22-calibre rifle, in his right hand. He looks around, searching behind the trees, the barrel of the rifle scything through the high grass, then walks down into the creek bed in Walker's direction, his head turning from side to side, the gun following his movements.

'I'll find ya, bitch,' he screams out. 'I'll find ya and then ya gonna pay.'

Walker's heart gives a jump: Barbara is alive.

Foley is getting closer. Walker can see that he has a deep red welt on the side of his face, his nose is swollen and one of his eyes too. He's talking to himself, occasionally raising his voice to scream 'Fucken bitch!'

Walker signals to Ginger to stay, then bends down and picks up a stone, weighs it in his hand before throwing it with a long, smooth movement onto the far-side bank. It lands with a crash and clatter; two galahs rise from the tree above with loud squawks and Foley spins towards the sound, bringing the rifle up and taking quick steps over the sand and up the opposite bank into the bush.

Walker picks up another stone, the only weapon he has, steps out and runs quickly across the bed of the creek towards where Foley has disappeared. He crouches low, pressing up against the sandy rise of the bank, the shade and the waist-high grass offering cover in the fading light. Ginger stays where he asked her to sit – he can see her ears pricked, alert, she's ready to come when called. On the bank above him he hears Foley crashing around, then the sound of the car door slamming shut and the vehicle moving again, towards the road.

He whistles for Ginger and runs quickly in the opposite direction to the car, staying close to the bank, his eyes scanning left and right for any sign of Barbara, any track or movement. The car stops again; he hears Foley shouting in the distance. He climbs the bank and beyond the stand of trees he sees the car's tracks have cut across open grassland from the direction of a tumbledown house and outbuildings.

He runs across the field as fast as he can, bent low, envious of Ginger and her easy speed, her low profile and dappled coat. She's hidden, invisible among the grass, while he's exposed. But the shadows are longer now, the sun almost ready to set, and he hopes it will be difficult for Foley to pick him out in the low light. His back is tingling the entire run. He can't hear the car or Foley for his breath and the sound of his heartbeat in his ears. Imagining the shot that will take him down gives him an extra burst of speed.

As he gets closer to the buildings, he sees that the property comprises an old house flanked by a few sheds. The door of the shed nearest him is open; there's blood on the doorframe, a small puddle on the ground beside it. He slows, makes a sign for Ginger to stop, forces his breathing to slow. It's possible that Foley isn't operating alone. He needs to approach carefully.

He drops to his haunches beside a clump of spinifex grass the same colour as his moleskin trousers. His pale-blue shirt, too, is less visible in the fading light. As his breath quietens he strains to listen, but there's no sound of the car, of Foley's voice, or other voices. He stands, treads as quietly as possible, drawing on the techniques that Blair taught him, taking smaller steps, his toes feeling the way, his weight on his back leg until he gets to the shed. He stays close to its far wall, hidden in its shade, casting no shadow that might warn someone of his arrival. As he slowly approaches the open door he can hear a low voice, whispering, a grunt of effort and the sound of something heavy being dragged, slowly, along the floor. He curses the fact that he doesn't have a gun, hefts the stone in his hand. It's a poor weapon but better than nothing. The dragging sound stops and he hears footsteps approaching the door. The steps slow as they come closer and a moment later a head peers around the corner. He steps forward, all his weight behind the punch before he realises its Barbara and pulls his arm back, fast.

The fear on her face, the absolute terror, just for one fleeting moment, is searing. She's wearing only a black bra and her trousers, carrying a chain in her hands that loops down to her leg.

'Barbara!' He steps forward, pulling her close.

Her body slumps into his, he can feel her trembling with relief. '*Gott sei Dank*,' she says, '*Gott sei Dank*.'

After a second, she steps back. 'Rita's here,' she says. 'She's really sick. I tried to carry her but she's too heavy. We need to get her away, we need to get her safe. Where's your car? We need to get her safe.'

She pulls him inside. The shed is rank, smelling of decay, blood, vomit and urine. In the gloom, just the other side of the half-open metal door, he sees Rita on the floor, her face and body covered in terrible bruises and a huge, badly infected wound on her thigh. Her face is white, bloodless. Barbara kneels beside her sister, talking quietly to her, touching her face.

'She had a fever but now she's cold – really cold.'

He crouches beside Barbara, touches Rita's throat, feels for a pulse. It's weak, erratic, but it's there. They need to call an air ambulance, get Rita to hospital as soon as possible.

The car is two kilometres away and night is falling. He can carry Rita that far. If they stay off the track, cut across the paddock towards the road, there's a good chance they can avoid Foley. And Grogan will be here soon. He'll be able to radio for help, call in an ambulance from the cruiser. As gently as he can, he picks Rita up, cradling her to him like a child, his heart breaking at the ruined body he's holding.

44

Dave Grogan is keeping his mind firmly on Surfers Paradise. The beaches, the nights at the casino, the look on Lisa's face when she sees their new home. His gun is a lead weight against his leg; he unholsters it and puts it on the passenger seat before reversing out of the police station driveway and turning right, onto the highway towards Smithton.

He's called it in, of course - not officially, but with those who count.

'This something to do with you? Is there anything I need to know?' he asked.

'Nah. Never heard of this Foley bloke. Nothing to do with us.'

'Righto.' He'd been relieved. Abducting a cop, even if it's a foreign one, especially if it's a foreign one, and if that's what this is and not just Walker getting the wrong end of the stick, is too serious to overlook.

'Don't forget this Walker bloke. Whatever his story is, he's been sticking his nose in our business. We're moving out but he still needs taking care of. You want to come to Surfers, right? Not end up in the bin.'

'Well, maybe this could be useful,' said Grogan. 'Things get confusing when there's an armed and dangerous villain around.'

'You're getting the hang of this, Grogan,' said the boss. 'I can see you've got a bright future ahead of you.'

So, he's taking it easy, keeping the speedo at 100 kilometres. If he's lucky, if he's late enough, Foley will do his dirty work for him. His heartburn is back. He pulls a new pack of Pepto-Bismol tablets from the pocket of his shirt, breaks one into his mouth, the chalky texture soothing. The sun is setting, the shadows are lengthening.

He calls Lisa. 'I got a call-out on the Smithton Highway, I won't be back in time for dinner.'

He feels the frigid air of her disappointment through the phone.

'I might have some good news for us,' he says. 'There's a job going in Surfers. I have a chance at it. They're putting my name forward.'

There's a long pause. 'I don't want to know,' she says. 'Until you have it signed, sealed and delivered, I don't want to know. I can't take the disappointment, Dave. If you don't get it . . .' Her voice trails off.

'Lisa?'

'I mean it. I won't – we won't stand it.'

'I'm going to get it. Don't worry, I'm going to get it.'

'Right,' she says. And hangs up.

He puts his foot down. That job is his. It has to be.

He's worried he'll miss the turn-off to Foley's place. Walker had said the sixty-five-kilometre mark but it's dark now and the mileage can be unreliable. Then he sees Walker's ute pulled over just beyond a turn-off. He slows down, realises he doesn't have a plan. Decides he doesn't need one. He's the law. He can turn up, guns blazing.

He turns the cruiser onto the gravel side road and is concentrating on avoiding the worst of the potholes when a white Hilux pulls out of the trees ahead of him and accelerates away at speed. It kicks up a cloud of dust, so he slows down, follows at a distance.

Ahead of him the Hilux turns left across a paddock and comes to a stop in front of a group of buildings, a small homestead, couple of sheds. Grogan pulls in behind it, puts the siren on, a couple of low woop-woops, the way he does when he's pulling over a driver on the highway, just to get the person's attention. The sound of the siren does something to people, makes them feel guilty, caught red-handed, even if they're only driving a few miles above the speed limit.

He realises that he's seen no sign of Walker. A moment's trepidation runs through him but he reminds himself that he's police. He's the long arm of the law. Whatever is happening out here, he's in charge. If this bloke has done away with Walker, he's done him a huge favour. A plan starts to formulate in his mind. Whatever happens out here can easily be attributed to whoever is sitting meekly inside the Hilux in front of him.

He picks up the gun and holsters it, opens the car door and walks towards the car. He can hear his mobile phone ringing in the cruiser behind him. Lisa probably. He keeps walking; he'll call her back on the way home. The bloke inside the car hasn't moved. Grogan can see through the rear window that it's Foley. He's just sitting there, looking straight ahead.

'Alright, Darryl, mate,' he says as he approaches the driver's-side window. 'Just following up . . .'

The words he'd been meaning to say disappear from his mind. He's looking down the barrel of a rifle, long and black and sleek. He's trying to process what to do next, how to handle this, when Foley says, 'I'm not your fucken mate,' and pulls the trigger.

• • •

Walker hears the shot. He's crouched in the paddock, a few hundred metres away, Rita still in his arms, Barbara beside him, Ginger, too, alert and listening. They'd been no more than a couple of hundred metres into the paddock when they'd seen the Hilux barrelling back towards the house and, with a surge of relief, the patrol car following in the dust cloud behind it. Grogan. Thank fuck.

The cars disappear from view behind the sheds and Walker realises he needs to call Grogan, warn him that Foley is armed. He's crouching there, listening to the dial tone in his ear, when the shot rings out. Then another. He freezes, shuts off the phone.

He has Barbara stay with her sister, signals Ginger to stay and guard them, and runs towards the house, keeping low and out of sight. He hears a car engine start up and a moment later the police cruiser reverses out. Walker relaxes with relief. He didn't think Grogan had it in him, to shoot a bloke like that. Not that he disapproves. If anyone had it coming, it was this psycho.

The cruiser slows and turns, an arc of headlights spilling across the dark paddock.

Walker speeds up, running into the light, waving his arms. Grogan is turning round, heading for the highway, but he can't leave. They need him to stay, to call for assistance for Rita, to help get her to hospital. The cruiser stops. The high beams flick on, illuminating Walker. He waves again using both arms and pointing in Barbara and Rita's direction. He steps out of the beam of light and runs back to them.

'What happened? What's going on?' Barbara is alarmed, fearful.

'Looks like Grogan shot him. Didn't reckon he had it in him. But he'll be able to help us, he'll be able to call for an air ambulance.' He bends down and picks Rita up again. Night has fully fallen. Twilight is non-existent this far north; the day turns from light to night seemingly at the flick of a switch. Luckily Grogan has left the full beam of the headlights shining on the paddock. Walker moves towards the car, carrying Rita, thankful for the light, which illuminates the hummocks of grass and spinifex and termite mounds.

It takes him a while to walk the short distance to the car. Rita isn't heavy, far from it, but she's in a bad condition and he's treating her as gently as he can, choosing his steps carefully so he doesn't stumble. He's close, no more than thirty metres away, before the car door finally opens. About fucking time, he thinks. Grogan had better have been using the time to radio for help.

It's hard to see with the lights bright in his eyes and he steps slightly to the left, taking himself out of the direct beam. Some instinct stops him in his tracks. And then he notices that the figure silhouetted in the light is taller and slimmer than Grogan. And the gun in his hand is no service revolver – the silhouette looks more like the long barrel of a .22-calibre rifle.

He steps quickly leftwards, further into the dark, as the man walks in his direction. Behind him he hears a shocked intake of breath. Barbara has seen him too. He lays Rita gently on the ground, commanding Ginger with his hand to sit by her. He crouches low and when Foley crashes through the grass, less than a metre to his left, Walker has no time to think; he propels himself upwards and launches himself at Foley's legs, tackling him hard, using his shoulder to bring the man crashing to the ground, the rifle falling with a soft thunk beside them. Foley falls heavily but he recovers quickly, kicking out sharply and landing a foot in Walker's gut, winding him. Instinctively Walker releases his hold, doubling up and gasping for air. Foley crawls out of his reach, his hands slapping the ground, frantically feeling for the rifle.

Walker forces himself to his hands and knees, lurches towards Foley, landing on his back. The man twists under his grip, he's stronger than he looks, and he has a manic energy. They grapple for a moment, Walker feeling Foley buck and twist underneath him, then something hits him above the eye with enough force that everything goes dark for a second. He loses his grip and Foley twists free, turning and smashing the butt of the rifle into his head again. Walker rolls over, semi-conscious, bringing his arms over to protect himself. He hears Ginger giving a deep-throated growl, then senses her standing above him, the noise of her anger reverberating through her body. Foley backs away and something in his action sends Ginger off. She's gone from above him, the sound of her growls fading as she leaps towards Foley.

There's an explosion of noise, a muted yelp and a thud.

'No!' Walker hears himself cry out, pushes himself to his feet.

In the glow of the headlights he can see Foley, standing, rifle in hand. Ginger lies at his feet, her body contorted. Foley swings the gun towards Walker. 'One move and I'll blow you away too,' he says.

Walker takes a half-step forward towards Ginger and another shot cracks through the night, a spurt of dust at his feet.

'Next one won't miss,' says Foley, advancing towards Walker, the rifle pointing directly at him.

Instinctively, Walker steps back, stopping when he feels Rita at his heels.

'Pick her up,' says Foley, jabbing the gun at him.

Walker bends slowly down. He doesn't have many options here. He's certain Foley will act on his threat; he's already shot Grogan. He needs to make a lunge for the rifle, time it right, but he won't be able to do that with Rita in his arms. He looks up. The barrel is pointing directly at him. He'll never make it. Foley will finish him.

'Fucken move it!' Foley shouts, his pupils dark holes, his eyes flickering and moving manically. He's tanked up on something, thinks Walker. That gives Walker some advantages but some big disadvantages too: he's dealing with someone who is unpredictable and irrational.

He bends his knees, picks Rita up in his arms, feels the barrel of the rifle against his neck.

'Move it.'

He's not sure where Barbara is and luckily Foley seems preoccupied with him and Rita. Hopefully he can buy enough time for her to get away. He walks slowly, running through options in his mind.

'Take her back to the shed.' The gun jabs again.

He changes direction, heading towards the shed on his left. As he steps out of the headlights' beam, he stumbles a few times until his eyes adjust to the night, and then he reaches the driveway, slightly less rutted than the bush around it. The darkness is useful, it gives him a few seconds' advantage. Foley's bullets won't find him quite as easily. As if he reads his mind, Foley steps closer, the barrel pressed hard against the base of Walker's neck.

'Don't even fucken think about dropping her or running.'

They've reached the shed, the door still standing open. Walker is wishing he'd spent more time casing it. All his attention had been focused on Barbara and Rita. He remembers a workbench, nothing more.

'Get inside,' says Foley, 'and put her on the ground.'

Walker has no option but to do as he's told. As they enter, Foley flicks on a light. The bare bulb is dim but it feels bright after the pitch-dark outside. Walker turns slowly; he wants to be facing Foley when he puts her down, it will be his only chance.

He's watching Foley as he puts Rita on the ground, sees the man's face change, fill with rage. 'It's the wrong fucken one!' he screams. 'You brought me the dead bitch.'

As Foley raises the rifle, Walker pushes himself to his feet, every muscle powering, driven by the urge to survive. Time slows to the pace of a heartbeat. His body connects with Foley's legs. Foley begins to fall, the gun goes off and Walker feels a searing heat, a vivid explosion of pain in his leg. He hears himself cry out. Foley hits the ground with a thump, kicks his legs, but Walker holds on for his life, every fibre of his being focused on not letting go. He has no plan, no coherent thought, just holding on, giving Barbara time to make it to the car, to make it to the highway, to get away.

He hears Foley grunt, an animal sound of pain, and feels the fight go out of him. There's a thump, then another, another, and another, then a wet-sounding crunch. The pain in Walker's leg is overwhelming and he lets go of Foley's lifeless legs.

Barbara is at his side. She's holding Foley's rifle by the barrel, the grip slick with blood.

'Lucas. Lucas. Can you hear me?'

He meets her eyes. 'Run,' he says. 'Run.'

'It's OK, Lucas. I think I killed him.'

She's kneeling beside him, looking at his leg. He sits up.

'Give me your shirt,' she says. He does what he's told, the pain dulling his thoughts.

He hears the fabric tear, feels her wrapping something around his upper thigh, tightly. Stemming the flow of blood.

'Can you stand?' she asks.

He nods. Putting pressure on his good leg, he gives her his hand and she helps pull him to his feet. Instinctively he puts down his right foot. The pain sears through him. He groans and almost passes out.

She helps him to the side of the shed and he balances there, holding onto the wall while she goes over and picks up Rita. He sees the effort it takes her, all her strength, but she does it, lifts and carries her sister, then walks slowly out of the shed. He tries to follow but he can't, the pain is too great. He slides to a sitting position, only half-conscious. After a moment Barbara is back. He feels her shoulder under his armpit, her arm around him, holding him up. Together they hobble out of the shed, towards the squad car, its lights still on, parked across the driveway.

Wednesday

45

Walker wakes to see a huddle of white-coated people at the foot of his bed. Sunlight is streaming through the window, there's a scent of antiseptic and cleaning products and the cool blast of an air conditioner. He can hear the low murmur of voices and the bleep and buzz of hospital machinery.

He searches his memories. An excruciating ride, the car jolting and bumping over the rough ground, pain blinding him. Barbara driving, talking to him, calling for help. Rita? An air ambulance? His memory is hazy. He searches further back.

'Foley!' He sits up. They'd left Foley there. He could be anywhere by now. Gone, free.

The doctors turn towards him, a nurse appears beside him.

'Lie down, Mr Walker, it's alright, you're alright.' She offers him water. He's incredibly thirsty, drains the small plastic cup in one large gulp.

'Where's Barbara? Where's Foley?'

The nurse takes the cup from him. 'Try to sleep,' she says. 'It's all OK.'

'No, it's not. I'm a police officer. There's a dangerous criminal . . .'

'Mr Walker, please, relax. You're in the Royal Brisbane Hospital. You've been in surgery – you suffered a major injury to your right leg. Your colleagues will be here shortly. Meanwhile, please relax.'

'Where's my phone?'

The doctors have moved on. 'I'll go and get your things,' says the nurse. 'Try to rest.' She pulls a light-blue curtain around his bed.

He lies down and when he wakes again Barbara is sitting beside him. Her head is bent; she's looking at her phone, texting. He sees the whorls and curls on top of her head, the messy spikes that she always ruffles up when she's thinking or anxious. He watches her for a while, until a yawn steals up on him and he moves. She looks up. The eyes that meet his are red, with heavy dark circles underneath.

'Are you OK?' he asks.

She smiles at him, lighting her face fractionally. 'Asks the man lying in a hospital bed with his leg half blown away.'

He looks at her. 'I'm fine, I'll be OK.'

'Have you spoken to the doctors?' she asks. There's something grave in her voice.

'No.' He looks down properly for the first time. His right leg is raised on a pulley splint, bandaged, and there's no feeling in it.

'Is it bad?' he asks.

'The bullet shattered your femur and damaged some nerves too. I don't know all the details, you need to talk with the doctors. They are saying you're very lucky that it did not hit the femoral artery. We would not have made it in time.'

'What does that mean? I'll walk again, right?'

She hesitates. 'I don't know,' she says. 'You need to talk to the doctors.'

He looks at his leg, stretched out. It will be fine. He will be fine.

'Rita?' he asks. 'I don't remember much . . .'

'She is in intensive care. They still don't know if she will be OK. She has been through so much. My parents are on their way. They will be here tomorrow morning. I'm not a praying person, but . . .' Her voice fades away.

'She's safe now. She's in good hands. She'll pull through.'

Barbara nods. 'She is safe thanks to you. I cannot thank you enough – we cannot thank you enough – for everything you did ...'

He squeezes her hand. 'It was mostly you,' he says. 'You never give up.'

She shakes her head. 'Rita is family but you risked your life for us.'

He changes the subject. 'What about Foley?' he asks. 'We left him there ...'

'You don't remember?'

He shakes his head.

'We met Paul Johnson at the turn-off. Where you left your car. He came out with one of his drivers. A hunting posse. He had talked to Terri and found out that she was arranging to meet Foley. Johnson decided to meet him instead. They were going to beat him. Perhaps they still did. I thought I'd killed him but I only knocked him out.' There's a grim purpose to her voice, anger not far beneath. Foley tortured her sister. Walker knows he wouldn't forgive him either if he was in her place.

'He's in hospital now,' Barbara goes on, 'in Too-*woomba*? He's not in good shape. They are managing his head injury; he is in a coma. Constable Grogan is alive too. He is here, in this hospital. The doctors told me he was shot in the groin and the abdomen but the bullets missed the vital organs. He was very lucky, apparently.'

She pauses.

'Berndt is dead,' she says. 'Foley told me he killed him and they found Berndt's car, all his things, at Foley's place. I saw Berndt's father, Carl, this morning. He had only just arrived, and to get this news ...' Her voice trails off for a moment. 'He's gone to Caloodie, they have people out looking for Berndt's body. And they think Foley abducted and killed Sheree Miller, Tanya Bowen and Sylvia Stevens as well, but you already know that, no? The police interviewed

Terri Johnson. He drives a white refrigerated truck, like the one on the dashcam video that you sent off. They think they can get a registration by enhancing it. They are waiting for Foley to regain consciousness, to talk to him . . .' Her voice trails off again.

He squeezes her hand again. 'He'll go to jail for the rest of his life,' he says, knowing it's cold comfort, that nothing can make up for the damage that Foley's done to so many young lives.

He hears voices outside; the curtain is pulled open. It's Blair, his face concerned, anxious, pale. Barbara lets Walker's hand go, stands back.

'You've caught yourself a beauty this time, cuz.' He can see the anxiety under Blair's smile.

'I'm fine. I'll be fine. It's all going to be OK.' He's reassuring Blair, reassuring himself.

'I have to go,' says Barbara. She steps over to him. 'We will talk, yes? I will call you and check in on you. Let you know how Rita is getting on.'

She leans down, kisses him gently on the forehead. The kind of kiss a sister gives. 'Thank you for everything, Lucas.'

He doesn't want her to go. 'You don't need to leave,' he says, reaching for her hand again.

She squeezes his hand. 'I do.'

And with that she's gone, and he's listening to Blair telling him that Ginger is fine, at the vet's; her injury will leave her with a limp but nothing more. And joking that Ginger loves him so much she had to get herself the same injury he's gone and got. Behind the smile, he sees something in his cousin's eyes. His stomach cramps up. 'Grandma?' he asks, but he knows the answer before Blair speaks.

'She's passed.' Blair's voice is low and full of grief and Walker feels a pain in his heart that is worse than anything his leg can give him. She's gone and he didn't say goodbye.

The day flashes by, doctors come and go, with conversations about splintered bones and nerve damage and rehabilitation. It's late afternoon when he sends Blair away. Michelle needs his help with the arrangements for Grandma's funeral and Blair is always twitchy when he's in the city, far from the bush and the open spaces.

'I'll be back for the funeral,' Walker says, knowing that it might not be true. He might still be in hospital, and truth to tell he's not sure he's ready. It will hurt too much and he's not sure he'll ever forgive himself for not being there to say a proper goodbye to Grandma.

'Righto,' says Blair. He pauses for a moment. 'Grandma said to tell you not to forget that Caloodie is your home, cuz. She's right, you know. We all want you to come back.'

Walker nods. 'Yeah, mate, of course, Caloodie is home.' But he wonders if that's still true, now that Grandma has gone. It was being with her that felt like home, and without her he's not sure.

Blair's not the type to make a fuss. He sits for a moment longer, twirling his hat in his hands, then stands, thrusts out a hand. 'See you around, cuz,' he says, and then he's gone.

Lying there alone, in the almost-silence, surrounded by the beeps and hums of the equipment around him, a soft squeak on the lino floor from the nurse's shoes, Walker feels a huge hole open up inside. He's alone. Grandma is gone. He didn't get a chance to say goodbye. He shuts his eyes but it does nothing to ward off the pain of losing her.

His phone beeps and rouses him. A text from Barbara.

Rita still critical but they think the worst has passed. How are you doing?

It lifts his spirits more than a short message has a right to. He's composing an answer when he hears steps outside. The curtain opens and the large frame of Dan Rutherford pushes through, pulls it shut behind him.

'Alright, Walker. I see you managed to keep your distance from the action as ordered,' he says, shaking his head. But there's genuine concern in his eyes when he asks, 'How is it?' – nodding at the leg.

'They're not sure yet,' says Walker. 'I'm going to need another operation, some physio. It's going to be a little while before I'm back in action.' He doesn't add 'if at all', the doctors' damning prognosis. I'll be back, he thinks, Terminator-style.

Rutherford pulls up the visitors' chair and sits down. 'I need you to debrief me on anything you came across concerning the Markovich operation,' he says. 'They've moved on, closed down the site.'

Walker's heart sinks. His night-time incursion has messed up Rutherford's operation. He lies there, wondering how to tell Rutherford that it was his fault, when the nurse with the squeaky shoes opens the curtain.

'I thought I told you, he's too sick for this right now.'

Rutherford looks sheepish. 'We're colleagues, I'm just checking up on him.'

'Not now you're not, he's in pain and needs to rest.'

Walker closes his eyes, feigns sleep, hears Rutherford protest once, then give in. 'It's important. Walker . . .'

'You see.' The nurse lowers her voice a little. 'He needs to rest.'

'When can I come back to talk to him?'

'Visiting hours are four to five p.m. tomorrow,' says the nurse, her voice fading as they walk away down the ward.

Walker keeps his eyes closed and soon he's not faking it anymore, drifting into a state of half-awake, half-dreaming, putting off everything he has to deal with until tomorrow.

Acknowledgements

Writing a novel is less of a solo project than you might think and this one wouldn't have come about without the guidance, support, love and encouragement of many people.

I owe my biggest thanks to Kassie Larkins, who, over many years of talking, support and encouragement, helped me find myself as a writer.

A huge thank you also to my parents, who supplied bookshelves filled with novels from my childhood onwards and who cheered me on from my very earliest writing attempts. And to Wolf, Dionne, Haidee and Mia, who hosted me while I was researching the first draft of *Outback* and gave me space, time and peace to write. It's only because of all of you, your moral support and quiet cheerleading, that I started, and then finished, the Walker series. I hope you like the final version!

In terms of policing, any procedural errors or other gaffes are all mine, but I want to say a big thank you to Danny and Gary, two Queensland Police officers who helped me with terminology, process and believability, and who introduced me to the state's biggest and best chicken parmi.

My agent, Jane Gregory, and Stephanie Glencross, Camille Burns and all the team at David Higham offered support and invaluable feedback and believed in this book from the start - it would never have been published without them.

Thank you to Jane Snelgrove, my editor at Embla Books, who took DS Walker to heart and helped me polish a first draft into this final version, and to copy editor Silvia Crompton for all her invaluable feedback. And to all the team at Embla Books - a professional, supportive and encouraging group who have found a way to present DS Walker that is better than I could have imagined. I'm excited and proud to be launching this first novel into the world. Heartfelt thanks to you all!

A Note from the Author

I grew up in outback Australia, in far north-west Queensland, in a mining town called Mount Isa – eagle-eyed readers will have spotted references to it in the book, though the fictional towns of Caloodie, Smithton and Hopeville are set some 500 kilometres or so south of the city.

We moved to Mount Isa in the 1970s when I was seven years old. We travel up from Melbourne on a four-hour flight, during which the crew feed us huge slabs of moist chocolate cake and the scent of cigarette smoke drifts over from the seats behind us. My brother and I squeeze into one seat together so that we can look out the small window at the world passing below, which turns from green to dusty cream and then to a startling rust red.

When the plane finally bumps and jolts to a stop, we emerge at the top of a wobbly metallic staircase. Two men are standing at the bottom, and I'm shocked to see that, although fully grown up, they are wearing shorts, with socks pulled up high on their calves so that only their knees, which are the same colour and texture as walnuts, are exposed. They squint up at us and we squint back at them, our eyes straining against the glare of the sun in the mid-morning heat.

Around us is a landscape that seems not so much foreign as extraterrestrial. As if we boarded our plane in Melbourne and have landed, a few hours later, on Mars. Fields of spiky pale grass, almost white in the blinding sunshine, sprout from oxidised earth. Low red hills rise in lazy, low waves behind them. The birds hovering in the sky above, brown goshawks, are like small fighter planes as they turn circles on the warm air, scanning for prey.

We move into a house that has a spinifex-covered hill directly behind the back garden, with caves and cliffs and tantalising places to explore. And this being the 1970s and outback Australia, we are given untrammelled freedom to do just that. We ride our bikes, climb hills, walk along sandy riverbanks and swim in waterholes and dams. We go barefoot most days – the heat obviates the need for shoes – and our feet become tough and calloused and almost always painted the same dusty red as the land around us.

We discover a stunningly beautiful, thriving, living world populated by a myriad of lizards, from as small as our pinkie fingers to as long as our legs. To this day I have a scar on my right index finger where a goanna, a metre-long prehistoric-looking lizard, bit me when I tried to feed it. We regularly see kangaroos and wallabies, flocks of galahs and cockatoos and swing-beaked pelicans paddling in the dam. Stick insects as long as a man's hand, biting green ants and poisonous redback spiders are everyday companions. Brown snakes are to be avoided, as are the sharp blades of the spinifex that scratch our bare legs and the ceaseless harsh sun that burns our fair skin.

Over the next fifteen years, the rugged beauty, indigo sky and wide horizons of the outback become home. Then, after university, I leave Australia, become a journalist, and travel the world. I live for twenty years in London and then in Berlin. But the outback always calls me home. It's a place where I feel grounded. Where I feel small in the same good way that I feel small when I'm floating in the ocean.

In 2019, just before the Covid pandemic locked us all in, I spent two months in north-west Queensland, getting over a heartbreak by taking a road trip across the country. And as I drove, as I spent nights and days surrounded by the beauty and rugged harshness of the country, DS Lucas Walker and this story came to me.

The follow-up to *Outback* is coming . . .

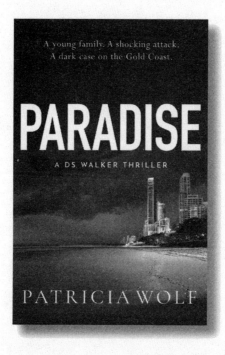

A young family. A shocking attack.
A dark case on the Gold Coast.

PARADISE

A DS WALKER THRILLER

PATRICIA WOLF

As DS Lucas Walker recovers from his injuries, he heads from Caloodie, Queensland, to the Gold Coast. Surfers Paradise: a seaside city where gleaming high rises fringe sparkling surf beaches, sunny days lead to wild nights, and criminals and bikie gangs mingle with tourists and dignitaries at five star hotels, clubs and casinos.

Before long, Walker is part of a team trying to solve a horrific home invasion and murder that has claimed the life of a young mother and left her nine-year-old daughter fighting to survive. Can he help them find the perpetrators, and keep the young girl safe? Meanwhile, Vandals head honcho Stefan Markovich is in town – and Walker once again finds himself on a dangerous collision course with the drug gang.

Weak from his injuries, and grieving, can Walker solve a case that is more shocking than anyone expected, and survive the dark underbelly of Australia's Surfers Paradise?

Don't miss the thrilling next instalment in the gripping and atmospheric DS Walker Thriller series.